The new Zebra Regency Romance logo that you see on the cover is a photograph of an actual regency "tuzzy-muzzy." The fashionable regency lady often wore a tuzzy-muzzy tied with a satin or velvet riband around her wrist to carry a fragrant nosegay. Usually made of gold or silver, tuzzy-muzzies varied in design from the elegantly simple to the exquisitely ornate. The Zebra Regency Romance tuzzy-muzzy is made of alabaster with a silver filigree edging.

"MERCIFUL HEAVENS," SHE THOUGHT, "HE IS UNDRESSED . . ."

She wondered how it came about she had not realized it beforetimes. He wasn't even wearing a coat, nonetheless a neckcloth, and his waistcoat of a fine buckskin was partially unbuttoned. His linen shirt was open at the neck. She could not tear her eyes away from the dark hairs which curled there.

Good heavens! She had never seen a man's chest before, and for some reason, she felt her heart begin throbbing painfully in her throat. Her gaze drifted to his trim waist and the snug fit of his breeches over shapely, athletic legs. Zeus, but he was a fine figure of a man! Quickly, she drank the rest of the brandy and turned away from him. Had he descended from his bedchamber dressed purposely in this manner?

Much to her consternation, Worthen glanced at her just as she was contemplating this most intriguing speculation, and she blinked at him, a blush suffusing her cheeks.

He lifted a cup to her in a silent toast . . .

THE BEST OF REGENCY ROMANCES

AN IMPROPER COMPANION (2691, $3.95)
by Karla Hocker

At the closing of Miss Venable's Seminary for Young Ladies school, mistress Kate Elliott welcomed the invitation to be Liza Ashcroft's chaperone for the Season at Bath. Little did she know that Miss Ashcroft's father, the handsome widower Damien Ashcroft would also enter her life. And not as a passive bystander or dutiful dad.

WAGER ON LOVE (2693, $2.95)
by Prudence Martin

Only a rogue like Nicholas Ruxart would choose a bride on the basis of a careless wager. And only a rakehell like Nicholas would then fall in love with his betrothed's grey-eyed sister! The cynical viscount had always thought one blushing miss would suit as well as another, but the unattainable Jane Sommers soon proved him wrong.

LOVE AND FOLLY (2715, $3.95)
by Sheila Simonson

To the dismay of her more sensible twin Margaret, Lady Jean proceeded to fall hopelessly in love with the silver-tongued, seditious poet, Owen Davies—and catapult her entire family into social ruin . . . Margaret was used to gentlemen falling in love with vivacious Jean rather than with her—even the handsome Johnny Dyott whom she secretly adored. And when Jean's foolishness led her into the arms of the notorious Owen Davies, Margaret knew she could count on Dyott to avert scandal. What she didn't know, however was that her sweet sensibility was exerting a charm all its own.

The Fanciful Heiress

VALERIE KING

ZEBRA BOOKS
KENSINGTON PUBLISHING CORP.

ZEBRA BOOKS

are published by

Kensington Publishing Corp.
475 Park Avenue South
New York, NY 10016

First printing: June, 1990

Printed in the United States of America

To Barbara,
fellow artist and excellent friend

Author's Note

To my knowledge, the village of Staplehope in Shropshire exists only in my imagination and upon the pages that follow.

Chapter One

Margaret Longville stood in a darkened corner of Mrs. Norbury's drawing room in Upper Brook Street. She knew she was the envy of half the young ladies present, for the season's finest Matrimonial Prize leaned provocatively close to her, speaking in a low voice, his gaze never leaving her face. She cared little for Lord Worthen's attentions, however, for though he was a Corinthian, a Leader of Fashion, as well as an object of every Matchmaking Mama in London, he lacked an essential quality that somehow everyone else seemed able to overlook: Lord Worthen was without honor, he refused to duel.

A soft rain pattered upon the windows behind Margaret as she stared up into Worthen's face, her fan resting gently upon her chin, her lips parted slightly. Several of his words occasionally reached her, striking an odd chord in her heart, but for the most part she was so enraptured by a series of brilliant images which had overtaken her mind, that she was not really listening to him. She knew he was serious about the subject upon which he was discoursing, for his dark eyes were very intense; but her thoughts had become engulfed by a vivid storm of purples and blacks, and by the image of a lone sea-faring vessel battling rain and wind.

In a small compartment of her mind, Meg composed a

line to describe what she saw. *The* Tormentia *floundered in the midst of monstrous waves, tossed like a battered cork upon a duck pond.* No, no—that wouldn't do. It was too silly. *Tossed like a feather in the wind.*

"Oh, the devil take it!" she cried aloud.

Lord Worthen lifted his brows in considerable surprise. "I beg your pardon?" he whispered.

Meg glanced about the crowded drawing room, guests chatting and gliding among rows of chairs during a pause in the musicale. She cried, "Oh, dear, I ought not to have said that, and I most certainly should not have interrupted you! Forgive me for such a wretched lapse of manner, my lord. Pray continue!"

The viscount smiled in a rueful manner and said, "Margaret Longville, do not tell me your mind has been engaged elsewhere for the past several minutes."

Meg blinked and responded with perfect sincerity, "I'm afraid I have been a trifle distracted. You must forgive me, but there was something about the mole— that is, I am sometimes given to a measure of daydreaming." She regarded the mole upon Worthen's cheek in a considering manner, tapping her fan against her lips. What an excellent, sinister Count Fortunato Worthen made. His looks were dark, for he had black hair cut fashionably *a la Brutus,* black eyes that always appeared intense and saturnine in the candlelit chambers of Mayfair, a noble, aquiline nose, a stubborn chin, and the final touch—an intriguing black mole upon his upper right cheekbone. Earlier in the season, when Lord Worthen had refused yet again to face Lord Montford in a duel, Meg had decided he would be the perfect villain for her latest novel, *Rosamund of Albion.*

His voice, bearing a hint of amusement, barely reached her brain, "You are quite adorable you know."

"Mmmm," Meg murmured absently, for her attention had again shifted to the *Tormentia.* Lashed to the main mast of that rain-soaked vessel was poor, fair Rosamund, the heroine of her fourth novel of adventure and romance. The rain beat upon Rosamund's delicate

8

features, drenching her silky, golden locks. Meg wondered if she ought to have Rosamund faint again, for that would be the third time in this chapter alone. Poor Rosamund fainted frequently.

The bonds tightened about fair Rosamund's wrists, cutting deeply into her skin. Again she cried out in pain as lightning rent the black clouds surrounding the sailing vessel.

Rosamund beseeched the devil standing before her, "Why will'st thou not release me? What have I done to deserve such cruelty?"

Count Fortunato leered at her, another flash of lightning revealing the ugly black mole upon his cheek. In a voice laden with menace, he replied, "Because the gods have commanded it. Vulcan himself has ordered me to bring you to the island of Lemnos where I have hidden your brother Ernest. And only when you agree to wed me shall you see your brother's face again."

Rosamund's voice rose to an anguished wail. "Never! I shall never marry the likes of you!" And she fainted yet again, her head drooping to the side, rain flailing her tender skin.

Margaret wondered briefly if rain could flail skin and then dismissed her concern as insignificant. She never bothered herself with the accuracy of her words, only with the potential "gooseflesh effect," as she was wont to think of it.

Lord Worthen watched the expressions rise and fall upon Meg's face. The passion he saw there tugged strongly upon his heart, and he wanted the right to ask her everything she was thinking and feeling. He had fallen deeply in love with her, pursuing her the entire season and delighting in the manner in which she would frequently stare at him, as though memorizing his every feature. Once he had teased her about her unabashed perusal of his face, asking her if he had soot upon his cheek. How delightfully she had blushed, nervously twisting one of her long red curls about her finger. Her speech had become tangled. She said she had been unforgiveably rude; she didn't know why she stared at him, forgive her, pray excuse her odd manners. The chit obviously was quite smitten with him, and yet never once had she given the least appearance of having set her cap for him: She had never swooned into his arms in an overheated ballroom, nor simpered her responses to a query regarding the weather, nor changed her opinions to suit his own. These were ploys he was used to experiencing, and Meg had made use of none of them. If anything, her conversation was enchantingly arch and usually quite intelligent, except in this moment now, when she again regarded his face almost unseeingly, her attention strangely distrait.

She was a lovely woman of six and twenty summers, dressed in a flowing gown of white muslin caught high to the waist with a dark green ribbon. Her long red hair, partially concealed beneath a striking turban of green silk, was pulled to the side and cascaded down her neck and shoulder. He knew a desire to touch her hair which sparkled in the candlelight. Her eyes were a clear light blue, dancing with life. Faith, how he loved her.

She was an exquisite creature, dressed modishly yet with a curious flare—a variety of headwear, from turbans to flowers, forming a prominent place in her wardrobe and lending her an exquisitely romantic appearance.

The truth was, in every respect Meg intrigued him. Even now she wore a gold shawl, not merely encircling her shoulders but twirled once about her left arm and draped elegantly over the other. Everything about her was inexplicably made for the eye, much like a painting of Turner's, brilliant and dramatic, bathed in light.

Her complexion was milky white. She was beautiful, intense, unconcerned about the opinions of others, and he loved her.

"Meg," he called to her softly, forcing her to attend to

10

him. "Will you not give me your answer or would you prefer I call upon your father tomorrow?"

Meg tore her mind away from Count Fortunato. Clearing her thoughts with a slight shake of her head, she answered simply, "I don't see why you must needs call upon Papa. What answer could he give you that I could not?"

Worthen nodded in approval and leaned closer to her still. In a warm voice, he said, "I have always been enchanted by your spirit. Even from your first season I have admired you. I remember most particularly when you told Lord Byron he ought to mend his dissolute ways before he tried to flirt with you again. You are everything I have wished for. But as you may imagine, I am anxious to know your answer."

Margaret swallowed very hard, for a certain suspicion entered her brain as she asked, "But what is the question? What do you wish to know?"

He started forward slightly and then laughed outright. "Meg Longville, I have just asked you to become my wife."

Meg was so shocked that she took a step backward and cried, "What do you mean, your wife? Are you saying you actually proposed to me? *You?* And in a drawing room, at a—a paltry musicale? Why, I've never heard of anything so—so unromantic in all my life!"

"Unromantic?" he asked, considerably bemused.

She smiled sweetly upon him and added, as though she meant to soften the blow, "There. You see how little we should suit, for you hadn't the faintest notion just how I might feel about a gentleman paying his addresses to me in a despicably dull drawing room."

Lord Worthen ignored the fact that the chamber was full to overflowing with members of the haut ton and quite improperly took her arm firmly in his hand. His voice was husky as he whispered, "You do not allow for a man being violently in love with you! Your beauty has robbed me of sensible action, and your fiery gaze fixed upon me so frequently this evening has been a complete torture to me this hour and more. I spoke because I could not contain my desire to make you my wife. You have used me unmercifully, Meg, to now answer me in this frivolous manner! Have you nothing more to say?''

Meg felt caught by something she did not quite understand. Worthen still held her arm and watched her with his eyes burning into her soul. He seemed overpowering in this moment, much as she had imagined Count Fortunato to be. She felt as though she had never really known Worthen before. And why, of a sudden, did she feel the worst sort of urge—good heavens!—to kiss him? The notion was ridiculous in the extreme, of course, for she did not, *could* not, love such a man as Lord Worthen.

''Meg,'' he whispered. ''You cannot mean to reject my hand.''

Meg felt a blush cover her cheeks, and for the longest moment, as she succumbed to the sheer force of his gaze, she was unable to speak. Finally her speech came in a halting gasp as she cried, ''I—that is, Worthen, I never meant to tease you! Indeed, now that I consider the matter, I realize how it must have seemed and—and how greatly at fault I have been. But I never meant to give you the impression that I was expecting you to offer for me. Never!''

''But what do you mean, you 'realize how it must have seemed'?''

''I—that is, oh, dear!'' Meg drew in her breath. She knew she could hardly tell him she stared at him so often because she wished to capture his every nuance within the character of the evil Count Fortunato. She searched her mind for some farradiddle to relate to him, when a familiar voice relieved her of the necessity of doing so.

Lord Montford's rich voice rolled over her as he asked, ''Are you in need of assistance, my fairest Margaret? Is this fellow importuning you? I should gladly call him out, but I daresay he would not listen to such nonsense as that.'' The baron's lip curled in disgust. He was a tall creature, his deep-set eyes cold and menacing.

12

Before Meg could speak, Worthen answered him readily: "You are quite correct, of course. I commend your perspicacity in finally comprehending it!" Only then did he see a most unhappy expression dart through Meg's eyes, almost of disapproval as she unfurled her fan in a loud snap and looked anywhere but upon his face. Now what had he said to provoke Meg to actually flare her nostrils?

Ignoring Montford, he addressed Meg firmly: "Will you not permit me a few moment's private speech?"

Meg took a small step toward Montford, and in quiet voice, her eyes downcast, she said, "I think not, Worthen. It would be very rude of me to ignore Lord Montford who, as you know, is a particular friend of mine. Besides"—and here she lifted cool eyes to meet his own—"I daresay there is nothing more to be said."

Lord Worthen watched her for a moment, his mind refusing to register the words she had thrown at him. *Nothing more to be said?* Impossible! He had been so certain of her interest. How could he have mistaken her so completely?

He realized to say more would only embarrass both of them and no doubt provoke Montford to again try his patience with another slur upon his honor. Bowing to Meg, he responded, "I shall, of the moment, be satisfied. But only for the moment." He shifted his gaze from her lovely face and continued, "Ah, I see Mrs. Norbury waving to me, for I have begged to hear her daughter perform a particular Bach prelude and fugue. Your servant, Miss Longville. Montford."

Meg nodded to him, a curious chill crossing her shoulders. She shivered in the warm drawing room and clutched her shawl more closely about her arms. How oddly her heart was behaving as she watched him make a polite progress across the room. He was very tall, his black coat cut to perfection across broad shoulders that tapered to a lean waist. He wore tight black pantaloons, encasing firm athletic legs. He had the easy grace of a gentleman who spent a great many hours astride his

13

horse or behind his matched grays which were famous in Mayfair for their breeding and spirit. If only Worthen had been—she almost smiled at the thought—more *worthy* of his rank and position in society, she would have almost considered his proposals. As it was, the thought of becoming his wife caused her to shudder.

Lord Montford asked, "Ought I to force the knave to face me in a duel, for I can see that you are uncommonly upset by your conversation with him? My dearest Meg, had I known he was causing you such distress I would have rescued you much sooner."

Meg regarded Montford with a slight frown. "You are very kind to be concerned with my honor, but I am certain Lord Worthen will very soon suspend his pursuit of me."

"He did not appear to be completely discouraged, but then you are of so sweet a disposition that I'm sure he could not possibly have read your hints properly."

Meg laughed at this. "What humbug! I should never describe my disposition as sweet, and as for Worthen, I spoke very unkindly to him. I've little doubt that after a moment's reflection, he will cut my acquaintance entirely. But you, my lord, ought not to address me with such an endearment as 'dearest.'"

Lord Montford smiled brightly. "Did I say, 'my dearest Meg'? The merest slip of the tongue. But here, take my arm, and I shall lead you to a very fine seat where you may enjoy Hope's performance in peace."

Meg smiled at him as she took his arm and said, "You are very good and always seem to know precisely what I need."

He patted her hand. "If we are to speak of a humbug, I shall remind you that I am not at all good!"

"Am I fairly warned?" she retorted in a bantering tone.

"Indeed, you are. However, I wish you to know that your interests will always be an object of my greatest concern."

"You are grown quite serious of a sudden, but I do

thank you for your solicitude. I have for a long time now valued your friendship a great deal."

He retorted, "And I wish that you could see me as something more than a friend, but I will not press you."

He was nearly as tall as Worthen, though not quite as muscular. His appearance was fascinating, for he possessed a pair of brilliant blue eyes which were at once piercing and appraising. His clothes, fashioned by Weston, hung on his sinewy frame in a rakish manner. His stance was wide, and whenever Meg saw him she had the impression of a hunter. Earlier in the season, she had gently set aside his hints that were she of a mind to accept him, he would offer her his hand in marriage. He had taken her rebuff in a gentlemanly spirit, but had made it clear he hoped one day she would change her mind.

Meg stole a glance at him as they wended their way through the chairs. He was handsome, certainly confident in his abilities. He had wit and charm, a fine property, and he frequently quoted Byron to her as well as John Keats. But above all, he was known to flout the king's law and engage in duels, both sword and pistol, a quality which appealed strongly to her sense of what was chivalrous and honorable. In short, he possessed every quality she could desire in a husband. Why, then had her elusive heart remained untouched by his quiet though persistent courtship? Wondering how he would respond to learning Worthen had offered for her, she leaned close to him and whispered teasingly, "I certainly hope that were you to pay *your* addresses to me, you would not do so in a drawing room."

He glanced down at her, his blue eyes narrowing suddenly. His words rolled easily from his tongue. "Were I to offer for you, Miss Margaret Longville, I would steal you away to the edge of the world, I would call upon angels to attend you, and upon bended knee I would beg for your hand a hundred times until you said yes."

"Oh, dear," Meg cooed, blinking several times rapidly. "Have I not known you, Montford?"

"Not nearly well enough." He lifted her hand to his

lips, saluting her fingers lightly. When he had released her hand, he said, "Forgive me, Meg, but am I to understand that Worthen actually offered for you?"

Meg laughed. "Yes he did. Can you imagine anything so absurd?"

Lord Montford did not answer immediately. His gaze searched the long chamber quickly until he found Worthen sitting in a chair beside Mrs. Norbury. The baron lifted a brow, his blue eyes cloaked. "No," he responded at last. "I can think of nothing more absurd, nor more unwelcome, and I feel most acutely for your discomfort in having to endure such a proposal. I know how much you despise that man."

Meg said, "I have always appreciated the fact that you, at least, understand my sentiments. I fear so many others do not see Worthen as you and I do. Hope Norbury, for instance, holds him upon a pedestal, likening him to the god of Mars, which always makes me laugh. Mars, indeed! It is very fortunate, I suppose, that he is as handsome as he is besides possessing a title, for I am certain he would not receive such accolades were he lacking either his strong good looks or his peerage. But I see Hope preparing her music, and I had best return to my seat."

As Meg sat down in a chair covered in silk, she approved Montford's choice to range himself with the gentlemen along the far wall in order that the ladies might have use of the chairs.

Meg sighed. The season had been such a disappointment. Time and again, in every doorway, she had searched in vain for her knight, but he had never appeared. Only Montford and, of course, Worthen.

Mrs. Norbury's voice, as she introduced the music her daughter, Hope, would now be performing upon the pianoforte, drifted over the audience. Several persons who had been sipping ratafia or champagne and chatting now scrambled to find their seats. Among them, Elizabeth Priestley, Hope's cousin, rushed to sit beside Meg.

The black-haired beauty grabbed Meg's arm and in an

16

excited whisper cried, "Do tell me everything Worthen said to you! I am all agog, as is half the room! Did he offer for you? Are you to be the next Viscountess Worthen? Oh, you are the most fortunate of creatures, for you will be a peeress! If only Montford had not interrupted you!"

Meg turned slightly toward her young friend, prepared to tell her everything. But the moment she met Lizzie's glittering blue eyes and the hungry parting of her lips, Meg playfully pushed Lizzie's hand away and retorted, "I will tell you nothing because the moment I revealed a single word of his lordship's, you would shout it to the entire room!"

"I would not! You know I would not! But never mind, for Hope is arranging her skirts and wriggling her fingers, and my aunt is glaring at me again!"

Meg turned toward the far end of the chamber, where Mrs. Norbury was indeed staring at Lizzie with a choleric eye and clearing her throat. Hope sat very straight upon the piano bench, flexing her fingers and breathing deeply in preparation for plunging into the keys. The piano of rosewood gleamed under the flickering of a branch of candles, the rain still pattering upon the windows. The chamber of yellow and blue silks rustled with the sounds of the beau monde as ladies unfurled their fans and gentlemen took hasty pinches of snuff and snapped their boxes shut. An assortment of coughs, giggles and sighs faded away as Hope began to play.

The prelude eased the audience along, some almost slumbering, but once the fugue broke upon the listeners, many leaned forward in their seats intent upon Hope's performance. Meg loved the music, closing her eyes and letting the relentless notes flow over her. After a moment, she opened her eyes, her gaze drifting slowly about the room until she found Lord Worthen. He, too, was listening intently to Hope. Meg still could not believe Worthen had proposed to her, and a tremor ran through her as she remembered the way he had held her arm and spoken so fiercely to her: *You do not allow for a man being violently in love with you.* How had she inspired so much passion in a man she believed to be lacking in any such capacity? Really she was flattered, but at the same time she felt as though forces were at work over which she had little control, much like Vulcan's command that Count Fortunato bring Rosamund to the island of Lemnos. And she trembled again.

Lizzie leaned very close to Meg, shuddering. In a whisper, she cried, "Do you *feel* the ecstasy of the music as well, Meg? Whenever I hear this particular piece, I am thrown into raptures!" Her fan moved at a wild pace in response to her heightened sensibilities as she continued to whisper, "I am always shocked when I hear Hope perform, for she is absolutely reckless, even daring! Look how she pounces upon the keys! My sweet, mousy little cousin, as bold as a lioness! Really at times I do not comprehend her at all."

Meg whispered back, "I am always astonished, just as you are. How is it possible for one so reserved and proper to summon such expression?"

Voices behind them, matrons intent upon dampening the spirits of the younger ladies, hushed Lizzie and Meg. Lizzie could not resist turning around and quite improperly pulling a face which further set the Tabbies to caterwauling.

After several ladies had performed upon both the harp and the pianoforte, the music at last drew to a close. Hope immediately sought out both Meg and her cousin, Lizzie. "I was never more nervous!" she cried. "Imagine Worthen begging to hear me perform."

Lizzie smiled broadly and exclaimed, "But imagine Worthen offering for Meg's hand in marriage!"

Hope, her soft brown eyes lit with excitement, extended a gloved hand toward Meg and pressed her arm. "Do not say he did so at last, Meggie? Oh, my dear, I thought he would, for he was always speaking so fondly of you! And are you to be married, or is Lizzie telling me yet again another horrid whisker!"

Meg frowned slightly. "He did offer for me, but whatever made you think I would accept his proposals?

18

We are not suited to one another, and you know very well what my opinion of him is."

Hope appeared quite astonished and said, "I suppose I had merely thought you had forsaken your notions of honor and duelling. I had thought you realized Worthen's value at last. You were forever staring at him, you know—and with such expressions upon your face! Really, Meg, if you did refuse him, I sincerely hope he does not feel himself terribly ill-used."

Meg was a little astonished by Hope's speech. Had she been so wretchedly indiscreet?

Lizzie clapped her hands. "I just knew he had offered for you, Meg. But what nonsense you are both speaking!" She addressed Hope: "If Meg refused Worthen, what difference does it make? He may have any female he wishes. I shall seek him out myself, for I should dearly love to become the next Viscountess Worthen. Of course I should be satisfied were he merely to form part of my court."

Hope shook her head at her cousin. "You've enough suitors to make even Venus jealous!"

Lizzie cried, "And this is but my first season. It has been the most amazing thing, for I have at least a dozen beaux." Her expression grew suddenly minxlike as she unfurled her brilliantly colored fan and began plucking at the narrow spokes. Her gaze remained fixed upon Hope as she continued, "However, I should gladly exchange them all for one particular gentleman, who shall remain nameless, but who I intend, given the slightest encouragement, to steal from you! No more dashing creature exists than your beau, and you are beyond reason fortunate to have claimed him for your own!"

It was now Hope's turn to lift her chin. Taking a deep breath, she retorted, "If you refer to Charles, I shall only say that I find your manner of speaking quite reprehensible. Steal him from me indeed! As though I owned him or something of that sort. He is his own man, Lizzie, and if you do not take greater care with your speech, you will very soon be thought of as a hoydenish young lady."

Hope was several years older than her cousin and did not hesitate to remind her at appropriate times of the difference in their ages.

Lizzie, who was shorter than Hope, merely squared her shoulders at this comment and with a sly wink said, "Hoydenish? How would you define that? Would a young lady who attended a masquerade at Vauzhall be considered a hoyden? Then such a female I am!"

Hope gasped, and Lizzie lifted a triumphant brow.

"It was perfectly acceptable, Hope," Lizzie declared, "for if you must know, Mama attended our party the *entire time*. However, I will admit that though a turn amongst the gardens upon the arm of Major Spickles would have been delightful, you will be happy to know I was forbidden even that! Oh, I see an acquaintance of mine, and I absolutely must speak with her, for she was at Astley's last night, and I heard that a man fell off one of the horses and was nearly trampled to death!"

Meg watched Lizzie go, feeling as though a shower of fireworks trailed after the impetuous young lady. She admired Lizzie's high spirits and boldness in staring down so many of the rigid dictums of the ton. She knew full-well that much of this speech had been purposely arranged in an effort to bring Hope's disapproving expression upon her face.

Lizzie had been quite successful.

Hope bit her lip and said, "From the time Elizabeth Priestley was able to walk, she was as wild as bramble vines. I am only shocked she hasn't fallen into some disastrous scrape before now!"

Meg heard but part of Hope's exasperated speech, for across the room, near the pianoforte, Meg could see her father speaking quite earnestly with Lord Worthen. A sudden fear rushed through her, especially when her papa turned around, caught her gaze and actually scowled at her.

Chapter Two

On the following morning, Meg sat before a large pile of linen sheets and table covers in her bedchamber. She was examining each one at length for a general thinning or actual tears in the finely woven threads. For the most part she took great delight in this homey task. Today, however, her heart felt very low as she fingered one cloth in particular which had been woven with the faintest impressions of roses all about the border. This table linen, a favorite of her mother's and now fraying in several places, brought her mama forcefully to mind. These memories shook her—remembrances that had been buried deep within her for years.

A sweet, final conversation had occurred between Meg and her mother just before her mama died some thirteen years earlier. Meg had forever based her values upon her mother's parting words.

"My dearest child," her mama had whispered, clutching her arm with her thin, wasted hand. "You must be very careful in your choice of a husband. He must be all that is honorable, a gentleman above reproach, esteemed amongst the men of his acquaintance, a knight willing to defend you against all the adversities of life. How else can a woman be assured of bearing her children in safety and peace? Choose carefully, my sweet Margaret!"

These words, addressed to Meg's half-child, half-womanly mind since she had been but thirteen years of age at the time, had imbedded themselves deeply within her spirit, setting her course for the second thirteen years of her life. She gauged every man who even touched the edges of her society against her mother's precepts. In addition, she imbued this ideal with the inevitable results of her rich imagination as she read the works by the author of the Waverly Novels. Her knight must be brave and courageous in every respect, and to this end she had begun weaving her own tales of love and adventure resulting in two published works of her own— a third taking shape in the form of *Rosamund of Albion*. The heroes of her novels became the epitomy of her mother's advice as well as a printed portrait of her own evolving, fanciful ideals of percisely what she wanted in the sort of man she wished to take as husband.

Her mother passed away that night, perishing from the horrid consumption, one of the most common and unhappy diseases of the day. Meg had adored her mother and promised her, with every ounce of her womanly heart, that she would marry a gentleman her mama would have honored and esteemed.

And with these thoughts, as she searched through the sheets and table covers, just as her mama had taught her to do, she remembered with great disgust Lord Worthen's proposal of the night before. How could he imagine that she would consider accepting his hand in marriage when he would not even give answer to Montford's direct challenge to his honor? Would such a man defend her own honor, protect her, cherish her? She thought not. And with a brisk nod of her curls and another promise to her mama to remain faithful to her final, parting wisdom, Meg continued her task.

Sir William Longville held the gold silk curtains back and stared down into Berkeley Square. He tossed off his

22

second glass of sherry just as Lord Worthen, astride a fine chestnut stallion, turned the corner of the square at a neat trot.

Sir William was a tall, large-boned man sporting a lightly silvered shock of red hair and a kind face. His eyes were clear blue, intense and frequently full of laughter. But of the moment his expression was clouded, his thick red brows drawn together, his teeth clenched. Letting the curtains fall back into place, he blew a breath of sheer frustration from his cheeks and returned his glass to a polished silver tray by the window.

Waiting for the viscount to cross the portal of his town house and mount the stairs, Sir William began pacing the library for the hundredth time that morning. The room was long, narrow and panelled in a fine oak wainscoting. Two wing chairs, covered in a warm gold velvet, flanked the fireplace. On a small writing desk near one of the chairs sat several volumes of mythology, one of which was open to an illustration of Vulcan, god of fire. Meg had been at work again.

Ordinarily Sir William took much refuge in this room, often falling sound asleep in one of the chairs. But today—good God!—he meant to give his daughter to Worthen if he would take her. Damn and blast, how had things come to such a pass as this? Meg would never forgive him.

He heard his butler's polite voice in the hallway and ran a finger just inside his neckcloth, feeling a familiar constriction that had afflicted him for several months now—a tightening of his cravat whenever he was faced with the difficulties of his household. He could not remember precisely when his neckcloths had grown uncomfortable, but he rather thought it began about the time in late February when his dearest Caroline informed him that he would be a father for the second time.

He scurried back to his decanter of sherry and quickly poured himself a third glass. Swallowing hard, he drank the nut-flavored wine and sighed deeply. He loved his

23

daughter; he loved his wife, but a worse mix you couldn't find—practical, measured Caroline and his fanciful Meg. *God help me*, he thought, *one of these days I'm sure to go off in a fit of apoplexy. Much either of them would care; they would be too busy arguing about bed linens and chamber pots to notice!*

There was only one solution, and Caroline had proposed it over a month ago. He must find Meg a husband. His daughter was a considerable heiress, possessing in her dowry through her mother a fine property that marched along Montford's lands. In addition, she was worth a very handsome thirty thousand pounds. Meg could snap her fingers at a dozen perfectly acceptable gentlemen if she would but choose to—and one of them a duke! Instead, she lived in that cursed fantasy world of hers, waiting for her ridiculous knight to come galloping up on his horse, throw her over his saddle and sweep her away. A deuced uncomfortable ride that would be, not to mention the fact he was likely to break her neck in such an attempt. But his Meggie never thought of life in these terms, only in whether or not a man could make her heart quicken!

In his marchings, Sir William paused in front of a globe of the world and could not resist kicking it. He sent the globe flying into the brass andirons fronting the fireplace. It bounced on the hearth and spun until it rolled harmlessly off onto the planked floor.

Lord Worthen's voice from the doorway brought a flush of embarrassment to Sir William's face. "I hope, sir, that I have not been the inspiration for your taking a vengeance upon the world, as it were!"

"What? Oh, damme, Worthen, I'm glad you've come." He moved to the door, his arm extended toward the viscount, and shook his hand warmly.

When he had settled Worthen in one of the chairs by the fireplace, he replaced the globe upon its stand only to discover India now bore a fine hole. After pouring out two glasses of sherry, he sat down in the chair opposite the viscount, absently retaining both glasses. Falling into a brown study, he grimaced, his gaze fixed upon a scuff mark at the tip of his right boot.

After a moment, Worthen's voice cut through his thoughts. "Would you care to part with one of those glasses? I shouldn't refuse a little sherry were it offered me."

"What? Lord have mercy I've grown addled these days." He handed the sherry to Worthen and stated flatly, "I won't mince words; I'm in the devil of a fix and you've got to help me. You see, that girl of mine is hopelessly muddled in her thinking, and I greatly fear last night she bungled her entire future."

Lord Worthen took the hint and suggested, "Would this have anything to do with my offer of marriage?"

"I'm glad you've brought it up."

Worthen laughed. "Your daughter did not seem interested in the least. In fact she seemed more insulted than anything else. If we were to speak of the art of bungling, I am sure I made an excellent mull of proposing to Margaret. She said such an offer was quite the most unromantic thing she had ever heard—or something of that nature."

"Well, as to that, you should have come to me first. I could have told you how to go on! You won't win Meg's heart with anything short of a suit of mail, a shield and a sword."

"I am beginning to understand a little of the difficulty before me, though I still cannot account for one particular aspect of her behavior of this season. You see, she was always looking at me, quite intensely. And I don't mean once or twice but nearly everytime we were together. To be frank, I had every reason to believe she had fallen in love with me. You can imagine what a shock her refusal was. However, I don't mean to give up my suit if that is your concern. I love your daughter very much."

Sir William sipped his sherry and regarded the viscount in a thoughtful manner. The wine eased through his veins, and he felt a great deal calmer; but there was more rough ground to cover, and he took a deep breath. "Meg's an heiress as I'm sure you already know," he said. "She has an excellent dowry which includes a certain property of ancient heritage, so you understand how careful I must be about the fellows who court her. I felt obliged to have my Solicitor investigate your situation, though I must say I wasn't surprised to learn that most of your lands are mortgaged to the hilt. You see, I knew your father quite well. A deuced miracle he'd kept any of it!"

"I won't cavil with you," Worthen responded. "My father ran his estate to rack and ruin. I must marry a woman of fortune. But I wish to assure you—"

"You needn't convince me of your motives. I've known you for a long time, before you was breeched, and I trust you. I am prepared to give Meg to you now. I am empowered to do so by the conditions of her inheritance, and given my own particular knowledge of my daughter, I believe you would suit her quite well. She is yours if you will have her." He felt his neckcloth again bite into his neck; but the words were spoken, and he wouldn't alter his course now, even though it terrified him.

Worthen choked on his last sip of sherry, unable to credit what he had heard. He queried, "What are you saying, Sir William? I don't think I quite understand. Will Meg not have a choice or the power to refuse me— again?"

"You've the right of it."

"Why? I don't understand? If I thought for a moment you had designs upon my title, I should leave your house this instant. But I know you don't give a fig for such things, any more than Caroline does. Why, then, do you wish Meg to marry me and why so hastily?"

Sir William rose to his feet and, taking Worthen's empty glass with him, marched to the decanter and refilled both glasses. "I've several reasons," he said. "Most of them of a personal nature which I will not divulge to you. As for the remainder, first, I think Meggie could love you. She may already do so and not be aware of it. She needs a strong man, for though she might wear her

26

ribbons and soft muslins and give all the appearance of being meek and malleable, damme, she's got a stubbornness like red sandstone. She's a passionate female, too, though I won't pretend she hasn't got a few horrifying notions that need to be drummed out of her. Did you know for instance that for a man to be truly a gentleman, he must be both scholar and athlete? Good God, that rules most of us out right there. If a man has a superior intelligence, generally he hasn't enough bottom to sit a saddle. On the other hand, if he rides to hounds, he hasn't the time or interest to learn his Greek letters." He brought both glasses back and handed one to Worthen. Sitting down again he continued, "Meg lives in a world of her own concoction too much of the time to suit me. And that leads me to my last point—Amelia Hartshorn."

Worthen heard the name and waited for Sir William to elaborate.

Sir William stared at him and sipped his wine but for a long moment said nothing. Finally he lifted a brow and said, "Have you never noticed the peculiar manner Meg has of gasping, shuddering and wearing her turbans at that intriguing angle? All for effect! I'm only astonished no one else has guessed the truth, though I'm nearly certain Montford is aware of it."

After a moment, a bolt of lightning flashed in Worthen's brain, and he again choked on his sherry. "Oh, dear God in heaven, was there ever a more hopeless sapskull than myself? Your daughter is Amelia Hartshorn, is she not? No wonder she chided me about having offered for her in so "despicably dull" a place as a drawing room. I should think nothing short of a misty, wooded dell would do for Miss Hartshorn."

"Then, you are familiar with my daughter's novels?"

"Only by association. You see, my sister, Augusta, could not be torn away from the last Hartshorn novel and snapped at everyone who so much as came within ten feet of her. She was deaf to even the most pitiful of entreaties from her youngest child!"

Sir William nodded as though he understood perfectly.

"Michaelmas last, I found Caroline curled up in our library at Staplehope very late at night, a single candle burning low in the socket, her eyes wide as saucers! She was reading one of Meg's novels, and she didn't even see me for a full five minutes." He smiled suddenly, staring into his wineglass. "Who would've thought my daughter would write stories, nonetheless have 'em published! Damme, I'm proud of Meg, but you do see what an enormous dilemma I face. How is any man going to measure up to her fictionalized heroes? I'll send one of my footmen over with her books later today if you like. I suggest you read them all so that you might be better prepared for dealing with my fanciful daughter."

Worthen was silent, wondering what to do. His gaze drifted toward the writing desk near his chair, and he happened to glance at a book open to an illustration of one of the gods of Olympus. Leaning closer, he read the words, *Vulcan, god of fire and of the working of metals.* Was Meg using Vulcan in her next novel? All of the poetry of the age was littered with mythological allusions, and it would be natural for Meg to include such characters in her books.

Learning of Meg's identity cast an entirely new slant upon his courtship of the elusive Miss Longville. He could quote poetry to her and should have been doing so since the season opened. He could speak as much nonsense as she wished to hear, and he would no doubt take great delight in doing so. He could win her heart if given the chance, only for the life of him he could not comprehend why a more romantic approach had not occurred to him before!

Turning back to Sir William, he said, "I don't like forcing Meg's hand in this manner. Could I not perhaps visit your house this summer and encourage your daughter's heart in my own way and in my own time?"

"I'll speak plain to you. I have a certain neighbor, who I believe is a particular nemesis of your own, who has made unwelcome overtures to Meg."

"Montford."

28

"None other, and I don't trust him. I had heard sometime ago that he had run into dun territory, and when his attentions toward Meg grew marked over these past two years, I had the same Runner see what he could discover about Montford. In the past several years the man has completely ruined his father's estates; they are mortgaged to the hilt. And from what the Runner could discover, he is deeply in debt to the cent-per-centers as well, which means that if my Meggie were to marry him she would be leg-shackled to a care-for-nobody gamester who wouldn't think twice about staking her dowry at Newmarket or one of the Pall Mall gaming hells! But my disregard for Montford has basis as well in the fact that I have known him to lie outright on more than one occasion. And though I am loath to condemn a man because his family's so recently acquired a peerage, I smell the shop as well as a great deal of ambition that has little to do with my Meggie's heart. I don't think he can make her happy, but he's just shrewd enough to persuade her to marry him. I think somehow he learned of her identity as Amelia Hartshorn because a few weeks ago he altered his pattern of courtship and even composed several lines of verse in her honor. Bah! I was ill just hearing Meg talk of it." He narrowed his eyes. "I'll never forget how my daughter's eyes fairly sparkled as she read the lines aloud—something about doves and foxes and bluebells. At any rate, I am fully persuaded that if I don't act soon, I don't know but what Meg will be bamboozled into believing Montford is her curst knight."

Worthen sipped his sherry, the image of Montford's deepset eyes overtaking his mind. Montford had not hesitated to interrupt his brief tête-à-tête with Meg at the musicale, nor to instantly cast a slur upon his own honor before he had gotten two sentences out. If ever he had regretted his vow never to duel again, he had regretted it last night. He wished, nay longed, to lay his sword alongside Montford's. Or better yet, to face him across thirty paces and level his pistol at the baron's jeering face.

At this unhappy thought, he leaned his head against the back of the chair and took a deep breath. Another image replaced Montford's—that of his brother stretched out upon a leaf-strewn forest floor, blood pouring from a wound to his leg. No, he would not duel, not even to protect his honor.

But what was he to do about Meg? He certainly would not give her up to the likes of Montford. He was the right man for her, he had no doubts on that score. And he always got what he wanted, one way or another. He never held back when it came to pursuit, whether it was on the hunting field or in matters of the heart.

With a sudden realization of how much enjoyment he would derive from entrancing Meg with sonnets, primroses and stolen kisses, he made his decision, saying, "I accept your offer of Margaret's hand in marriage."

Sir William let out a great sigh of relief. He felt as though a tremendous burden had just been lifted from his shoulders. "Damme!" he cried. "But you'll not regret it! Can you be prepared to take her as wife in let us say three weeks?"

Worthen laughed outright. "You do not think Meg would need a little more time to adjust to the notion of becoming Lady Worthen?"

"Better to bowl her over and be done with it! I know my daughter. Three weeks, not a day less!"

Worthen inclined his head. "I certainly have no objection! I only hope Meg will not despise me for this day's work."

Sir William again felt a tightening of his cravat, and he swallowed uncomfortably. "You'll have a devil of a fight on your hands! Well! I am content, or reasonably so. Send your Solicitor around when it is convenient."

Worthen said, "There is just one thing. You will tell Meg about my estates? I would not want her learning upon our wedding day that I had need of her dowry to salvage my lands."

Sir William waved a negligent hand. "Yes, yes, of course! I'll see to everything."

A gentle tapping on the door startled both men as Meg's voice begged entrance.

Sir William leaned forward in his chair, clamping a firm hand about Worthen's arm. "Not a word until I've spoken to her," he whispered. "I'll give you a few minutes with her now, but remember: Amelia Hartshorn!"

Meg was so startled to find Worthen closeted with her papa in the library that she dropped several bulky linen sheets that had been awkwardly slung over her arm. "Papa!" she cried. "I did not mean to intrude!"

"Nonsense! Come in, my dear. We were just speaking of you!"

Meg responded quickly, "I am hardly gowned in a manner to receive company." She was dressed in a faded blue muslin gown, her hair caught high upon her head with a white ribbon. Several strands of hair had escaped, and she felt untidy in Worthen's presence, especially since he was dressed immaculately in a dark blue riding coat, buckskin breeches and gleaming top boots. Her heart lurched within her in a traitorous fashion as he rose to his feet and bowed to her. He was a remarkably handsome creature, she thought for the hundredth time. She wondered why she felt suddenly frightened by his presence. She tried to back out of the room, as a small animal might when it becomes aware of a trap, but her papa nearly leapt upon her, holding her by the waist and informing her Worthen desired to speak with her.

"No, Papa!" she cried in whisper. A flush covered her cheeks as she amended, "I mean, I am certain Lord Worthen can have nothing to say to me which could not also be said in your presence."

Sir William gave his daughter's waist a friendly squeeze. In his jovial manner, he said, "Nonsense. Worthen is a great friend of mine, and he has begged a few words with you. I'll not deny him that." And he was gone, the door closing ominously behind him.

Meg gulped as she glanced in Worthen's direction. Her

papa had been as mad as fire when he learned she had refused so notable a Matrimonial Prize as Worthen. Though she tried to explain her sentiments that she could not esteem Worthen, her father had merely flared his nostrils, slammed his copy of *The Morning Post* down upon the dining table and stormed from the room. Meg gulped again. What had the two men been discussing? Certainly nothing less than the details of Worthen's proposal of the night before.

Well, she had no intention of giving the viscount another opportunity to renew his addresses, regardless of her father's desire to see her wedded to the wretched beast. In a polite manner she stated that she had a great many household duties to attend to and she hoped he would understand that she had scarcely a moment to spare.

She dropped to her knees, and as she began folding the sheets, she spoke in a hurried voice: "I don't know how I came about to be so clumsy. We are closing the house, you see, for Caroline has not felt very well of late and she wishes to return to Staplehope as soon as possible. I long to return home as well. Of course it is too early to begin collecting the brambleberries for jelly, but this time of year I am always in the attics seeing what might be given to the poor and what ought to be burnt in a bonfire."

As Worthen watched her, he made a great effort to see her now as Amelia Hartshorn, authoress. Did she long to hear poetry whispered in her ear? He walked toward her slowly and, in a quiet voice, said, "You are far too pretty to be submerged in such tasks. You ought to spend your hours walking barefoot through fields of bluebells or perhaps sitting beside a quiet pool and letting just the tips of your curls dangle in the water."

He took a crumpled sheet from her hands and, turning away from her, shook it to its full length. Facing her again, he knelt in front of her and shaped the linen fabric, frayed in several places, into the semblance of a pool of water. He gestured to the sheet. "Such as this pool of water."

Meg was so astonished at his form of address, as well as by his actions, that she stared at him, her mouth slightly agape. "A pool of water?" she queried.

He gestured again to the sheet in front of her. "Yes," he said, regarding her intently. "If you were to recline beside this pool, would your copper locks dangle into the water? Are your curls of such a length? I have longed to know, this entire season and more."

Meg felt a familiar tingling sensation take root in her imagination. She tilted her head slightly, a dizziness affecting her senses, her heart beating rapidly within her breast. Worthen's image grew misty, a soft glow shimmering about his entire person. How very odd! "Yes," she responded in a whisper, "I think my hair would just touch the water, but I am not wholly certain."

"I should like to see your hair unloosened about your shoulders and framing your beautiful face." His voice was very low; his gaze never left her eyes.

Meg responded, "My hair is rather frizzy when it becomes wet."

He leaned toward her, from across the pool, and said, "A halo of spun copper just after a rain."

Meg felt her heart constrict in a blissful manner as she said quietly, "Oh, what a pretty turn of phrase. I did not know you could speak so poetically, my lord."

He reached over to her and touched her hair. "I was used to compose all manner of verse when I was young. Sonnets as every lad must compose when he is in the throes of a first love."

"And was such a love also red-haired?"

He shook his head. "Alas, I am afraid not. But shall I confess the entire truth to you? I fell madly in love with my sister's governess, Henrietta Andover, a beauty of five and twenty. I had been sent down from Eton for putting ink on the headmaster's chair."

"Naughty boy," Meg said softly, not wanting to break the spell.

"Miss Andover had very straight black hair, and I remember seeing it once tumbled about her shoulders. I thought I should go mad. How long is your hair, Meg? Would it fall now into our pool? I should like to know. Just once, I should like to see your hair as free as your spirit."

Meg was caught entirely by Worthen's manner of speech. Somehow in a few words, he had obliterated her intention of leaving the library as quickly as possible. Instead, he had caused her to abandon every maidenly consideration, and without the least hesitation, she quite scandalously reached up and pulled at the ribbon that held her hair in place. When her locks were loosened, Worthen began tugging gently upon her curls to bring them down about her neck and arms. She was entirely vulnerable, he realized, and he could scarcely tolerate the thought of Montford speaking false endearments to her.

Meg looked at her hair and said, "I fear it does not even come close to the water."

"If you reclined on your elbow, perhaps?" he suggested gently. He didn't think he could bear to see her lying beside the rumpled sheet, and he hoped she would demur. Instead, she immediately lay down, her head cradled upon her elbow. She pulled her hair forward across her arms and draped it into the pool.

The tingling sensation Meg had been feeling grew stronger, and a vision formed suddenly in her mind—an image of fair Rosamund reclining in innocence beside a pool. Tears of heartrending grief dropped one by one into the water. Rosamund's thoughts were all of how she might vanquish the evil Count Fortunato, when suddenly the beast appeared before her!

"Rosamund, you are caught! You shall not escape from me now!"

Rosamund screamed, but no one heard her pitiful cries in the cedar forests of Lemnos. Vulcan kept the populace from his gardens; the servants were loyal to their god. She cried, "What do you mean to do with me?"

He glared down at her, his eyes dark with passion. "I mean to make you my wife."

He frightened her so, and she fainted, yet again.

Only vaguely, did Meg realize that Worthen had crossed their pool and was now leaning over her.

"Meg," he breathed into her ear. "I mean to make you my wife."

Fear coursed through Meg's heart as Worthen's choice of words struck her. She tried to move, but his breath upon her ear had somehow made it impossible. What had come over her that she had placed herself in so dangerous a position? His lips moved lightly over her ear and her cheek. His mouth was unbelievably soft.

Meg whispered, "You should not. Oh, my goodness!" His lips brushed her mouth lightly. Her breathing became almost painfully difficult as he kissed her gently.

"Meg, you must marry me." He kissed her again.

"No, no," she answered, her voice faint. She couldn't move. Count Fortunato had cast a wicked spell upon her as well. She felt his powerful arm slip behind her waist as he lifted her from her reclining position to cradle her in his arms.

Worthen felt a fire rush over him, of hunger and longing, of extreme desire at the extraordinary female in his arms. The very thought of Montford holding her in his own arms caused him to cry out, "I won't let another man have you. Do you understand?"

Meg felt lost in his arms, almost powerless. He kissed her very hard, bitingly hard, his lips bruising her own. She felt more than just a mild tingling now as an urgency welled up within her. She felt compelled to return his kiss, and yet she knew she should not! Horrified at the strength of her sudden and inexplicable desire, she pulled away from him, but he would not release her.

Meg blinked several times until Worthen's black mole came sharply into focus, and she gave a little cry. Placing a hand upon his chest, warding him off, she cried, "You—you are seducing me, you knave! Montford asked me last night if I desired he should call you out, and now I regret that I did not immediately set him upon you."

He kept her imprisoned in his arms, refusing to let her go, though she began struggling against him. "Am I the villain in this piece, Meg?" he asked. "Be careful that you do not mistake your man."

"Evil one!" she cried in dramatic accents.

He released her then, and she hurriedly rose to her feet, affecting a proud, injured countenance. "Despicable cur!" she cried.

He rose to his feet, planted his boots in a wide stance, folded his arms across his chest, lowered his head slightly, and scowled at her in a purposely fierce manner. He nearly laughed when she clutched her bosom and gasped, "Leave me at once, you—you beast!"

Worthen was enjoying himself hugely as he regarded her with what he hoped was a villainous expression. He advanced on her again, slowly and steadily. She walked backward, all the while demanding to know what he was doing, what he meant to do, and why he would not leave her in peace.

When he had trapped her beside the little writing desk, he spoke in a low, husky voice, leaning very close to her: "Because I love you and I mean to have you."

"You are a monster!" she cried.

He swallowed very hard, for he was filled with a measure of amusement that threatened to ruin this exquisite moment. "I am a monster, my dearest Margaret, and you've only begun to discover the depths to my depravity."

She closed her eyes and, flinging her arm toward the door, cried, "Begone! At once!"

He loved her, every expressive inch of her, and it was all he could do to keep from gathering her up in his arms and covering her with kisses. Restraining this mad impulse, he took a deep breath and said, "I shall leave you, but only because I know that I will be with you again in but a few days."

Meg opened her eyes and, lifting her chin, said, "My

family is removing to Shropshire in the morning. I have already told you so."

He happened to glance at the book on the table and, smiling wickedly, said, "I will come to you, Meg. Vulcan has commanded me to take you as wife! I will not disobey the god of fire."

Meg gasped and closed her eyes, feeling very much as though she might faint. In the barest whisper, she said, "I shall pray for your soul." She heard a strangled sound issue from Worthen's throat, but before she could see the effects of her words, he abruptly left the room.

Worthen walked quickly down the stairs to the front door. He held his breath the entire time for fear if he breathed, laughter would erupt from him. Only when he was standing upon the flagway, did he give vent to his amusement in a series of muffled barks to which the butler expressed his sincere hope that his lordship was not being afflicted with the influenza!

When he had mounted his horse and was trotting around the square, Worthen glanced back at the town house. He saw Meg standing at a window on the first floor, a maid beside her nodding vigorously to her instructions. He loved Meg, he wanted her, but what right had he to force her into a marriage she did not wish for. No right whatsoever.

At that moment she happened to glance toward him and immediately clutched her bosom, stepping away from the window.

He began laughing heartily. It was wrong, the engagement was a horrid thing, but he could not help himself. She was too adorable, too caught up in her quirky view of the world, for him to resist the forthcoming struggle of wills.

Laying his crop smartly across his horse's flank, the chestnut stallion broke into a canter, and Worthen leaned into the wind, his blood racing, his heart readied for the battle that lay ahead of him.

Chapter Three

Nearly a sennight later, as Meg made her way to the stables, she suddenly stopped in mid-stride. She had forgotten her riding crop and turned briskly upon her heel heading back to the morning room where she had left the crop on the day before. For several days now, since her return to Shropshire, she had ridden out every morning after breakfast. She was in high gig, for the sky was clear save for a few scattered puffs of clouds, and she could be assured that for at least an hour, she would not be brangling with Caroline.

She held the long flowing skirt of her black habit slung over her arm and walked swiftly toward the back terrace. Something odd was afoot at Staplehope Hall, but what, precisely, she was still not certain. Frequently, she would find the maids clustered together in little knots, whispering. Invariably, upon her approach, the young women would giggle, bob their curtsies and scurry away almost as though they wished to avoid her.

Meg supposed such odd behavior was in response to the news that Caroline was increasing. However, it was a little strange that the entire household would be fluttering about when the baby was not due until November. Why, even the butler, a stately, imperious creature known fondly as The Brute behind his back, was often found smiling when he would usually scowl. He even forgave one of the footmen who had been so bold as to steal a kiss from the scullery maid!

As Meg mounted the terrace steps, she was struck yet again with the beauty of the ancient, brick mansion. The style was typical of the Elizabethan mode, and row upon row of small-paned rectangular windows smiled onto the soft, Shropshire hills. The house looked to the west, the wild Welsh mountains not far distant, and took every storm full in the face.

Meg walked quickly through the halls toward the morning room, which had been her own special habitat since she could remember. Over the years she had converted the large, airy chamber to a library of sorts where she closeted herself, hours on end, and brought to life the characters of her novels.

The sound of her riding boots tapping down the hall echoed across the tiles in a swift, marching cadence. Meg was happy to be home, even if she and Caroline still dissented over matters of housekeeping.

Just before she reached the morning room, a footman opened the door and walked out of that chamber bearing a stack of paintings, of watercolors, her own special watercolors.

Meg froze in her steps, her gloves held in one hand, her heart lurching within her. "James! What are you doing with my paintings?" Meg asked, her brows lifted in surprise.

James turned a bright red color. "I do be sorry, miss," he answered promptly. "But I think ye ought to speak with Lady Longville. She's within." He bowed slightly and stepped away from the door.

Meg moved slowly toward the room and asked in a quiet voice, "Where were you taking them?"

The footman, his blue eyes wide, gulped. "To the schoolroom, miss. Should I continue on my way, then?"

Meg paused before the door, her hand upon the brass doorhandle. Turning back to the footman she regarded him for a moment, unseeing. Caroline was in the morning room. *Her* room. No one, not even the servants were allowed in her chamber save one particular maid who knew precisely how Meg wanted the room cared for.

"Miss? You look a little pale. Do ye mean to faint? Ought I to call for yer abigail?"

Meg shook her head slowly. "No. No, of course not. I am perfectly well." She tried to smile, though she was uncertain how well she succeeded, for a frown appeared on James' brow. She said, "I suppose my stepmama has a little surprise for me. Please go about your business as you were directed."

Meg turned back to the door and, after taking a deep breath, opened it gently. The chamber was a comfortable size, well-lit since it faced the west, and alive with activity. Caroline stood in the center of the room, her hands upon her hips, looking up at the mantel. Two footmen were working diligently to remove the remainder of more than two dozen framed watercolors that had adorned the wall above the fireplace for more than ten years. These paintings would hardly fetch a tuppence were they to be sold, but Meg cherished them. She had painted each one when she was a child of ten or eleven, seated all the while beside her mama, who instructed her diligently in the use of the watercolors.

Meg felt a pain strike her heart as the memory of her mama's voice rippled through her mind. *Meggie, my sweet, let the colors flow over the paper. You work too hard to get the images correct. All that will come in time.* Images. The image before her was horrifying in the extreme.

To the left, where fine bookshelves lined the south wall, two maids were busily packing hundreds of Meg's books into three large trunks. On the opposite side of the room, a veritable flock of maids was assembling her collection of rocks, butterflies, seashells and every other precious relic from childhood that Meg displayed throughout the room. These articles were being put into several wicker baskets that dotted the thick Aubusson carpet in front of the maids.

"Ah, that is so much better!" Caroline's voice rang through the room, full of relief. She was still regarding the mantel before her.

Meg tried to speak, but found her throat constricted painfully. A maid cried out, "La, but it be Miss Margaret. She weren't expected back fer nigh on an hour! We be in the basket now, for sure!" Another maid told her she had just made a joke as she pointed to the baskets at her feet.

Another voice, in a hushed tone, added, "She's all white, even her lips! Lord ha' mercy, I think she's like to faint!"

Upon these words, the bustle of the room drew to a halt. At the same moment, Caroline turned abruptly, her eyes wide with horror as she cried out, "Meg! I didn't see you; I didn't expect you!"

Meg finally found her voice. "Obviously not," she cried. "Could you not have at least spoken to me first about your schemes?" And with that she wheeled about and quit the room, tears burning her eyes.

Caroline's voice called after her, "Margaret, wait. You don't understand! Oh, blast that husband of mine."

When Caroline caught up with Meg, she had already run halfway down the first row of terrace steps. Caroline called to her from the doorway, "Meg, wait! One moment, please. Let me explain."

Meg turned on her sharply. "Explain, what, Caroline? From the time you first arrived you made it quite clear I no longer had a place at the hall."

Caroline advanced into the sunlight, her black hair silken and gleaming. "That's not true. Well, perhaps it is a little. But you can't imagine how loyal the servants are to you. I feel as though I have had to fight for every command I've issued. Perhaps I should have asked you about the room, but your papa said it was not necessary, that he would discuss the matter with you himself; only now I can see he has not!" She took another step toward Meg. "Everything is being removed to the schoolroom, carefully, I assure you. And the schoolroom is quite well-

41

lit and comfortable—" She broke off as Meg's expression grew reproachful.

Caroline sighed. "I can see I have erred, but your father—"

Meg stared down at the brick steps at her feet, her throat still painfully tight. "The schoolroom?" she queried. "Is that how it is to be? I vow I felt more grown up when I was thirteen than at this moment when I am six and twenty."

Caroline reached out to her, a hand extending forward then falling back to her maroon silk skirts. "I am not entirely at fault, Meg. Your father promised me that after breakfast he would go to you immediately. I do not know why he failed to do so." She clasped her hands before her, her own lips pinched as though she held back a biting epithet upon her husband's character. After a moment, she added somewhat cryptically, "I told him he should speak to you. He should have done so while we were yet in London."

"Papa took his favorite rod from the gardener's shed more than an hour ago," Meg informed Sir William's bride. "He is now no doubt fallen asleep upon the banks of the river."

Caroline pressed a hand to her head. With another sigh, she said, "He is not one to face matters squarely, is he?"

Meg lifted her gaze to regard her stepmama steadily and said, "I still don't really see what he has to do with the morning room. We have been at odds for over a year now, you and I. You would be much happier were I to leave Staplehope. But I think your manner of intruding in the morning room, where I harbor everything that is precious to me, is beyond what is kind."

Meg left Caroline standing upon the terrace. She did not go to the stables. Instead, she lost herself in the large yew-hedge maze that formed the back wall of the extensive gardens behind the hall.

Once there, she sat upon her favorite bench in the very

center of the maze and leaned her head back to watch a few scattered clouds roll over the wide valley. How had things come to such a pass as this that Caroline must actually invade her special workroom with an army of servants?

How long she sat there, she did not know, though after a time, perhaps an hour or more, she heard her father's voice calling to her. Meg found it impossible at first to answer him. She was too hurt, too angry.

After a moment, Meg heard him cursing the maze roundly. "Damn and blast!" he cried. "Should have had the gardeners tear this curst thing out last summer when I'd a mind to. Meggie, damn it—that is dash-it—answer me! Where are you? How do I get to you? And don't try gammoning me, for Caroline watched you enter the maze!"

Meg heard him grunting for a moment, and then cry, "Let go of my coat, you confounded, dirty, old, bug-infested *weed!* I'll have the gardeners burn you down! I swear I shall! *Meggie!*"

Meg smiled faintly. She loved her father, but he could be quite a nuisance upon occasion.

She spoke, finally, directing him toward her as best she could. He still took several minutes to locate her, all the while muttering several pithy comments about the sort of mind that would create such an irritating arrangement of shrubbery.

After some five minutes more, he arrived at the center of the maze. When he finally turned the last corner, his face was red from exertion, his dark blue coat covered with dust and leaves from pressing through the narrow alleys of the maze. "There you are! At last!" he cried, an expression of immense relief on his face. "Never could abide puzzles of any sort!"

Meg sat on a carved stone bench with her knees up and the voluminous skirts of her riding habit tucked about her ankles. Her pose was not at all ladylike, but of the moment she hardly cared.

Sir William did not hesitate to sit beside her and pat her knees. "I've made a mull of it, pet. I am sorry. I should have come to you much sooner—right after breakfast, in fact!" He shook his head, puffing out his cheeks. "Caroline was as mad as fire when she found me reeling in the biggest trout I'd ever seen! Got away, of course. Not Caroline!—the trout, I mean! Ah, Meg, the entire episode is my fault. I don't mean the trout, I mean your scrap with my poor wife! Damme, I've made a complete shambles of the whole thing." He leaned forward, his hands on his knees. He was still breathing heavily from having run back and forth through the maze. He continued, "Meant to speak to you about the morning room. I'd say I forgot, but the fact is, I didn't. I just didn't know how to tell you. Caro wants the morning room for—" He broke off, his eyes widening. He seemed to be having difficulty shaping his thoughts. "That is, she wants the chamber for—for—well, never mind that! She can do without your room, I suppose. It isn't as though the house will be full to overflowing with guests." He chewed on his lower lip, scowling. Finally, he said, "Meggie, I just don't know what to say!"

Meg smiled through sudden tears. Her father was an odd mixture of loveable parts and pure exasperation. She asked, "Do you wish me to leave Staplehope, Papa? I am certainly able to form my own establishment if that is what you wish. I know Caroline is not content with my being here. And—and I am not unaware that the servants take my part when they ought not to. Caroline has a right to feel out of reason cross with my presence. I'd been mistress here far too long, I fear."

Sir William uttered a groan that sounded like a cat in severe distress. Setting Meg's knees gently aside, he gathered his little girl up in his arms. "Meggie, my dear," he said, his voice unsteady. "I don't want you to go. I love you. You're my daughter! It's just that, damme, you need a home of your own, a husband, children—"

"Papa," Meg said quietly, interrupting him. "I'm not certain that I wish to marry. Ever since Phillip died—and don't tell me it's been five years and I should have finished grieving for him a long time ago, for it still feels like yesterday to me!" Meg paused and when her father did not attempt to convince her she should feel otherwise, she began again, "But ever since he died, I haven't felt the least *tendre* for any of the gentlemen of my acquaintance. I loved Phillip so very much, and he was all that I had ever wanted in a man. He was tall and handsome, and had *such* a devil-may-care attitude! He rode brilliantly and was forever reading poetry to me and pinching my chin." Tears trickled down her cheeks suddenly at the memory of her first love, her lost love.

Sir William held her tightly. "I know, I know," he said. "Phillip was a good lad. A—a trifle hot-at-hand perhaps, but he certainly would have found a solid footing soon enough, only—dash-it, Meg. I want you to be happy, I do. I just wish you would have accepted Worthen. He's a good man, and I think you could love him if you would but try!" He leaned slightly away from his daughter and peered down into her face.

Meg shook her head at him and laughed lightly as though the idea were absurd. "You know I cannot abide that man."

Meg was about to playfully slap her papa's arm with the riding gloves she still held in her hand, but something in his expression startled her. "What is it?" she cried.

Sir William gulped and pulled away from her suddenly, rising to his feet. "Why, nothing! Nothing at all!" He pressed his hand against his neckcloth, and Meg tilted her head slightly, watching him twist his neck about in a circle as though to ease a cravat that was strangling him. How very odd! He had been going through this particular motion quite frequently of late. Everytime she was with Caroline and her father, in fact. Caroline would look at him in a meaningful way, and her

45

father would clear his throat and either glare at his wife in return or twist his neck about, the way he was doing now.

Meg rose to her feet quite slowly. "Papa!" she cried. "Whatever is the matter? If it is the morning room, of course I shall relinquish it to Caroline. I may feel badly about giving up a room that has been my haunt for times out of mind; but I know what my duty to your wife is, and I shall not hesitate to do it."

Sir William nodded, almost absently, his face wrinkling into a perfectly wretched frown. "I'll speak to Caro about permitting you to remain where you are until—let us say until the end of the summer. Would that please you?"

Meg nodded, relief flooding her. "That would be wonderful," she cried. At least then she would have time to adjust to the notion and perhaps find a more suitable chamber other than the schoolroom. Anywhere but the schoolroom!

The center of the maze was a gravelled square fit for pacing, and Sir William suddenly took advantage of it. He marched to the south, turned sharply around and marched to the north. When he had repeated this process several times, mumbling beneath his breath as he paced to and fro, Meg cried, "Papa! I've never seen you so agitated. This goes beyond the matter of the morning room, doesn't it? Only tell me, what is wrong?"

Sir William's face grew quite red, and finally he turned upon Meg, his eyes fairly bulging as he cried, "Why could you have not accepted Worthen! Ah, Meggie, I can't bear it!" And he ran from the maze, making only one wrong turn—but swearing loudly when he realized his error—before leaving the obnoxious yew hedges.

Meg sat down upon the stone bench, confused and worried. She had never seen her father in such a state before. What could he possibly mean that he couldn't bear it? Bear what? For the life of her, she could not comprehend what was going forward. She stared at the small gravel at her feet, trying to make sense of all the undercurrents in her father's words, as well as in his twisting and pacing. Something more was disturbing him than just the morning room, but what she could not imagine.

A fine mist clung to the valley in which the village of Staplehope was situated. Lanterns outside The Vine Inn at nine o'clock in the evening winked through the light drizzle, beckoning travellers. Staplehope Hall, one of three principal houses in the long, wide valley, was located some three miles south of the village, upon a rise on the eastern slope. Meg opened the door of the morning room, clutching her amber shawl tightly about her shoulders, and peered out into the mist. Beyond the bluebell wood directly to the north of the hall, she could perceive the faint outlines of the second principal house of the valley, Burnell Lodge.

She stamped her foot in impatience. "Charles Burnell, where are you?" She spoke quietly into the damp night air, feeling more irritated than she ought that her dear friend from childhood had not signalled her from the library on the first floor of the lodge. He had promised to visit her this evening, to tell her himself whether or not Hope Norbury had agreed to become his wife. Charles apparently remained longer at the Norbury's than he had anticipated.

Years ago, when Charles and Meg were children—and the best of friends—Sir William had cleared a path across his lands to the lodge. Shortly afterward, Meg had devised a simple signalling system, a lamp in the window, and Charles would answer with a lamp of his own, await a second signal from her, then run to visit her in her morning room. Tonite, the windows of the ledge were dark, and Meg could hardly bear the suspense of waiting to hear whether or not Charles would very soon be leg-shackled to Hope.

Meg sighed, a familiar restlessness again assailing her.

Clouds blanketed the valley, dulling noises and further depressing her spirits. As beads of mist began collecting on her face, she closed the heavy wood door slowly and leaned against it. Supper earlier that evening had been somewhat painful, Caroline's anger ill-concealed, though directed oddly toward Sir William. When the small, irritable family party had finished dining, Meg immediately made her excuses—that she wished to continue working on the next scene of her novel—and quickly stole away to her quiet refuge.

The paintings had been restored to their place above the mantel, though the arrangement was quite different from before and two of the pictures hung crookedly. The books and other assorted collections were hapazardly replaced, all a reminder that this chapter in her life, the comfort of Staplehope, was quickly drawing to a close.

How she loved this chamber, her reclusive haunt for over thirteen years. She moved to stand beside her favorite chair that was as unattractive as an old, shrunken apple. It was overstuffed, a little lumpy in places, and sported a gnarled, red velvet upholstery. Caroline had gasped when she had first seen it, for it was quite ugly. Meg remembered standing beside the chair, patting it gently with her hand, as though she meant to sooth its wounded sensibilities. She loved her chair, her room.

Meg returned to her writing desk, where the pages of her current novel littered the aged and scarred wood. Ink spots and scratches had stained the desk and given it a battle-worn appearance which pleased Meg almost as much as her lumpy red chair.

Sitting down before the desk, Meg tried to concentrate on the manuscript before her, but the Muse was elusive, her thoughts jumbled. Something nagged at her like a bothersome gnat flitting about her curls and refusing to go away no matter how many times she batted at the irksome creature. Worthen came to mind suddenly. Her papa had mentioned him only this afternoon. She drummed her fingers upon the papers before her and narrowed her eyes. Perhaps the viscount meant to come to Shropshire afterall. Well! Heaven help him if he did, for she would be only too happy to ring a peal over his head and send him about his business, the beast!

As Meg regarded the scattered sheets of paper before her, she picked up her pen and dipped it in the inkwell. Her thoughts were full of Worthen now, and she could not help but remember their last encounter and how completely he had bewitched her, even kissing her so passionately, and that in her papa's library! She still could not comprehend how he had managed to turn her head, to actually persuade her to recline beside a silly sheet on the floor and pretend it was a pool of water. Her head became quite dizzy for a brief moment as she remembered the gentle touch of his lips upon hers. The memory of his kisses overtook her, and she closed her eyes, a shiver travelling all down her spine. She pressed her fingers to her lips. Phillip had kissed her once, but it had been nothing like the sensation of Worthen's—oh, but what was she thinking! She turned her thoughts sharply away from these treacherous reflections. She realized yet again her own vulnerability, that her feminine heart could be swayed by such tricks, especially when she despised him so very much. Worthen was clearly a dangerous man and not to be trusted. What if he did come to Shropshire? How would she protect herself from his libertine manner of addressing her? A shot of fear raced through her heart as she realized she had no one to protect her, not even her father, for he had made it clear she could please him best by agreeing to marry Worthen.

She held a hand to her bosom. If only a chivalrous knight, someone like Phillip, would take up her cause, watch over her, be at hand at every turn to rescue her from Worthen's evil machinations. Someone like Emmanuel Whitehaven, for instance, the hero of her latest novel.

She sighed deeply as she thought of Emmanuel and leaned her chin in her hand. In her mind, he was dashing, his white-blond hair flying away from his face as though he had been astride Pegasus, riding the heavens above Mount Olympus. Emmanuel would have known what to do with Worthen, just as he knew precisely how to manage the wicked Count Fortunato.

A sudden inspiration struck Meg, and she again dipped her pen into the inkwell, the words for the next scene of her novel flowing quickly onto the page before her.

Count Fortunato took great delight in slapping his walking stick along the flagways. He strolled down the streets of the litttle harbor village of Lemnos. Click, click, click. In a fortnight's time, Rosamund would be his. Vulcan himself would perform the ceremonies.

A hand shot out, pulling him sharply up by the arm, his walking stick clattering to the cobbles.

"So, it is you! We meet at last, you villainous knave! Where is Rosamund of Albion? Where have you hidden her and where is her brother Ernest?"

Count Fortunato stared up at the godlike creature before him and gasped. Zeus! It was Emmanuel Whitehaven himself, his blond hair a flame of justice about his handsome face, his expression a veritable portrait of angelic vengeance.

"I—I don't know what you're talking about, Whitehaven! I haven't seen Miss de la Mer in months."

Emmanuel narrowed his eyes, pulling Fortunato's arm hard toward him so that he looked directly into the count's eyes. "Tell me or I shall bring every known deity here to hold court over your bold-faced lies."

Fortunato swallowed hard, his face flushed. "You've—you've mistaken your man. I don't know what you mean!"

Emmanuel stepped back, released the count's arm, and readied his fist, but not before Fortunato drew a concealed knife from the inside of his black cape. Lunging at the blond giant, the count drew blood. As Emmanuel staggered back, the count fled into the shadows of a nearby alley and disappeared into the scum and sewers of Lemnos.

In another chamber, directly above the morning room, Lady Longville, born Caroline Jane Bradley, sat before her dressing table, her brushes and combs spread out neatly before her. Her maid, known solely by her surname, Pierce, stood quietly behind her, brushing her hair and braiding it with great care. Pierce was a somewhat humorless creature, a native of Kent, and suspicious of these Shropshire foreigners. Though she was completely loyal to her mistress, she had but one desire, to return to Kent where the weather was mild and the servants spoke *English*. Shropshire was too close to Wales for her liking, and the village folk were hopelessly tainted with a heathenish Welsh ripple to their speech which she could not abide! Tonight she was pinch-lipped. She had told the housekeeper she wished to visit the town of Salop, for the servants were always exclaiming over it. The housekeeper had laughed condescendingly. "But you've been there already, Miss Pierce. Shrewsbury. Didn't ye know?"

Well, how was she to know that these foreigners would have more than one name for their towns. It was just one more example of their strange ways. She was loyal to Miss Caroline, but she missed the cherry trees, hop fields and coast houses of Kent where she grew up.

"Salop, indeed!" she muttered.

"What was that, Pierce?" Caroline asked.

"Nothing, madame! Nothing at all."

Caroline knew her dear old Pierce was unhappy, but she simply couldn't let her leave. Not yet at least. She, herself, still felt unsettled at Staplehope, and to be without her familiar if somewhat crusty Miss Pierce would be more than she could bear. She was struggling mightily to establish herself at the hall without completely alienating the household staff or Meg, and it was comforting to retire to bed each night with Pierce waiting to fuss over her. If only she and Meg could be friends.

Caroline regarded herself in the mirror while Pierce brushed her long black hair. She was as different from Meg as any two women could be, at least in appearance. She was short while Meg was tall. Meg's figure was lithe and graceful while she was almost athletic in build, certainly solid. Meg had clear blue eyes, and her own eyes were a mottled green in color. Her brows were thick and black while Meg's were delightfully arched. Meg's hair was full, red and easily shaped into the current modes. Her own hair was as straight as thatched straw, and she had had to find her own fashion. After a time, she had given up tying her hair in rags or burning it with curling irons in order to bring a little curl to her coiffure. Instead, she had created for herself a more severe style, braids and elegant coils which turned out to suit her organized, precise manners very well. She knew she was considered to be a handsome woman, but Meg was beautiful and had more adoring suitors and worshippers than she would ever know. That was what she liked best about her stepdaughter, Meg was without the least measure of conceit, nor was she aware of the fiery passions and admiration she evoked from the scores of gentlemen who literally dogged her heels the entire duration of the London season.

Caroline sighed as she watched her maid's white hands move steadily over her hair. Meg was certainly a unique female. If only they had more things in common. In fact, they shared very little save their love for Sir William as well as one particular flaw which Caroline hoped she had long since worked out of her own character—a certain fanciful quality that in years past had brought to Caroline her own share of heartache. Everytime she heard Meg discuss tenets of chivalry, she cringed a little, not wishing to remember a certain epoch of her own young womanhood when these ideals ruled her life, eventually leaving her scarred forever. The truth was, she saw a part of her former self in Meg, and this vision frightened her. She feared greatly that Meg would have to suffer as she had suffered. If only there were some way she could reach Meg before tragedy struck or before Meg committed a foolhardy act for which she would be forever remorseful.

Pulling her woollen wrapper tightly about her as her maid carefully braided her hair, Caroline reviewed the events of the morning with a shudder. She was still out of reason cross with her husband for not informing Meg of her impending marriage.

After Pierce secured a mobcap over her coiled braids, Caroline sent her away. The moment the door closed behind her faithful abigail, she sighed deeply and put her head in her hands. What was she to do? For the past six days she had wheedled and cajoled Sir William in an attempt to get him to attend to a duty he obviously felt was impossible to perform. But after all her efforts, he had not even approached Meg after supper, and Caroline was furious. Worthen was due to arrive on the morrow at The Vine Inn, and Meg still did not know of her engagement! Caroline knew something must be done, but what?

When Sir William had first told her the news that Meg was to be married, she was so happy she actually leapt into his arms. She could not believe it was true, that the difficult relationship she had endured with her stepdaughter for the past year would be so beautifully resolved. She and Meg might even become friends once they did not share the management of the same house. All season Caroline had hoped against hope Meg would choose to marry Worthen. From the earliest weeks of the season, she could see that Lord Worthen had fallen in love with Meg, but from all the evidence, she did not think Meg returned his sentiments. Her stepdaughter may have watched the viscount frequently, but Meg was such an oddity that Caroline did not place much faith in that. And other than a propensity to stare at Worthen, she felt Meg showed none of the usual signs of having tumbled in love: She never spoke of Worthen except to complain of his unchivalrous tendencies, there were no heart-burning recountings of a shared waltz, and not once did Caroline detect the least glimmer of enchantment in Meg's eye upon the mere mention of Worthen's name. No, Meg evinced none of the traditional hallmarks of love. For some reason, for all of Worthen's abilities, he had still not touched Meg's heart—at least not perceptibly.

Caroline's excitement over the news of Meg's betrothal lasted but a few minutes. She was shocked to learn that her husband had actually given Meg to Worthen without Meg's consent or knowledge. Meg would not submit tamely to such a high-handed scheme as this. She was fearfully independent and headstrong, more than her father realized.

Caroline's first question had been "But what did Meg have to say to you, Will? I am astonished that I did not hear her protestations raised to the rafters when you first told her. Surely, she does not care for the idea of being forced into a marriage with a man she professed only this morning to dislike?"

Sir William answered, "Meg hasn't said anything about the engagement because she doesn't know of it yet. And damme, if I don't think I'll just wait to tell her when we are all settled comfortably at Staplehope again! Yes, I'll just wait a day or so."

He had certainly fulfilled this part of his intention. It was a full sennight later, and Meg was still unaware that she would very soon become Lady Worthen. Sir William, so noble and worthy in other respects, was proving to be quite henhearted when it came to matters concerning his beloved daughter.

Rising to her feet, a measure of frustration and rage overtaking her, Caroline knew precisely what she must do next. She refused to countenance her husband's silence any longer.

Beside her dressing table sat a large vase of peacock feathers. On an impulse, Caroline pulled one of the feathers from the vase and marched to the door that led to her husband's chambers. She knocked firmly, and when she was bid enter, she walked to the center of the room, slapped the long peacock feather against the palm of her hand, and glared at Sir William.

"I am greatly aggrieved," she cried.

The baronet sat in bed, his spectacles low upon his nose, a book open on his lap. A branch of candles sat on a mahogany table beside his bed, the flames shadow-dancing on the wall behind the table. As he regarded his wife, he appeared to grow nervous beneath her gaze and pulled his cap from his head, his thick silvery red hair sticking up at odd angles. "My love!" he cried. "What is it!"

Caroline spoke with great innocence, mocking him. "What is it? What is it? *What is it?* Sir William Longville, get out of that bed at once! I will not have it! Your daughter must be told the truth, and you will tell her now!"

Sir William closed the book on his lap and folded his hands rebelliously atop the book. "I will not," he responded curtly. "I shall leave everything to Worthen. He, as you know, is a very capable man and will comprehend best how to handle my Meggie."

Caroline, who ordinarily had great respect for her husband's abilities and the manner in which he conducted himself among his acquaintance and staff, marched over to the bed and smote him on the top of his head with the peacock feather.

He laughed. "Whoa! What are you up to, my fiery, little Caro?" He reached toward her, as though he meant to grab her and pull her into bed with him, but she stepped quickly away, slapping at his hands with the feather.

She cried, "If you do not go to Meg at once, I shall leave your house and never return. I won't live with a man who would treat his daughter so shabbily! And don't tell me Worthen shall handle everything! Pitching it a bit rum, Will! You know very well a man of Worthen's stamp would expect Meg to be informed of her engagement before he arrived at Staplehope!"

The laughter slipped away from Sir William as he watched his bride of one year intently. Blinking several times, he said, "You seem very set on this."

"I am!" Caroline cried. "Meg deserves better from you and from Worthen for that matter!" Levelling the peacock feather toward the floor, and referring to the morning room situated directly below their adjoining bedchambers, she added, "Go to her! I promise you I mean what I say, and I shall not hesitate to leave Staplehope if she is not told the truth tonight!"

"You cannot be serious!" he cried. "Well! I think it only fair to warn you that I permit no one to force my hand."

"So that's how it is to be," Caroline retorted, her eyes wide. "You may force your daughter's hand, or anyone else's whenever you choose, but we are all to treat you with a different sort of respect and kindness? I think not!"

"Meg's case was quite different as you very well know. But as for this engagement, I have already made up my mind as to how the matter is to be settled!" He picked up his book, opening it in a measured fashion. Pretending to scan the pages, he added, "And now you may leave Staplehope if you so desire. I shall not hinder your going. You must certainly follow your own conscience."

Lady Longville threw the peacock feather upon the floor and cried, "You are an extremely stubborn man, William Longville! But I can be equally as mulish, when the occasion requires it!"

She marched back to her room, ringing for her maid. She purposely left the door ajar, standing near the doorway so that her husband could see her. When her maid appeared, she spoke in a carrying voice: "Pierce, you will be happy to know I am quitting Staplehope Hall as of this moment. I intend to remove permanently to Kent and reside with my mother. Please see that my baggage is packed and a travelling chariot brought round at once. I shall spend the night most happily at The Vine Inn."

"Madame!" the maid cried, a smile lighting her features. "Do you actually mean we shall return to civilization? To Kent? Oh, madame! At once, madame!"

From the corner of her eye, Caroline could see her husband jump from his warm bed, barefooted, and throw his dressing gown about his large frame as quickly as he was able. Pierce had already begun pulling great piles of clothing from Caroline's bureau when Sir William reached the doorway adjoining his wife's bedchamber. "Good God!" he cried, addressing the maid. "What are you doing? Go back to bed, you foolish woman. Your mistress is going nowhere!"

Pierce paused in her frantic movements, Caroline's undergarments held in her arms and stacked clear to her chin. Her dark eyes were anxious as she waited for Caroline's response.

"Stay, Miss Pierce!" Caroline called to her maid.

The maid breathed a sigh of relief and walked quickly to the bed, where she dumped the clothing, returning to the bureau at a decided trot. She muttered, "We ought never to have come to this heathenish place! Salop, indeed!"

Sir William ignored the maid and regarded his wife with a deep frown furrowing his brow. In a small voice, he asked, "Would you really leave me, Caro?"

"I'm afraid so, Will," Caroline responded softly. "You've used Meg abominably."

Sir William drew in a deep breath and threw up his hands. "Damme, I should have said something to Meg before we left London. I've been a coward; and though I can't say that I regret arranging this marriage, I know Meggie will be hurt, and I don't want to see her blue eyes reproachful and sad." He uttered a faint groan, then said, "I'll go to her now. You were very right to pinch at me."

Caroline threw her arms about her husband's neck, an odd constriction in her throat. "Thank heaven," she cried, her eyes filling suddenly with tears. "I was afraid I'd have to return to Mama, and you know I could not tolerate living in the same house with her again! I should rather die first!"

Sir William held her very close, and, in front of the grievously disappointed Miss Pierce, planted a warm kiss upon his wife's willing lips. After the maid took this as her cue to leave the room, closing the door with a snap as she did so, Sir William shook his head and cried, "Meg'll be as mad as fire!"

Caroline pinched his cheek and smiled up into his face. "You're such a gudgeon! You know you should not have foisted this marriage on her, and now you must pay the piper! Well, I can't help you in that respect"—and here her voice dropped very low—"but I shall be waiting for you to return to my bedchamber if you so desire. I would be most happy to mend any of your sensibilities that might become bruised in the forthcoming fracas."

"Caroline!" he cried, his voice suddenly husky. He leaned forward to kiss her again, but she slipped from his arms and pushed him away with a shake of her head.

"You'll not get another kiss from me, Will, until you've spoken to your daughter!"

Sir William puffed the air from his cheeks, shook his head and, after tying his dressing gown firmly about his waist, walked purposefully from the room.

Chapter Four

"Meggie, may I speak with you for a moment?"

Meg whirled around in her chair, startled by the unexpected sound of her father's voice. "Papa!" she cried, smiling suddenly. "I did not even hear your footsteps coming down the hall! Of course, I've been quite engrossed in writing a particularly exciting portion of my next novel." She smiled at him, pleased that he had come to visit her, though she found it quite odd that he appeared as though he had already been retired for the night. He wore a blue brocade dressing gown, and his feet were bare! His hands were thrust into the oversized pockets of his gown, and he wore a tentative smile, though his eyes were a trifle haggard.

He crossed the room and kissed her forehead lightly. Speaking in a gruff voice, he said, "I'm sorry for leaving you so abruptly this afternoon and for—for causing strife between you and Caroline." Meg looked at him steadily, startled by the intensity of his manner, his shoulders hunched and tight, his gaze piercing.

Meg said, "Papa, I know something is wrong. I wish you would tell me what it is. For days now I have felt uneasy, and yet no one will speak to me. You seem to be bearing some unknown burden while the servants!— why, they seem almost excited, as though an event of great moment were about to transpire."

Sir William turned away from her, walking toward the fireplace and clearing his throat. A small fire burned in the grate, and he paused before the hearth, his feet white against the blues and reds of the carpet. "I've something to tell you, m'dear. I should've told you much sooner, but I lost heart after we left London. You were so pleased to be returning to Staplehope, and I couldn't bring myself to speak to you! I wanted you to enjoy being home, you see."

His back was to her, and Meg could not see his face in order to judge by his expression the meaning of his words. She hadn't the faintest notion what he was talking about.

"Papa," Meg chided. "What could you possibly have had to tell me that could have diminished my love and enjoyment of Staplehope?"

She thought she heard her father groan, but she couldn't be certain since he was still turned away from her.

"You won't like it at all, Meggie. You'd best brace yourself for some difficult tidings." He straightened his shoulders, clasping his hands behind his back. Finally he took a deep breath and said, "Worthen will be here tomorrow."

For a long moment, Meg waited to hear more. When she realized this was all the news her father had to impart to her, she laughed outright, saying, "Why, you big goose! Is that all? Had I known, I could have relieved your mind of its cares much sooner! Worthen told me himself he intended to come to Staplehope. And how could I possibly be upset about that?" Knowing her father admired the viscount, she added graciously, though the words cost her a small parcel of pride to utter, "Lord Worthen is welcome in our home at any time."

Sir William turned around sharply, an oddly joyous expression on his face. He appeared as though he would speak, then stopped himself. His face fell instantly, and he stated, "You knew he was coming, then, but not the reason why."

Rising to her feet to stand beside her chair, Meg wrinkled up her nose and said, "He was so very bold as to tell me he would come to Shropshire to make me his wife—as though I would ever consent to anything so absurd—so I am not entirely surprised that he decided finally to journey here. I only hope he does not suffer greatly at my indifference. He travels here to no purpose."

Sir William winced. "You do dislike him dreadfully, don't you?"

Meg watched her father begin the now familiar twisting movement of his neck. She wondered why they were speaking of Worthen. It was always Worthen. She was sick to death of hearing his name. She was fatigued with her father's hints that she ought to have accepted his hand in marriage, that he was a good man and that somehow she was at fault for not seeing his value. How could she make her father realize she could not esteem him?

After Sir William finished rolling his neck, he regarded his daughter quite seriously. He paused for a moment, took another deep breath and plunged into his speech. "You are to wed Richard Blake, Viscount Worthen, at St. Michael's Church in a fortnight's time. And the reason Caroline was so busy removing your things from this chamber was because she intended to use the morning room to receive guests following the ceremony. I've arranged everything with Worthen. He is arriving tomorrow, as I already told you, and we shall announce your engagement to our neighbors as soon as his lordship wishes it so."

There was a clock on the mantel that had ticked away the hours and seconds of Meg's life ever since she could remember. But the second hand stopped suddenly, or seemed to. Time stopped, and the chamber dulled about the edges of Meg's vision. A hard knot formed in her stomach, and she felt as though a spirited horse had just kicked her very hard, knocking the wind from her. She found it nearly impossible to breathe. Was it possible that her papa meant to force her to marry Count Fortunato?

Instinctively, she grasped the back of her chair to steady herself, for she no longer had any physical sensation. Her entire body felt numb; she could not even feel her feet touching the floor.

"Papa," she whispered, "I don't understand. What do you mean? I refused his offer of marriage the night of Mrs. Norbury's musicale. Worthen knows I do not wish to marry him! You know it as well!"

"Yes," Sir William said, his voice sounding oddly distant. "But the next day, after he proposed to you, he came to call on me at my request. I asked him to take you as wife, and though he was not precisely pleased with the idea at first, I was able to persuade him. He loves you, Meg. He will make you a fine husband."

Meg shook her head in disbelief and cried, "I won't marry him! I don't love him. I can't respect him in the manner a woman ought to esteem her husband. You can't truly expect me to wed Worthen, can you? I won't do it, I tell you!"

Meg expected her father to leap into a series of cajolings and explanations in an effort to win her support for his schemes. Instead, his entire being was quiet in a fashion she had seen but once before, and he frightened her. In his bearing was a stubbornness and determination that told her he would not be moved from this path easily if at all. Years ago, he had appeared thusly, his face set, his blue eyes burning fire. A mob of angry, destitute cloth weavers had entered the village of Staplehope intent upon some grievous mischief. They were displaced workers, heading north in hopes of finding employment in the much despised factories of the North Midlands. Their own trades in Gloucestershire had been replaced recently by modern mills and weaving looms.

Meg remembered her father standing resolutely in the

middle of the High Street, no nonsense about him, waiting for the mob to challenge him. Charles Burnell's father and the first Lord Montford stood beside him as well. They were all prepared to do whatever was necessary to protect their small village and their homes from devastation.

The mob met her father's unwavering stance. After venting their rage in shouting curses and threats at the resolute men of Staplehope, the seething, furious mob turned back down the High Street and disappeared from the village, leaving the populace and buildings unharmed.

Though Meg hardly represented so fierce an enemy, she realized the gravity of her father's intentions because he looked just as he had so many years ago— unmoveable, determined. He would see her married to Worthen.

She sank back into the chair in front of her writing desk and stared at his bare feet. Her mind moved rapidly, searching for something, anything, some line of reasoning that might force him to change his mind. But none surfaced to rescue her.

"I don't understand!" she cried at last. "Why have you done this to me? Why have you intruded into my affairs when you were always so insistent that I chart my own course? And why, of all men, Worthen?"

Sir William answered succinctly, "Because I promised your mother, on the last day of her life, that I would see you properly married and also because I refuse any longer to permit you to live your life with your heart buried in your novels. As for Worthen, he is a great man, a fine man, the husband I wish for you! I had wanted, hoped, that love would find you naturally. But there's something odd about your heart, Meg. It's as though you're shut off from life! Worthen can change that, I know it!"

Meg felt tears of anger and humiliation sting her eyes. "I won't marry him," she cried. "I detest him. He is scarcely a gentleman in my estimation."

"Scarcely a gentleman?" Only now did Sir William raise his voice. He repeated her words: "Scarcely a gentleman? Margaret, you've lost your senses. How can you possibly think that of Lord Worthen? Have you not known him in all these past weeks, nay years? He's a finer man than a hundred I could name. He's a man of great honor."

"Honor!" Meg retorted angrily. "Has he somehow bewitched you as well? How is it the entire beau monde regards him as a paragon of virtue?"

Sir William breathed heavily through his nostrils as he said, "Has it ever occurred to you that perhaps you are the one who errs in judgement rather than hundreds of our friends and acquaintance?"

Meg sat stiffly upon the chair, her hands pressed together on her lap. She felt an ire rise from deep within her as she retorted, "I can speak only for myself. But I have seen him permit other men to shame his character, and he does nothing but smile at them and pretend their words have no effect! I do not call that honorable!"

Sir William's voice rose further. "Margaret Eleanor Longville, I've endured a great deal of your nonsense far longer than I ought. And now see what comes of it. I suppose next you will tell me that in your opinion, Montford is a better man."

Meg rose to her feet again and responded enthusiastically, "I should do so instantly! I have discoursed at length with Lord Montford on many fine and pure subjects. I have listened to the exemplary tone to his mind, and I approve of the value he places upon chivalry and one's duty to one's family. He would not hesitate to challenge any man to a duel who would defame his honor!" She sighed, her voice growing softer. "Phillip was just such a man. I know that he engaged in several duels while he was in London years ago. I know that Montford does the same, even today. I also am fully aware that Worthen turns off such challenges with a light jest while the gentlemen of his acquaintance laugh at him."

Sir William's expression had grown stoney, his complexion almost gray. He reverted to his quiet manner as he asked, "You mean Montford and his set make sport of him?"

Meg lifted her chin. "As it happens, yes. And upon occasion I have laughed with them."

Had Sir William felt any reluctance about the engagement he had arranged between his daughter and Worthen, it was more to the effect that perhaps he had not dealt kindly with the viscount. He shook his head at Meg and said, "I have been negligent in my rearing of you. I suppose your mother would have recognized the nonsensical turn to your thinking and would have long since eradicated the absurdities I am now hearing pour from your lips. Your judgements have grown clouded by the novels you read and those you write. You haven't a degree of understanding as to what duelling is really like."

He took his hands out of his pockets and slapped his thighs saying, "Well, I shan't cry over spilt milk, but I can make certain you marry a man of whom your mother would have approved heartily. You shall wed Worthen if I have to lock you in your chambers until the church bells peal over the countryside. And as for Montford, my dear Meg, I would recommend most strenuously that you look beyond his platitudes and into his heart. If you can find that it still beats with any regularity, I would be greatly surprised."

He turned, preparing to quit the room when Meg ran to him, pulling at his arm and forcing him to stop and attend to her. She felt desperate and cried, "Papa, don't you see that I am endeavoring to make certain I marry a gentleman of whom Mama would have approved? The truth is, I don't wish to marry either Montford or Worthen. I long for adventure, and perhaps this would be the right time to embark upon one. Why, Charles and I have had a scheme in mind for years to purchase a yacht

65

and sail all around the world. Would you not permit me to do that?"

He looked down at her, laughing lightly and stroking her cheek. "You would sail around the world?" he asked incredulously. "You and Charles? Neither with the least experience on a sailing vessel? And you! Meg, you grow queasy in a small boat out here on the River Tun! I should like to see you in a yacht, with the swells at thirty feet and the boat bouncing around like a helpless little duckling on a storm-tossed pond. The seas can be ominous when the wind whips the water to a frenzy!"

Meg swallowed hard, her stomach turning over at the very thought of being in a boat. Licking her lips she answered in a small voice, "I haven't the least doubt that in a very short time I should gain my sea legs."

"Well, as to that, who can say. But the fact is, I'll not even bother to discuss this scheme of yours. You are to marry Worthen, and in time I am convinced you will grow to love *and* respect him."

"Worthen is a beast," Meg cried, frowning. "Why, had you seen what he did to me in the library while you were scarcely out of the chamber five minutes, you would be shocked!" She then clamped a hand over her mouth. She did not wish to be called upon to relate to her father the precise details of Worthen's manner of kissing her.

Sir William could not keep from smiling. *Good lad,* he thought. He then cleared his throat and donned a more sober aspect. "Nevertheless, I'm certain whatever he did was merely in hopes of showing you how much he loves you." He regarded his daughter, who was deeply distressed, and on an impulse said, "I will allow one thing, however—one way in which I would release you from this engagement."

Meg turned beatific eyes upon him. "What?" she cried. "Tell me! I would do anything!"

He smiled. "All you have to do is convince Lord Worthen to end the engagement. If he decides he no longer wishes to take you as wife, I certainly would not hold him to such a poor bargain."

Meg was first relieved and then a little startled. "What do you mean, a poor bargain!"

He did not hesitate to answer her: "You're spoiled, you know. You fight doggedly for what you want with little consideration for anyone else, and you see life through the eyes of the heroines of your novels rather than through your own eyes. You've some odd notions, Meg. I should like to put it to you this way—have you ever seen a man bleed to death from a sword wound to his throat?"

Meg took a step backward, clutching her own throat as though she had just received the wound herself.

Sir William smiled, his eyes narrowing as he continued, "The blood gushes out, not one fine trickle over which a delicately nurtured female can pat a neatly folded linen cloth, but a river, a man's life-blood. Well, I have seen just such an occurrence, for my uncle died with his throat torn open. I was twenty at the time, and duelling was famous sport then, the ground upon which a fellow marched and proved his manhood. I never thought much of duelling after that, however. You see, I am inclined to agree with King George—duelling is a heinous practice. I only wish, for my aunt's sake, that duelling had been outlawed years ago."

He saw that his words were settling nicely into Meg's mind as he watched her complexion turn chalky white. When he was certain she would not faint, he bid her good night, expressing his hope that her dreams would all be peaceful, and quit the morning room.

Meg moved slowly to her comfortable, familiar red chair and sank into its lumpy depths, wishing that the chair would fold up all around her and hide her from her father's words. A man bled to death? Good heavens, what a truly wretched thought! Well! She would by far rather not think on such a morbid subject. In her novels, no one really bled very much or died, and the villains generally drifted away on a slave ship.

She gave her head a strong shake, wishing to dispel the gloomy pictures her papa had planted there. After a few minutes, she was able to turn to the difficulty before her—how to persuade Worthen to release her from the engagement. Really, it should be a simple matter, Meg concluded after some thought. Worthen was a sensible man, or could be when he wished to be. And once he was fully convinced she could not love him, she was certain he would bow graciously, bid her *adieu*, and quit Shropshire forever!

With that settled, Meg returned to her writing desk and plunged into the creation of another scene whereby Rosamund of Albion considered any number of perfectly gruesome tortures which she imagined inflicting upon the person of Count Fortunato.

When fifteen minutes had passed, Meg glanced up from her work and looked in the direction of Burnell Lodge. There, through the drizzly darkness, a faint light gleamed. "Charles!" she cried aloud in the empty room. She nearly overset her chair as she leapt to her feet and held aloft her oil lamp, moving it in front of the window several times. The light in the distance responded, shifting slightly, and Meg repeated her own signal. Much to her relief, the light at the lodge disappeared entirely. Charles would be with her now as quickly as he could.

In no less than five minutes, the door to the morning room flew open. Charles Burnell appeared in the doorway, a grin on his face, his fair cheeks red from running. He was out of breath, obviously happy to be with her, and exclaimed, "I was afraid you were abed. I am sorry, Meg, but I had so many things to think about that I actually walked poor old Saracen all the way from the Norbury's house back to the lodge."

He was considered a short man, being just two inches taller than Meg, and to some degree he resembled her. He had red, curly hair which, after his jaunt through the misty night, was curiously sprung about his head. His light blue eyes were frequently full of laughter, his complexion was unmarred by even the faintest spot, and it was often remarked upon how much the pair of them could have been brother and sister. That Sir William and Mrs. Burnell were cousins, both stunning redheads, explained the similarities.

Meg looked at her friend fondly and cried, "Saracen must have been tossing his head the entire way, stupid boy, begging you to give him his head! And you knew how much I wished to see you. Besides, I have the most amazing news! And do shut the door before my gown is soaked through with all this dampness! Oh, do tell me everything! Are you to be married? What did Hope say?"

Charles Burnell closed the door behind him, and Meg could see instantly that all had not gone well. He was still dressed in his black evening attire, a black coat with a double-notched lapel, a white waistcoat, an intricately tied neckcloth of the finest white linen, black pantaloons fitting his athletic legs to perfection and black half-boots which were now littered with leaves and humus from the footpath through the wood. He reached down to brush off his shoes and said, "I didn't even ask her, Meggie! I don't know what happened, really. There I was in high gig! I'd spent an hour tying this cravat which is supposed to be the mail coach but which looks more like the *trone d'amour,* my valet took another half hour arranging my hair, I was wearing my best blacks and all Hope could do was sneeze!"

Meg moved slowly toward her red chair and gestured to a wing chair opposite the fireplace. Once Charles had picked the last leaf from his boots, he crossed the room to the chair and fairly tumbled into it, stretching his legs toward the fire.

"I am sorry," Meg commiserated. "But I don't quite understand. What has sneezing to do with offering for Hope?"

Charles scowled, glaring at the fire moodily. After sighing deeply, he said, "Because she can't abide Byron and roses!"

Meg waited for him to speak, to explain this cryptic phrase. Suddenly, he was on his feet, marching about the room and running a wild hand through his hair. "I meant to ask her, but I just couldn't, though I'd sufficient opportunity. We even stood on the terrace together looking out at the valley. We could see lights from the village and even the dancing lamp of a late-arriving vehicle. Did you know from the Norbury's terrace you can actually see a coach progress from the far end of the valley all the way to the village? Come to think of it, I wonder who would be travelling at this late hour. I wonder if it's anyone we know!" He shook his head. "At any rate, there we were, Hope and I. And we were actually alone. I even held her hand. Her fingers trembled; I felt so much love for her that I could scarcely restrain all the thoughts that wanted to pour instantly from my heart. I leaned close to her, whispering, *She Walks in Beauty Like the Night*. You know that poem of Bryon's! Well, Hope caught her breath, and at first I thought she was pleased with my attentions. But do you know what she said to me?" He paused in his rantings beside Meg's chair, staring down at her, his blue eyes aflame.

Meg had to crane her neck to look up at him, but she was entirely spellbound by his story. She shook her head and blinked. She had never seen Charles quite so distressed before. "No!" she cried. "I cannot imagine what she said! Tell me at once or I vow I shall perish with anticipation!"

Charles took a deep breath, his chest swelling, his eyes narrowing. "She said something to the effect, 'I have never found the night to be beautiful. If anything fearful, and when the owls screech in the woods, I shiver in my nightclothes. Even in the summer when it is hot and uncomfortable I quake at the night sounds. Now, if Byron had said, *She Walks in Beauty Like the Day*, I could understand his enthusiasm. I have simply never comprehended Byron's melancholia! I think he would benefit greatly from a little sea bathing or perhaps the mineral waters at Bath! What do you think?'"

Meg groaned loudly, covering her face with both hands. Charles placed a sympathetic hand on her shoulder. He said, "Have you ever heard anything so pitiful in your life?"

Meg could not restrain a giggle and choked back the laughter that welled up within her. "I am sorry," she said. "I didn't mean to laugh. It is just that I have never heard anything quite so absurd. And though I must confess that I am particularly fond of that poem, I cannot help but think Hope may have the right of it. Byron might be able to benefit from—from—" She could not finish the thought, for she broke suddenly into a trill of laughter. *"Sea bathing!"* she cried, and clutched her sides as she rolled in her chair. "Oh, poor Charles! To be making such pretty love to a girl only to have her talk about screeching owls and the waters at Bath!"

Charles, who was grinning broadly, turned away from Meg, his spirits falling again as he muttered, "You do not know the whole of it. So then I thought I might take her in my arms and perhaps even kiss her and then offer for her. And just as I slipped an arm about her waist, she said, 'Charles, I didn't tell you, but I have completed my sampler. Imagine, I have been working on it for a year now.' She was out of my arms before I even had a chance to kiss her cheek. I followed her inside, and she brought her needlework to me. I was struck by the message which was a quotation from *The Moor of Venice* and quite appropriate given my current struggles with her. It read, 'How poor are they that have not patience.' I wondered if I was indeed impoverished, for I was growing more impatient by the second. The sampler was done all in green. There was not a single stitch of any other color. I asked, 'Could you not have included a flower on your sampler? A rose perhaps?' She replied, her brown eyes wide and innocent, 'Why, Charles, you know very well roses make me sneeze.'"

"Her mother wheezed slightly and began enumerating the various ways in which each of the members of her family suffers from such a sneezing malady, concluding with a nod of her head, 'I am convinced it is the pollens!'"

"Oh, Meg. There I was, prepared to pour my heart out to this beautiful, doe-eyed creature, and she and her mother must speak of pollens. I was never more mortified nor disheartened!"

Meg frowned slightly. "Charles, it almost sounds as though Hope did not wish for you to offer for her."

Charles scratched his head. "Damme—that is, dash-it—if I don't know but that you have the right of it. She seemed to realize I was unhappy, for when I took my leave of her, she walked into entrance hall with me and in a quiet voice asked if anything were amiss.

"Meg, you know how pretty she is, and I have loved her for so long. She had but to stare at me with her large brown eyes and my knees nearly gave out beneath me. But when I took a step toward her, she backed away slightly, her nose all wrinkled up, and she sneezed—not once, but three times. Next to my elbow, on a large, round table in the center of the hall, sat a vase of yellow roses! Damme, if I'm going to offer for a girl who has just sneezed on my very best coat!" He then glanced teasingly at Meg and added, "Why, that would be almost as shabby as offering for a lady at a musicale!"

Meg gasped at his words. For the moment she had forgotten about her engagement completely. "Oh, Charles!" she cried. "I wish you had not mentioned the musicale. I have the most wretched tidings imaginable."

Charles seemed considerably more relaxed than when he had first entered the room, and upon Meg's words he did not hesitate to return to the blue velvet chair opposite Meg and reseat himself. "Do not tell me Caroline wants you to perform upon the pianoforte at some soiree or other. I don't like to mention it, Meggie, but if she wants you to play, she's probably deaf!"

"Thank you very much, Mr. Burnell. Your compliments do turn a girl's fancy!"

He inclined his head in a stately manner, and Meg laughed at him.

"I was only teasing you a little," he amended. "You play tolerably well—"

"I am nothing to Hope!"

"No, you're not!" he responded with great candor. "Nor is anyone else in London for that matter. But what is your wretched news? I take it neither of us has had the most propitious of evenings!"

Meg grimaced. "You will not believe what has happened. My father has given my hand in marriage to Worthen, who is due to arrive in Staplehope tomorrow morning. We are supposed to be married in a fortnight's time."

Charles sat staring at Meg, unblinking for several seconds. After a moment, he laughed uneasily and said, "You're bamming me! Come, come, tell me the truth!"

Meg leaned forward slightly. "Papa was afraid to tell me the truth until but a half hour ago. I knew he was angry with me for refusing Worthen in the first place, but it never occurred to me that he would decide to give me to the beast!"

Charles drummed his finger on the padded arm of the chair and said, "For a female who is supposed to be married soon, and that to a man you despise, forgive me for saying so, m'dear, but you seem uncommonly placid. What? No spasms?"

Meg waved a negligent hand. "As to that," she said firmly, "I have no intention of wedding Lord Worthen. And though I begged my father to break the engagement, he absolutely refused. You can imagine how distressed I was. But that changed when he told me that if I could persuade Worthen to end our engagement, he would not kick up a dust." She sighed in a rather bored manner and said, "I doubt that it will be any great feat to convince his lordship that we ought not to marry. I was considering composing a letter to him, much to that effect, when I saw your lamp in the window."

Charles leaned forward slightly and said, "Meg, do you know Worthen very well? I mean, you have conversed with him frequently over the past several weeks. I know, for I have seen you together often enough. What I am getting at is this—have you learned anything of his character? Would he simply end an engagement were you to try to reason with him?"

Meg laughed lightly. "Why on earth would he not? Surely he can be as sensible as the next man!" A vague doubt, however, began nagging at her. She remembered a conversation she had had with him at Almack's one evening. She was searching for further clues to his character in order to develop Count Fortunato and asked Worthen whether he enjoyed hunting or not. For some reason, she had expected a man whom she believed to be a coward, to say he never hunted. Instead, Lord Worthen had turned to face her fully. He stood very close to her and, holding her gaze in a frightful manner, said, "Miss Longville, your questions intrigue me immensely. The fact is, I enjoy a good hunt more than most, I think. If one is skilled in the chase, one invariably traps one's quarry. But the real secret is never to quit." He had lowered his voice after that and, leaning uncomfortably close to her, added, "I never quit, Margaret. Never."

His breath had burned her ear, and she pressed a hand against her ear with these thoughts as though the memory had the same effect as the original deed.

Gulping, she said, "Now that I think on it, Charles, I wonder. But why do you wear that furrow between your brows? Speak! Tell me precisely what you are thinking."

Charles said, "I remember sitting beside him once at White's. Montford held the bank, and the wine flowed almost constantly. I was about rolled up by two o'clock, but the pair of them sat at the faro table for hours on end. I'll never forget Worthen sitting there, his back as straight as a soldier of the Horse Guards. Twice he lost everything, punting on tick, but he succeeded in beating Montford and five other hardened gamesters all to flinders.

"When we arose from the table, the sky was gray and several sweeps had just arrived to clean the chimneys. The point is, any lesser man would have quit as I had. But there's something about Worthen, a certain doggedness—I don't know, maybe I'm making too much of the incident, but if he means to have you, Meg, I would hazard a guess that you will need more than just your abilities with the quill to deter him from his purpose!"

Meg felt as though Charles' words had just turned her to stone. Her arms felt heavy with fear, her legs immobilized. She knew instantly he was correct in his perceptions, and an awesome dread filled her. "Charles!" she cried. "I know you are right; I just never considered it before. And somehow I have the worst prescience that I ought to leave! That if I don't, I will be trapped in this engagement! He's a beast, I tell you." Pressing a hand to her bosom and closing her eyes dramatically, she shuddered.

"Meggie!" Charles cried as he gripped the arms of his chair. "Do not tell me he—he accosted you!"

Meg gulped. She wanted to tell Charles about how he had forced her to recline beside a sheet in the library, but she had this vague sensation that he would not at all understand why she had willingly lain down upon the floor. "No," she answered slowly. "I mean—I have just now comprehended his character. He will stop at nothing to make me his wife. That much he has already told me, only I don't think I really believed him until now."

She stared at the floor, her limbs still oddly stiff, her eyes unblinking. After a moment, she lifted her gaze to meet Charles' concerned blue eyes, and she said, "If you and Hope were to be married, I would not even suggest this to you. But do you remember how we have always talked about purchasing a yacht in Bristol and sailing around the world? Well, why don't we do it? I'm not wanted at Staplehope, I don't wish to marry Worthen, and it seems to me that a little time and distance between you and Hope might be quite beneficial."

Charles was on his feet in an instant, his expression joyous. "By Jupiter, Meg!" he cried in his impetuous manner. "The very thing! How? When?"

Meg turned her gaze to the fire, her eyes wide, her heart ablaze with excitement. "Midnight!" she squealed. "We should leave at midnight with nary a word to anyone! They'll all think we've been stolen by gypsies or something like that! The whole valley will be in an uproar, and no one will have the faintest notion where we've gone or why! Oh, Charles, we'll have such an adventure!"

Charles looked down at her and said, "I've never seen your eyes glow quite like this before, Meg. We should go, and who can stop us? By the time Worthen arrives here tomorrow, we will be secreted in Bristol. Oh, do let us grab Fate by the coattails and fly!"

Just as suddenly as his exuberance had exploded across his face, his expression grew grave and concerned. He said, "But don't you get violently ill even in a small boat?"

Meg rose to her feet, smiling triumphantly as she said, "Well, a yacht is hardly a small boat, now is it? Now you go home and fetch your papa's travelling carriage. I shall pack a bandbox or two, and I shall meet you up on the carttrack that runs behind both our properties—you know, the one near the edge of the bluebell wood. There's plenty of shrubbery about to conceal you from either of our houses."

Charles beamed. "I always knew you was a game one, Meg! I'll meet you there at midnight!"

Chapter Five

At thirty minutes past the midnight hour, Richard Blake, sixth Viscount Worthen, fell into a fit of laughing that brought tears to his eyes. An unknown guest at The Vine Inn, situated in a room next to his, pounded on the common wall between them. Worthen had been laughing frequently and loudly throughout the past hour, and his neighbor was heartily sick of it.

"Yes, yes!" Worthen shouted over his shoulder, toward the wall. "I'll try to be quiet!" But spurts of laughter escaped him as he read the next line, *The gander of geese took flight, their long necks stretched heavenward. A hundred fowlings, each carrying in its bill a portion of the square, webbed, ship's net in which Brianna and her dear brother Marcus huddled together. They were lifted from the deck of the ship by their white, winged angels. As Brianna looked up, the sight of two hundred little orange feet struck joy and awe into her heart.*

Worthen collapsed onto the desk in front of him, burying his head in his arms and laughing until he thought his chest might ache forever. He could not imagine how a hundred geese could ever fly together in such close proximity, nonetheless actually choose to carry an impossibly thick, coiled rope between each of their bills. This was the third of Meg's novels, and he was charmed, delighted, and vastly amused.

He sat at a small writing desk across from a fine, mahogany four-poster bed. Above the desk was a small window, hung with bright chintz curtains of red and yellow, that overlooked the cobbled court of the ancient timber-framed inn. From the window, he could see the brew house where the innkeeper made some of the finest ale he had ever had the pleasure of drinking.

He lifted his head finally and sat back in his chair, smiling idiotically to himself. Meg's novels had been a complete enlightenment, both to the extent of the difficulties before him as well as to the treasure he had found in Margaret Longville. The heroes of her stories invariably performed impossible feats of daring—such as climbing the sheered-off face of a rock cliff barehanded, or confronting alone the sharp swords of fifty merciless Turks, all at once, of course, or leaping across thirty-foot chasms with "the grace and ease of the most proficient ballet dancer!" That one in particular had caused him to whoop loudly, the guest in the next chamber shouting at him to "stubble it, man!"

He began laughing again. Oh, lord, if he didn't stop thinking of all the absurdities, he would laugh until he perished. He refused to go on in this manner and mopped away the last of his tears. He drew in a deep breath, closing the third novel slowly. Despite his original intention of reading her stories with the strict purpose of discovering the secrets of Meg's mind, he found his heart stirred frequently by the quality of love she portrayed in each of her novels. Meg, he now realized, had a large, wonderful heart, capable of great feeling. He had suspected as much, but now he knew it was true. If only he could find a way into her soul and capture her love for himself. But how?

He fell silent, leaning back in his chair and smoothing the soft calfskin cover of the book with his hand. His darling, adorable Meg! However was he to win such a creature? Now he understood so many of Sir William's concerns and frustrations; for although Meg was loving, her concepts of the practical world left a great deal to be desired: Geese could never fly in such a pattern as one great wing-flapping mob. He almost began laughing all over again.

He tapped the cover of the book with his finger, his brows creasing suddenly into a frown. There was something more within the pages of all three books that baffled him, a lingering, vague pattern of a lost love. Worthen could sense Meg's loss. Was this the real enemy then, he wondered, a phantom from her past?

Whatever the case, he meant to conquer her—geese, lost love, and all.

He had arrived early at Staplehope for no other reason than that he could not stay away. He had become obsessed with the thought of his quarry—Meg's guarded heart—and intended upon the morrow to lay siege to her battlements.

He had sent his valet to bed and sat in his chamber, wearing a maroon dressing gown over a fine linen shirt, fawn-colored breeches, and Wellington boots. As he looked down at his boots, he felt quite ridiculous. For the past two hours and more, he had intended at every moment to remove them, but Meg's books had kept the task at bay.

He turned in his chair and began struggling with one of the snug, black leather boots, when the clatter of a vehicle upon the cobbled court, and the sudden sound of angry voices, caused him to turn his attention to the window and the court below. He was situated on the first floor of the building—the ground floor below and the attics above. As he peered out the window, he was met with a sight that caused him to exclaim, "What the devil? Good God, what next?" For there, in the dimness of the court, stood a fine racing curricle, burdened with half a dozen fat bandboxes strapped haphazardly upon every available space of the carriage. The occupants were both flame-haired and squabbled in hushed cries which did little to keep their voices from filling the entire courtyard. Within a minute, they had roused from their slumbers two stableboys, and the ostler, and a light appeared in the innkeeper's bedchamber near the kitchens.

"Master Charles!" the ostler cried, carrying a lantern forward and peering at the woman beside him. In a voice of pure astonishment, he exclaimed, "Miss Margaret? Whatever are ye doin' with this Jackanapes? And ye be shivering mightily."

If Worthen had been in doubt of the identity of the travellers, he was no longer. It was Charles and Meg. His betrothed sat stiffly upon the left side of the curricle, her cloak pulled tightly about her neck, and on the right, Charles Burnell glared at her.

Worthen was startled. Was it an elopement? he wondered. After a moment's reflection, he dismissed this thought entirely. Charles and Meg were the best of friends, but hardly inclined to see one another as marriage prospects. They frequently pinched at one another, even in London, in a purely sibling fashion. On the other hand, if it was not an elopement, then Meg was running away—from him.

With this thought, a devilish spark lit suddenly in his breast, for he loved an excellent chase. And what pure enjoyment he would have in pursuing this lovely red fox.

He stamped his left foot back into his boot and rose hastily from his chair. His thoughts were precise as he moved to the mirror and checked to make certain his appearance was in order. It would not do for a serious hunter to approach his quarry with his hair sticking out awkwardly from his head nor to have a stain upon his shirt. At first he meant to tie a hasty neckcloth, but instantly he knew that in order to achieve the effect he wished for, the appearance of deshabille was more likely to bruise Meg's senses than a neatly tied cravat. He quickly donned his black silk cloak which always billowed about his person when he walked and created a devil-may-care appearance. His heavy greatcoat would have been entirely too cumbersome to wear, particularly if he found an opportunity to accost Meg.

Just as he was about to quit his chamber, he remembered his pistols. On an impulse he took one of them in hand and headed for the court.

Meg ignored the ostler and his shock at seeing her at so compromising an hour with only Charles in attendance and climbed carefully down from the curricle. She was seething with fury. Once on the cobbles, she placed her hands upon her hips, glared at Charles and cried, "You cowhanded whipster! You almost overturned me on the High Street!" She gestured toward the street with an outflung arm.

Charles, who was red-faced, sat stiff-necked in the carriage. Through clenched teeth, all the while trying to keep his voice low, he said, "If you hadn't packed the entire contents of your bureau in these curst band-boxes"—here his voice rose all by itself—"I could have easily navigated that corner without lifting a wheel!" He tossed the reins to one of the stableboys and leapt down from the carriage. All over the inn, a variety of windows began to glow with freshly lit candles.

From the moment Meg arrived at the carttrack with six of her bandboxes in hand, she had been furious with Charles. Instead of the warm, comfortable travelling coach that he had promised to bring, he had harnessed a pair of black geldings to—of all the absurdities—his racing curricle! The vehicle may have been light, well-sprung and fast, but Meg had worn only a thin cloak to protect herself against the dampness of the late spring night. And where was she supposed to have stowed all of her baggage?

But worse, when Charles saw all that she carried, he immediately snapped, "Now, why the devil did you bring all of that rubbish?"

Meg had been horrified. They may be escaping from

81

Staplehope, but she did not intend to live like a gypsy. "These are my essentials!" Meg responded tartly. "But pray tell me, Charles, what happened to your papa's travelling chariot! You told me you would bring it. At the very least, on such a damp evening as this, I expected a brick for my feet."

"A brick for your feet? Meg, we are going on an adventure not a holiday! You'd better adjust yourself to that notion this very instant. I brought the curricle because we need to make haste. The more I thought on it, the more I realized your father would be in pursuit the moment he knew you'd gone. And as for my father." His blue eyes opened very wide. "Damme, I won't think on that! He'll have my head if he ever catches me!"

Meg agreed that their situation was desperate but insisted Charles strap each of her boxes onto the carriage. The result was awkward and ridiculous in appearance. They had not travelled but half a mile when the box containing her brushes and perfumes fell to the ground. Charles had to stop the carriage, wasting a full fifteen minutes of travelling time, to restore the box to its original position on the curricle.

All the while Meg chided him from her seat as she held the horses in check. "We wouldn't have the least difficulty if you'd brought the proper carriage. And do hurry up! These horses of yours are fresh beyond belief and refuse to stand still!"

"They ain't used to cow-handed treatment!" Charles responded caustically.

"Charles Burnell, you're a buffleheaded clunch and you know it!"

After that, silence had reigned for another half mile, until Meg began shivering. They had originally begun journeying south, toward Bristol, but when another bandbox fell off the curricle and Meg could not keep her teeth from chattering in her head as she shivered and slapped her arms in an attempt to keep warm, she cried, "I won't go another mile in this curricle. Let us turn around and go to Staplehope. You spoke earlier this evening of a coach travelling through the valley; perhaps it was a post-chaise and we could hire it!"

"That would suit me just fine!" Charles retorted as he picked up the bandbox off the gravelled road and shoved it toward Meg. "And you may hold this on your lap until we get to The Vine!"

Meg had merely glared at him, lifted an imperious brow, and arranged the box carefully at her feet.

As Meg stood on the cobbles of the courtyard, she was about to continue haranguing Charles about his driving ability, when the ostler intervened, "I don't like to separate cats and dogs when they take to spittin' and growlin' at one another, but we've an inn full of guests who don't take kindly to having their slumbers disturbed. So, if ye please, Master Charles, will ye lower yer voice and explain if ye can, why ye're travellin' in this odd fashion with Sir William Longville's daughter?"

These last words were spoken with great emphasis, and Charles flushed a dark red. He stammered, "I, that is, I am escorting Miss Longville to—to her aunt's house in Bath, and we—that is I decided I ought to be taking her in a closed carriage. Have you a post-chaise we might hire, perchance?"

The ostler swung his lantern in a casual movement that sent shadowy lights dancing over the cobbles. He cried, "Well, if that ain't the worst Banbury Tale I've ever heard!" He had known both Meg and Charles since they were children. Walking toward the horses' heads, he patted the lead horse, who promptly blew at him and stamped his hooves.

The ostler clucked at Meg and Charles and added, "Well, I might have a carriage, but wouldn't ye prefer to take yer da's travelling chariot? I know that coach well, nicely sprung and Miss Meg wouldn't suffer the carriage sickness like she usually does in them yellow bounders! Or would yer da' have any reason fer objectin' to yer using his coach? Eh?"

Charles' face burned on and on, and Meg could see that he could think of absolutely nothing else to say.

Taking a step toward the ostler, Meg pressed her hands together in a beseeching fashion and cried, "My aunt's case is indeed desperate. Charles thought the curricle would be fastest. My poor aunt, that is my poor Aunt Sophia, is in dire need of my care. She is ailing, you see—near death! We must leave immediately!"

"Whiskers, again, Miss Meg?" He clucked his tongue.

Meg smiled faintly at the large, burly man and said, "You were always up to every rig and row, weren't you? Well, the truth is, I can't tell you why I must leave Staplehope in such an unseemly manner, but I must. My case is desperate."

"And have ye an aunt in Bath?"

"No. You know very well I do not!"

The ostler shook his head, but could not keep from smiling. "Well, as to the coach, 'tis a private carriage belonging to that gentleman there. Ye may ask him, I suppose, if he will lend it to ye."

Meg was slightly startled, particularly by the expression on the ostler's face. He rubbed his stubbly chin with a hamlike hand, his lips curled in a faint smile. She could but only guess at his thoughts. Ignoring the somewhat knowing glint in his eyes, Meg prepared herself to begin bargaining for use of the gentleman's carriage.

Before she turned to face the stranger, she arranged a pretty smile on her face. Perhaps the man could be persuaded to aid her cause if he knew she was being pursued mightily by a very wicked man and that she must at all costs escape his clutches this very night. She heard his steps, the firm brisk sound of boots upon cobbles. When she was satisfied that her expression had every chance of softening the man's heart, she turned around.

Nothing prepared her, however, for the sight that met her eyes. For there, walking quickly toward her, his silken cloak floating about his broad shoulders, was none other than Lord Worthen. He smiled at her, his head lowered slightly, his black eyes amused and taunting.

Charles muttered, "Lord have mercy, we are in the basket now!"

"You!" Meg cried, her heart leaping within her from sheer fright. "But how did you get here? I mean, you weren't expected until tomorrow!" As he drew near the curricle, he came within the small circle of light emitted by the carriage lamp, and Meg shuddered as she saw the mole upon his cheek.

"My love!" Worthen cried. "What a sweet sight you are for my poor eyes." He moved very close to her, and holding her gaze, he took her chin in hand and kissed her firmly on the mouth. When he was done, leaving Meg so astonished that she did not even step away from him, he added, "I've thought of nothing else but you since last we met—and kissed! But what is this!" he cried with a smile and gestured to Charles' curricle. "Were you hurrying to meet me upon the road? What a sweet gesture, my darling Meg!"

Meg finally took hold of her senses and took several steps backward, bumping into Charles. "You—you beast!" she cried. "Charles, will you not protect me from this savage, silk-tongued creature?"

Charles place a protective arm about her shoulder and swallowed very hard. "I say, Worthen!" he cried. "You ought not to have kissed—that is, I request you cease accosting Meggie this instant." Glancing over his shoulder, he addressed the ostler: "I suggest you throw this man from your inn at once! He is an importuner of ladies as you can very well see for yourself!"

Worthen chuckled. "Come, come Burnell. You can do better than that. An importuner of ladies? You might perhaps wish to call me a libertine?"

Charles frowned at him. "Well, as to that, you're no such thing. I won't call a man something he ain't."

Worthen smiled suddenly and said, "You'll do, Burnell! But I will not desist from torturing Miss Longville, not for you, nor anyone. I love her and I claim

85

her as my own."

Charles stood his ground. "Again, I suggest you leave, my lord. Meg has told me all about this dastardly business, and as her friend, I cannot countenance it."

"Why, Charles," Meg cried, greatly pleased. "How very gallant of you."

Worthen's voice intruded. "Is it, Meg?"

As Meg turned to regard Worthen, she nearly fainted at the sight of a pistol he held easily in his hand, the barrel levelled at Charles. She lifted her brows, her surprise equalled only by her doubt that he had the courage to use such a weapon. "You've gone mad!" she cried at last.

Worthen held her gaze steadily. "Have I? Well, it hardly matters. The fact remains, I mean to stay and I will not permit Mr. Burnell, or anyone, to stop me."

The ostler moved away from the horses to stand beside Charles and stared down at the pistol. "By all that's holy, he's got a pistol!"

Charles addressed Worthen: "You wouldn't shoot me, would you?"

Worthen replied, "Let me ask you this, do I have the right as a gentleman, as a man of honor, to keep my betrothed from eloping with you or anyone else for that matter?"

Charles frowned. "Well, as to that, we weren't eloping. You must know we weren't. How could anybody think such a ridiculous thing as that?"

The ostler, who now wore a grin on his face, said, "And what do ye think me thoughts were when I seen you with Miss Meg? I says to meself, 'Rupert, them children will be married over the anvil in but a day or two unless I stop them.'"

Charles looked at the ostler with an expression of horror in his eyes. "Married!" he cried. "Why, I would rather wed you, Mr. Barnes, than Meg." When the ostler burst into a loud guffaw and returned his attention to the horses, Charles turned back to Worthen and bowed slightly. "I don't wish Meg to marry against her own wishes, but I do see that my own words were hastily spoken and that my actions could be misconstrued."

Meg was not at all pleased with the progress of this unhappy encounter with Worthen. Seeing that Charles had lost command of the situation, she lifted her chin and said, "I don't see why you must needs wave your pistol about our noses—"

"No, my dear, there you are out!" he cut her off. "One does not wave pistols about. That is an expression better left to the novelist. One holds a pistol quite steady if one is wise."

Meg responded coolly, "If you think I mean to stand here and discuss the proper use of pistols, you are greatly mistaken. I am only surprised that you even possess such an article."

Worthen replied, "I have not used one in years if that is what you mean. But I have since decided that I have neglected the more violent forms of sport and mean to reacquaint myself with them. Shall I, for instance, begin by shooting Charles here for trying to steal you away from me?"

Meg tried to read the expression on Worthen's face, but found the task to be impossible. His eyes were almost cold, and she bit her lip slightly, not knowing what to think of him. At first she was certain he was making sport of them both, but seeing the hard cast to his eyes, she simply did not know what he was really thinking nor what he intended to do.

"Don't be absurd!" she cried, at last.

"Come, that is no answer for me. You must choose for me, my dear. Shall I avenge my honor and kill the man who dared elope with the woman promised to me by her own father? I assure you, fifty years ago, a gentleman would not hesitate to do so."

Meg opened her mouth to speak and then closed it suddenly. Had the situation involved anyone else but Charles, she realized with a start that she might indeed have recommended a duel. But as she glanced at Charles, the idea suddenly seemed to lose a great deal of its mysterious pull; besides, they were not eloping as Worthen very well knew. She said as much, then added, "He was merely taking me to Bristol where we fully intended to purchase a yacht. As it happens, both Charles and I have long planned to journey about the globe."

The ostler struck in suddenly, "You, Miss Meggie? On a ship? With the waves up and down, up and down, and the boat shifting about like a—"

Meg swallowed very hard. "That will do, Barnes!"

He laughed and was about to say something, when a man from the first floor, in a silk nightcap, leaned out the window and cried, "If ye don't settle your business in good time, I shall fetch Staplehope's constable meself, and he shall throw all of you in the lock-up—if this godforsaken village has such an amenity." He then pushed his spectacles high upon his nose and cried, "By God, that's the man who has been laughing all evening! I'll have your head, by God I will. I've business in Shrewsbury tomorrow and—"

"Enough, man!" Worthen cried. "We will retire immediately, I promise you."

"Well, and I should hope so, indeed. Laughing and shouting into the early hours of the morning. If I'd wanted such a rackety way of life, I'd've removed to London years ago." He slammed the window shut.

Worthen lowered his pistol finally and gestured with a sweep of his arm for Meg to step into the inn. The ostler, however, had a different idea entirely and stayed Margaret with a hand upon her arm. He addressed the viscount: "Beggin' yer pardon, me lord. But I've a question about yer engagement to Miss Meg. I've heard nobbut a thing! And given the lateness of the hour, ye must understand, the Longville family has been part of our village fer nigh on a dozen generations!"

Worthen bowed to him slightly then addressed Meg: "Well, my sweet, are we engaged?"

Margaret wanted to refute Worthen, but she realized suddenly that were she to deny her engagement, the ostler would feel compelled to take her part, and given Worthen's current unpredictability, she feared a riotous scene would ensue. "We are to be wed," she said, at last. "Most regrettably."

Worthen smiled suddenly, his eyes alight with laughter. He did not take his eyes from Meg as he addressed the ostler: "I'll see both *Master* Charles and Margaret home, so you needn't worry further about either of them."

The ostler grunted and, after looking at both Meg and Charles in turn, said, "Of course, m'lord."

Meg suddenly felt sick at heart, for she had failed utterly in her attempt to escape from Staplehope and from Worthen. She shivered and was surprised when Worthen handed his pistol to Charles, removed his own cloak in a whisper of silk and whirled it deftly about her shoulders. The effect was immediate, for the cloak was warm, and she sighed. "Thank you, Worthen."

She then felt his hand take her elbow as he guided her toward the inn and exclaimed, "You are half frozen, Meg! Whatever possessed you and Charles to travel in his curricle?"

Having found a sympathetic ear, even if it belonged to Worthen, Meg immediately launched into a recital of the wretched decision Charles had made in bringing his racing curricle instead of his papa's fine travelling chariot. Worthen shook his head, agreeing with her that Charles should have been more considerate of her person, then assured her at length that had he intended to run away with her he would most certainly have provided her with a very large fourgon strictly for her use. "Then you could easily transport every gown you owned if you so desired."

As they crossed the threshold to the inn, Meg looked up at him and gave him a reluctant smile. "You are being nonsensical, of course."

"On the contrary," he responded, his voice dropping very low. "A lady should always have her comforts about her. I suppose it was my mother's favorite dictum, and I have grown over the years to realize that she was quite right. A woman is much happier when she is cossetted. And when a woman is happy, the entire house is happy."

Meg touched the lining of his cloak, which she discovered to be a very soft fur, and she sighed.

, He leaned close to her ear and whispered, "I could make you happy, Meg, if you would but let me try."

His breath on her ear disturbed her immensely. She wished he would not speak to her in so cozening a fashion. She did not know how to answer him.

Charles, however, interrupted them. "Worthen! If you aren't a complete hand! This pistol ain't even loaded."

Over his shoulder, still holding Meg's arm firmly as they walked to the parlor, Worthen retorted sharply, "And do you think I would risk Meg's life for one second? Then you know very little about me, indeed!"

Meg glanced up at the man walking beside her, his eyes now straight ahead as he met the smiling visage of the innkeeper, Mr. Crupps, and begged the stalwart man to have brandy and ingredients for a rum punch brought round to the best parlor.

What manner of gentleman was he who would boldly face Charles with a pistol only to later announce that he had kept it unloaded for fear that he might otherwise endanger her life? She shook her head, trying to make him out, but she could not comprehend him at all.

Chapter Six

Once before the fire, Meg gave up Worthen's cloak as well as her own, thanking the viscount for his attendance to her comforts. She could not refrain, at the same time, from casting a reproachful glance upon Charles, afterward turning toward the fireplace. Mr. Crupps, who had quickly surmised the situation—having learned from Cook at Staplehope Hall that Miss Margaret was to be wed to a lord—was instantly in obsequious attendance upon the whole party. He built up the fire himself and provided a footstool for Meg's feet. He did not quite understand all that had transpired to bring Miss Longville to the inn at so late an hour—and *that* in the company of Master Charles!—but he was content to smile and bow to Lord Worthen and to pinch his missus on the cheek when he returned to the kitchens, exclaiming, "We've got a lord at our inn, we've got a lord!"

"Aye," his missus answered him dreamily. "We have and that! I ought to fetch me sister from Salop. She likes to touch them, ye know what I mean? The last time she visited here, she kept bumpin' into Montford whenever he came in for yer ale. She says it heals her gout, though I told her she ought not to drink so much of her blackberry wine."

For her part, Meg was grateful that the innkeeper neither scowled at her as the ostler was inclined to do,

91

nor gave any other indications that he found her actions at all questionable.

She sipped a small glass of brandy, enjoying the fiery liquid in her throat. Finally her limbs grew warm, and she turned her attention to Charles and Worthen. The latter was carefully measuring out the ingredients for his own special rum punch, and she smiled at Charles, who watched everything he did with a fierce expression on his face. After a time, Charles even went so far as to withdraw a piece of paper from his coat pocket. Using a stubby pencil, he made several detailed notes, nodding his head vigorously to Worthen's instructions.

Men were such oddities, she realized, interested in rum punch and horses and arguing over which tailor was the best in London. With a start, Meg suddenly became aware of the state of Worthen's dress.

Merciful heavens, she thought, *he is undressed!* She wondered how it came about she had not realized it beforetimes. He wasn't even wearing a coat, nonetheless a neckcloth, and his waistcoat of a fine buckskin was partially unbuttoned. His linen shirt was open at the neck, and her gaze became fixed upon Worthen's chest. She could not tear her eyes away from the dark hairs that curled there.

Good heavens! She had never seen a man's chest before, and for some reason, she felt her heart begin throbbing painfully in her throat. Her gaze drifted to his trim waist and the snug fit of his breeches over shapely, athletic legs. Zeus, but he was a fine figure of a man! Quickly, she drank the rest of the brandy and turned bodily away from him. Had he descended from his bedchamber dressed purposely in this manner? Every instinct told her he had, and Meg felt acutely that she was in danger of succumbing to his quite masculine manner of flirting with her—nay!—of seducing her, the beast!

The brandy seemed to have dulled a little of her maidenly shyness, for given the opportunity to examine Worthen at length, she could not resist doing so. Every other minute, she would look back at him as she did now. Even his boots fit well-muscled calves. The cuffs of his shirt were turned loosely up from his wrists. Upon inspection, she saw that even his arms were covered with a fine mesh of black curly hairs. She tilted her head slightly, wondering how much of his body was covered in such a fashion. Without intending to, she emitted a sound somewhere between a sigh and kitten's meow.

Much to her consternation, Worthen glanced at her just as she was contemplating this most intriguing speculation, and she blinked at him, a blush suffusing her cheeks.

He lifted a cup to her in a silent toast, inclining his head, his gaze never leaving her face. His fist was settled on his waist, his feet planted firmly apart.

Meg knew a sudden need to keep him at a great distance, and she shifted her gaze back to the fire. Her cheeks still felt uncomfortably warm and further deepened in color when she heard Worthen chuckle.

Once Charles had partaken of the punch and exclaimed over it, the party moved back to the curricle. Worthen had his own horse saddled, and the trio returned at a brisk trot to the carttrack behind Staplehope Hall. Even Worthen agreed that the less said to anyone about the aborted flight from Shropshire, the better. He also promised to grease the palm of at least two stableboys, an ostler, an innkeeper, and of course the innkeeper's wife, when he returned to The Vine.

When the party drew to a halt, Meg kept Charles from descending the curricle, and as Worthen drew his horse alongside the carriage, she said, "I'm certain Charles can see me safely to the terrace steps, my lord. You may return to the inn now, for I know you must be greatly fatigued after your journey from London."

It was very dark, and Meg could not read his expression; but she could hear the amusement in his voice as he responded, "How very kind of you to be so solicitous for my well-being. But I feel it my duty, as your betrothed, to tend to your safety myself. I wouldn't think of leaving you at such a moment." He leaned forward in his saddle and looked around Meg. Addressing Charles, he asked in a friendly fashion, "Mr. Burnell, would you be so kind as to assist me in taking the bandboxes back to the hall?"

Charles, who had been humming all the way home, having imbibed several glasses of punch, leapt lightly down from the curricle and promptly gathered up all the bandboxes. In a loud whisper, he cried, "I'll take them to the morning room, Meggie!" And before she could beg him to remain with her until Worthen left, he was off and trotting down the path, one of the bandboxes balanced on his head.

Worthen dismounted his horse and tied it to a shrub near the carttrack where it was free to nuzzle the long grass at its feet. He crossed the distance to the curricle in several long strides and helped Meg descend.

Meg had only one purpose, to remove speedily toward the hall, intercept Charles, and keep him beside her until Worthen quit the grounds. She moved swiftly by Worthen, walking toward the maze and the gardens, all outlined dimly in the dark. The low, drifting clouds began to part suddenly, and a half moon shone upon the path at Meg's feet. She heard Worthen following her down the path. His voice was low as he said, "You're mine, Meg. You cannot escape. I'll not let anyone have you! I've travelled these many miles for only one reason, to make you my wife, and nothing will keep me from my goal. Nothing."

Meg reached the maze and moved more quickly now, breaking into a run. Her heart raced as Worthen pursued her, always on her heels and laughing low. She felt partly silly and partly frightened out of her wits. Where was Charles? They could still leave Shropshire once Worthen returned to the inn. But what if Worthen caught her before Charles returned? What if he forced Charles to leave?

She wouldn't think of that, she decided, as she entered the formal gardens of clipped s-shaped hedges and gravel paths. The fragrance from a dozen rose bushes permeated the damp air. The moonlight lit the paths about the garden, and Meg turned too abruptly near the roses. Her cloak caught on a thorny stem.

She gave a frightened cry, tugging at the cloak. When she finally freed herself, she was about to tear down the path, but Worthen was upon her, catching her about the waist and holding her to him. His breath carried just a hint of lemon and rum as he spoke her name. His lips were on hers almost instantly, and a fire burned upon her mouth as he kissed her very hard. She was his prisoner, for his arms were fastened about her and she couldn't break free, though she struggled against him.

But her struggle lasted only a second or two. His mouth was too sweet to be resisted for long, and she found herself throwing her arms about his neck and returning his kisses madly. She was lost in an impulse she could not explain. Her heart was her enemy, she realized, betraying her at every turn. She was for some inexplicable reason entirely vulnerable to his madcap ways and to his kisses. She did not understand what was happening to her.

"Meg!" he cried. "You do love me! Tell me you love me as I love you!"

"But I don't, I can't," Meg cried as she tried to break away from him. "I cannot love you! I have already told you so."

The moonlight shone on her face, and he said, "I shall make you love me, Meg. I can you know. I have discovered your secrets. I know who you are now! A witch, a Fury who has reached past the mists of Olympus to haunt me. You belong to me Meg, and I shall never be satisfied until you are my wife."

Meg's heart stilled within her as she looked into the shadows of his face. There was no sign of teasing in his voice; he was serious. She felt her heart beat against her ribs. "You are a devil!"

"As you will," he responded quietly and released her. "I will call upon you tomorrow, and as for tonight, do not think you can escape me again. I shall not leave here until the sky turns gray with the dawn."

Meg gave a cry and turned away from him, running down the path to the terrace behind the hall. An hour later, as she stood at the window of her bedchamber, she saw Worthen standing where she had left him, beside the roses. She pulled a chair forward, stationing herself at the window. She knew he wouldn't stay the rest of the night; she had only but to wait until he slipped away, and she would return to Burnell Lodge.

Meg felt a hand on her shoulder and awoke with a start. She glanced up into the face of her abigail, Bonnie, who said, "Miss, have ye been sittin' here the entire night?"

Meg said, "I—I couldn't sleep and the moonlight was so beautiful. I had the most fantastic dream." She sat up with a start. "Oh, lord, it wasn't a dream!"

Bonnie said quietly, "The gardener nearly shot a man in the gardens early this morning, until he saw the finery of the man's clothes. He thinks the man was your—your betrothed." She regarded Meg hopefully, her lips parted slightly. The whole household was in an uproar.

Meg rose from the chair, staring out onto the gravelled paths of the garden. She looked at the very spot where Worthen had kissed her last night and shuddered.

"And another thing, miss! Charles Burnell is asleep in yer morning room, and he had all of these things with him!" The maid gestured toward the door, and Meg turned around to look at her bandboxes.

Meg said, "I suppose the entire house knows of this."

Bonnie moved to stand beside her mistress and said, "I'll confess we're all a bit curious. Did ye mean to elope with Charles and instead fall asleep? Or were ye intending to run away with the tall man in the garden."

She approached Meg and began unbuttoning Meg's carriage dress by long habit. "It all seems so romantic, and already the maids are half in love with the mysterious man from the garden. I wonder who he was."

Her query was edged with excitement as the gown fell all about Meg's feet and she stepped out of her dress.

Meg again turned to look out the window. The mist from the night before was gone entirely, and the horizon of beech trees rose to meet a sky of deep blue. Her spirits feeling very low, Meg sighed gustily and responded, "Lord Worthen."

The maid gasped ecstatically. "Oh, I knew it was him!" she cried. "Why, I've gooseflesh prickling all over me! He's that handsome he is, and imagine him waiting all night for ye! La, Miss Margaret, ye've caught yourself a man, and all!"

Chapter Seven

Later that afternoon, Meg sat in the large, well-appointed drawing room of Staplehope, sipping her tea. Lord Worthen had arrived some few minutes earlier to pay a formal visit upon the ladies of the hall, and Meg watched him cross the threshold with a feeling akin to panic. She had decided shortly before nuncheon precisely what her next step must be. Somehow, she must attempt to reason with Worthen, to convince him that they were ill-suited and that he ought, as any sensible man would, to simply give her up.

However, from the moment Worthen stood before Caroline, took her hand and bowed over it, Meg's attention had been caught by an undercurrent she did not comprehend. The three of them—Caroline, Worthen and herself—were now grouped near a round table in the center of the room. The fine inlaid table held a generous assortment of fruits, a variety of biscuits which Cook had been preparing all morning in honor of "havin' a lord at Staplehope," a dish of sweet Devonshire cream and enough tea to serve half the families of the valley.

Sir William, however, had chosen to seat himself at the far end of the room near the fireplace. He wore his habitually tolerant expression, his attention, as usual, never entranced by the chatter of polite society. Caroline, to give her much credit, accepted her husband's dislike of certain of society's less amusing forms and required his presence in the drawing room only when absolutely necessary. Even then, she did not expect him to speak unless he wished to.

On the surface, then, everything was as it should have been: Sir William was disinterested, Worthen, polite and Caroline, gracious.

As for Meg, well, she sipped her tea, and watched, and was intrigued beyond measure. She stared first at the two spots of color upon Caroline's cheeks and then at the intimate manner in which Worthen looked at Caroline, a friendly, warm smile on his lips. That they had known one another for several years was common knowledge, but suddenly Meg knew that their association had been something more than mere friendship could boast. Had Caroline loved Lord Worthen at one time? The notion seemed ridiculous to Meg, partly, she supposed, because Caroline had married her father.

Worthen said, "You look remarkably well, Caro. I should say that marriage becomes you."

Her blush deepened. "Thank you, Richard."

Richard. Meg glanced at her father to see how he would respond to Caroline's use of the viscount's Christian name, but her father now wore an expression that indicated his boredom was progressing at a quick pace. His eyelids had begun to droop, and he had placed his elbow on the arm of the chair, his chin tucked in his hand. He was dreaming, no doubt, of the quiet pool on the bend of the River Tun in which the largest, most delectable trout could be had merely by casting a line.

As if in response to Meg's projected thoughts, Sir William sighed longingly.

Caroline again addressed Worthen: "Hope Norbury's birthday ball is tomorrow night. Several days ago I informed Mrs. Norbury of your impending visit, and she said she would of course be delighted to have you attend." Caroline regarded him just over the rim of her teacup and smiled suddenly. "You are a favorite of hers,

99

you know!" And she laughed.

Meg was startled by Caroline's laughter, which sounded so very youthful and quite unlike her. She glanced at Worthen and noted a peculiar light in his own eye, of a shared thought or secret. Meg felt uncomfortable suddenly, as though she had just sat down on a pincushion.

Worthen responded with a laugh: "Do not begin teasing me, Caro. I have long since grown to admire Mrs. Norbury."

"Yes, but you called her fusby-faced and that within her hearing!"

Meg's attention was riveted to Worthen. Had he actually called one of the highest sticklers of society fusby-faced? Impossible! How very rude, how very ignoble, how very intriguing!

Worthen wore a slightly pained expression, his brow furrowed slightly. "I was incredibly young then, as you very well know!" he cried. "I was hardly out of my salad days and as stupid as any other young man who arrives in London with too many sovereigns in his pocket and a belief in his invulnerability. Besides," he looked at Meg and added, "you hardly advance my cause with Margaret by revealing an event I have long since regretted."

For some reason Meg blushed. She knew so very little of Worthen, and these remembrances, shared between old friends, forced her to see the viscount as merely a man, a man who might have been much like Charles ten years ago.

Caro seemed to recollect her own purposes in desiring to see Meg married to Worthen. She blinked several times, straightened her shoulders slightly and, in a more composed manner, said, "You do well to rebuke me." Turning to Meg, she added, "You must forget what you have just heard. It was all a very long time ago." But Caroline could not keep a soft smile from her eyes as she continued to sip her tea.

Worthen said, "As to the ball, I received a card of

invitation not an hour ago and have already sent a note round saying that I would be most happy to attend Hope's party. Of course I begged to hear Hope perform again."

For several minutes more, the conversation travelled almost exclusively between Caroline and Worthen as the pair of them discussed at length Hope's abilities as a pianofortist. Meg was disinclined to join in the discussion because she did not wish Worthen to feel especially welcome by her at Staplehope. She tapped her foot, suddenly impatient to speak privately with him in order to finish this dastardly business; but alas, Caroline was fastidious in her manners, and the matter of the impending wedding would not be broached for a full fifteen minutes at the very least.

Sir William, for his part, was silent, his attention now fixed upon a small mahogany table next to him. His chin was still nestled in his hand as he cast his gaze over his arm. Every once in a while, he would take the crumbs of a biscuit from his plate and place them on the table.

Meg alternated her own gaze between watching the progress of a small white mouse toward Sir William's crumbs and the soft expression of Caroline's face as she chatted with Worthen. Of the latter, she could not help but wonder, her curiosity prickling her, whether or not Caroline and Worthen had once loved one another. It seemed very likely.

The chamber was situated facing the long, gravelled drive. Several tall groups of windows, all set with small, rectangular panes, permitted light to possess the room the entire year round. An Aubusson carpet of blue and gold lay regally upon the polished wood floor. The furniture in the room was mainly gilt and blue brocade with accents of gold and white silk. The windows were flanked by gold silk drapes, heavily tasselled, and about the walls a dozen fine paintings and portraits bespoke an age gone by. Even the gardens were arranged in the formal manner of seventy years ago. Still, the drawing room was friendly, the portraits of Meg's ancestors reflecting a happy people.

Sir William again pushed several crumbs toward a large, ornate music box and whispered, "There, there, little fellow! If you don't eat a bit of this, I'll tell Cook, and she'll be after you with one of the stable dogs!"

Meg shifted her gaze quickly to Caroline to see her response. Caroline glanced at her husband, her expression at first slightly exasperated, but as she watched him turn in his seat, leaning over the edge of the settee, his coattails appearing crushed from being poorly situated in the cushions, Caroline's emerald eyes crinkled with affection. Meg knew in this moment the extent to her stepmama's love for Sir William. Her father possessed enough irritating traits to annoy even the mildest of females, but Caroline, for all her meticulous ways, could even forgive him this quite rude manner of receiving the man—a Peer of the Realm at that—who was shortly to become his daughter's husband.

Caroline loved him, indeed!

"What was that, my dear?" Caroline spoke quickly. "Were you speaking of the dogs?"

Sir William jumped in his seat slightly, then picked up his teacup and took a sip. He stretched his long legs out, glancing at Meg and winking at her. "Nothing of consequence. Say, I wonder if Hope will be performing tomorrow night. Have you heard her play upon the pianoforte, Worthen? Very clear and precise with something a little more! Odd thing since Hope is such a *mousy* little thing!" He glanced over his shoulder again.

Meg shook her head at her father and chided him. "Papa!" she cried. "You are being too severe with regard to Hope and very naughty! A mousy thing indeed!"

She then addressed Caroline: "If you must know, your dear husband is feeding a mouse over here and has been doing so ever since we returned from London."

"Meg!" Sir William called to her in a reproachful manner.

Caroline glanced at her husband, lifted a brow and

said, "So you are the culprit!"

Meg giggled and happened to glance toward Worthen, who, she found, was watching her with a warm smile that reached clear to his eyes. She felt the funniest sensation pass through her at his expression, her stomach tightening in an odd fashion. He looked very handsome in the warm light of the room. He was dressed in a coat of blue superfine, buff pantaloons and Hessian boots that gleamed to a high polish. His neckcloth was intricately tied in exacting folds, his shirtpoints were precise, and his dark hair was brushed elegantly about his temples.

He was a fine figure of a man, quite immaculately groomed, and much to Meg's surprise, he did not give the least appearance that he had spent the night standing in the gardens of Staplehope.

Meg could not resist asking, "And did you sleep well, my lord, for I have been given to understand you arrived at the inn sometime yesterday?"

He nodded, a teasing glint in his eye. "Yes," he responded. "I did arrive last night, a couple of hours before midnight. As for sleeping well, I must confess that I was tormented by the most persistent nightmare: I was caught in the gardens of a large, brick house and could not escape. I was only able to sleep, as it happens, when in my dream the gardener, who tends his roses with great care, shoved a blunderbuss in my face and told me to take myself off at once. 'We'll have no wastrils at t'hall!' he cried. He was very insistent. I left at once."

Caroline's attention was caught immediately. "What a very odd dream, to be sure, Worthen!" she cried. "For our own gardener frightened off a vagrant only this morning, just before dawn!"

Worthen turned to regard Meg, holding her gaze steadily, and she blinked twice then turned to look at Sir William, who was staring up at the white, molded ceiling. "There are a dozen cherubs up there. Have you ever noticed that? Little winged boys carved into the corner of each square."

Meg glanced at her father, then addressed Caroline: "You will learn of it soon enough. I tried to run away with Charles last night to Bristol. Worthen stopped us and escorted us home. Indeed, Charles had had too much rum punch and fell asleep in the morning room. And though Worthen needn't have, he waited all night in the garden to make certain I would not escape again." She lifted her chin, casting a reproachful glance in his direction.

"Margaret!" Caroline exclaimed. "Oh, lord! No wonder the servants were whispering and wide-eyed throughout breakfast. So, you have set the countryside by the ears! Well!"

Sir William merely clucked his tongue.

Meg said, "You know I want nothing of this engagement, and if you please, I would beg a few words with Worthen—in private!" Here she looked directly at her father, who merely waved his hand and said, "Of course."

Caroline sat forward on her seat immediately and cried, "But I don't see why you must needs do that. I wished particularly to speak to you both about the wedding itself. We ought to begin making arrangements."

Meg turned her gaze upon Caroline and said, "I have no intention of marrying Worthen and will do all I can to end this engagement."

Sir William shook his head at his wife. "Never mind, my dear. Let her have her head. A chat with Worthen can do little enough harm."

Caroline sat back in her seat and sighed heavily. "As you wish."

She watched them go and was a little startled when she heard Worthen address his betrothed: "But you have delighted me, my dearest Meg, in wishing a few moments alone. Do you mean to express your love to me? Just remember I am bashful . . ." And the rest of the words trailed into the hall toward the morning room.

Sir William looked at his wife, and they exchanged a

sudden smile. "He'll do, by God!" the baronet cried.

Caroline agreed heartily.

Once Worthen entered the room, Meg closed the door firmly behind him. "You? Bashful! I might as well describe your coat as being a delightful scarlet in color!"

But Worthen did not appear to hear her, for he stood very still, very tense, as he glanced about the morning room. For a long time, he didn't speak, and Meg was suddenly embarrassed that she had brought him to her haunt. Why had she done so? she wondered with a start. What possessed her to have brought him to the very place where he could see her life and her soul spread before him.

Suddenly, she was afraid of his scrutiny. She moved to stand beside him and glanced up at his face. She could not tell what he was thinking. His expression was unreadable, his dark eyes narrowed slightly as he gazed at nearly every object in the chamber in turn.

"You live here," he said, though his words seemed to be a stray thought spoken aloud.

Meg felt suddenly naked as his gaze shifted about the room. Her scattered treasures would have no meaning to anyone but herself. The arrangement was haphazard and untidy. Every object was a reflection of her heart. Oh, why had she brought him here when she could have easily taken him to her father's library!

When his gaze lit upon her red chair, her knees positively trembled.

He must have realized she was silent, for he looked at her with a measuring expression. He smiled suddenly, and Meg caught her breath. "This is a fine chamber," he said, and as though he comprehended her perfectly, he walked directly to the red chair and sat down.

Meg tilted her head slightly and cried, "Oh!" She was only vaguely aware she had uttered this exclamation and moved to the nearest bookshelf on the wall to her left and began straightening a row of books. The maids had replaced a number of the books upside down, and Meg felt a great urgency to right them, if for no other reason than to avoid seeing Lord Worthen ensconced in her favorite chair.

Why had he sat in her chair, she wondered, and that so purposefully? She felt as though some secret part of her had been discovered and violated by this strange man. She glanced at him over her shoulder for the briefest second and returned her attention immediately to the books. He was staring at her, his expression lit with amusement! Well! He may have seen a part of her that she had much rather wished unknown to him; but the deed was done, and she refused to fret over it.

She had business of no small import to conclude with him. Turning around abruptly, she squared her shoulders, held his gaze steadily and said, "I wish to speak to you, Lord Worthen, about ending this engagement!"

He nodded, the fingers of his left hand caressing the smooth surface of the worn velvet upholstery.

Meg felt the faintest blush touch her cheeks as she watched his hand for a moment. He remained silent, and she felt compelled to ask, "You do agree that our engagement is an absurdity, do you not? You must know that I do not love you." His hand left the velvet fabric and found its way to his lips. His fingers touched his lips as he continued to watch her.

Meg placed her hands behind her back. She knew very well what he was about. He wished to distract her, the beast. And she did not think it at all wise that she look at his fingers or his lips, for then she might remember the kiss they had shared—oh, what a devil he was!

His deep voice filled the room suddenly. "What a comfortable chair. It seems to suit me somehow!"

The afternoon sun shone through the windows in golden shafts to heat the carpet on the floor. A beam of warm light struck one of his boots.

Meg felt as she often did in his presence of late, as though she were trying to walk quickly through mud and with each step her feet grew more and more sluggish. The sensation was nightmarish in quality, except that she wasn't afraid, just lulled to a state of quiet vulnerability. She spoke accusingly: "You are sitting in my favorite chair, you know."

He gave no response but merely smiled at her in a content fashion, like the cat who had just caught and eaten the mouse.

How on earth was she to reason with a man who refused to address the issue. She shook her red curls, turned away from him, and stepped toward the door of the morning room. The chamber seemed unaccountably warm to her suddenly as she opened the door and threw it wide. She drank in the air, hoping that her mind would become better focused on how to address Lord Worthen. That he was obstinate she had finally grown to comprehend, but she had not realized how elusive he could be as well, as slippery as an eel.

She took a deep breath, steeling herself to try again. She must find a way to break the engagement. Whirling around to face him, the soft silk of her light green morning gown whispered about her ankles. She found, much to her horror, that he had risen to his feet and was fast approaching her. She felt just as she had last night, when he had chased her and caught her. Why did she always feel like a trapped animal with him?

She held her hands directly out in front of her, warding him off. She averted her gaze, squeezed her eyes shut and cried, "No!" She suppressed the worst urge to turn on her heel and take flight into the bluebell wood.

She felt him take her hands, holding them firmly, his lips kissing each of her fingers in turn. "My darling Meg," he spoke in a whisper. "You are adorable beyond words!"

She couldn't bear the sensation of his lips touching her skin. With her eyes shut, she spoke in a small voice: "Worthen, please release me from this engagement. I don't mean to bruise your sensibilities, but I cannot marry you."

His lips continued softly violating her fingers, and she felt so dizzy and miserable that she knew in a moment she would be crying. She opened her eyes and watched his gentle manner of saluting her fingers. She continued, "I, that is we should not suit. I swore I would never marry where I did not love. I loved once. We were engaged. It is not your fault that you are nothing to Phillip." Her voice was low and taut.

He stopped kissing her fingers suddenly and met her gaze. "Phillip?" he queried in a whisper. "I do not know of anyone by that name."

"He is dead—these five years and more."

Worthen still held her hands and pressed them, saying, "I am sorry. I didn't know—"

"Phillip Harcastle," she breathed, smiling into Worthen's face. She felt a freshening of relief, for she had caught his attention at last. She continued, "I loved him beyond measure. We understood one another so well. He perished very nobly rescuing a small boy from a ditch full of flood water. Phillip drowned—" Meg's voice broke as she averted her gaze and swallowed very hard.

"Meg, I feel for you most acutely—" He broke off suddenly, his eyes searching her face. A strange expression overtook his features as he released her hands. "Phillip Harcastle? Very tall young man, a favorite with the ladies—not *Harcastle?*"

"What is it?" Meg cried. Worthen's expression was one of disbelief.

He closed his mouth firmly. After a moment, he said, "We are at phantoms, Meg. How can I win your heart away from a ghost, an image that glows all the wrong colors as well?"

"What are you talking about? What do you mean, colors? Ghosts are white or misty."

"You compare me in your mind to Phillip, and I have come up wanting," he said, refusing to explain the meaning of his words.

She opened her mouth to speak, but he cut her off.

"No!" he cried, lifting an abrupt hand, silencing the

words readied on her tongue. "Don't try to explain your meaning, for I can see your heart in your eyes. You don't esteem me, do you?"

He did not wait to hear her answer, and he laughed aloud, turning back toward the room. "Sometimes the irony one meets in one's life is painfully sharp, and this is just such a one!"

Meg felt more hopeful in this moment than she had for a long time. She knew he could be reasonable, and she could tell that he was finally beginning to comprehend that they should not wed.

But he whirled back to her, the expression on his face intent, a dangerous shaft of light in his eyes. "So, you do not esteem me! Well, that is most unfortunate for you. But I am afraid that I am not concerned with your perceptions of my worth. I want your heart, and I will have it!"

He advanced on her, and Meg opened her eyes wide. "Then you will not relent?" she asked, astonished. "I knew you were stubborn, but this is absurd!" What manner of man was he?

She took a step backward as he continued, "I will not release you from this engagement for so paltry a reason as this, my dear Miss Longville. You will have to try much harder to rid yourself of me than to merely compare me to your former beaux!"

Meg was horrified. Why, any reasonable honorable gentleman would have acquiesced instantly! But not Worthen, as Meg had to remind herself again and again. At every turn he proved himself without the true honor of a gentleman.

She backed away from him as he began advancing on her. She intended to run from him, for she was swift on her feet and knew the twists and turns of the bluebell wood better than he did. But even as she mentally commanded her feet to move, he caught her easily about the waist, laughing very low as he pulled her close to him.

"You were not fast enough, Meggie. But feel my arms about you. They are real, not the ghostly visions of a lover who has not arms to hold you, who has only memories to keep you bound to him. Feel my legs against your own. They are strong, and they are willing to walk beside you until you are gray and withered with age. Feel my chest, Meg." He hugged her hard, his breath on her ear sending the worst shiver down the whole length of her body. "My chest beats with a living heart that wishes to share your troubles and triumphs, to share your life. I am flesh and blood, Meg, not a schoolgirl's daydream. My bed can keep you warm at night. I want you to bear my children, to rule my house, to beat my servants if you so desire. And by God you will be my wife or I shall die making it so!"

Meg sighed softly, his words like cool water pouring over a scorched desert. She wished of the moment only one thing, to have his lips pressed upon her own. She knew it was wrong, for she hated the man he really was. But this man, who cozened her and spoke words that she ached to hear, words Phillip should have spoken to her had he lived, was just as he said—alive beneath her touch.

He moved his lips to her cheek and kissed her gently. She was trembling, and when a tear met his lips, he brushed it lightly with his mouth.

Only then did she tear away from him. This time he did not try to stop her as she ran to the woods, to safety, to the quiet of her own thoughts, to the desolation of what she realized suddenly, achingly, was her acute loneliness.

But she would not settle for any man, not for Worthen whom she could not respect. If only he were not so brutal with her sensibilities. Did he realize how vulnerable she was? He was seducing her, and the tension of the thought forced her to run more quickly away from him, pressing steadily up the hill above Staplehope, the beechwood rippled with sunlight, the bluebells bobbing frantically as her feet rushed swiftly by.

She despised him, loathed him and ached for him.

Chapter Eight

On the following night, Meg watched Hope Norbury's expression fall dramatically as Charles led Elizabeth Priestley out for a second dance, a waltz in fact! Hope stood between her mother and Caroline, a stiff smile fixed to her face, her fan moving in a halting fashion across her features. She was dressed all in white, an unhappy choice since the gown tended to enhance Hope's pale complexion instead of bringing to life the rich brown of her hair and the hidden sparkle of her soft brown eyes.

Meg thought a daring royal blue would enliven Hope's features immensely, and she wondered whatever had possessed Mrs. Norbury to permit her daughter to wear such an indifferent costume. Certainly the color white lent Hope an angelic appearance, but next to Lizzie, who was romping about the ballroom floor in a décolleté gown of orange-blossom sarsanet decorated with a net shawl covered in silver spangles, Hope appeared dull indeed.

And Charles seemed to have judged the ladies already. He had not even danced once with Hope yet. But who could blame such a firebrand as Charles for choosing lively, playful Lizzie over Hope, who paled by comparison?

Meg stood beside Mr. Norbury, curiosity burning in her breast. Whatever did Charles mean by singling Lizzie out—and that at Hope's birthday ball? Why, half the ballroom was staring at Hope, nodding toward her and whispering. Surely Charles was not unaware of the great stir he was causing by shunning Hope and flirting quite outrageously with Elizabeth!

Mr. Norbury, a man of dry wit and a burgeoning stomach, rocked on his heels slightly as he addressed Meg: "It is always the same in summer, is it not, Miss Longville?" He pursed his lips and twisted them to the right and the left. "One has such infinite opportunity to observe and admire the great variety of fowl that traverse our valley. Though they do *gabble* and *monger* more than I care for. In particular, I grow positively weary of the incessant cries of the blackbirds." He levelled his gaze at a group of thin older women who sat upon straight-backed chairs on the opposite side of the ballroom floor. One lady, a spinster of long-standing, was dressed in black bombazine, another lady, a widow of two years, was still dressed in black silk, and the third woman, a pinched matron of advancing years, wore a black cashmere shawl over a violet satin gown, her expression severe and disapproving. Together, the ladies glanced at Hope, Charles and Lizzie in turn, clucking their tongues and shaking their heads in a reproving fashion. Charles had clearly given them more pleasure than a gathering amongst the families of Staplehope had provided in a very long time.

Margaret glanced up at Mr. Norbury, whom she admired a great deal, and responded, "I have little interest in ornithology, Mr. Norbury, though I have noticed that a certain bird, wild and unpredictable, seems to be migrating south at an unseasonable time of—of evening."

Mr. Norbury twisted his lips again and harrumphed. He offered Meg his arm and begged her to take a turn about the room with him. He asked, "Would you happen to know the cause of so abrupt and inopportune a migration? I daresay there shall be a flood—of tears that is—this very evening! A man ought to be prepared for

112

any and all natural—or domestic—disasters if he can."

Meg hesitated, remembering all that Charles had told her not two days ago. How much ought she reveal to her host? Finally, she said, "I cannot speak for the parties concerned, but I have noticed a grave difference in temperament between the—dare I say it—lovebirds."

Mr. Norbury chuckled and groaned. "That was poorly done, Miss Meggie, however apt." He sighed. "But I think you've the right of it. I, too, have noticed a large disparity between my daughter and her favorite beau. Of late, such differences as one might suppose first drew them together have grown even more marked—much to Hope's detriment, unfortunately! To be quite honest, I should have been very grateful to Charles if he could have brought out a little more of Hope's liveliness. As it is, why, she's more stiff and reserved than I have ever known her to be. And as for Charles, do but look at him! A great deal of his former steadiness is gone. He's making a cake of himself chasing after Lizzie's skirts." He lifted his quizzing glass to his eye and stared at Charles. "Good God! Why, the man looks like a regular Pink of the Ton! And I was used to think him a gentleman with some sense at least!"

In terms of proving Mr. Norbury's opinions, the moment was fortuitous, for Charles held a giggling Lizzie very tightly about the waist and was laughing at some joke she had made, his laughter audible even above the orchestra as they whirled about the ballroom floor. Only then did Meg realize he was wearing yellow pantaloons, a bold-striped waistcoat, and several fobs dangling at his waist! He almost looked the dandy, just as Mr. Norbury had said! Even his red hair gleamed from a liberal use of Russian oil.

Meg glanced to the top of the ballroom where Hope remained as though fixed forever in one spot. She noticed that Hope's brown hair was fixed neatly—too much so for her round features—into a braided coil at the back of her head and that her white gown was cut

113

severely high upon the bosom; a necklet of pearls faded into her white skin. Her beauty was lost in such a costume, and Meg was disturbed deeply by what she saw. She knew in her heart that Hope loved Charles, but why, then, did the passionate *artiste* upon the pianoforte attempt in every other respect to appear almost spinsterly, decorous and dull? Meg could not comprehend it at all. She remembered Hope's comments—Byron and sea bathing—and it struck her suddenly that Hope had become quite prosy and missish. She had not been so very bad before, just as her father had said. But why had she changed? Surely Hope, who was quite intelligent, could see that her actions as well as her manner of dress would only serve to cool her beloved's ardor.

Mr. Norbury, who saw the direction of her gaze, spoke in a whisper: "I told her not to wear that old white gown. Her pretty face had disappeared entirely. She needs color and lots of it." He glanced at Lizzie, who was passing very close to them again, her bright laughter rolling to the high ceiling of the chamber as she squealed at some teasing remark of Charles'.

He clucked his tongue and said, "Good God, there's a handful! And my own niece! She's rather like my sister, Hetty—her mother, you know—a dazzler but one to jump off at the most freakish of starts! Charles is in the basket now if he means to pursue that bit of baggage!"

"Mr. Norbury!" Meg exclaimed. "How can you say such things about Lizzie when she is your own blood relation!"

"Easiest thing in the world. I only wish my brother-in-law hadn't stuck his spoon in the wall, for Lizzie needs a strong hand, and she won't listen to me! And as for Hetty! Well, she lives half the time at Carlton House and the other half with Sally Jersey. I don't mind having Lizzie underfoot so much, save that she leads these fellows about by the nose and I can scarcely tolerate watching the slaughter!" He then gave a crack of laughter. "Although I must admit at times I am vastly entertained!"

Meg laughed. She knew Mr. Norbury frequently quarrelled with Lizzie, and though he foretold a disastrous end for her, he would often pinch Lizzie's chin and seemed to take as much delight in her fiery disposition and outrageous manners as any of the young gentlemen did who kept his drawing rooms and gardens full to overflowing.

"Someone ought to warn that boy away from her!" he announced. "I wouldn't like to see Charles get all tangled up with Lizzie. She's had her cap set for him since the beginning of the season, and damme if I don't think he deserves better than my hoydenish niece!"

Meg was a little startled. Lizzie had professed an interest in Charles, but Meg had not taken her seriously. As for herself, she admired and enjoyed Lizzie's high spirits, perhaps even as much as Mr. Norbury did, but truly she did not think Lizzie would make a suitable wife for Charles.

She wanted to ask Mr. Norbury precisely what he meant regarding Lizzie, but at that moment a commotion at the entrance to the ballroom separated them. Mr. Norbury saw two guests arrive whom he felt both compelled and inclined to greet—Lord Worthen and his brother, Geoffrey Blake!

Meg remained where he had left her, near the long French doors on one side of the ballroom. One of the doors was open slightly, and she felt a fresh breeze touch her back as Worthen greeted Mr. Norbury.

The viscount bowed in his polished manner, presenting his brother with a smile of affection on his face.

A young lady standing near Meg exclaimed, "Lord, but they are both so devilishly handsome! Oh, Sukey, do but look at the one who is sporting a cane!" The females sighed together. "Do you suppose he was a soldier at one time? How utterly romantic—to have been wounded in battle. Perhaps even Waterloo!"

Meg's gaze drifted to Mr. Blake, who leaned slightly upon his cane. He was as tall as Worthen, with the same

115

dark coloring. His chin, however, was not at all in Worthen's strong, stubborn mold, but was a softer, kindlier oval in shape. Of the two men, she thought he was even more handsome than his older brother. She could not suppress a sigh. Blake was a fine, dashing figure of a man, and the cane upon which he obviously relied heavily merely accentuated his masculine bearing. She did not know the circumstances surrounding the injury to his leg, but had heard that he had been wounded in a trifling hunting accident. She smiled faintly. Certainly to have been wounded in battle would have been a great deal more interesting, but the mere fact that he was lame created a mysterious quality which few females could resist. In fact, Meg was certain that a great deal of Byron's abilities to incite devotion amongst the females of the beau monde was not his famed poetry, but his lameness. Even she was not indifferent to his exceptional figure and address. In fact, had the famous poet not been of such a dissolute character, she would have certainly encouraged his advances.

Sukey exclaimed, "Oh, yes! He most certainly must have been a soldier!" Her voice dropped dramatically as she whispered ecstatically, "Unless of course he injured his leg in a duel."

Her friend gasped and answered her in the same hushed cry: "Oh, yes, it must have been a duel! Certainly a duel! Who is he, I wonder?"

Meg narrowed her eyes slightly. A duel? Could Blake have been wounded in a duel? Would his brother have permitted him to duel? She doubted it.

Mr. Norbury led the brothers toward Caroline, Hope and his wife.

One of the young ladies next to Meg cried, "Oh, do but look at Lady Longville! She's grown quite pale upon seeing that man with the cane. I wonder if she will succumb to a fit of the vapors!"

Just as these words were spoken, Caroline's knees buckled. Only Worthen, acting with great presence of mind, prevented her from crumpling to the floor as he caught her easily in his arms.

Whatever was the matter with Caroline!

Meg felt several things at once—but the foremost was her concern for Caroline, whose delicate condition was becoming more apparent every day. Meg hurried across the room, not wishing to give form to the other thoughts that crowded in on her suddenly. The fact was, Caroline had fainted shortly after she had seen and recognized Geoffrey Blake. And at the last instant before Worthen caught her, she had cast a beseeching, pained glance at the viscount. Caroline, then, had known both of the brothers at one time.

Whatever did it all mean?

Meg could not explain the suddenly sick feeling she experienced. Perhaps the intricacies of her mind had already sorted through the mysteries before her and had drawn a conclusion. But whatever it might be, she did not wish to know. Not yet. Shutting her speculations from her mind, Meg turned her thoughts and efforts toward assuring herself that Caroline would be all right.

All about Worthen, a dozen females suddenly grouped themselves, fluttering at his heels as he walked slowly from the ballroom with Caroline in his arms. Mr. Norbury's three blackbirds pattered from the room as well, the spinster wafting her vinaigrette near Caroline's face and another calling out loudly that a cake of pastilles would be just the thing.

Meg followed the crowd of some dozen ladies as they moved into the hall and could only wait in the background as several of the matrons saw that Caroline was laid upon a chaise longue in the drawing room. Worthen was forced to leave almost immediately afterward when several of the ladies began clucking at him.

The spinster's vinaigrette, containing a sponge soaked in aromatic spirits, had its usual effect. Caroline's eyelids fluttered, and very soon she opened her eyes. When she

117

learned she had fainted, her expression grew quite disgusted.

"I have never fainted in my life!" she exclaimed. But some realization seemed to descend upon her as her clear green eyes grew slightly hazed. When she saw Meg, she said, "That was Geoffrey. I haven't seen him in years. Of course Worthen would want him here. I'm sorry, Meg, to have made such a spectacle of myself when it is all such ancient hist—" she broke off as she realized that some dozen of her acquaintance and neighbors about Staplehope were listening intently to her speech. She fell into a fit of coughing, then amended her words carefully. "That is, when women have been forever bearing children. It is such an ancient condition."

The several matrons who attended her seemed in full agreement with this observation and broke into a clacking of anecdotes all relating to the difficulties of childbearing and raising. But Meg knew that Caroline had meant to say something else entirely, and she was suddenly afraid to know what it was. That it pertained to Worthen and his brother, Meg understood perfectly well.

When Caroline had fully recovered her spirits, making light of her fainting spell, Meg met Geoffrey Blake whom she found to be a composed, reserved young man, with a family of five children and a wife who would very soon be brought to bed with a sixth. He positively delighted in twitting his brother on anything and everything, and the result was that Meg saw a slightly different viscount than she had ever known in London. Worthen was easier with everyone it seemed, yet anxious to see his brother well-accepted in Sir William's circle of acquaintance. In this, Meg sensed something more and was certain of it when she happened to see Worthen regarding his brother—the latter of whom was speaking with Hope Norbury—and an odd expression of pain crossed Worthen's face. It was gone as quickly as it had come, but Meg had seen it as clearly as she had seen Caroline's expression just before her stepmama had fainted.

When Geoffrey fell into a conversation with Mr.

Norbury about the various angling spots about the countryside, Meg could see that Worthen finally felt free to leave his brother to his own devices. He sought her out immediately, sweeping her from Hope's side and leading her out to a waltz.

He held her firmly, his hand upon the small of her back, as he whirled her about the floor. They moved easily together, and some of his own enthusiasm seemed to communicate itself to her feet, for she danced in a rustle of her emerald green silk gown as though this were the last dance her feet would know.

"Ah, Meggie, can't you feel how we belong to one another?" Worthen's eyes glittered in the crowded ballroom.

"Your mind makes far greater leaps than your feet, my lord! It would be more appropriate to say that we dance well together, would it not?"

"Where is your poetic soul this evening, my love! We belong together, you and I!"

Meg smiled and then laughed. "You have had a great deal too much of Mr. Norbury's champagne. Now, as for this engagement, dear sir . . ."

He closed his eyes and gave a gusty, playful sigh. "That is the first time you have called me 'dear.' I shall remember it all my life."

"Not only did you ignore the point of my conversation, but you are also being nonsensical."

"I am a man in love with the most beautiful ninnyhammer that ever existed. I may say what I wish! I have every right to be nonsensical!"

Meg took exception to his first remark. Tilting her head, she cried. "What do you mean, ninnyhammer!"

He smiled in a devilish manner. "A woman would be a ninnyhammer to refuse me, especially when I make love so prettily."

"You are conceited beyond measure, Lord Worthen."

He lowered his voice. "You enjoy my kisses. Admit that you do!"

Meg was shocked and nearly faltered in her steps as she

119

met his laughing gaze. She never expected him to speak of such things. He may have taken advantage of her upon several occasions, but to actually refer to his wicked deeds was quite another matter. She stammered, "I—that is—Worthen! How am I supposed to answer you?"

He was suddenly intense and frightening. "Say yes. Say yes to my kisses, to my love, to my embraces, to my heart, to my hand in marriage."

"And I suppose now you will tell me I actually have a choice?" She spoke firmly, hoping to fluster him even if but a little and perhaps enough to force him to relent.

He merely laughed and held her more tightly still. "No, you haven't a choice in the least."

Meg replied quietly, "Beast." But her heart held little anger. He was too congenial, too happy for her to feel animosity toward him. She sighed, wondering how she was to rid herself of a man who continually kept her off balance.

The music drove them relentlessly about the long chamber, the swish of slippered feet on the floor and the chatter of contented partners soft sounds that pursued them. Meg let herself simply enjoy the dance. Perhaps later, when some of the guests began departing, she could take him to a secluded corner and tell him the truth.

Since her last encounter with him, when she had fled into the woods, afraid of succumbing to his advances, she had been strengthening her resolve to tell him the precise nature of her sentiments. But everytime she thought of facing him and informing him of her opinion a terrible knot formed in her stomach. How could she possibly say to him, or to any man, *I have found you cowardly and lacking in other gentlemanly attributes; these are my reasons for being unable to love you.* Even now, as she looked up at him, his arm still guiding her easily about the ballroom, her heart wavered. Yet what choice had he given her? Surely, if he knew her honest opinions of his character, he would be more than happy to give her up.

When the waltz ended, Meg sat down near the entrance to the ballroom and waited for Worthen to return to her with a cup of iced champagne. She arranged her emerald skirts, fanning herself lightly. She tapped her foot to a lively Scottish reel, which Lizzie had begged the orchestra to play, and watched with mounting horror as Charles went down a third—a third!—dance with Lizzie. The entire ballroom rose to a quiet frenzy of gasps and bosom-clutching whisperings. It just wasn't done!

Charles had dealt Hope, with whom he had not danced once during her birthday ball, a final blow. Meg watched him, startled that he could be so cruel. Did he even know of the pain he was inflicting?

And Hope! She stood beside Worthen's brother, her eyes suddenly glassy in appearance as she watched her beau take his place across from Lizzie. Hope curtsied slightly to Blake and stumbled once as she fled the ballroom, her white shirts in hand.

As she disappeared into the hallway, Meg turned reproachful eyes upon Charles and saw that he had watched Hope leave the chamber, his brow knit with concern. He glanced about the room and had the grace to blush as he realized he was being regarded most sternly by at least a dozen matrons. Meg knew instantly that he was not completely aware of how great a solecism he had committed.

The next moment, he was smiling at Lizzie, fairly skipping to the light, fast music. Whatever decision he had made with regard to Hope appeared to be final.

Worthen returned with the champagne, and instead of sitting beside Meg, he begged her to excuse him, for he wished to speak with Hope. Meg took the cup, curious as to why he felt a necessity of attending to Hope, but also thankful that he was doing so. She wondered if he knew what had happened and realized somehow he must have learned of Charles' treachery because he returned to the ballroom shortly afterward with Hope on his arm.

In a matter of seconds, they, too, joined the several lively young couples who were creating a great rumpus on the ballroom floor. Even the blackbirds were tapping their feet, smiles now creasing their wrinkled faces as they watched the hero of the piece, Lord Worthen, escort the jilted heroine—poor, poor Hope Norbury—down the dance.

As for Charles, he was doomed to receive many a snub before the evening drew to a close.

After the dance, Meg watched Worthen converse for a few minutes with Mrs. Norbury and Hope. The results of this conversation were soon known. Hope was to perform, at the express request of Lord Worthen, upon not the pianoforte, but the harp!

A buzz raced through the gathering crowd. Hope, it seemed, had prepared a surprise for everyone. For the last two years, she had been studying the harp assiduously, and tonight she meant to perform for those she loved best—the families about Staplehope.

The crowd responded with delight and amazement and was soon stuffed into the drawing room.

Meg stood in the shadows at the entrance to the drawing room. She searched all the faces of the gentlemen, standing or sitting, in an effort to find Charles and to speak with him. She wanted desperately to discover what had happened to cause him to treat Hope so shabbily. But she could not see him anywhere within the drawing room.

Her heart fell. Was Charles with Lizzie? A quick scan of the long, elegant chamber gave her the answer.

Retracing her steps to the ballroom, she arrived there in time to see Charles steal through the French doors with a giggling Elizabeth Priestley upon his arm. She immediately followed after them.

One thing she knew for certain, she could not permit Charles to refrain from being present at Hope's performance. Tongues would wag unceasingly for weeks, and Hope would be obliged to bear the brunt of it. And if she had to drag Charles by his curly red hair, she would do so.

As for Lizzie, she felt ready to give that bit of baggage a hearty scold!

Chapter Nine

Meg crossed the ballroom floor swiftly and followed Charles and Lizzie out onto the terrace.

"Don't be a goose!" Lizzie cried, smiling up into Charles' face with her clear blue eyes flashing. "Who will notice if either you or I are not present. Surely no one will care in the least. It is Hope who will have command of everyone's attention. And I only want command of yours."

Charles reached down and pinched her chin. "You know very well that you and I, most particularly, will be noted more for our absence than if we sat right next to your aunt during the entire performance."

Meg did not hesitate to intrude as she spoke quietly: "There you are! I found you at last. Do not tell me you haven't been told of all the excitement. Hope is to perform on the harp! You shall miss her entire performance if you do not hurry!"

Charles released Lizzie's firm grasp on his arm and whirled her around. "There, you see, Lizzie! If Meg was aware of our absence, then I daresay your aunt is as well."

Lizzie, who did not seem to be in the least disturbed that she had been discovered in a scandalous tête-à-tête upon the terrace with Charles, breathed a sigh of relief and cried, "Oh! Thank heaven it is only you, Meg! I was afraid for a moment that my uncle had come to scold me." She turned back to Charles. "Come, then! I suppose we ought to go listen to my cousin play, though I daresay if I have heard the piece she is to perform once, I have heard it a thousand times." Lizzie led the way back through the

French doors and onto the ballroom floor. She continued, "You simply cannot imagine what it is like day and night —the twanging and drumming of strings until even my teeth ache. Do you enjoy the harp, Charles?"

"I don't know," Charles answered. "I haven't really thought about it. I suppose it sounds as every other instrument sounds—as well as it can, in its way."

Lizzie smiled at him. "Well," she said, "I am at least happy to hear you express an indifferent opinion, for when we are wed, I shan't ever play the harp or the pianoforte for that matter."

Meg was so astonished to hear Lizzie speak in this manner that she paused midstride and was not surprised that Charles did so as well. They both stared at Lizzie, who continued walking toward the hall by herself, giggling. When she arrived at the doorway, she turned back to them, an impish smile upon her pretty face as she said, "Oh, my, I do believe I have quite shocked you. But then even if you did ask me to marry you, Mr. Charles Burnell, perhaps then I would have to say no." And she was gone.

Meg looked at Charles, who returned her stare with a somewhat guilty look. "I know what you are thinking, Meggie, that I am in the devil of a fix with that female. And you know something, you are right. But for the first time in my life, I don't care a rush! If I can marry Lizzie, I will. By God, I will!" He began walking away from Meg, and after he had taken several steps, he turned back and added, "I have come to the conclusion that Hope and I would never suit. I am much too fond of the beauties to be found in the night sky to give it up forever. You, at least, ought to be able to comprehend my sentiments."

He turned as if to go, but Meg called after him. "Wait, Charles. At least enter the drawing room with me and allay a little of the gossip. This is Hope's birthday, afterall."

Charles paused and, after a moment said, "Yes, of course, I suppose it is the least I could do."

Meg hurried to catch up with him, and slipping her arm through his, she said quietly, "I do understand why you feel as you do, but could you not have spared Hope a little? She was positively devastated tonight."

Charles ran a hasty hand through his thick red locks as they continued walking toward the hall. "I suppose you are right, but it is so very difficult to explain all that I feel. I should have spoken to her beforehand, but I had no opportunity to do so. I only decided this morning that I should break with her. And it is not as though we were engaged."

"No." Meg laughed at him. "Except that the entire village has been laying odds upon the event for the past six months and more."

Charles responded testily, "I cannot help that. Is it my affair if everyone has little else to do than to speculate upon Hope's future or mine?"

"You might have danced at least one country dance with Hope, and as for the Scottish reel, oh, Charles, it was poorly done."

He nodded and sighed. "I agree with you there. I was in the middle before I realized what Lizzie and I had done. The reel was Lizzie's idea, you see. And we were having such a jolly time! You know how spirited she is! Our feet were running across the ballroom floor before I had had time to recollect this was our third set together. Lord, I'd never danced more than two, even with Hope. I could see we'd set all the Tabbies to caterwauling. I can't tell you how glad I was to see Worthen lead Hope out! So you see, no harm done!"

Meg looked at her friend from childhood. She knew him well, that even though he professed a certain measure of indifference and even spoke lightly of his treatment of Hope, he was still laboring under some very strong emotion. She did not condone what he had done, nor did she feel the least good would be accomplished by taking him to task. Instead, she asked, "Do you love Elizabeth?"

Charles gave Meg a crooked smile and squeezed her arm as he responded, "I haven't the faintest notion what love is. All I know is that Lizzie makes me laugh a great deal, she is full of fun and gig, and as for Byron, she has

125

begged me to read any and all of his poetry to her at the earliest opportunity. I could not ask for more in a female."

When they reached the entrance to the drawing room, they stood together at the back of the room. Lizzie was nowhere to be seen, perhaps having removed to the ladies' sitting room. At the front of the audience, Worthen stood near the harp, his quizzing glass in hand, his attention riveted to Hope's rippling fingers. He was completely mesmerized by her performance as was the entire room, and within a minute, both Meg and Charles had been equally drawn into the sweet flow of Hope's rendition of a Mozart sonata, cleverly arranged for the harp, probably by herself. Her fingers were magical, the music pulsing steadily, the notes ringing clear in the red and blue drawing room. Mrs. Norbury and her husband stood aside, across from Lord Worthen, also watching their daughter intently, a fond light of pride glowing from each parental face. Mr. Norbury slipped his hand within his wife's, who turned to look at him, her eyes shimmering with tears.

Meg's throat grew very tight at the fondness she saw reflected there. She could not keep from glancing at Charles to see if he had noticed this affectionate gesture on Mr. Norbury's part. But Charles' gaze was fixed upon Hope, who leaned into her harp with great vigor. As he watched Hope give of herself fully to her music, Charles' face grew grief-stricken. His brow was knit painfully, and the expression in his blue eyes was the sharp hurt of a young man who has seen his first love slip away from him.

Meg turned her gaze away from Charles. The pain she saw there struck deeply into her own heart. She knew he loved Hope, but after seeing how much he took delight in Lizzie, she felt he was right in letting Hope go. With this thought, she could not keep from regarding Worthen again, her own heart feeling oddly constricted. Why was he so intent upon having her when they were so ill-suited themselves? And why did not Worthen see their differences as she did?

When Hope struck the final chord of the sonata, the room broke into a wild burst of applause, and afterward a general hubbub of conversation ensued. Charles pulled Meg toward the back wall of the drawing room as many guests began sauntering back to the ballroom.

He asked her in a whisper: "And how rages your battle, Meggie? Do you still wish me to cart you off to Bristol?"

Meg sighed. "No. Somehow, I intend to reason him out of the engagement."

Charles frowned as he watched Meg. "And have you done so yet?"

Meg laughed. "No, I have not, and how right you were. He is a remarkably stubborn man. When I reasonably pointed out to him that I did not love him, could not love him, could not *esteem* him, he so much as told me he didn't really care what my sentiments toward him were— he would marry me anyway!"

Charles cried, "Even when you told him what you really thought of his character? That you believe him to be a man lacking in some of the nobler virtues?"

Meg said, "I have not told him the extent to my sentiments. I did not wish to unless it were necessary. I am beginning to see, however, that I will have to. He will be greatly shocked. I know he does not view himself in the same manner. He is rather assured in his opinions of himself."

Charles shook his head. "It is always the way with these great men. They have been so used to the laurels of their station in life that they frequently have greatly distorted views of themselves." He frowned slightly as he continued, "But are you certain in your opinions of him?"

Meg laid a hand upon the sleeve of his coat and spoke in a low voice: "Montford so much as challenged him not a sennight past, in defense of me, of course, and all that Worthen did was smile at him and say something trifling in response. If the situation had been reversed, I know that Montford would have instantly accepted the challenge thrown at him. But Worthen acted as though Montford was beneath his notice. I tell you, Charles, I could hardly bear looking at him."

Charles shook his head. "What is to be done, then?" he cried. "It is not for you to marry a man so lacking in spirit and dash. Why, you should be heartily disgusted with such a man within a month of your marriage!"

Guests filed past them in waves of rustling silk and exclamations over Hope's performance. A number of people remained in the drawing room, crowding about Hope and praising her for her talent and her performance.

Charles, whose gaze had been fixed upon Worthen for a moment, turned back to Meg suddenly and cried, "I know precisely what must be done, Meg! I only wonder that I did not think of it sooner! And you will be greatly surprised! Oh, what fun we shall all have now!"

Meg cried, "But what is it, Charles? What do you mean to do?"

Charles tugged at her chin in a friendly manner. "I shan't tell you a thing. But I promise you that in a few days I shall have a great surprise for you!"

With that Meg had to be content, for he immediately bowed to her, saying he must atone a little for his sins of the evening, and began weaving his way through the crowds toward Hope. Once near her, he bowed to her and begged for a dance, but even at this distance, Meg could see that his manner was both distant and rigidly polite.

Hope responded graciously, curtsying to him slightly as he walked away. Later he would claim his dance, and perhaps then some of the Tabbies would be satisfied with his actions. But Hope would not. Her gaze was nothing short of stricken as she watched him walk away, her heart sitting ever so briefly but painfully in her eyes. Poor Hope! For all her appearance now of serenity, as she turned back to the throng about her, Meg could see that this birthday would long be remembered as the worst one she had ever had to endure.

When the hour had grown quite late, and the orchestra's instruments had fallen wearily out of tune, Meg completed a sedate country dance with her father. Afterward she watched him leave the ballroom to go in

128

search of his wife and to ask the coach to be brought round. The hour was considerably advanced, and Caroline needed her bed.

Meg realized that if she were to make a push to end her secret engagement with Worthen, she must do so very soon. She began searching the ballroom for Lord Worthen's tall figure. She was situated near the entrance to the ballroom but could find him nowhere.

With a start, she felt a feminine arm about her waist as Lizzie whirled her about suddenly and fairly squealed, "Oh, do but look at him, Meg!"

"Lizzie, what are you about?" Meg cried with a laugh, startled by being nearly toppled over as Lizzie pulled her around to face the doors near the terrace.

She remained standing behind Meg, and cried, "Over there, by the doors. Do you see how the breeze makes the curtains billow? Well, look who is sitting just beyond them, leaning upon his cane." She sighed gustily. "How very handsome he is! I think he is even more dashing than Lord Byron!"

Meg found the object of Lizzie's exclamations as Lizzie continued, "Was there ever a more romantic creature than Geoffrey Blake? Oh, if he weren't married, I should set my cap for him. Look how sad his expression is!"

Meg responded, "Perhaps he is caught in a fit of melancholia because he is unable to dance with the pretty ladies of Staplehope!"

Lizzie sighed gustily, but at that moment, Worthen, who apparently had overheard their brief comments, spoke in a flat voice: "You are both mistaken, I am afraid."

Lizzie and Meg turned as one, with Lizzie's arm still bracing Meg. The ladies spoke in unison, asking, "What do you mean?"

Worthen withdrew a small, enamelled snuffbox from his coat pocket and took a pinch of snuff. He said, "I don't like to destroy your illusions, but I doubt that my brother is of the moment regretting he cannot dance. You see, his hip is quite weak, and if he strides about for too long a time, he ends up in a great deal of pain. I have been begging him to return to the inn this hour and more. I fear he is in much discomfort, but he will not spoil my evening! So, you see, he is hardly thinking about the dances he is missing!"

Meg knew that Worthen had meant to dampen their ardor for his brother's romantic appearance, but his words only heightened their sympathies for the young gentleman as well as their view that he was somehow extraordinary. Again, as one, they turned back to look at Blake, their heads nearly touching as they cried out a very sad, "Oh, poor dear!" their voices again resounding as one.

Meg continued, "Poor, poor man, without even his wife to comfort him or his children to prattle about his knees and give succor to the wounds of his life."

Worthen gave a crack of laughter at this dramatic speech and could not withhold his comment. "As to his wife, undoubtedly you are correct, for she is a woman of great forbearance and understanding. But as to his children, four of whom are the naughtiest boys in England, I should say he felt the evening's trials were a fair Holiday." He sauntered away, and both ladies glared after him.

Lizzie's gaze followed him, her expression indignant. "He is of a practical turn, is he not, Meggie! I think you are well rid of him, but why has he come to Shropshire? Does he mean, do you think, to pursue Hope? He certainly appears to admire her prodigiously."

Meg was at first relieved by these words, for it meant that the village was as yet unaware of her engagement to Worthen. On the other hand, when Meg considered the thought of Worthen pursuing Hope, she knew the faintest prickle of jealousy which caught her completely by surprise. That Worthen joined Hope and Mrs. Burnell as they stood near the orchestra, contesting lively as to whether the last dance of the evening would be a quadrille or a waltz, only added to Meg's sudden dislike of the idea that Worthen could possibly find Hope attractive. She then took herself sorely to task for a notion that was ridiculous in the extreme. Why should she give a fig what sort of female Lord Worthen found intriguing when she meant to get rid of him herself? And wouldn't it be a wonderful thing, even at this late hour, if the viscount were to give his heart to another?

This thought, far from setting her sensibilities on an even course, merely caused Meg to snap at Charles when he approached her suddenly and asked her if she had as yet convinced Worthen they ought not to wed.

Many of the guests had already taken their leave when Mrs. Norbury announced the final dance of the evening. Worthen begged this dance of Meg, and just as they were to take their places for a quadrille, she suggested that they take a little air out on the terrace.

He was at first surprised then immensely pleased as he took her arm firmly in his and guided her quickly toward the long French doors opposite the entrance to the ballroom.

Worthen drew her to a shadowed place at the far end of the terrace. The dark night sky was free of even a scattering of clouds as well as the light from the moon. The stars did not seem to mind, for they twinkled brightly above the soft hills that surrounded the village of Staplehope.

Worthen immediately took Meg's hand and kissed her fingers, but she drew her hand away abruptly and said, "You must not, my lord, for I have brought you here to a purpose. There is something you must know."

He stroked her cheek with his gloved finger and, in a low voice, asked, "And what is that, my dearest Margaret?"

Worthen edged closer to her, a wicked smile on his lips. She knew what he intended, and she instantly placed a hand upon his chest, firmly holding him away from her. He seemed surprised by this move on her part, and upon seeing the serious expression on her face, he relented and ceased his advances.

"You won't like what I have to tell you, but since you have continually refused my requests to release me from this engagement, I feel compelled to tell you the precise nature of my reasons for rejecting your suit both now and when we were last in London." At first, she meant to simply state her opinions, but after a moment's consideration, she said, "Do you remember last season—over a year ago now—when we were at Almack's and Mr. White bumped into us while we were sharing a waltz?"

The pleasant expression on Worthen's face fled instantly. He grew equally serious, as though he comprehended the full direction of her thought. Nodding, he responded, "Yes, I remember the incident clearly. Mr. White is a friend of Montford's, I believe."

"As to that," Meg responded, "I cannot say. But as to what happened next, I think you ought to know that I found your actions incomprehensible. Mr. White apologized to me, of course; but he accused you of boorishness, and you merely smiled at him."

Worthen took a deep breath and leaned an elbow on the stone railing of the terrace. Meg waited for him to speak, to defend himself, but he said nothing.

Finally, she asked, "Why do you merely stare at me, Worthen? You are a man of intelligence; what do you have to say in defense of yourself?" She suddenly realized that she truly hoped he would have a sensible answer for her; she wanted to believe the best of him.

He said, "I have heard nothing yet to which I need give an answer of any kind. Mr. White did not deserve a response from me—not then and certainly not now."

Meg was angered by the rigidity of his spirit. Why would he not tell her what she wished to know? She said, "As you wish then, I will phrase my question more bluntly. Why, after he had called you a boor and then taken your kerchief from your pocket and dusted his shoes with it, did you choose to ignore him? Why did you not call him out? The situation demanded it!"

He answered her with a question of his own. "Is this all that concerns you? That I do not offer satisfaction to every scoundrel in London who would demand it of me?"

"He laughed at you and walked away, and you did nothing."

"He deserved nothing better from me."

"And had he offended me, would you have done nothing more?"

"Since he did not, I cannot possibly give you a meaningful answer."

"I ask you to suppose; I ask you to tell me what you would intend to do. If you say you love me, and were a Mr. White, or anyone else, to approach me and offend me—and that, in your presence—what would you do?"

Worthen smiled. "I might blacken his eye and perhaps draw his cork." He seemed certain she would be gratified by this.

Meg was deeply distressed and humiliated. "You would brawl as any mere commoner? You would engage in a bout of fisticuffs and thereby permit my name to be bandied about every male coterie in England?"

Worthen felt her words as though she had struck him forcibly across the mouth. "What are you really asking me, Margaret? And why, if I were to strike a man for accosting you, would you not consider yourself avenged?"

Meg lifted her chin haughtily. "I would be humiliated beyond words. A true gentleman would never take up a lady's cause by employing so savage a means as his fists."

Worthen's expression grew grave. "What you are really saying, Margaret, is that a true gentleman would engage in nothing short of a duel."

Margaret let out a great sigh, relieved that they had finally arrived at the heart of the matter. "Yes," Meg responded, her voice quiet. The sounds of the quadrille drifted into the night air, cutting through the silence that separated them.

He commanded her: "Tell me everything, Meg. Tell me now what thoughts reign in your heart."

Meg took a deep breath and stated her case: "I believe you lack honor, Lord Worthen, that you are afraid to face those who would discredit you. I have thought so these several months and more. You know I have cause—great cause. Mr. White was only one of many incidents over the past twelve months. What I don't understand is why

133

your heart fails you. I have been given to understand by Charles and by my father that you are a man of great abilities—either as a swordsman or with your pistols.

"Another more recent example, however, comes readily to mind. You know that Lord Montford is a particular friend of mine, and though I was not content that he should have uttered his challenge to you during Mrs. Norbury's musicale, the fact remains that he cast a decided slur upon your honor. I heard him do so! And all that you did was remind him that you would not face him in a duel! I was never more mortified, especially since you had just asked for my hand in marriage. Do you not see, then, how absurd your request for my hand in marriage seemed to me?" She paused for a moment, then asked, "Would you not at least admit that other gentlemen whom you esteem, upon receiving such a challenge, would not have hesitated to tell Montford to name his seconds?"

"Yes," Worthen responded quietly. "A number of my friends and acquaintance would have long since called Montford out."

Meg spread her hands out and said, "These, then, are my heartfelt reasons for rejecting your suit, now and forever. Had I been a different sort of female, with a lesser regard for matters of chivalry and honor, I don't doubt for a moment that I would entertain your suit with much pleasure." She found sudden tears bite her eyes. "I am most willing to believe you have some reason for ignoring the taunts of your peers, but I cannot approve of or admire the manner in which you conduct yourself among the beau monde. I ask you then, again, in light of what I have just told you, will you not release me from this engagement?"

Meg waited for his answer. That he was giving careful consideration to her words she could see, for his brow was deeply furrowed and his jaw worked strongly. She had spoken bluntly because she saw no other way. But what was he thinking?

Lord Worthen turned slightly away from Meg, a fury

mounting within him that he did not feel entirely capable of controlling. Her words were sinking into him as though a claw were attached to each one. He knew she had been strongly resistant to his advances, but upon his soul, it had never occurred to him that she saw him, or his actions, as ungentlemanly or dishonorable. Good God! She might as well have called him a coward! Was there any word more despised by a man who valued his beliefs, his integrity, his ability to battle the adverse winds that stormed every man's life?

The woman he intended to make his wife believed him to be nothing less than a coward and all because he refused to let a dishonorable muckworm like Montford, or White for that matter, bait him into a duel. Meg could not know that the situation had even worse aspects to it. She could not know, for instance, that her particular friend was well aware that Worthen would never give him satisfaction and used this knowledge to his own advantage whenever the occasion arose. Somehow, Montford had learned the truth about Geoffrey's hunting accident and knew of the vow Worthen had taken afterward never to duel again as long as he lived!

Worthen stared into the shadows beyond the terrace. A topiary garden of tea pots and oversized birds sat in the center of the garden. Beyond the wide boundary of a clipped yew hedge, the straight trunks and thick foliage of a forest of beech trees, black in the darkness of the night, mounted steadily toward the hill that rose some nine hundred feet above the valley floor. The dark appearance of the woods reminded him suddenly of a night ten years ago, when a shot rang frightfully among a similar forest of trees and his brother Geoff fell to the ground, his voice crying out in anguish.

A thousand times, Worthen had relived the horror of that night. He had not slept for weeks because the dreams tore at him and he awoke in sweat-laden nightshirts. A thousand times he had undone the deed in his dreams, and only one thought saved him: At the last moment, when he had levelled his own duelling pistol at Geoffrey, his blood hot from jealousy, he had distorted his aim by some instinct he could not comprehend and, instead of killing his brother, merely lamed him for life. Oh, God! Lamed him for life! His own brother!

And Meg believed him to be a coward! The fury he felt raged in him to so strong a degree that he gripped the stone wall of the terrace before him until his hands and arms ached. How had it come about that of all the females in Mayfair—of which, given his peerage, he could certainly have had nearly anyone he desired—he chose instead a woman who held beliefs so contrary to his own. And her opinions were so unusual for a female. In general, the ladies of his acquaintance detested the practice of duelling. His own grandmama, for instance, despised it so much that when she learned her youngest son was to engage in a duel, she had the servants tie him up in one of the gardening sheds for a full week to prevent the duel.

But it was not for Meg to abhor the vicious practice of taking a man's life with a sword or pistol merely because he spoke with the wrong inflection in his voice, or jostled you in a doorway, or called you a boor, took your kerchief and wiped his shoes with it. There was no doubt in his mind that had he called White out, the man would have later been buried in the churchyard of his own village— and to what purpose?

Could the gods have been more cruel to him, though, than to have caused him to fall in love with a woman who extolled duelling? He felt as though the guilt of that last duel with his brother had been hurled in his face yet again by this great irony.

"My brother was lamed in a duel," he said at last, his voice hoarse. "It is not common knowledge, and as you can imagine, I have a great antipathy for duelling."

He turned to look at Meg through a blur of his mounting hatred for Montford, who had forced this issue unwittingly between himself and Meg. He searched for a way to answer her. As he began speaking, his voice sounded so hushed that he would not have been surprised if Meg could not hear him at all. "You must wound or kill a man yourself at thirty paces, Meg, before you pass judgement on me or any man who stands against the practice of duelling. You don't know what your beliefs really mean. And to judge me entirely by this, frankly, I had given you much more credit than perhaps you deserved. But if you think for one moment that I will release you from this engagement because you have judged me—and that erroneously—to be a coward, you are mistaken. And now, I must take Geoff back to The Vine Inn, where he can rest a hip that was ruined forever in a duel. Understand at least this much, that for the rest of my brother's life, he will never dance again, he cannot run, he lives with pain daily, and I grieve for his loss daily. The surgeon has said that by the age of fifty, he will be confined to a Bath chair. Is this romantic, Meg? Is this honorable?" He was unable to say more, for his heart burned in this throat. He turned away from her abruptly and left her standing alone on the terrace.

Meg felt numb, by both the vision of his face as he relived some horrible memory—perhaps the very duel in which his own brother was lamed—as well as by his words. Would Geoff truly live out the final score of his years in a Bath chair, like an invalid—because of a duel? Through the curtains, she could see Worthen approach his brother. As Geoff rose from his chair, he winced and fell backward, leaning heavily on his cane. Meg felt sick at her stomach suddenly as Worthen slipped an arm under Geoff's elbow and helped him to his feet. And she had thought Geoff such a dashing figure with his cane. But for ten years he had not danced and would never dance again!

Meg whirled away from the sight of Worthen supporting his brother from the ballroom as she wiped tears from her cheeks. Her uncle's words of two days ago came back to her in a torturous wave: "Have you ever seen a man bleed to death?"

Chapter Ten

"Are you certain you do not wish me to fetch one of the dogs?" Mrs. Potts asked. She was the housekeeper of Staplehope and of the moment sat at the end of the settee in the drawing room, the upper part of her body twisted completely around as she leaned as far as she could over the side of the settee. She looked down at her mistress, who was crawling on her knees behind the table and searching the floor.

"No!" Caroline cried. "I will not have one of Sir William's dirty hunting dogs in this house. If we must, we'll have Cook bring us a piece of cheese. The gardener said he had a trap we could make use of if we wished."

Mrs. Potts groaned faintly and removed a kerchief from the sleeve of her gown of black bombazine.

Caroline lifted her gaze swiftly to Mrs. Potts. "Good heavens!" she cried. "Whatever is the matter!"

Mrs. Potts rolled her eyes slightly and slumped back down into the settee, the kerchief pressed delicately to her lips. She was a slight, fine-boned woman with a sharp hawklike nose and large, gray eyes. Moaning again, she spoke dramatically: "Do not ask me! I beseech you not to mention the gardener or his traps to me. The last time we used one of them, the poor mouse, who had perished in the most grotesque fashion imaginable—his head nearly cut off in his attempt to get at a square of moldy cheese—was not found for days! The wretched thing was discovered in the linens. I suffered the vapors for weeks afterward!"

"Oh, dear!" Caroline exclaimed. "Well, perhaps I can lure him out with one of Cook's fresh biscuits and entrap him in a box. But wherever does Sir William's little mouse reside?" She searched the area around the end of the settee where her husband had been seated two days earlier. She found neither a trace of the mouse nor a place where he might have made his abode. She rose to her feet, and with her hands planted on her waist, she cast her gaze about the fireplace, but could see no secretive caches where a mouse might hide. She said, "We simply must be rid of that creature before Saturday. I will not have Mrs. Burnell or any of the other ladies fainting because our little guest chooses to make an untimely appearance!"

"Ah." Mrs. Potts nodded as she wafted her vinaigrette beneath her nose. "I am so very happy for Miss Margaret. Imagine, marrying a Peer of the Realm. And your party is a splendid idea. By the way, I was speaking to Cook only this morning, and she assured me that she could have enough white soup prepared by Saturday for supper afterward. She also wished you to know that she could most certainly arrange a dinner for twelve if you wished it. She seemed a little affronted that she had not been asked to do so."

"Sir William and I considered serving a dinner, but we decided that keeping the party a surprise would be just the thing to celebrate Meg's engagement," Caroline responded with a forced smile. She had the worst feeling that the party would be a disaster, but she did not wish to communicate her sentiments to the staff. She continued, "Besides, Sir William has already made arrangements for the three of us to dine with Lord Worthen at The Vine Inn that evening. We won't be returning here until after all the guests have arrived. Worthen and Meg are to know nothing about their engagement party until the moment they cross the threshold to the ballroom." She paused, wondering if she was doing the right thing.

Caroline had concocted this scheme after she overheard Meg's disastrous conversation with Worthen on the night before. She had not meant to overhear their argument, but she was just returning from the gardens where she had taken a quiet, secluded stroll to try to arrange her thoughts a little. Geoffrey's sudden appearance had shaken her to the roots of her soul.

Just as she had put her slippered foot on the bottom step of the stone stairway, she heard Meg's voice. Even she had not suspected the depth to Meg's convictions. Later, when she related the whole to Sir William, he had agreed readily to her plan to honor Meg's engagement with a party and in this fashion hopefully move the impending marriage to a safe conclusion within the confines of the church of St. Michael's.

Caroline had felt so many things upon listening to the entire conversation between Meg and Worthen. Mostly, however, a tremendous amount of guilt had overwhelmed her. She was as much to blame for Geoffrey's lameness as either of the brothers. She had known of the duel several days before it actually took place. Was it really ten years ago? It seemed like only yesterday. And even though she had tried to stop the duel—sending a missive to Worthen by Lord Montford's hand—the evil had already been accomplished. The gentlemen would face one another with pistols; Lord Montford had told her that both men proved intractable.

Caroline had been as flirtatious as Elizabeth when she was very young and first come out. She was also as fanciful as Meg—two horrendous flaws which she had been working steadily since to overcome. The brothers had vied for her hand, and she had revelled in their attentions, playing one against the other. They were not her only suitors, but she so enjoyed seeing the devil's light gleam in their eyes that she encouraged their competition whenever she could. A duel and Geoffrey's lameness had been the result.

It seemed so odd to her, that Fate had somehow brought them all together again, as though history demanded they rework past events into a better future. When she had heard Meg's opinions of Worthen's character, she had been horrified. It was all too ironic, too horrific, too familiar to bear with equanimity. Had the gods chosen to punish them all over again?

But whatever hand the gods of Olympus might have in their lives, Caroline knew she must help in whatever way she could to further this faltering romance along. Of course she wanted Staplehope to herself, but her heart now demanded that Worthen receive his due—the woman he loved.

After the duel, Caroline had faced the worst truth of all. Her own heart had long since been given to Worthen, but her silliness, her foolishness, had cost her his love. She could not face him after Geoffrey's lameness was confirmed by three of London's most famous surgeons. Her flirtatious disposition died on that day, and she had worked ever since to keep her vanity from ever causing harm to another again.

But would Meg suffer the same fate? Would her own misguided beliefs and frivolous romanticism cost her Worthen's love, too? Caroline did not want that to happen.

She nodded briskly, her course set, and she addressed Mrs. Potts: "I hope they will both be greatly surprised and pleased by our efforts!" Still her heart quavered within her.

"Oh, indeed I'm sure they will!" Mrs. Potts answered as she tucked her kerchief beneath the wristband of her sleeve.

Caroline frowned at the table in front of her. "But where is that mouse? I cannot bear the thought of seeing him sit upon one of our guests' shoulders and beg for biscuits!"

Later that afternoon, Meg rose abruptly from her

writing desk, picked up a pen that had broken twice in the past five minutes and threw it toward the fireplace. Much to her amazement, the pen landed squarely upon a neat stack of coals, having cleared the screen by a mere fraction of an inch.

"Well!" she cried aloud in the empty room. "And that is the only thing I have accomplished in the past four hours."

She turned to look at the twenty or more pages spread out on the desk before her. The sheet on the top was dotted with ink spots and crawled with a variety of scrolls, swirls and several incomprehensible sentences. Her hand had been unable to connect with her brain, a condition she had been suffering from the entire afternoon.

Putting the lid back on the inkwell, Meg rummaged in the top drawer of her desk for a length of black ribbon—a color well-suited to the dark thoughts that weighed heavily upon her spirit. When she found the ribbon, she tied the most recent pages of her manuscript together, picked up a pencil, a light blue cashmere shawl, and promptly quit the morning room.

She felt restless and to a degree quite sick at heart. This was the state in which she had found herself shortly after her quarrel with Worthen. Afterward, no amount of sleep, or reflection, or rumination or even the fiercest jaunt about the country lanes on the back of her favorite mare had diminished the sense of turmoil boiling within her. She could not set aside her own convictions, nor could she dismiss the horrific nature of how wretchedly the practice of duelling had affected Worthen and his brother.

All night, even in her dreams, a battle had raged in her mind. When does a man's honor require satisfaction? Worthen seemed to have concluded *never!* But she could not agree with him. She was terribly sorry that Geoffrey had been hurt; perhaps the object of their quarrel did not warrant so violent a step.

Oh, she did not want to think about it anymore! All she

knew was that before this engagement had been forced on her, her world had been very neat and tidy, with her values arranged in great detail to coincide with the high-minded rules of chivalry. But in a mere fortnight, she had been asked first whether she had ever seen a man bleed to death, and then forced to witness just how a man lamed in a duel must evermore cope with his existence.

As if in response to all these thoughts that kept whirling around in her head and never lighting long enough to sort themselves out so that she could adjust her thinking, Meg picked up her skirts with her free hand and ran toward the yew-hedge maze. She wanted to lose herself for an hour or so and not have to think of anything. But the image of Worthen's face kept rising before her. She could not seem to forget the horrible expression he wore as he told her how Blake had become wounded, and she ran harder still.

When at last she arrived at the center of the maze, she flung the manuscript down on the stone bench and curled up beside it, her knees tucked beneath her. Using her cashmere shawl as a pillow, she rested her head against the back of the stone bench and kept her gaze fixed upon the beechwood rising to the east. The sun was far to the west and warmed her face, her hair and her arms, and within a few minutes she had fallen fast asleep.

She awoke to the gentlest tugging on her arm.

"Meggie," a soft voice called to her. "I must speak with you. Will you not wake up?"

Meg blinked her eyes open and stared into Hope Norbury's kind face. Hope smiled at her in an encouraging manner. The sun had nearly set, and a breeze was blowing steadily, cooling the center of the maze.

Meg sat up quickly. "Oh, my goodness. I must have slept! How very odd and it has grown so cold!"

Hope unfurled Meg's shawl and placed it about her shoulders.

"Thank you!" Meg cried. "But however did you find me? Oh, my dear, you've been crying." She reached a hand toward Hope and pressed her arm.

143

Hope gave a little laugh, her eyes filling with tears. "I have cried harder today, as well as last night, than I have in all my life. I've become a veritable watering pot, and the worst of it is I cannot seem to stop." Her eyes overflowed, and tears coursed down her cheeks.

Pushing her manuscript aside, Meg pulled Hope to sit beside her and immediately slipped an arm about her waist. She spoke softly: "There, there! Don't cry anymore or you shall have me weeping right alongside you."

"I am sorry," Hope said. "I promised myself I would be very good—"

"Nonsense. You may shed as many tears with me as you like. I was only teasing you."

These words, however, seemed to have a calming effect, and Hope was able to take a deep breath and compose herself. At least for a moment, anyway.

She wore a light brown pelisse of twilled cotton and withdrew a cambric handkerchief from her pocket. She dabbed at her tears and said, "Your stepmama told me she thought you might be found here, and I did need to speak with you, Meg. You see, I think I have lost Charles forever. I never meant to go so far in my little scheme. I have erred greatly, and now I believe it is too late to do anything about it."

Meg sat very still and, after a moment, asked, "What do you mean that *you* made a grave error?"

Hope turned to Meg, her eyes again brimming with tears, her nose turning a bright pink as she said, "I know how it must have seemed to everyone last night, that Charles was using me abominably. And though he might have restrained himself a little—that Scottish reel for instance was entirely unnecessary to make his intentions clear!—the fact remains that it is I who pushed Charles away! A dozen times, purposefully. I knew the other night that he had come to offer for me—the matter was as good as settled between us—but I was so frightened!" She laughed suddenly. "I even sneezed on him and said I didn't find the night beautiful! Meggie, you know how I

144

love the stars and the moonlight atop our hills—"

Meg caught Hope's arm with her free hand and said, "But I didn't know. How is that? Do you mean you lied to Charles? I don't understand!"

Hope could not continue as she pressed the kerchief to her mouth and gave in to a deep sob. Meg held her close, her own emotions rising readily to the surface as tears spilled down her cheeks. Whatever did Hope mean that she had pushed Charles away? And did Hope appreciate the beauty of the night? But of course she did. Any young lady who could enrapture an audience with her gift of music in the way that Hope was able to simply could not be impervious to the charms of moonlight dusting the beechwoods. Oh, why was nothing as it should be? Why was everyone behaving so oddly? How was it the perfect little bows of her life were being pulled apart everytime she turned around? Hope should have come here crying about a jilted love instead of admitting she had meant to snub Charles.

With this thought, Meg was startled. Why would Hope wish to reject Charles in the first place? He was a fiery, honorable, exciting young gentleman who would not hesitate to defend Hope's honor if he needed to. What cause could Hope possibly have for rejecting Charles' suit?

After a few minutes, when her sobs subsided and she had blown her nose at least half a dozen times, Hope explained, "It was my fault entirely that Charles began pursuing Elizabeth. To some degree I even encouraged it, for frequently of late—even when we were in London—I would leave them alone together. I was being very wise, you see." She laughed at herself suddenly, then continued, "I had decided Charles had grown too unsteady for me. He had taken to attending the Five Courts and had begun speaking some of that horrid boxing cant; even his clothes had grown so very odd. Did you notice his yellow pantaloons last night? But beyond that, he had become such great friends with Lord Montford, and though I know that you are also a friend of his, I could not help but notice that much of his set frequents the more notorious private gaming establishments, not to mention that they are gone to Newmarket during the season every other sennight."

Meg cried, "You cannot possibly think that Charles has become a gamester?"

"Oh, no! Nothing of that sort, at least not yet. Oh, I don't know what to think, now or then. It is just that he has become so much like Phillip that I am afraid he will suffer the same end, and I could not bear it! You were so very strong, Meggie, but I know that I could never be stalwart and brave as you were—indeed, as you are!"

Meg did not think she had heard correctly, and she asked, "Do you refer to *my* Phillip? To Phillip Harcastle?"

Hope rose to her feet quite suddenly, holding her kerchief to her forehead as though trying to forget a terrible memory. She said, "Phillip was incredibly handsome, was he not? Oh, lord, we were all in love with him, and he belonged to you! I was but nineteen at the time, and you were scarcely much older." She shook her head, smiling sweetly as she continued, "He used to pinch both my cheeks at once and call me Hopeless, and then claim he was hopelessly in love with me. He was so charming, and we were all so very sad when he died." She turned away from Meg and began slowly traversing the small, gravel square, walking to and fro, her shoulders drooping slightly.

Meg could not keep her gaze from Hope's face. Somehow she knew something dreadful was forthcoming, something she did not want to hear. She tried to rise to her feet, to stop Hope from speaking, but she felt frozen to the cold stone bench. The breeze riffled the edges of her manuscript, and she shivered mightily.

Hope said, "Even Papa, who did not like Phillip in the least, said that he felt certain "the young chap would have come about," if given the chance. I just never understood how you bore it? I remember asking you once, shortly after the funeral, whether or not you

146

wished to share your grief with me, but you shook your head. You seemed so calm, but Meg, how did you bear it?"

Meg looked up at Hope and said, "You mean, how did I bear his sudden death?"

Hope waved a wild hand about. "I mean," she said, "how did you bear knowing how he had died."

Meg swallowed very hard, her knees shaking. "You mean how did I bear knowing that he drowned."

"Yes and that he had been half-foxed, was deeply in debt to the cent-per-centers and fell into a ditch after being chased for several miles by their henchmen? How did you bear knowing that your beloved had become so very bad? You were so noble," Hope said, turning away from her as she continued walking slowly around the bench. "I tried to be like you with regard to Charles; but he had begun going to a gaming hell in Pall Mall, and I suppose I simply could not remain constant to him in the manner you had remained ever faithful to Phillip. Do you see what I mean?"

Meg nodded, feeling numb to her toes.

Hope sighed. "But now I feel I was very wrong to have given Charles up so easily. You see, I had a long conversation with Papa last night, and he explained to me that your Phillip had always been in and out of mischief from the time he was at Eton—that I had been unfair in comparing the two men. So, you see, I am the one who has erred, and I am afraid it is too late. Charles seems to have fallen violently in love with Lizzie!"

She turned toward Meg, tears again streaming down her cheeks.

Meg instinctively held her arms out to Hope, and her friend ran to her and buried her head in her shoulder. Above the quiet sound of Hope's tears, Meg kept hearing everything Hope had said, and she felt as though a stone wall had just crashed down on her. Phillip had not died rescuing a small child, then. He had been drunk, deeply in debt and died when his debtors insisted he discharge his debts.

147

How noble, Meg thought with great irony. The dashing, winged angel who had become Phillip in her imagination suddenly flew too close to the sun, and all of his wax wings melted away. Phillip toppled to the earth, where he had always belonged. Even before Hope spoke the truth about her beloved's death, Meg knew what the truth was. She couldn't say precisely how she knew, but now little events began lining themselves up in her mind, small things really, like the servants whispering and looking at her not with grief, but with a fear that one of them would unwittingly impart the truth to her, like the funeral where so many faces were shocked but not really grief-stricken or even surprised, and like her father's words from just a few days ago, "he was a good lad, he would have come about."

Hope had begun growing considerably calmer as Meg patted her shoulder. She did not want Hope to know that it was she who had shattered her illusion regarding Phillip, and she said, "So what are we to do about this dreadful mistake you've made. You could have come to me, you know. I could have told you about Charles. He is rather clutchfisted when it comes to money. He is forever telling me that Montford grows out of reason cross with him when he will wager nothing more than five pounds." She giggled. "That is hardly the makings of a gamester, now is it?"

Hope pulled away from Meg, leaning back onto the stone bench. She emitted a watery laugh, saying, "No, it is not! I daresay I have not given him enough credit, have I?"

Meg, whose heart had grown heavy, shook her head slightly and said, "No, you have not. It was very unfair of you to—to compare Charles with Phillip." She remembered suddenly the look of disgust on Worthen's face as he had said, "Phillip Harcastle." A wayward tear escaped Meg's eye. "I try to think only the best of Phillip, you know. That is what I have done from the beginning. However, I think you are much wiser than I am, for I refused to see that Phillip's ways had grown erratic. Now, when I look back, so much is obvious to me, but at the time, I closed my eyes."

Hope said, "You were so very brave. You never shed a tear, even in the chapel."

Meg spoke quietly as the sun disappeared behind the hills: "I was blind."

Hope was silent beside her, and Meg turned her thoughts to Hope's dilemma. She remembered Lizzie and shuddered slightly. She knew suddenly that she did not want Charles to marry Lizzie. She said, "Hope, you must tell Charles how you really feel about things, the night, for instance!" She laughed. "What I mean is, you can't keep pretending you don't respond so eagerly to life, not when you bowl us over with your music. Charles longs to know that part of you. I have seen that much in his eyes, only last night in fact when he watched you perform on the harp."

"I am afraid," Hope responded simply.

Meg cried suddenly. "So, who is not? You are vulnerable to so much hurt when you open your heart to someone. It is frightening beyond belief, and sometimes it is safer to stay in your own neat little box than to give yourself fully to someone else. This much I will say for Phillip; he never withheld his love from anyone, though I do remember wishing he had not flirted quite so much as he had. Well, he may have been raucously unsteady, but we loved him, didn't we?"

"Oh, yes!" Hope cried. "I wish he would have lived to have come to his senses, married you and made you happy! I suppose you would have had a dozen children by now."

Meg smiled. "Oh, yes. At least a dozen, and I would be as round as our Cook here at Staplehope!"

Hope laughed merrily, for Cook was as delightfully chubby as one who enjoys preparing food had a right to be. She tucked her kerchief in the pocket of her pelisse, rose to her feet and said, "Well, it is getting very cold and very late. I should be going. And I do thank you for your advice."

Meg stood up, wrapping the blue shawl tightly about her shoulders. Picking up her manuscript, she said, "Perhaps you should stay to dine with us, and then we'll see you home later in the barouche."

Hope nodded in agreement.

As they moved toward the archway in the hedge that led the way out, Meg said, "There is just one more thing I feel I ought to say to you. I trust you will take this in the spirit in which it is meant, for I do think you are a very pretty young lady; but if you could possibly dress occasionally in a more brilliant color, such as royal blue or even a deep magenta—"

Hope lifted her hand, cutting Meg off as she let out a trill of laughter. She cried, "You will not credit what Papa did last night. He came to my chamber, went directly to my wardrobe and rent my white gown in two! Can you imagine? He then took most of my gowns—all maidenly pale pinks, light blues and yellows—tossed them in a heap on the floor and said he meant to burn each one unless I gave them to the Poor House. He said these dull colors, including this brown I am wearing, all pull my face down instead of bringing out the fine color of my complexion and my eyes. I was so startled, and yet, I had to agree with him. He then said that Mama had been foolish beyond permission to have gowned me in such insipid fabrics for so many years." She sighed with pleasure as they began wending their way through the maze. "You will laugh when you hear that he took me to the dressmaker's this very morning! Mrs. Barnes was very shocked to have a man selecting the fabrics—even if he was my father—and you know how disapproving she can be! Well, it was very amusing, for when he said he wished to see me have a cherry-red velvet habit, she nearly fainted."

Hope prattled on in this happy manner for some time. Meg was pleased to see her spirits recovered.

Chapter Eleven

Lord Montford lay facedown on a dull, brocade sofa in his study. He heard a faint, persistent rapping that irritated him beyond words. He was in a state of half-sleep, and at times the noise sounded very close and at other times as though it came from the window across the room. He could not place it; his mind was cloaked in a fog.

"Begone, you rascal!" he cried aloud, an effort that only served to cause his head to pound.

The rapping grew more insistent. He should open his eyes, he thought, and face the devil that hounded him, but he could not make his eyelids move even a fraction of an inch. He moaned, tasting a mouth that felt cottony, and he grew to an awareness that his head ached miserably. The wretched brandy they served up at Mrs. Bolles' gaming establishment had cost him both the last of his quarterly income as well as his habitually clear head.

It all came back to him in a rush! Why, you'd think he was a damnable Flat after the way he'd played last night! After he'd gambled his last guinea, the candlelight began dancing eerily about him. His friends—friends, bah!— laughed at his drunkenness as he stumbled from the gaming hell. The fresh air outside only caused him to reel about awkwardly and cast up his accounts into the gutter.

The Watch nearby almost clubbed him until the man recognized who he was.

"M'lord!" the fat watchman had cried.

"Put me in a hackney," Montford responded with a groan.

When the watchman was about to close the door of the coach, Montford leaned out slightly and said, "Thank you, man. You've done me a great service." He reached into his pocket but found nothing there. "Damn and blast! Not even a groat to repay your kindness."

"Yer rolled up, m'lord. Off with ye now. To bed afore ye lose yer coat an'shirt as well!"

Montford did not remember arriving back at his rooms. And now, several hours later, he was being set upon by some curst fellow demanding admittance to his study! If it was his manservant, Brown, he would impale him with his short sword, by God he would!

The rapping continued until his head nearly exploded. He tried to sit up, but the pain was only made worse with the effort.

A voice now accompanied the rapping, and he recognized Brown, who cried, "My lord, a rider has just come with a message of some import. My lord!"

Montford licked his lips and groaned. He tried to wake up completely but was finding the task almost impossible.

When the rapping began all over again, Montford was sufficiently in command of himself to cry, "Enter!" though afterward his head throbbed painfully.

His valet crossed the room and squatted in front of the couch. Montford remained in a prone position and squinted his eyes at his manservant. He asked, "What is it you miserable whelp? You had better have good cause for waking me in this monstrous fashion!" He closed his eyes again, wincing.

Brown spoke quietly, but his voice was intense. "M'lord. A rider from Staplehope has just arrived with a missive for ye. The man thinks it's concerning that female what you've been courtin' recently. He were instructed to return to his master—Barnett is his name—with word that you've received this letter. You may send a letter in return if you've a mind to."

"Staplehope? Barnett?" Montford responded, his mind sluggish. "Good God!" he muttered. "Barnett? I don't know a Barnett. Staplehope?" He leaned up on his elbow and finally took the missive from his valet's hand.

Breaking the seal, he opened the letter and glanced first at the signature—*Charles Burnell!*

Burnell! He sat up suddenly, the fog clearing quickly away from his mind as he realized Charles must have some word of Margaret for him. He no longer cared that he felt like the devil and rose abruptly to his feet, the blood rushing to his head.

He read the letter quickly and exploded, "Damn!" Words poured from him, hot and angry. His valet opened his eyes wide and backed toward the door in case a fast exit became necessary for preservation of life and limb. His master rarely displayed his temper, but when he did, the whole building was like to be shaken to the ground. He slipped through the doorway and closed the door, breathing hard.

"Whew!" he cried and hurried down the hall toward the kitchen at the back of the small town house. He had a sudden desire to talk to that rider and find out all the news from Shropshire. He was ever one to advance his position if he could by knowing just the right details in order to make clever suggestions to his master now and again.

Montford poured out a glass of brandy from a sideboard near the window of his rooms in Half Moon Street. He stood in front of the window, his legs planted in a wide stance. He read the letter again. So, Worthen thought he had won the prize, but according to the letter, they would not be married for several days yet.

He took a sip of the brandy and let it roll about in his mouth, then swallowed. He was sick to death of this existence. He'd been short of the ready for months now, and his pursuit of Margaret Longville had not gone as well as he had expected, nor nearly well enough to keep his creditors entirely at bay. He had intended to be leg-shackled to Meg by now, but somehow she had proved surprisingly elusive.

He needed her handsome dowry to replenish his pockets, but his desire to wed her went much deeper than that. He wanted the ancient lands that belonged to her through her mother, and he wanted her connection to the established families in England. As for Meg, herself, he was uncommonly attracted to her, a sensation, he was convinced, that meant he loved her.

He reread the letter shaking his head in disbelief. He uttered a disgusted grunt! It was always the way among the beau monde. The ancient families, those who had been landed for a dozen generations or more, clung together, refusing to allow the newcomers an equal place in their coteries. He knew, for instance, that Sir William had hated his father and had carried over his resentments to the son. What had he ever done to deserve the snubs that Sir William had given him? Just because his father had inherited his money from shipping, instead of rent-rolls, he had never been included in the baronet's intimate circle. Even when his father had received his peerage, a rank above Sir William's, the baronet still treated him with cool, polite indifference.

There was certainly one means of righting these wrongs—Montford would marry Sir William's daughter.

In response to the letter, the baron sat down and wrote a carefully contrived letter stating his intention to return to Staplehope posthaste. His final remarks pleased him immensely: "You did right, my good and most excellent friend, to inform me of the impending marriage. I have stood as friend to Miss Longville for several years now, and in many respects we are of one mind: I know well her sentiments regarding Lord Worthen. Of course you know it has been my desire since ever I can remember to marry Margaret. I had hoped one day to win her hand for myself. I am appalled, just as you are, to learn that she is being coerced into a marriage she does not want. I would bring Worthen to account for this dastardly act of his,

154

but you know well how little he values such gentlemanly forms. And this is his worst act of all, is it not? Poor, poor Margaret. I feel most acutely for her. She must believe herself friendless, and to that purpose, to show that she stands not alone in this world, I intend to come as quickly as possible. If I travel post, with a curricle and four, sleeping as I am able, I should arrive in Staplehope by Saturday at the latest. Yours, etc. Montford."

Montford sealed the letter and sent it to the waiting rider.

He watched Burnell's servant dig his heels sharply into the flanks of a sweating black gelding. One thing he omitted from his letter to Charles—if he found it necessary, he would elope with Margaret himself to achieve his ends.

On Friday, three days after Hope's disastrous birthday ball, Meg paced the grand entrance hall of Staplehope, waiting for Lord Worthen to arrive. She paused before a large, gilt-framed mirror on the wall opposite the door and tugged gently at two long red curls that dangled on either side of her face to the décolleté of her gown. Some of her hair was caught high upon her head, dressed in a wild mass of curls and stuffed full of fresh flowers— bluebells, rosebuds and sweet peas. The remainder of her long red locks cascaded in a riot of curls about her shoulders. As she regarded herself in the mirror, she was infinitely pleased with her summery appearance. She thought Rosamund herself could not have appeared to better advantage than this! She was dressed in a gown of light green muslin for an al fresco picnic that Worthen had suggested. The gown was a little impractical in that it was gathered in a hundred tiny folds at the back of the waist, flowing down to her ankles in a fulsome demi-train. The hem of the gown rippled in row upon row of tiny ruffles. The effect when she walked was enchanting, for the gown positively danced behind her. She meant, however, to suggest to Worthen that the nuncheon take

155

place upon a grassy bank so that she would not capture unwanted leaves in the rolling bulk of her skirt.

"La, Miss Margaret!" her maid cried. "Ye do look fine as a sixpence if I may say so meself. His lordship is sure to be pleased, an' all!" Bonnie sat in a tall, mahogany chair near the entrance to the drawing room. She was dressed in a plain round gown of brown stuff made high to the neck and wore a small poke bonnet over her tidy, braided brown hair. She would accompany the couple on their expedition.

Margaret still stood before the mirror and pinched her cheeks slightly. She wondered if Worthen would indeed be pleased with her toilette, and she realized suddenly that she wanted him to be pleased. This thought caused her to meet her own gaze in the mirror and shape a silent question with her lips: *Do you love him?*

She squeezed her eyes shut, not wanting to love him, not wanting to give her heart to a man she did not believe fully met her ideals. Yet Phillip had met her ideals, and the truth was, he had been a notorious gamester. Papa had told her everything! He had gone through his inheritance, mortgaging his properties to the hilt, then selling them off one after another. Phillip had been the personification of her ideals, but his character had been sadly wanting.

As for Worthen, she did not know what to make of him. She was clearly drawn to him as she had never been drawn to any man before, not even Phillip. But the sensation was so very brutish and made her distrust both her own senses as well as her judgement. Phillip had treated her as though she were delicate and fragile—an angel to be treated with the loftiest respect and worship. Worthen, on the other hand, grabbed her roughly and spoke of bearing his children and beating his servants. He was so much of the earth that he frightened her. But this she did know, she would marry no man under such circumstances. Today, she meant to appeal to him yet again to at least give her more time to comprehend him as well as to adjust to these more recent revelations

156

regarding Phillip. Perhaps she could love Worthen, but she did not want to be forced into any marriae. It went sorely against the grain with her. Surely he could comprehend that!

She had not seen him since Hope's ball. The next day he had sent a message round informing her that his brother had taken ill with a mild influenza and that he intended to remain with him until he had recovered from his illness. Meg knew instinctively that though Worthen was indeed tending to his brother, he was also to a small degree avoiding her. He had been furious during the last quarrel. She knew he did not trust himself to speak to her with any degree of equanimity.

Meg chewed on her lip, her gaze shifting to the left to watch absently as a little white mouse scurried around the corner of a cherrywood table near her. "Shoo!" she said quietly. "Before Caroline discovers your presence. Else you are doomed my friend! Now, shoo!"

She sighed. Her world had turned topsy-turvy overnight, and she was all at sea! She didn't know what to think anymore, about Phillip or Worthen or even Charles with his yellow pantaloons! She wished Montford were here to help her sort things out, to help her make sense of all that she had so recently been told.

The sound of a carriage in the drive broke her reverie. She whirled around, her heart beginning to quicken in her breast as she started toward the door, then stopped. What was she thinking? For a moment, she saw herself throwing the door wide and running down the steps to greet Worthen! She placed a hand on her cheek and gave a little cry.

"What is it, Miss Margaret?" Bonnie asked, rising slowly to her feet. "Ye look quite ill, of a sudden."

With her hand still on her cheek, Meg turned toward her maid and said, "Oh, nothing of significance. Merely that I think I've gone mad!"

Bonnie sighed and nodded in a knowing fashion. "He's that handsome, he is, Lord Worthen. I'd go mad too if I had to look at him fer hours at a time!" She sighed again and cooed.

As the carriage drew near, Meg was struck by the volume of noise the horses were making. For so brief an outing, two horses were certainly adequate, but by all accounts, Meg thought the viscount had hired at least an additional two—perhaps with outriders!

She was very curious and could not keep from stealing into the drawing room and peeking between the curtains to see what sort of carriage Worthen had hired.

"Merciful heavens!" she cried. Never would she have believed such a sight had she not seen it with her own eyes. Even the gardener, working across the drive in a grove of fur trees along with several hired laborers, ceased his toils to stare at the equipage approaching the entrance steps.

Worthen sat quite forward and erect in a light blue barouche drawn by no less than six white horses—each with a pink plume on its head! Meg felt a fluttering of her heart as a familiar sensation assailed her, a tingling throughout her entire body—the way she always felt in the midst of creating the most romantic scenes of her novels. Her arms grew weak, her legs faltered beneath her and she dropped onto the arm of the settee situated fortuitously right next to her. "Oh," she sighed, pressing a hand to her bosom. "Six white horses, just like my first novel where the hero spirited the heroine away—away from the clutches of the evil Duke de Moreno—away to the safety of his abode in the heart of England!"

She felt a glow surround her. She could scarcely swallow so delighted was she at the prospect of what would undoubtedly be one of the finest al fresco nuncheons she would ever enjoy in her entire life!

"Whoa!" She heard Worthen's voice through the panes as the equipage pulled up before the steps of the hall. Much to her surprise, she noticed that the expression on the viscount's face was one of intensity as he kept all six reins tightly in hand. "Whoa!" he called again, pulling sharply on the reins as the horses refused to obey his first command.

A groom appeared around the corner of the hall, racing at a mad pace toward the horses. He lost his hat as a breeze freshened suddenly, but he ignored the hat and approached the horses quickly, taking the halter of the lead gelding and holding him steady.

The tiniest doubt entered Meg's brain that perhaps six horses would not be entirely comfortable on such an outing, but when she saw the large hamper strapped to the back of the barouche, her doubts dissipated instantly. Worthen may be sadly lacking in the finer qualities of chivalry, but he certainly knew how to appeal to a lady's imagination, as well as her appetite.

When the horses were finally held in check by the groom at their heads, Worthen glanced about the front of the hall and saw Meg sitting by the window, her hand still pressed to her bosom. He smiled suddenly and inclined his head. He then stood up, and Meg saw that he was wearing a sturdy cloak, slung over one shoulder only, a russet coat, buff breeches and gleaming Hessians. Her maid was so very right. He was handsome and dashing, and she felt her heart slip yet again as he doffed his hat to her, bowed very low, and fairly leapt to the gravel drive. His cloak flew out behind him as he landed squarely upon the stone walkway near the steps.

Meg lifted her brows, startled! Why, it was done in just the same manner as the hero of her first novel! She wondered briefly if Worthen had read her books, then dismissed the thought as silly. Most men laughed at such novels. She inclined her head to Worthen in response and adjusted her countenance to one of quiet reserve as he quickly ran up the steps. She did not wish to appear to be encouraging him, particularly when he seemed so happy to see her.

A brief shot of doubt assailed her. He seemed overly congenial, she realized suddenly. She could not believe he was no longer angry with her. She had certainly made her opinions of his character clear and what man would ever be content to have the woman he professed to love express such sentiments?

But when she greeted him in the entrance hall, he said, "Will you ever forgive me for speaking so harshly to you at Hope's ball?"

Greatly relieved, Meg replied, "Oh, yes, Worthen, of course. I do understand that you have reasons for your dislike of chivalry in general. But we can at least be friends?" she extended her hand to him.

Meg thought for the barest second that she saw a hard glint enter Worthen's eye, but he possessed himself of her hand quickly and was very soon—in front of two grooms, her maid, and the butler—placing a firm kiss upon her fingers.

She felt her cheeks warm with a blush. She pulled her hand away and cried, "What a lovely day for a nuncheon out of doors!" She moved toward the threshold and heard his low laughter as he followed behind her. Moving quickly, he caught up with her as she began descending the steps, took her arm and escorted her to the waiting carriage. Her maid followed several steps behind them.

Meg eyed the horses warily, for several of them were tossing their heads and stamping their feet. The groom held on firmly to the halter of the lead horse, but she could see that he was straining with the effort to maintain control of the six horses.

Within a few minutes, Meg was seated comfortably in the barouche, her maid planted in the small seat behind her. Meg told Worthen she was delighted with the horses just as the viscount took the reins in hand and sat down beside her. He leaned well forward, his entire body tense. He glanced at her, inclined his head acknowledging her pleasure and, with a laugh, said, "I only hope you enjoy the drive as much as their appearance. They are as fresh as bedamned! What a team!"

Meg noted that he did not even apologize for his use of such language and suddenly felt the worst qualm assail her stomach.

Worthen nodded to the groom, who was sweating with the effort to keep the horses in check. As he released the lead horse, he jumped away from the equipage, apparently

MORE PASSION AND ADVENTURE AWAIT... YOUR TRIP TO A BIG ADVENTUROUS WORLD BEGINS WHEN YOU ACCEPT YOUR FIRST
4 NOVELS ABSOLUTELY *FREE*
(AN $18.00 VALUE)

Accept your Free gift and start to experience more of the passion and adventure you like in a historical romance novel. Each Zebra novel is filled with proud men, spirited women and tempestuous love that you'll remember long after you turn the last page.

Zebra Historical Romances are the finest novels of their kind. They are written by authors who really know how to weave tales of romance and adventure in the historical settings you love. You'll feel like you've actually gone back in time with the thrilling stories that each Zebra novel offers.

GET YOUR FREE GIFT WITH THE START OF YOUR HOME SUBSCRIPTION

Our readers tell us that these books sell out very fast in book stores and often they miss the newest titles. So Zebra has made arrangements for you to receive the four newest novels published each month.

You'll be guaranteed that you'll never miss a title, and home delivery is so convenient. And to show you just how easy it is to get Zebra Historical Romances, we'll send you your first 4 books absolutely FREE! Our gift to you just for trying our home subscription service.

BIG SAVINGS AND FREE HOME DELIVERY

Each month, you'll receive the four newest titles as soon as they are published. You'll probably receive them even before the bookstores do. What's more, you may preview these exciting novels free for 10 days. If you like them as much as we think you will, just pay the low preferred subscriber's price of just $3.75 each. *You'll save $3.00 each month off the publisher's price.* AND, your savings are even greater because there are never any shipping, handling or other hidden charges—FREE Home Delivery. Of course you can return any shipment within 10 days for full credit, no questions asked. There is no minimum number of books you must buy.

4 FREE BOOKS

TO GET YOUR 4 FREE BOOKS WORTH $18.00 — MAIL IN THE FREE BOOK CERTIFICATE T O D A Y

Fill in the Free Book Certificate below, and we'll send your FREE BOOKS to you as soon as we receive it.

If the certificate is missing below, write to: Zebra Home Subscription Service, Inc., P.O. Box 5214, 120 Brighton Road, Clifton, New Jersey 07015-5214.

FREE BOOK CERTIFICATE

4 FREE BOOKS

ZEBRA HOME SUBSCRIPTION SERVICE, INC.

YES! Please start my subscription to Zebra Historical Romances and send me my first 4 books absolutely FREE. I understand that each month I may preview four new Zebra Historical Romances free for 10 days. If I'm not satisfied with them, I may return the four books within 10 days and owe nothing. Otherwise, I will pay the low preferred subscriber's price of just $3.75 each; a total of $15.00, *a savings off the publisher's price of $3.00.* I may return any shipment and I may cancel this subscription at any time. There is no obligation to buy any shipment and there are no shipping, handling or other hidden charges. Regardless of what I decide, the four free books are mine to keep.

NAME

ADDRESS _____ APT _____

CITY _____ STATE ___ ZIP _____

TELEPHONE (___)

SIGNATURE _____ (if under 18, parent or guardian must sign)

Terms, offer and prices subject to change without notice. Subscription subject to acceptance by Zebra Books. Zebra Books reserves the right to reject any order or cancel any subscription.   069002

GET
FOUR
FREE
BOOKS
(AN $18.00 VALUE)

ZEBRA HOME SUBSCRIPTION
SERVICE, INC.
P.O. Box 5214
120 BRIGHTON ROAD
CLIFTON, NEW JERSEY 07015-5214

afraid he might be trampled to death.

The horses fairly leapt forward, breaking into a trot. The carriage lurched. Meg clutched the side of the barouche and heard her maid cry, "Oh, lord! We're like to be killed!"

Worthen's voice cried out, "Onward, oh, ye fleet of foot!" And he laughed into the breeze as Meg stared up at him, aghast. What devil had possessed him to treat her own safety and comfort with such recklessness?

Every turn in the road soon became a nightmare for Meg and her maid as the six white horses flew down the road away from the village. Meg begged Worthen to slow the horses down, but he looked at her all wild-eyed and said, "Never! They shall speed us, Margaret, to our fate!"

Meg replied in a small voice, "I had rather walk, if you please!"

"Nonsense!" he cried, laughing into the wind. "Do you not love the sense of adventure these horses bring to a simple al fresco nuncheon? When we are wed, I shall see that every outing shall be filled with just such excitement. I have not known you these many years and more without comprehending your love of adventure, and I mean to see that you are satiated with daring expeditions and journeyings to dangerous ports! This is only the beginning! Do you know, for instance, where we are going?"

Ahead of them on the road was a slow-moving cart. Meg began breathing quickly. "No, my lord, I haven't the faintest notion what our destination might be! I had supposed we would dine along the grassy slope to the south of the beechwood. I had meant to speak to you before we left Staplehope, but I think the sight of your horses distracted me. Worthen, they are rather spirited, aren't they?"

"Only half-tame! I purchased them from a friend of mine not two days ago. I really haven't had time to break them in, as it happens! But that merely adds to the excitement, don't you agree?"

"Undoubtedly," Meg responded in a whisper, her

heart pounding against her ribs. "But do you not think we might return to the hills behind Staplehope? I am certain you would find the location I have in mind much to your liking! There is a small Roman ruin nearby." She felt frightened out of her wits and had only one purpose—to be rid of the barouche and horses as quickly as possible, to feel the solid, unmoving earth beneath her feet again.

He retorted with a cry, "An insignificant ruin on a hill? What a wretchedly dull idea! That will not do for us, my dearest Meg. We are going to the mill on Horsley stream!"

Meg glanced quickly at Worthen. "The mill?" she asked, dumbstruck.

Her maid uttered a cry of anguish and exclaimed, "But that mill is haunted! There's a tale that the old miller hung himself from the rafters after his wife were murdered by gypsies. Their specters walk about the grounds at night! Tis a terrible place, I tell ye! Ye cannot mean to take Miss Meg to Horsley Mill!"

"Worthen, we cannot possibly—" Meg broke off as the cart loomed closer still. She said, "Ah—Worthen, do you not see Mr. Mitchett ahead of us? His cart is moving prodigiously slow!"

Worthen clucked his tongue. "The simplest trick imaginable to pass him!"

Meg watched as sweat began beading on the viscount's brow, and she was not convinced. He guided the horses to the right of the cart. She saw the tanner glance over his shoulder, and his dark eyes grew wide with horror as he pulled his poor, plodding hack toward the ditch on the left.

"You'll force Mitchett off the road!" Meg cried. "Do stop the horses. Oh, do stop, I say!"

Worthen cried, "But this is an adventure! I will not stop!"

Hunched over the reins, Worthen lowered his head slightly and held the horses firmly in line. He murmured to himself as the wind pressed against him. "Steady, now—"

The horses eased alongside the cart with but inches to spare. Meg, as though drawn by a force she could not withstand, leaned over the side of the barouche and looked down upon the wheels of the cart. They were nothing to the spinning whirl of the barouche.

Meg cried, "We will lock wheels!"

Worthen eased the barouche to the side slightly, and the faintest whisper sounded as the hub of the barouche's wheels grazed the cart's wheel. And then the cart was left far behind.

Meg leaned back in the velvet lining of the barouche and felt so sick she nearly swooned. She started to beg a vinaigrette from her maid, but when she turned around to regard Bonnie, she found that her maid was leaning upon the back of her seat, her kerchief pressed to her mouth, her eyes shut tight.

The horses began to slow as a lane came into view. With great skill, as well as monumental effort, Worthen guided the six horses onto the lane, several of their pink plumes dangling awkwardly over ears that twitched.

Meg breathed a sigh of relief when they were finally travelling along the road. The lane twisted and turned, and much to Meg's horror, Worthen soon had the horses moving at a fast trot.

"What are you doing?" she cried.

He merely laughed at her, and Meg soon felt that he had some purpose in mind other than merely an adventurous nuncheon. The faster the horses moved, the greater a dust the horses kicked up. The lane was dry and had not been modernized with crushed rock as had been many of the roads about Shropshire. The barouche was soon covered in a cloud of swirling dust, and Meg squeezed her eyes closed and coughed into her kerchief.

Lord Worthen, who coughed himself, cried aloud, "Is this not enchanting!"

Meg scowled up at him, but refused to say anything lest she fill her lungs with more of the dust.

Several minutes later, the horses finally crossed a stone bridge, and Meg sighed with relief. The lane was rutted beyond belief, and between the dust and the dips in the road, Meg was heartily sick of Worthen's notion of an adventure, when the mill came into view. Suddenly, despite the difficulties of the journey, Meg was glad he had brought her to the ancient, stone flour mill. It was charming beyond words.

As the dust settled into the grass about the outskirts of the mill, Meg drew in her breath and let it out with a long "Oh!" Again, she pressed a hand to her bosom and cried, "I will confess that your horses were almost more than I could bear, but this! Why, the ivy has nearly covered the north wall, and the waterwheel does not move at all anymore."

The stream rippled over large gray stones and passed around the base of the wheel. Only a dapple of sunlight broke through the beech trees which over the years had encroached on the mill. In addition, a yew hedge had nearly overtaken the entrance to the mill. But a path was clearly visible, giving indication that the haunted, abandoned structure was visited more frequently than was at first supposed.

Worthen turned to Meg and said, "I knew you would like this spot when I was first told about it. However, it will take a little time for me to both situate the horses and to prepare a place within the mill for our nuncheon."

Bonnie cried, "Oh, miss! Ye're not goin' inside, are ye?"

Margaret turned back to her maid and exclaimed, "Of course I am! I am not so henhearted as you!"

Bonnie pursed her lips together and sat very straight as she replied, "Well! However improper it may be, I will not go inside that mill!"

Worthen could not resist saying, "You are the perfect chaperone, then, and I consider myself indebted to your, er, henheartedness!"

Bonnie gasped, and even Meg could not restrain a giggle.

The horses, after having pulled the barouche some four miles in all, were less restive than when the team first arrived at Staplehope Hall. Worthen handed Meg and her abigail down from the barouche and afterward tethered the horses to some shrubbery near the mill.

Bonnie, true to her word, remained outside the mill. Just as they crossed the threshold of the old building, a clap of thunder resounded in the distance, and almost as quickly clouds obscured the sun, casting the mill in gloom.

Meg clasped both her hands to her bosom as she regarded the dim interior. "What heaven!" she cried as she glanced about the roomy, empty chamber, where a series of large gears and wheels inhabited the center of the mill.

She sniffed suddenly as a rank odor assailed her. "Oh, my! I wonder what that could be?"

Worthen stood behind her and asked, "What is that, my dearest Meg?"

"That peculiar smell."

He spoke with a negligent tone to his voice: "Well, I'm sure that several generations of rats have inhabited this place. On the other hand, it could be the miller's method of warning us that we should not tarry. What do you think, my sweet?"

He stood behind her and placed his hands on her arms. Stepping very near her, he felt her shudder slightly, and he asked, "You aren't really frightened, are you?"

Meg responded with a sigh, "Deliciously so. If only the odor were not quite so pungent."

He whispered in her ear, "You will grow used to it in time, I'm sure."

Meg saw clearly that he meant to begin his antics again, and she had already determined she would not permit him to do so. She stepped away from him, briskly crossing the room to the far wall. A small, broken window overlooked the stream, and she peered out, watching the water bubble around the rocks. She felt an odd movement at the back of her demi-train, and she uttered a cry. "I felt something touch me!" She whirled around halfway, lifting her skirts slightly. She was appalled at what she saw, for though whatever had scurried past her was no longer present, the dirt and dust of the floor had soiled the ruffles and demi-train of her gown. "Oh, no! Do but look at my poor muslin! Why, it's filthy."

Worthen appeared as though he were trying not to smile when he said, "I suppose there has not been a housekeeper here for many years."

Meg grimaced at him. "Well of course not and stop funning me. I just didn't expect it to be quite so dirty inside."

Just then, she heard a scuttling sound overhead and glanced up at the rafters. She saw nothing, but instinctively moved toward Worthen. "Rats?" she queried.

He slipped an arm about her. "Undoubtedly. And though I can see they disturb you, I am wont to call them friends, for they have brought you back to my side."

He turned her toward him, and she looked up into his face, her eyes wide. "Aren't you afraid they will pounce on us?"

Worthen gave a crack of laughter. "They are more frightened of us than we are of them. They will hardly attack us, though I won't hesitate to defend you should the need arise." He gestured to a large case of polished burlwood that he had brought with him into the mill.

Meg looked at the box and tilted her head. "You've brought a pistol with you!" she exclaimed, surprised.

"Of course," he said simply. A roll of thunder was heard a little closer now. The air seemed still suddenly within the mill; no vagrant breeze whisked through the open door or broken windows. Meg's heart felt very quiet as she looked into Worthen's face. In the shadows, the mole upon his cheek was scarcely visible, and she could hardly read the expression in his eyes.

"I never meant to speak unkindly to you the other night," she said.

His voice was low and rich in the dark room. "I know. I think I understand you, Meg. I know that goodness reigns in your heart, that you don't possess a malicious thought." He searched her gaze, and continued, "We do not stand so very far apart as you seem to think. Only, give me a chance to close that distance, to draw near enough to you for you to comprehend me as well as I do you. My only desire is that you would believe in me but a little."

Meg swallowed very hard, wanting suddenly, desperately, to believe in him as well. She didn't speak, but leaned toward him, a small gesture upon which he did not hesitate to act. He gathered her up in his arms, holding her in a crushing embrace. Lifting her chin with his hand, he placed a firm kiss on her mouth. He drew back suddenly, as though he meant to say something, as though he meant to release her, when he caught his breath and exclaimed, "Do you know how beautiful you are, how you torture me especially with that expression on your face? Answer me this, if you've enough courage, do you want me to kiss you again?"

Meg, whose entire being felt drawn to him with an urgency that tore at her soul, merely slipped an arm about his neck and placed her parted lips upon his. She heard him groan as he held her more tightly still, pressing his mouth hard upon hers. If only love could be as simple as this moment, Meg thought, then all her decisions would be simple. But she wouldn't think of that now. Not now, not when he engulfed her with his embrace. He was so very strong, his legs pressed hard against hers, his arms pulling her waist tightly against him. She had never been quite this entwined in his arms before, never quite this lost, and she did not want the moment to end. The mill grew darker still as clouds moved relentlessly from the west. It would be raining soon, and perhaps they would have to spend hour upon hour in this fashion. The thought was too delicious to endure as he began placing gentle kisses on her cheek.

"My darling, Meg. Won't you forget your silly notions and love me?"

The sweetness of his embrace ended abruptly with these words. She turned her head away from him. So he thought her silly. How could he think her silly and still profess to love her?

He drew back, releasing her slowly and looking down at her. Again, he appeared as though he meant to speak, and then he stepped away from her and spoke in a happy manner: "I shall retrieve the hamper now, if you like?"

Meg nodded absently as he bowed to her with a flourish and quit the mill. Again Meg was aware of the musty, almost foul smell to the grinding chamber. She was cold suddenly as a new, different breeze, redolent with rain, blew through the doorway.

They were far too different to ever belong to one another truly. He thought her notions silly. What more needed to be said? Her heart felt very low as he reappeared in the doorway, the large hamper cradled in his arms.

When he set the wicker basket on the floor and spread out a fine, linen tablecloth, he took a linen napkin and, much to her surprise, lifted the hem of her skirt and removed some of the debris that had collected there.

"Oh, no, Worthen, do not bother with that," she cried, a little embarrassed by his attentions.

He said, "I know very well, Meg, that all this dirt bothers you. It is one of the misfortunes of adventures, however, that they are invariably dirty." He held her gaze for a moment as though trying to impart a silent message to her, then continued his task.

Meg stared down at his head while he brushed her gown. He was so incomprehensible to her! Honestly, one moment he offended her beyond bearing and the next he was unutterably solicitous. Suddenly, she wondered if he did not, afterall, have some method to his madness. What was he really trying to say to her? Everything he had done and said from the moment he arrived at Staplehope now seemed to Meg to have been designed for a purpose. Whatever did he hope to accomplish?

"Worthen, look at me," she commanded him. He glanced at her sharply, and she asked, "What are you about?"

The air between them seemed to crackle. Perhaps it was the approaching storm. He bade her sit on the linen cloth, and he walked purposely over to his case of pistols and withdrew both of them. He began preparing each of the fine duelling pistols, loading them with shot and pistol balls. She knew he was thinking about what he wished to say to her.

When he joined her by the hamper, he set his pistol close at hand and began drawing out a fine nuncheon of cold chicken, apricot tarts, fresh bread baked only that morning by the innkeeper's wife, jellies, a variety of fruits and fine champagne.

He served Meg and said, "I have given a great deal of thought to all you said to me a few nights ago. I had composed several lengthy treatises on the subjects of honor, duelling, the lost art of chivalry. I had intended to give at least one of them to you and perhaps argue with you about your viewpoint."

Meg ate a slice of the chicken and sipped her champagne, watching him all the while. He spread butter on a thick slice of bread and continued, "Then I realized that the task was hopeless. Your beliefs stem not from experience but from the culling of words from a novel or two. After we have eaten, Meg, I want you to fire one of my pistols. I want you to know what it sounds like, how it feels when it recoils in your hand."

Meg looked at the pistol laying next to him, and she was suddenly mesmerized by it. She wrote of pistols but had never handled one herself, not even her papa's.

She looked at Worthen strangely, tilting her head as she did whenever she was mystified, and said, "Did you know before you brought me here how badly the interior smelled?"

He nodded.

"You've purposely arranged this nuncheon to show me several things, have you not?"

He nodded again.

Meg set down her glass and said, "I wish to shoot your pistol now." Her hands were folded neatly on her lap, and her mouth felt suddenly very dry.

Worthen rose with alacrity and helped Meg to her feet. He retrieved the pistol and handed it to her. He said, "Squeeze the trigger gently; there will be a loud retort. Aim there." He pointed to where an old wood box, shredded with age, sat in the corner of the chamber. "Look along the site at the top of the pistol. You may fire anytime you please."

Meg felt light-headed, giddy almost, certainly faintly nauseous as she lifted the pistol and extended her arm straight out. What a delightful al fresco nuncheon this had become, she thought with irony. A putrid mill crawling with rats, impending rain, six horses that nearly ran the tanner off the road, and now she meant to fire a pistol at a box. Hardly the makings of a romantic adventure.

She held the pistol as steady as she could, taking care to look down the site and line it up with the box at the far wall. She did as he had told her, to squeeze gently. It seemed forever before the pistol responded to her touch, and then she thought a cannon had been discharged in the small mill. "Good heavens!" she cried aloud, her arm and hand shaking. She was surprised she still held the pistol in her hand as she looked at it in awe.

"It was so loud and deafening!" She peered at the box and saw a blackened mark.

Worthen said, "Here, shoot this one now!" He was handing her his second pistol when a rat, startled from his place of safety behind the box, suddenly darted toward Meg. Worthen instinctively lifted the pistol and fired.

Meg saw the rat and heard the sharp retort at the same time. She covered her ears, and then she saw the dead rat smeared on the dirty floor and quivering in its lifeblood.

Worthen caught Meg as she fell into a swoon.

The maid appeared at the door suddenly and cried, "My lord, ye've done killed Miss Margaret."

Chapter Twelve

On the following day, Meg sat at her writing desk, her elbow resting on the desk pad. Her left hand clutched a small vinaigrette as well as a soft cambric kerchief and was curled deep within her cheek. With her right hand she wrote furiously, the words pouring across the pages as quickly as she could dip her pen into the ink well. She had locked her door and refused admittance to anyone, even Caroline or her father, both of whom at various times had wished to know if she was feeling better.

Feeling better? How could she feel anything but ill when the memory of that rat—oh . . . Meg pressed her kerchief to her mouth and immediately lifted her vinaigrette to her nose. The pen dribbled ink on her last sentence, but she was so afraid of fainting again that she did not care in the least. She did not ever wish to faint again if she could possibly help it.

Worthen was a beast to have killed that poor creature, even though he had explained time and again that they were disease-ridden vermin and he feared for her health if the animal had chosen to bite her. She didn't care whether they were dangerous or not. All she knew was that she had awakened in his arms, feeling as though she had been knocked about the head several times. Her senses had been unsteady for a long while afterward.

The journey home had been even worse than the

rackety trip to the mill. The rain had swept over the countryside in a loud torrent, the calash had become stuck, and both ladies were completely soaked by the time they arrived back at the hall. Poor Bonnie was sick in bed this morning with a putrid throat! But the worst had been the six excitable horses, which jumped about with every bolt of lightning. Twice Meg was certain they would be thrown into a ditch.

Meg had never known a more miserable nuncheon than this. And by the time they had reached the hall, she was furious with the viscount for having subjected her to so many discomforts and all because he felt she had needed some obscure lesson or other!

Meg did not wish to spend one more second of her existence thinking about that cruel man. She turned instead to her novel, which was nearly complete. She smiled ruefully, thinking that if nothing else had been achieved by the adventure, her fury against The Beast now drove her toward finishing her story. The hero, Emmanuel Whitehaven, had been able to rescue poor little Ernest from the count's palace on the island of Lemnos, but the vile Fortunato had again spirited Rosamund to a place beyond Whitehaven's reach. She revelled in her use of her most recent disastrous expedition to the mill to exemplify Worthen's—that is Fortunato's—despicable character:

Rosamund shuddered violently as Fortunato pushed her into the rat-infested flour mill. Everywhere she looked rats shrunk from sight. She was frightened nearly out of her wits, but more so by the evil monster standing before her, leering down at her with his black devil's eyes, than by the poor creatures languishing in the abandoned mill.

The water turned the wheel in a droning monotony, and Rosamund cried, "Do not touch me! You are a great evil in this land, and Whitehaven will see you banished forever from

172

Lemnos and from Albion."

The count spoke quietly: "But Whitehaven is not here to protect you, is he? Only I am here, full of love for you, my dearest Rosamund—"

"Love? Ha!" Rosamund cried. "You cannot possibly have the least notion of what love is! Is it love, for instance, to bring a woman to such a place as this?"

The count cried, "The highest form of love, for now I am alone with you and who will intrude?"

As the count advanced on her, the last sight Rosamund had was of the dark, brooding mole upon Fortunato's cheek. She felt her mind drift to a blissful emptiness as she fainted yet again.

Meg set her pen down. *As she fainted again.* How many times had Rosamund fainted already? More than a dozen. Poor Rosamund. Suddenly, all the fire went out of Meg's heart, the inspiration of the moment gone almost as quickly as it had come.

Her anger spent, Meg thought of her heroine and the ridiculous propensity she had for swooning whenever she found it convenient. A month ago Meg would never have been so critical of poor Rosamund, but now she wondered if it weren't a trifle poor-spirited of her heroine always to be escaping from danger by swooning. But beyond this, how had Rosamund ever survived so many spells?

Meg stood up from the desk and moved to sit in her lumpy red chair. She closed her eyes and leaned her head back against the overstuffed cushions. Finally, she felt able to think without having her thoughts whirl madly about in her brain.

For the first time in her life, she had fainted. When she awakened to the aromatic spirits of Bonnie's vinaigrette, she felt dizzy and sick, almost ready to swoon again at the least provocation. Bonnie had tended to her, all the while looking over her shoulder as if the miller and his wife were ready to jump out at them. Worthen had buried the remains of the rat, pouring champagne over the darkened boards in an effort to clear some of the blood away.

Only as the rain threatened them, did Worthen make a push to get both ladies in the carriage, and then the calash had become stuck. Meg had blamed Worthen, believing he had planned it all. She had said as much to him, but he had replied, "The rain came of its own account, and as for the calash, you will have to speak to Mrs. Norbury, for the barouche belongs to her!"

Meg opened her eyes, feeling suddenly quite uncomfortable. She had behaved in a childish manner, and no matter how many times she told herself Worthen was completely to blame, she knew he had never for a moment thought he would have to kill a rat. As for the weather, Meg's temper had merely gotten the better of her.

She was heartily sick of the entire business, she realized as she sighed deeply. Worthen seemed intent upon making her love him, and to some degree she knew his antics had succeeded with her. But what female would not be flattered by such attentions as Lord Worthen was wont to give a lady! Undoubtedly, however, the moment they were wed, he would no more concern himself about the dirt upon her muslin gown, for instance, than he would whether or not the sun would rise in the east that day.

Meg rose to her feet suddenly, unwilling to endure such thoughts any longer. Her life had been so very peaceful before Worthen intruded. She must find a way to rid herself of him, but how? Charles was right; he was dogged when in pursuit, and perhaps even more now when she resisted him so strongly.

A rapping on the door startled Meg from her reverie. She had been reclusive long enough, and she moved to the door, saying, "One moment, if you please." When she reached the door, she unlocked it and opened it wide.

She was startled as she looked into deep-set blue eyes

174

and, with a joyful cry, exclaimed, "Whitehav—that is, Montford! Whatever are you doing here? Oh, you are most welcome, indeed!"

Beside him, Caroline stood, a thin smile on her lips as she said, "Lord Montford has just now arrived in Staplehope and wished to call upon us. I explained that you were not feeling very well today." She glanced at Meg with a curious expression on her face.

Meg sighed with satisfaction, thinking momentarily of Emmanuel Whitehaven. Were the baron's hair a white flame about his face, he would look just like Whitehaven. She addressed him: "I have merely been a trifle blue-devilled this morning. But now I am perfectly well, I assure you."

Montford did not hesitate to ask, "Enough to take a turn about the gardens, perchance?"

"Oh, indeed yes!"

Caroline spoke hesitantly, as though she was unsure whether or not Meg ought to be alone with Lord Montford: "The paths are still a trifle damp from the rain, Margaret. Perhaps Montford would take a little tea with us in the drawing room instead."

"Oh, no," Meg cried gaily. "He must see the roses. And the sun is shining, so we shall be very comfortable. Besides, I believe Montford has a particular fondness for roses."

He lifted his brow slightly but answered smoothly, "Ah, yes, the flower of love!"

Meg slipped her arm through Montford's as she moved into the hall. Caroline preceded them, asking the baron, "You will stay for nuncheon, then?"

Lord Montford said, "I would be greatly pleased, Caro."

Meg turned sharply to look at Caroline upon this familiar use of her stepmama's name. Caroline blushed faintly, but her smile held just a hint of pleasure as she met Montford's gaze and held it for the barest moment.

Meg felt jolted yet again by the odd coincidence that

Caroline seemed well-acquainted with Montford in much the same way she had been known to both Worthen and Geoffrey Blake.

Just before they moved out onto the terrace, Caroline addressed Meg: "I don't think his lordship has yet been informed about all our news here at Staplehope. Perhaps you ought to tell him everything."

Meg looked up at Montford and with great emphasis said, "I shall certainly do so." She then pulled him firmly by the arm, leading him toward the terrace steps.

He laughed lightly and teased her with, "Had I known you would be so warm in your greetings, Miss Longville, I should have returned to Shropshire long before this."

Caroline watched them move quickly down the steps. The sun seemed to dim suddenly, as though a cloud passed in front of it, but the sky was was completely clear. She felt her heart twist strangely as she watched Montford pat Meg's arm in almost a fatherly manner. Her friendship with Montford had grown distant following the duel between Worthen and his brother. The baron's presence was a continual reminder to Caroline that she had been unable to halt the bitter feud between the brothers. The letter she had written had been entirely ineffectual.

Later, Montford had returned with the unfortunate news that Worthen had merely burnt the letter and had spoken the ominous words, "She is too late with her supplications!" Montford had then held her sweetly in his arms, conforting her. He had also begged for her hand in marriage, quite passionately, too. When she refused, he had been all that was gracious and gentlemanly.

When they reached the hedges sculpted immaculately into s-shapes, Meg whispered, "I cannot believe you are here! Did you know that I had great need of you? How

176

could you have known? I have so much to tell, most of which you will not credit!"

He squeezed her arm and spoke in a low voice: "I will not try to gammon you, Meg. The fact is, Charles sent for me."

"Oh!" she cried. "Yes, of course. He said he would have a surprise for me, but that was but four days ago. Do not tell me you were in London and got here so quickly?"

His voice grew husky. "I came as fast as I could. Nothing could keep me from your side at such a time. Only what can be done? I was shocked to hear that your father and Worthen had joined ranks against you. I would never have believed your dear papa capable of such treachery toward one so sweet as yourself—but as for Worthen, I am of a mind that he somehow coerced your father."

He held her arm tightly, and when Meg looked into his eyes, she saw them dark with meaning. Something inside her shifted uncomfortably as though an idea she wished kept buried was trying to force its way into her heart. She answered him in an equally low voice as their feet crunched the raked gravel path. "I—that is, I know that Worthen said he resisted the idea at first. I must be fair, my father pushed for the union."

"But Worthen must have instigated it somehow—a hint here or there. His mind moves in this manner."

Meg swallowed hard, fighting his words, wanting to speak the truth clearly. "No. It was all Papa. I am certain of that."

Meg felt Montford's arm stiffen. She glanced up at him and saw that his jaw had grown quite rigid. He said, "For some reason, I believe he was afraid you were falling in love with me."

He looked down at Meg and caught her gaze. The sunlight sparkled in his eyes, and Meg wondered about him, whether or not she could love him. A breeze pulled at her summery gown of lavender and yellow calico. She felt a blush creep up her neck.

"Could you love me, Margaret?" he whispered, leaning close to her.

His breath touched her ear, and she shivered slightly. She answered quietly, "I don't know. I do count you as one of my dearest friends. Perhaps—in time."

"But you are short of that particular quantity, are you not?"

Meg sighed.

He pulled back slightly and again squeezed her arm. "Then, at least let me help you now. Only tell me what I can do. When is the wedding?"

"A sennight, no more, on Sunday next. Oh, Montford, I cannot marry him. He is heartless and brutal—"

"He has not hurt you in any way?"

"No! That is, I refer to his manner of address."

"Ah. He has kissed you, then, taking spurious advantage of this disgraceful engagement."

Meg blushed again. "I should not be speaking to you of such matters. Only, what am I to do?" She felt sudden, unexpected tears sting her eyes.

"It only makes it worse, you know." They had reached the roses, and he stood beside a large bush covered with deep red flowers. The fragrance caught on the breeze and swirled around them.

Meg withdrew her arm from his and dabbed at her eyes with her kerchief. Only then did she realize she still held both her kerchief and vinaigrette tightly in her hand. She said, "What do you mean, it is worse if I cry?"

He glanced at her. "No, I did not mean that at all. I was referring to a rumor I had heard in London. Of course, I suppose that you are well versed in Worthen's precise financial condition."

Meg sniffed once and reached out a hand to touch the velvety petals of one of the roses. "I have not even thought to discuss such matters with Papa. I don't give a fig about money. It is my heart that feels so lost."

"Then, you do not mind that his properties are heavily mortgaged? Your heart is very generous, Meg, but then I have always known that to be true."

Meg's fingers froze upon the red petals of the flower before her. She looked up at Montford and said, "My heart would always be generous where I loved. But what do you mean, heavily mortgaged?"

Montford drew his brows together. He took one of Meg's hands and said, "I do not wish to be the one to bring you pain, my dearest Meg, for I can see now that you have been kept from the truth. But I will speak the truth; you must know all. Worthen must marry an heiress. I suspected it, and upon your behalf I had my solicitor make a few discreet inquiries. His estates, probably through his own gaming propensities, are in a sorry state indeed. His father was a notable gamester in his day. The son undoubtedly followed in his path."

In all her six and twenty years, Meg had never known any fortnight to have contained more pain than this one. The warm summer breeze might as well have carried snow flurries, for her entire being felt as cold as though winter had stolen into her heart. Worthen needed her dowry? Oh, it could not be true, and he never said anything to her. Meg supposed suddenly that he meant to inform her upon their wedding night. *Oh, yes, and once my estates are repaired, perhaps we will have enough money for a new gown for you once each year.*

"Why, did not your father tell you?" Montford asked, still holding her hand. "My dear, you do not look well. I have given you a great shock."

Meg felt dizzy and immediately snapped open the vinaigrette. "I will not become another Rosamund!" she cried.

"Rosamund?" he queried. "I do not know the lady. Is she a friend from London?"

Meg steadied herself and withdrew her hand from Montford's warm grip. "It is nothing, merely someone I knew once who was always falling into a swoon when she confronted her difficulties."

Montford laughed softly. "I should be here to catch

179

you, Meg."

She looked up at him and smiled. "You are very good to me. I do not deserve such a friend as you."

"And you, my dear, are so much more deserving than this! My blood burns within me when I think of you being forced into a marriage, particularly with one so unworthy of you! Had it been anyone else but Lord Worthen, I don't think I would be quite so appalled and furious." His eyes glowed with the fervor of his words. "He cannot possibly love you. He hasn't the proper spirit to appreciate your gentle, virtuous nature." He paused for a moment and, leaning close to her, said, "I worship you, Meg—the air you breath, the sparkle in your eye—my only desire is to enshrine you in my house as you have long resided upon the altar of my heart. Do but say the word and I will spirit you away from all this unhappiness. Believe me when I say that for months now, I have thought only of you, of winning you. Tell me I may hope. You have but to give me the veriest hint, and I would arrange an elopement. We could go to Paris—"

Meg gasped and stepped slightly away from him. "You would ask me to elope with you?"

He stayed his ground, not reaching so much as a hand toward her, and spoke firmly: "I despise the idea as much as you do. But if it were necessary and if you thought you could love me . . ." He let the words drift between them.

Meg turned away from him. Would she risk marriage to Montford to escape from Worthen? She did not know. She did not really wish to marry either gentleman.

His tone became rather tender as he said, "Do you not think it would be romantic, Margaret, to be whisked away, near dawn's light, in a warm, comfortable town chariot—well-sprung, of course—a brick for your feet against the morning's chill, and to dash off through dew-drenched forests and fields clustered with lambs and ewes. With you, I would find such an adventure more blissful than I could endure, the happiness it would bring me—"

He broke off as a familiar voice called to them from the terrace. "Meggie! Bring your guest and come in for a little tea!" Sir William waved at them, and Margaret found herself blushing as she waved back and immediately turned down the garden path. "We should go," she said. "Papa will not like it that I am conversing with you alone in the gardens."

Montford sounded very sad as he said, "Your father has never approved of me, has he?" He then sighed deeply.

Meg could not answer him, for she knew well her papa's sentiments. Instead, she took a deep breath and said, "You may rest assured, however, that I choose my own friends. I only wish for the opportunity to love and marry where my heart leads me. It would matter little, in that case, what my father's opinions were."

He spoke earnestly: "I honor you! Oh, indeed, you are the finest of women. You have but to speak the word and I will give you—"

She smiled sweetly upon him, but placed a finger upon his lips to silence him. "Yes, I know," she said. "Dew-drenched forests and hills dotted with lambs and ewes!" Just before they ascended the terrace steps, she stayed him slightly with a touch upon his arm. "You have described to me a picture of pure enchantment, my lord, another example of how well you know the workings of my heart. But I am uncertain, as you may imagine. Know this, however, that I am heartily gratified by your presence here at Staplehope."

In the center of the private parlor at The Vine Inn, covers were laid upon a square table. The chamber was large, comfortable and panelled in a light walnut. The fireplace crackled with a tidy fire, and on a sideboard, a rich sherry sparkled in a crystal decanter. In the middle of the table sat a vase of bluebells and ferns. *A charming picture, all!* Meg thought, as she was ushered into the room with her father and Caroline. She was still exceedingly angry that not only had her father and her betrothed failed to inform her of Worthen's need to replenish his pockets through his bride's dowry, but that all this time, Worthen had hypocritically told her he loved her. *How very convenient!* she thought, *and how easy to fall in love with thirty thousand pounds!*

Meg wore a polite smile as she met Lord Worthen's gaze. He stood by the fireplace, awaiting his guests, dressed in formal evening attire. He inclined his head to her, but she could see by the narrowing of his eyes that he at least suspected she was discontent. Next to him, seated in a chair and tapping his cane against the side of his shoe, was Geoffrey.

Just as Worthen started to speak, Meg interrupted him quite peremptorily and addressed his brother.

"And how do you go on, Mr. Blake? I hope you are feeling much better, for I was given to understand you had been ill."

Geoffrey glanced up at his brother and could not restrain a smile. Looking back at Meg, he responded, "We have both suffered a trifle since we last met, have we not, Miss Longville?"

Meg was startled by his question and would have answered him, but he clucked his tongue at Worthen and said, "I told you not to take her to the mill. Shabbily done, brother dear! Next time, you must ask me how to properly entertain a lady."

Meg extended her hand to Geoffrey in greeting. She tilted her head slightly and asked, "You knew what he was about and you disapproved?"

He had a decided twinkle in his eye as he took Meg's hand and whispered, "My brother is dreadfully high-handed. Do not for one moment give him his head. Hold the reins tightly, m'dear!"

Meg laughed outright and said, "And why is it, Mr. Blake, that you had to marry so early in your career, for I can see that you and I would have gone on together prodigiously well!"

He smiled, his face alive with good humor, as he said, "I am afraid my wife would have a tale or two for you, and then you should no doubt count yourself fortunate indeed!"

"What a rapper!" Meg answered him with a smile. She then turned to Worthen and said, "Had you one particle of your brother's grace and manners, I should have long since followed you anywhere!"

"Meggie!" her father chided her. "Is that any way to speak to Lord Worthen?"

But Worthen only laughed as he addressed Sir William: "She is right, you know. In matters of deportment, I fear my talents are sadly lacking. I can only claim a devoted heart." And he bowed to Meg.

She lifted a brow and tried for a light tone. "Oh, indeed?" She turned away from him and walked to the window, where she stared out onto the street, refusing to say another word.

Geoffrey looked up at his brother, who wore a frown on his face, and whispered in a teasing manner, "You should not have shot that rat! She seems uncommonly aggrieved."

Worthen shook his head. "No. I think this is something else. But what?"

As though in response, Sir William said, "We had an interesting caller today, Worthen."

Lord Worthen turned to greet both Sir William and Caroline as he pulled a chair toward the fire for the latter. Bowing over Caroline's hand, he asked, "And who was that?"

Caroline spoke mildly: "An old friend."

Sir William rocked on his heels slightly, his hands behind his back. Casting a scowl toward his daughter, he said, "Montford. Montford was here today."

Silence reigned in the parlor for several seconds, long enough for Meg to turn back toward the rest of the party. She met Blake's surprised stare, Worthen's frown, her father's scowl and Caroline's expression of perplexity.

She lifted her chin and said, "Montford and I are great friends. I was delighted beyond words to see him. Besides, he had the most fascinating things to tell me." She then smiled sweetly upon them all.

The innkeeper appeared at the door bearing a silver tray, five etched crystal glasses, and a bottle of champagne. He was a short, rotund man of advancing years, with a balding pate and friendly blue eyes.

Meg gasped and said, "Oh, no! Worthen, you should not have ordered anything quite so dear as champagne. However will you afford it?" She pressed a hand to her cheek.

The innkeeper seemed quite startled by this remark, frowning and tisking at her. Again, the rest of the party turned to stare at her. Caroline's face was red as she exclaimed, "Margaret!" And though her mouth remained agape, no other words followed.

Meg looked around at everyone, her eyes wide and innocent. "If I am to be a married woman shortly," she said, "I ought to begin thinking in such terms as spending and saving. How much does that champagne cost, Mr. Crupps?" She blinked at the innkeeper, her expression serious.

He merely shook his head at her and spoke severely: "That's not a matter I intend to discuss with ye, missy."

Margaret blushed faintly at this rebuke, but she could not keep from smiling a little. Behind her, she heard Worthen utter a crack of laughter.

Dinner languished, for though it was well-prepared, and Mrs. Crupps had prepared two enormous courses, Meg continued to speculate the entire time on the cost of turtles, oysters, lobster and everything else that appeared before them. Mr. Crupps frowned at her several times, but she appeared unable to comprehend his meaning and continued estimating the cost of an entire service of dinner plates. "Perhaps we should never entertain our friends, Worthen. What think you? We could save a great deal by ignoring all of our acquaintance entirely."

But Lord Worthen, who was making a hearty meal, did not appear in the least distressed by either her choice of conversation or her interest in home economies. He responded politely, "I should cherish every possible moment alone with you. Your idea does have some merit, afterall."

Meg was not at all pleased with this mild response. She had hoped at the very least to make him as angry as she felt. But apparently he was not to be so moved—drat the man!

Her father, however, was not so even-tempered as Lord Worthen. By the time a platter of fresh fruits, tarts and biscuits was brought to the table, Sir William's expression was so strident that Meg finally let the subject drop.

The party prepared to return to Staplehope, where they would enjoy a few games of whist and later a light supper that Cook had been preparing for days. Sir William found an opportunity to draw Meg aside and threaten to whip her if she did not improve her manners at once—at once! "Especially since Caroline has planned so special an evening."

Meg spoke mockingly: "I am sure I can smile at Worthen over whist if that is what you require."

Sir William leaned his face close to hers. "I've had just about enough of your surly behavior this evening, Margaret Eleanor Longville."

Meg did not move away from him one inch but met her father squarely. She said, "If you wanted your daughter to be prettily behaved, then why did you not tell her that she was being married for her dowry! Do you despise me so much, Papa?"

The color drained from Sir William's face as he uttered a groan. "Hell and damnation! We are at that! I suppose Montford told you."

"Yes, as it happens, he did! He, at least, has proven to be a true friend. By why must I hear such a thing from him or anyone else, Papa? First you inform me, a day

185

before Worthen arrives, that I am to marry him. Then Hope tells me the truth about my sweet Phillip, and now Montford must tell me that Worthen needs to marry an heiress in order to rebuild his estates!" She drew in her breath, her voice catching on a sob. She glanced down the hallway where Caroline was speaking animatedly with the brothers. "I should have been informed long before this!"

"Ah, Meg, I should have told you!" Sir William cried as he ground his teeth and winced.

Meg, who had been harboring a faint hope that Montford did not have the right of it, felt her throat tighten. She spoke in a whisper: "So Lord Worthen does have need of my dowry? Then, how can he speak of loving me?"

"Meg, I won't pretend I've not done wrong, but you can't think worse of Worthen for it! I know he loves you."

Meg responded, "Hah!"

"Well, aren't you the conceited one, then. Faith, child, he could have had any of a dozen wealthy females, with merely the nod of his head. And why he would want to wed the most disagreeable female in London, I'll never comprehend." Sir William pursed his lips together. "Bah, why do I even try to reason with a stubborn, mulish chit like you!" He turned toward the court where his large travelling chariot waited. He said, "Come, Meg. John Coachman is nodding to us, and your stepmama's guests are waiting!"

"What guests?" Meg asked, feeling more ill-tempered than she had in her entire life.

But Sir William had apparently endured enough of his daughter's ill-temper, for he refused to answer her.

Chapter Thirteen

The moment Sir William's coach turned up the drive of Staplehope Hall, Meg realized something was not as it should be. Looking toward the house, she saw that all of the chambers on the first floor were aglow with candlelight, a circumstance odd in itself. Only during the reception of a large number of guests would the hall be lit in such a fashion. In addition, Caroline, who sat across from her, clasped and unclasped her hands nervously, her green eyes positively glittering. For a moment she thought something odd was afoot, but then she realized that no doubt Caroline had merely wished to honor Lord Worthen and his brother.

Whatever the case, Caroline seemed to have gone to some effort to see that the gentlemen were well entertained. Meg wished her stepmama had been less attentive; she did not want Worthen to feel at all welcome at Staplehope.

Within the coach, the gentlemen were behaving just as Meg expected them to.

Of course her father ignored her completely, averting his gaze out the window and sitting with his arms folded across his chest. Geoffrey, however, seated beside Caroline, maintained a steady, polite flow of anecdotes and comments upon the weather. Meg observed that his address was impeccable. He was congenial as always, even though he spoke almost exclusively to the air since the rest of the party each seemed absorbed with his or her own concerns. Even his brother did not attend him, for Worthen sat turned toward Meg, offering only one comment in response to one of Geoffrey's remarks: "I will say this! For so mild a June, the climate has suddenly grown positively frigid."

Meg knew he was referring to her own dear self, and she merely cast an irritated glance upon him. After that, she ignored him entirely. She meant, given the first opportunity, to rake Worthen over the coals and to delight every moment in doing so.

Once inside the entrance hall, Meg ignored the servants dressed in their finest livery and waited for the proper moment to arrive in which she could address Worthen in private. He seemed just as eager to be alone with her, though his reasons were obviously quite different from her own.

He helped her off with her peach satin cloak and whispered over her shoulder, "How beautiful you are!" She was gowned in an emerald sarsanet, beaded with seed pearls upon her puffed sleeves. She wore a necklet of emeralds and a white ribbon wound throughout her hair.

Worthen added, "I only wish I could be alone with you. First, that I might hear all your grievances and fishwifery harpings. Then afterward so that I might kiss you."

Meg turned on him, her light blue eyes blazing fire. She whispered back, "You may not wish to hear all that I have to say to you, my Lord Hypocrit!"

Caroline hurried up to Meg at this point and said, "Margaret, I have just realized that Lord Worthen has not yet seen our ballroom. Perhaps you would like to show it to him."

Meg looked at her, a little surprised but grateful. Caroline must have somehow sensed that a quarrel was imminent and wanted to give them the opportunity to enjoy it in private.

Caroline's parting comment as Meg led Worthen down the hall was, however, a trifle bemusing. Caroline cried, "Meg, do try to smile, if but a little!"

Worthen took her arm and held it firmly. Just before they arrived at the ballroom doors, Meg thought she heard a muffled laugh. One of the servants, perhaps? She was about to say something when Worthen suddenly took her roughly in his arms and kissed her once, very hard. He then released her. She was about to cry, *You beast!* but Worthen hushed her with a hand over her mouth, laughing at her and holding her gaze intensely.

He whispered, "Remember, your stepmama said you must smile!"

Her heart was nearly ready to burst with fury, until she saw him incline his head toward the doors. Another muffled cry was heard from within the ballroom. Meg rolled her eyes, whispering, "Oh, no! Do not tell me that within are a mountain of Caroline's guests! Oh, lord. No wonder the servants have been in a frenzy these past three days!"

Worthen chuckled deep in his throat.

"So, you are amused," she said, her tone sarcastic.

As he threw open the doors, he smiled wickedly at her and said, "Just when you wanted nothing more than to comb my hair, you must now enjoy our engagement party!"

The sight before Meg was both infuriating and lovely, as a crowd of all her friends and acquaintances swirled suddenly about them both, shouting their congratulations and wishing them every happiness in the world.

And Meg smiled, just as Caroline had told her to.

The ballroom was decorated in over two dozen bouquets of roses, ferns and ivy placed along all four walls at varying intervals. The walls were hung with yards and yards of spangled lavender netting. The atmosphere was festive; the lights of hundreds of candles lent a brilliance to the dancers who moved in the intricate pattern of the quadrille.

Meg had shared the first waltz with Worthen, and immediately afterward Montford had made certain that most of her dances were taken up by the other gentlemen present.

Worthen had given the baron a slight bow of recognition at the outset of the ball. Meg noticed that he seemed careful to avoid speaking to Montford, and she felt all her former sentiments regarding her betrothed surface again. But above all, she was still hurt and angry that after all of Worthen's protestations that he loved her, his real aim had been her dowry. She should have known that such a man who would coerce an unwilling female toward the altar would of course have his eye to her fortune. What other reason could such a man have than this?

Whenever she crossed his path throughout the course of the evening, she was smiling and polite—she had little desire to give the tittletattles the least morsel of gossip— but behind her smiles, she made it quite clear to him that matters were not at all settled between them.

She was currently dancing the quadrille with Mr. Norbury. When the movements of the dance brought them together, he smiled broadly at Meg and said, "Have you seen my daughter?"

The dance parted them, and Meg searched the length of the ballroom for Hope. When she found her, she was astonished at what she saw. Hope was dressed in a brilliant dark pink gown, nearly the shade of brambleberries, with a fulsome demi-train billowing behind her. Her soft brown hair had been fashionably cut and wisped in delicate curls about her face. Almost, she looked as charming as Emily Cowper, and Meg smiled at the wonderful transformation. A dozen beaux had gathered about her skirts and were begging for her favors. Hope was smiling and happy.

Meg turned back to Mr. Norbury and nodded her

approval. She wondered suddenly what Charles would think of his former love and whether or not he had already seen Hope.

After the quadrille, Meg sought out Charles only to have Montford catch her arm and beg her to take a turn about the ballroom with him. He said, "Have I told you yet, how elegant you appear this evening?"

Meg replied, "No, you have not, but pray, proceed at once! You have full command of my attention!" She flung open her fan and waved it across her face. Over the edge of the fan she smiled at him.

Montford squeezed her arm daringly. "You rob me of breath, Meg, and leave me with but one desire, to sweep you away from Staplehope. Tonight, my carriage awaits if you are willing!"

Meg was startled. "You are not serious!" she cried. She blinked several times at him. Was he really asking her to elope? "Montford, I never meant—that is, I hope you do not think that I was encouraging such an action—"

He laughed lightly. "I am only teasing you—at least, in part. The truth is I have brought my curricle, a vehicle I am certain you will agree is hardly the proper mode of travel for an elopement."

Meg looked into his teasing eyes and queried, "Have you, perchance, spoken with Charles?"

He threw back his head and laughed. "What a gudgeon to have tried to whisk you away in a racing curricle!" He then watched her intently. "I blame myself, however! Had I been here, I could have taken you to Bristol in short order. I still can if you are of a mind to." Meg began to protest, but he said, "Not an elopement. I would merely help you escape this wedding if it should become necessary."

Meg felt as though the room had been stuffy and someone had just opened a window permitting a fresh breeze to blow over her. A great tension seemed to ease itself from her body. Charles would forevermore be suspect were she to disappear again, but who would think of Montford stealing her away? "Sir!" she responded immediately. "I am deeply indebted to you for such a suggestion. And just as you said, should it become necessary, I will indeed ask for your assistance."

He inclined his head. "Let nothing more be said between us, then. You have but to send me word and I am at your service."

Worthen approached them suddenly and took Meg from Montford's side, saying, "Mrs. Norbury has asked to speak with Margaret. You will permit her to attend that lady, will you not?" He regarded Montford squarely.

The baron smiled easily and said, "Of course." He did not hesitate, however, to take Meg's hand and to kiss her fingers. Afterward, he sauntered away.

"Insufferable," Worthen murmured beneath his breath.

Meg took Worthen's arm stiffly. "Indeed?" she responded quietly, offering him a challenge. "He, at least, has not forced me into an engagement I do not want."

Charles Burnell stood beside Lord Montford, a few feet away from the orchestra. The baron was extolling Meg's virtues, and though he, himself, had a fondness for Meg, he had never been able to see her as more than his muddy-stockinged playmate from childhood. His gaze was fixed not upon Meg—as was Montford's—but upon a ravishing creature a mere ten feet away, gowned in a flaming pink balldress and surrounded by suitors. Ever since he had made his defection clear, several of his friends had spoken privately with him, indicating their desire to court Hope Norbury. Charles had been stunned. It had never occurred to him that should he step aside, his sweet, little Hope would be inundated with so many ardent suitors. He saw her, suddenly, in an entirely new light and felt a pang of regret at his sudden decision to drop his pursuit of her.

Charles of course released any claim upon Hope; he wished the very best for her—but that was before tonight. He swallowed hard as he watched her gentle manners grow more teasing as she rapped one of the members of her court with a mother-of-pearl fan. She was so deuced pretty with her cropped hair, and her gown was quite dazzling! He knew a sudden desire to walk right up to her and run his fingers through the soft curls that surrounded her face.

A giggling, schoolgirl's voice called to him from the opposite side of the floor. "Charles, my darling, do come here!" Charles heard the voice and recognized it as Elizabeth's, but he was so caught by Hope's remarkable appearance that he could not tear his gaze from her.

Montford pulled on his coat sleeve and said, "Miss Priestley is calling you, Burnell."

Somehow the baron's words broke the spell that kept Charles' attention fixed upon Hope, and he was able to follow the direction of Montford's gaze. When he saw Lizzie, he cried, "Good God!"

Montford laughed. "A trifle bosky, wouldn't you say? A real baggage, that one!"

Charles stiffened as he bowed slightly to the baron and said, "I hope to make Miss Priestley my wife, though I suppose you could not know that since you have so recently arrived in Staplehope."

Montford stared at Burnell and cleared his throat. "You and Elizabeth? But I thought—" He broke off and lifted a brow. After a moment he smiled. "I only meant to say that Elizabeth is a young woman full of fire but nothing a man of your stamp could not handle."

Charles meant to defend Lizzie, but at that moment she tripped slightly and hiccoughed. "Oh, dash-it-all, she is something of a baggage, is she not!" he cried.

Montford laughed and slapped him playfully on the back. "Come, let us both tend to her. She does seem to require a strong hand of the moment, if nothing more than to support her while she walks!"

As they moved toward Elizabeth, Charles could not keep from casting one more glance toward Hope. He was a little startled to find that she was watching him. When he met her gaze, she curtsied ever so slightly to him, then lifted her fan to her lips and smiled sweetly upon him.

He felt as though she had struck him somehow, hard in the stomach. But the moment passed quickly as Hope turned her attention to a heavily freckled youth who began leading her out for a country dance.

Lizzie called to him again, afterward emitting a bosky laugh that echoed loudly in the ballroom. "Why, Charles!" she cried, "you have been neglecting me! Come, let us find a little more champagne." She happened to glance at Montford and, lifting a brow, cried, "Why, it is you, my lord! Whatever are you doing in Staplehope! I was certain you would remain in London forever. Mrs. Bolles is charming, is she not?" She hiccoughed and giggled again.

Montford narrowed his eyes slightly and said, "She has charming little card parties, if that is what you mean."

Lizzie giggled again and took both his arm as well as Charles'. "You are a wicked, wicked man, Lord Montford. I know very well you have been chasing the widow for months now!"

Charles stared at Montford, a little surprised by this revelation, but Montford caught his gaze over Lizzie's black locks and shook his head. Charles nodded, understanding perfectly that his dear little Elizabeth was suffering from the dubious effects of too many cups of champagne. He said, "I wonder if we might not procure a little coffee!"

After a few minutes, Montford and Charles were able to persuade Elizabeth to sit in a comfortable chair in Sir William's study. She giggled frequently and flirted with both men in turn until her aunt appeared and begged her to try to control her laughter, even if she was unable to curb her hoydenish manners!

Mrs. Norbury addressed Charles: "And if you would, please see that one of the servants brings her a little coffee." She shook her head at Elizabeth as Charles quit the room and would have rung a peal over Lizzie's head, but she was drawn away soon after by a request from Mrs. Burnell. It seemed that poor Miss Fitzwell had fallen into a swoon after having been attacked by Sir William's pet mouse!

The moment the study was empty, Elizabeth turned her gaze upon Montford. He was standing by the window, his hands across his chest, staring at her. She rose from her chair, ran to the door, and shut it quite boldly.

She smiled coyly and said, "I have not really had so much champagne as you think. But I do enjoy playing as though I have! Do you not think me very wicked?"

"Very!" Montford responded, never letting his eyes leave her face.

"You are quite the handsomest man I have ever known, my lord. Do you mind that I speak in this manner to you?" She walked slowly but quite steadily toward him, her hands clasped behind her back. She wore a décolleté gown of midnight blue satin, setting her white skin and black hair off to perfection. It was both exquisite and completely unsuited to her tender years. White was the accepted mode for maidenly young ladies, or a pale pink or iced blue. The gown Lizzie wore was clearly outrageous.

His gaze slipped over her womanly figure, and he asked, "How old are you? If you are nineteen, I will be greatly surprised."

"Just barely. But what is age?"

"It depends upon the task at hand. A young man, for instance, is much better fit to chop down a tree than an old man."

"And—" Elizabeth interjected quickly, "a young woman is better fit to fill a nursery than an older woman. I know what you want—you'll never get it. Meg will

195

never have you. You will have to steal her from under Worthen's nose!"

She stood very near him now, only a small table separating them. Atop the table sat a crystal bowl of pot pourri. Lizzie sank her hand deeply into the dried flower petals and spices and said, "My dowry is not so large as Meg's, but it would certainly go far toward eliminating a detestable mortgage or two."

He regarded her askance. "What are you at, Miss Priestley? Almost I feel as though you are offering for me."

Lizzie said, "You may kiss me if you like."

Montford laughed. "You are not serious!"

"Oh, indeed I am. You have something I want, you see."

He nodded in a knowing fashion. "Of course. You wish for a handle to your name."

Lizzie said, "You would enjoy kissing me, I'm sure, even if it is very, very wicked."

Montford said, "I may be many things, Elizabeth, but I would never do such a thing to my friend."

"And you are a liar, too. I do like you, Montford, and I think we have a great deal in common!"

He laughed outright at this, then altered the course of their conversation. "But what of Charles? I understand I can wish you joy!"

Lizzie said, "If you will not kiss me, I suppose then I will have to marry Mr. Burnell. It's a funny thing about Charles. I don't think I actually love him; but you see he was Hope's beau for so long, and I couldn't bear it. He never would look at me, and so you see I simply had to have him. I mean to marry him, too. Perhaps after we are married I will be able to encourage him to take an interest in government. That is, of course, if you will not kiss me."

Montford said, "You are a baggage, Miss Priestley, and unfortunately, I haven't the least desire to, er, *kiss* you."

Elizabeth, who hated having any of her wishes denied, grabbed a fistful of flower petals and flung them in his face. Montford laughed at her, which only caused her to turn quickly on her heel and flounce toward the door. A footman appeared in the doorway, bearing a tray of coffee, and Lizzie, in her wholly inconsiderate manner, hit the tray, knocking the coffee to the floor. Then she was gone.

The footman, mortified at the incident, began apologizing for his clumsiness, but Montford cut him off and said, "Never apologize for a lady's temper!"

"Yes, m'lord," the footman cried as he dropped to his knees and began tamping a linen napkin upon the stained carpet.

After Charles had signalled a footman to provide coffee for a lady in Sir William's study, he saw Hope disappear into Meg's morning room. He felt his heart beat strangely within his breast. He knew he should return to Lizzie's side, but he could not resist the impulse of following after Hope. He glanced quickly behind him to see if anyone was about, and when he saw that his movements would go unnoticed, he ran down the hall and within seconds was secluded in the room with her.

Once inside, he saw her standing before the fireplace, her head bowed. His first thought was that she was meeting someone secretly here. He asked, "Are you alone, Hope, or do I intrude?"

Hope whirled about, staring at him as though she were seeing a specter. She held a hand to her bosom and said, "Yes, that is no. No, of course you do not intrude. Did you suppose I was meeting someone here? But whatever are you doing? Where is Elizabeth?"

Charles did not know what he was doing in this quite scandalous *tête-à-tête* with the very woman he had spurned not five days ago. He said, "I merely wanted to tell you how pretty you look this evening. I have never seen you appear to such advantage. Why, you have more beaux than even Lizzie."

Hope lowered her gaze to the floor. She stood very still,

as though she was uncertain what to say next. Finally, she said, "Charles, I lied to you—a hundred times and more, in my words and deeds. Will you ever forgive me?"

Charles felt again as though she had struck him a blow. He advanced into the room and said, "Whatever do you mean? I don't understand. For you to tell a lie would be impossible. And don't try to gammon me! Remember, I have known you since you were a child."

"Nevertheless," Hope responded, "I have lied. I have pretended not to feel things when my heart overflowed with feelings and desires." Her complexion was flushed, Charles noted, but not with embarrassment. No, it was something more.

As he drew near to her, she stepped away from him and moved purposefully toward the door. She opened the door and said, "There is nothing more beautiful to me than a night sky full of stars. Unless of course the moon is full and the countryside glows with its light."

Charles frowned. He did not quite understand what she was doing or why she spoke of the night as she did. He could not believe what he was hearing. "But you told me not six days ago that the night frightened you."

Hope swallowed very hard, her eyes brimming suddenly with tears as she closed the door. She said simply, "I lied, Charles."

He stared at her, disbelieving. "But I would have offered for you that very evening had you professed then the very things you are telling me now."

Hope said, "I know. My faith in you had faltered terribly, you see. I was afraid somehow that you had become reckless like Phillip Harcastle. And you had become such good friends with Montford, who everyone knows is a confirmed gamester. Only afterward, when I spoke to Meg, did I realize how greatly I had erred. Charles, I love you."

Charles ran a fitful hand through his thick hair. He shook his head in disbelief. "You thought I had become a gamester?"

"Yes, until Meg told me how you will scarcely wager more than a few pounds upon anything."

He shifted uneasily on his feet and chided her gently: "You are mistaken about Montford. He is no such thing, I assure you."

Hope leaned against the door and said, "It is only gossip I am sure! The truth is I don't give a fig whether he is a gamester or not. I only wanted you to know what my sentiments really are."

Charles knew an intense longing to take Hope in his arms. He was just about to respond to this impulse when Lizzie's voice intruded. "Why, Hope Norbury! To think of you trying to get up a flirtation with the man I intend to marry. And how very odd to think of you possessing even the smallest amount of spirit to actually tell a man—who no longer has an interest in you—that you love him. I am amazed; I am prepared to shout it to the entire ballroom."

Charles was about to silence Elizabeth, but Hope merely set her shoulders and crossed the room to Lizzie. Here she stood before her cousin and threatened her. "You won't say anything, Lizzie, or I shall gladly tell everyone that you . . ." she whispered in Lizzie's ear. "You would not!" Elizabeth cried. "You haven't an ounce of courage, and you would no more relate such a story than—"

"Oh, wouldn't I just. I have learned, you see, a great deal from you, and I mean to make use of it."

Hope lifted her head very high and walked regally from the room.

Elizabeth pulled a face, but turned her attention back to Charles. "And as for you, oh, wayward one, do take me back to the ballroom and dance with me or I shall go in search of more champagne."

Charles, who had half expected to find himself in the midst of a violent argument with Elizabeth, emitted a heavy sigh of relief and offered his arm to her.

Chapter Fourteen

All the guests had gone, save Worthen. Even his brother had returned to The Vine. Meg paced the carpet in front of the fireplace, her temper worn thin from the fatigue of a long day. She listened to Caroline speaking inanities to Worthen, who in turn was laughing at something or other she said.

When there was the barest lull between their conversation, Meg ceased her restless marching and said, "Are you not tired from the evening's exertions, Caroline? Are you not longing even now for your bed?"

Caroline cast a startled glance upon Meg. Blinking twice, she responded, "I—that is, I suppose we are all fatigued." She rose to her feet and addressed Worthen: "How silly of me to keep you, Worthen, when the hour has grown so late. You must be wishing for your own bed as well."

Caroline smiled nervously at Meg, then held out her arm to the viscount as though she meant to escort him to the door.

Worthen took the hint and stood up, but Meg said, "Oh, no, Lord Worthen. You cannot leave just yet. I simply must have a word with you, if you please!"

He glanced at her and bowed, saying, "It would be a pleasure—" He paused for a moment, his eyes twinkling as he added, "At least I *think* it would be a pleasure."

Meg refused to smile at him, stating that he knew very well they had a matter of some import to discuss.

He took his snuffbox from his pocket and, taking a pinch, said, "Ah, yes, the price of lobster, as I recall!"

Meg sniggered, "Oh, yes, at the very least we must discuss the cost of lobster patties!"

Caroline began to reseat herself, appearing quite conscious as she did so. Meg sensed that her stepmama had no desire to leave her alone with Worthen, not for propriety's sake but because she feared Meg would disturb the wedding plans. But Meg addressed her respectfully as she said, "If you please, I really do need to speak with his lordship in private. I won't be long, I promise you." When her stepmama hesitated, she added, "He is, afterall, my betrothed, and we are to be married in but a few days."

Reluctantly, Caroline rose to her feet and, in a quiet voice, said, "Of course. But—" She lifted a hand toward Meg, as though she had something important she wished to say, then let her hand fall, the pinched expression on her face giving way to one of surrender. She curtsied to Worthen slightly as she extended her hand to him. "Good night, then."

Meg did not speak until the sound of Caroline's slippers upon the tile of the grand entrance hall faded away completely.

She stood in front of the fireplace, a steady log fire crackling behind her skirts. Worthen, who had stood up when Caroline quit the room, turned to face her, his features lit with a measure of amusement that merely set the hackles to rising upon Meg's neck.

His lips twitched as he spoke in a firm manner: "And now, pray tell me what is wrong before I go off in a fit of apoplexy. Your hints all evening have kept me in the worst state of apprehension. You have no idea!"

Meg said, "Yes, I can see that you are shaking in your boots."

Worthen nodded. "Indeed, I am, though I had hoped

you would not have noticed. Now, what is the matter, though I have a good notion, given your sudden concern with the cost of shellfish, that it has something to do with money!"

Meg clasped her hands tightly in front of her and was about to speak when he added, "No, no! Do not hold anything from me. I wish to know every thought that has been rattling about in your brain this entire evening!"

Meg responded sharply, "If you would but give me a chance, I should not hesitate to do so."

He lifted a hand and said, "One moment, if you please. I think I would rather have you scold me while seated. You don't mind if I sit down, do you?"

"Oh, my dear sir," Meg responded sarcastically, "I would by no means suspend any comfort of yours." She gestured to the settee. "Pray seat yourself. Shall I ring for the butler to bring you a footstool? Perhaps a posset might give you succor as well."

"It is an idea," he said. He then glanced at the settee with disdain and crossed the room to a gold velvet wing chair near the fireplace and promptly sat down. "Ah, that is much better. Besides, now the fire has set your face aglow. You see, from the settee, the light would have been positioned behind you and your face cast in shadow most of the time. How could I then see the tremulous images of love that might pass across your lovely face from time to time?"

Meg rolled her eyes. "Well, are you content now with where you are sitting and where I am standing?"

He nodded, his expression serious, though his eyes twinkled with amusement. "Pray speak! You may now give me that dressing down that has been readied upon your tongue for the past several hours."

Meg was heartily sick of his manner of jesting and faced him with her hands on her hips. She did not say anything for a long moment, but merely stared at him. Finally, she said, "Of all the fine speeches you have made me over these past several days, there must have been one I missed through some freak occurrence of deafness, for I do not remember it at all. Would you please repeat it for me?"

Worthen cocked his head. "And which one might that be, my dearest Margaret?" He squinted his eyes as though searching his mind for some clue to her riddle. After a moment, he said, "Would it have been the speech about how I expect my wife to save every groat she can, either by purchasing cheap, intolerable candles or by doing the family laundering herself, or was it perhaps the treatise on—"

Meg cut him off with an upflung hand as she cried, "Enough of this folly! What I wish to know is this; how dare you kiss me and make pretty love to me, begging me all the while to adore you desperately in return, and somehow forget to mention that you are under the hatches!"

"Oh!" he cried, his expression one of false astonishment. "Did I forget to tell you that? Well, how silly of me! I shall immediately tell you then—my pockets are to let, my estates are all to flinders, I haven't a feather to fly with and obviously my only interest in you is your dowry of twenty thousand pounds!"

"Thirty!" Meg corrected him.

"Thirty? Well, is this not a day of bright fortune for me, then. I now have another ten to squander as I please! Ah, could love hold greater sweetness than this!"

Meg regarded him askance as she stepped toward the fireplace, her hands clasped behind her. "Well, you needn't be so flippant about the matter. I have cause to be greatly aggrieved, as you well know."

"I can't see why, Margaret. I would not be the first man to marry a woman's purse!"

Meg gasped. "You are nothing but a miserable fortune hunter. How my father is able to esteem you I will never comprehend. I'll never wed the likes of you if I have to escape from Shropshire—"

He shook his head. "You tried to do so once already, if you recall!"

Meg said, "Well, I shan't fail a second time, I can

assure you of that. I have made up my mind entirely. I won't wed you; I will never do so. You have no sensitivity whatsoever. You even shot a rat, right at my feet, and all for effect!" She waited for him to speak, but he merely stared at her, a hard cast to his dark eyes. Finally she cried, "Well, have you nothing to say for yourself?"

"I see," he said slowly as he rose to his feet. "So that is what you really want me to do—to defend myself against your ill opinions of my character. Do you know, Margaret, all evening I have had this piercing sensation that you wished more than anything to make me angry. And, all evening, I have laughed at the notion because I know that the error was in fact quite simple and human and could be set to rights with but a moment's intelligent conversation. Instead, I find merely that you want an excuse for brangling with me, but why? Well, I want you to know, whatever the case, you have succeeded in enraging me. I cannot remember being so angry in my entire life than in this moment."

Meg stepped away from him as she saw his nostrils flare and quiver.

He spoke in a low voice: "How dare you treat me with such contempt as you have displayed just now. How dare you assign to my motives the worst, most dishonorable of intentions." He advanced on her, and Meg backed slowly away from him. "How dare you accuse me of wrongdoing before you even know whereof you speak. What have I ever done, Meg, to give you such a poor opinion of me. But as for defending my actions to you, or anyone else, I will not do it! Not now, not ever! You have a mind prejudiced against me, whatever your reasons, but do you know what I really think? I think you are afraid of me, of what you might be feeling for me, even now!"

Meg had continued walking backward and now bumped into the mahogany table. The music box atop the table emitted several high, sweet notes from this jarring movement. She was as much startled by the sudden sound as by the burning quality in Worthen's dark eyes. Her throat dry, she rasped, "What a ridiculous notion!

Why should I have the least fear of you?" Her tone was even, but her knees had begun to tremble.

He smiled suddenly, but his expression was cold as he responded, "Because I am real, because I have no pretenses and because your heart already belongs to me, though you refuse to admit it. But I will tell you what is more ridiculous than your being afraid of me—the fact that you will take for your dearest friends anyone who will flatter your vanity and pretend to worship you."

He stood over her now, his breath warm on her face. She cried, "You refer to Montford, I suppose." She leaned her hands on the table behind her for support, the music box again clicking another solitary note.

"Who else? Who else would have rushed to Staplehope merely to inform you in a *friendly* manner that I must have your dowry. What a decent friend he is. What else did he tell you, Meg? Did he tell you that I am unworthy of you? Did he tell you he worships you and that only a saint would deign to kiss your feet?"

Meg drew in her breath sharply, remembering that Montford had indeed said that he worshipped her. She whispered, "Montford says that he loves me, if that is what you wish to know. And yes, he worships me. And what possible fault can you find with that?"

"Because when you worship an earthly creature, eventually the creature falters and becomes unworthy of your devotion. There is no place in love for worship, Meg. Did you worship Phillip, for instance? And what if you had wed him, only to discover that he had feet of clay and that he was being crushed beneath a pile of debts of his own making? Would you still be able to love him then? I think not."

He grabbed her roughly about the waist and said, "Well, let me tell you that I don't worship you, Meg. But I would kiss your feet; not in some ethereal, meaningless symbol of devotion, but because I adore your imperfections, your fragility, your foibles, even the fact that you are so blind. I adore your temper and your hateful manner of assigning virtue to evil and evil to virtue. You

205

are so very human and I love you and I would kiss your feet because they are made only of clay."

Worthen picked her up bodily and slid her onto the settee beside the table. The words he had spoken worked strongly upon Meg's heart. She had never had a man speak to her in such a fashion before. She had always supposed that worship formed a great measure of love, that it was a spiritual devotion that drew a man and woman together. Instead, he spoke of adoring her temper when he should have said he despised her for it! She could hardly see him for the tears burning in her eyes. He was the complete opposite of everything she wanted in a husband, and yet why then was her heart longing to hear more? At the same time she was frightened out of her wits at what he meant to do next. Would he kiss her? Would he once more tear at her sensibilities by again accosting her lips? She desired nothing more, and yet her mind told her to beware.

When he dropped to the floor in front of her and in a gentle motion picked up her slippered feet, Meg almost screamed at what she knew would follow. She would go mad, she was sure of it, and she cried, "No, Worthen! Please do not! Please spare me this. Get up! Get up at once!" Tears began streaming down her cheeks as he looked up at her.

He said, "The next time Montford tells you he worships you, I want you to remember that I adore your feet of clay." And he placed a tender kiss on the top of each foot.

He stood up then and pulled her roughly off the settee and into his arms. Meg had little strength to resist him. He had worn her down, word by sensible, passionate, hated word. He drew her to him in a firm embrace and spoke harshly: "I love you, Meg, and I shan't rest until you tell me the same!"

He kissed her then, crushing her in his arms, his mouth a searing burn upon her lips.

A great pain welled up within Meg, rolling over her like a powerful ocean wave about to break. She gripped the hair at the nape of his neck, pulling it hard as she returned his kiss, her mouth pressed hard against his own. She felt his hands move from her waist to her hair as he ran his fingers into her curls. His kisses grew gentle, and after a moment, he kissed her upon the cheek, saying, "I won't deny that I need your dowry. But I need *you* far more. Love me, Meg."

The wave broke suddenly, crashing down upon Meg. She pushed away from him, a sob escaping her.

He let her go.

Meg ran up the stairs to her bedchamber and buried her face among the dozen embroidered pillows that covered the emerald green counterpane atop her bed. She cried until she could cry no more. Finally, she fell into a sound sleep, stirring only once when one of the maids covered her with a thick woollen blanket.

The next morning, Meg awoke to the sound of a lark outside her window. The sun shone brightly in a mosaic on the carpet upon her bedchamber floor. She squinted at the shaft of light as memories began drifting into her mind. She did not try to stop them, but let each one rush over her: Phillip teaching her how to waltz; Montford begging to call Worthen to account; the wild look in Worthen's eye when he had kissed her last night—and the feel of his lips through the silk stockings on her feet.

She groaned, her heart a misery within her. What manner of gentleman was he to so wreak havoc on her soul? If he hadn't kissed her feet—her clay feet, the members of her body that represented to him all of her faults—she would certainly have already sent a note round to Montford, begging him to take her away from Shropshire.

But Worthen had kissed her feet; he had told her in a thousand ways he loved her exactly as she was, that he worshipped her about as much as he worshipped the gravel path to Staplehope. Even Phillip had called her an angel, and Montford, well, he called her good, and she wasn't good. She had a temper of no mean order, she was spoiled, and she wanted her way no matter what!

Phillip, she now believed, had loved her without ever really knowing her, perhaps in the same way that she loved him without having the least comprehension that his prediction for cardplay indicated the soul of gamester. Perhaps he would have come about in time, but what if he had not? Meg knew she would have felt dreadfully cheated by such a flaw in her beloved's soul.

As for Montford, he loved her while ignoring who she really was.

And Worthen. She pressed a pillow over her head. Worthen loved her because of who she was, and the thought sent a wave of fear pounding into her brain. She was afraid of him, she realized, just as he had told her she was. She feared his ability to cut through her every thought and expose the secret places of her heart—the hidden longings about which no one knew.

Later that day, Meg received a note from Worthen saying that his brother had received word that his wife had entered her confinement. Blake felt it necessary to return to Oxfordshire at once and attend her. Worthen meant to escort him but would return by Tuesday, hopefully with news of a happy birth. He would be an uncle for the sixth time, and he delighted in few things more than seeing his niece and nephews. He was sorry to leave Meg at such a time, but he knew she would understand his going.

Meg read the note, seated in her red chair, and breathed a sigh of relief. She would not have to face him again for two days, enough time to sort through her thoughts and gain the composure she had lost since Worthen's untimely arrival a sennight earlier.

Perhaps then she would know what she ought to do and whether or not she should call upon Montford to spirit her away from Shropshire!

Chapter Fifteen

As Worthen aided his brother to descend the stairs, an arm held firmly about Geoffrey's waist, he spoke in a low voice: "So you see, I am caught in the worst predicament possible. At every turn, she wishes me to account for my words and actions. And you know quite well how little I relish doing so, ever! I don't think she respects me, even a little."

Planting his cane firmly next to his infirmed leg, Geoffrey eased himself down the next step. "She is quite a spirited female, Richard." He chuckled softly. "I can't imagine any other young lady taking you to task for ordering champagne."

"No," Worthen answered quietly. "The accepted order was for a female to bat her lashes, simper and exclaim. Meg does none of these things."

"Ah." Geoffrey nodded. "I wondered how long it would take you to grow weary of such affectations."

Worthen supported Geoffrey's arm as well and said, "I could never abide missish young ladies, as you very well know. But Meg's extraordinary indifference to my rank is rooted, I am sorry to say, in her low opinion of my worth."

"You did not advance your cause, brother dear, by agreeing to this wedding. Forcing the hand of such a female would be akin to whipping her!"

Worthen was astonished and cried, "Do you really think so? Have I erred so greatly?"

Geoffrey stayed his brother suddenly, leaning against the stairwell, his complexion pale. He winced slightly as he said, "Confound this hip of mine."

Worthen groaned slightly, and Geoffrey looked at him. "Do you still blame yourself? I had long since believed we'd settled that!" He then gave up the use of his cane entirely and let Worthen support him down the remainder of the stairs.

Worthen said, "It was my pistol ball that ruined your leg. Nothing, no amount of forgiveness on your part, can alter that irrefutable fact."

Geoffrey laughed lightly. "Well, I'm certain my own stubbornness, jealousy and otherwise childish behavior had nothing to do with our duel either, so you may have it as you wish: You are entirely to blame for ruining my entire existence."

Worthen could not help but laugh at this, but his laughter would always hold a hollow ring.

Mr. Crupps walked up to them and bowed. "Yer carriage is ready, m'lord, Mr. Blake."

Slowly, Geoffrey progressed down the hall toward the court where the horses were stamping their feet ready to be gone. His cane clumped heavily on the wood floor. Worthen said, "We were both a pair of cawkers, weren't we? Hot-at-hand. How did we permit things to come to such a pass?"

Geoffrey grunted in response. After a moment, he said, "And which of us do you think Caro would have chosen, had we not nearly killed one another? If you are not forgetting, my dear brother, I grazed your skull and ruined your coat, shirt and neckcloth with my efforts."

"Yes, I had a fierce headache for a fortnight afterward. As for Caroline, who will ever know? I was unable to even speak with her that first year. Besides, she was as devastated as either you or I were. Not only that, she changed so very much afterward; her flirtatious manners disappeared almost completely."

Geoffrey interjected, "And she started wearing her hair in careful braids instead of that wild manner she had of jumbling her locks atop her head and stuffing her curls with every manner of flower. There is only one thing that has bothered me about the whole affair. She could have stopped our duel with the merest lift of her finger, but she didn't. Why?"

Worthen shrugged. "She was full of mischief, just as we were. Perhaps she simply didn't believe we would actually try to kill one another off."

When they reached the coach, both Mr. Crupps and Worthen found it necessary to aid Geoffrey in ascending the coach steps. His short sojourn in Staplehope had taken something of a toll, and even though he professed his sincerest regrets that he could not remain for the wedding, Worthen detected in his manner a desire to return to his home where his servants knew instantly how to attend him.

When the steps had been let up and the door shut, the postillion gave the lead horse's flank a resounding whack, and the coach soon moved out of the yard. The hour was advancing quickly, and the soft hills surrounding the green valley glowed in the lingering sunshine. As the coach moved in a southerly direction, Staplehope appeared on the eastern slopes, a gracious Elizabethan mansion standing proudly against the hills. The beech trees beyond the hall shimmered with sunlight as the afternoon breeze swept down the valley and over the thick woodland.

Worthen regarded the house from the window of the coach. What the devil was he to do about Meg? He was passionately in love with her, with a woman who, in the core of her being, did not trust or respect him. Was there nothing he could do about that except continue to prove the quality of his love for her and hope that one day she would realize his worth?

Geoffrey noticed the direction of his gaze, and he

watched his brother thoughtfully for a moment. Finally, he said, "You are grown uncommonly proud, Richard. I have never noticed it until now. You refuse to defend yourself to Meg—the one thing she demands of you—but has it ever occurred to you that our society, as much as I revel in the relative comfort it has provided me, my family and the majority of my friends and acquaintances, lends little occasion for the demonstration of character? Afterall, Meg has only your word—and that against Montford—for the sort of man you are. I recommend you tell her why you refuse to accept Montford's challenges, and White's and the rest of their lot. She needs to have reason to believe in you, to esteem you. Why, for instance, could you not have simply said to her last night, 'Your father promised me he would tell you of my need for your dowry before you returned to Shropshire'?"

"It seemed so pointless, I tell you. She was determined to believe me at fault. I want her to believe in me without need for perpetual justification and action. A man's character should stand alone, without need of such supports."

Geoffrey glanced at the pink brick mansion and said, "If she is unable to esteem you and you are unwilling to humbly tell her what she wishes to hear, then perhaps you had best give her up."

Richard said, "I will never give her up! Besides, how can a man of honor speak what in his heart he does not believe?"

"Hmm," Geoffrey murmured. "Stubborn as well as proud. A dangerous combination, Richard. If you remember, we fought a duel built upon two such foundations."

"You cannot mean to compare my pursuit of Meg with a foolish duel you and I shared ten years ago?"

Geoffrey held his brother's gaze steadily. "I just did."

*   *   *

Two days later, Meg thought their little party, astride four handsome horses, cut a charming dash through the countryside. Lizzie's black, shiny hair streamed over a shocking, yet quite exquisite, habit of red velvet while Charles, outfitted in a subdued costume of blue riding coat and buff breeches, rode a feisty chestnut. Worthen, dressed in buckskins and a russet coat, sat upright, in full command of a glossy black stallion.

Her own bay mare, Bluebell, trotted skittishly beside the stallion, and Meg knew all the delight of having the wind tug at her red curls tucked precariously beneath her black riding hat. A fluffy white ostrich feather curled from the brim of her hat downward, touching her cheek. Her habit was of royal blue velvet, trimmed with black piping, and the long skirts hung gracefully to one side of the horse.

A curl slipped from beneath her hat to dangle to her shoulder, and Meg smiled. She might be facing a prolonged imprisonment within the walls of Worthen's country estate, but she would at least enjoy this outing which Charles had planned for them. Lord Montford to some degree had greatly eased her mind where her approaching nuptials were concerned. If for some reason she found it impossible to dissuade Worthen from the unwelcome union, she knew Montford would stand fast and would spirit her away from Staplehope before Sunday, before she was leg-shackled to a man toward whom she was ambivalent at best.

"I have been to this abandoned quarry but once!" Lizzie exclaimed. "Do you know what I heard only a sennight past that a naughty little boy slipped on the sheered slopes and nearly fell to his death. I was never more shocked!" She clasped a hand to her bosom and rolled her eyes, clearly delighting in the near catastrophe.

Charles spoke in a firm voice: "Well, I am certain nothing of that order shall befall any of us today. I shall see to it!"

Lizzie, who had cantered slightly ahead of him, looked back over her shoulder at Charles and cast him a dazzling smile. "How very gallant of you, Charles. But if you think for a moment I shall not walk the length of Devil's Path, you are greatly mistaken."

Charles' face took on a sudden glow as he kicked his horse's flanks and caught up with her. "I admire your spirit exceedingly, Miss Elizabeth Priestley. And I would not for a moment think of preventing you from enjoying such an adventure as this!"

Elizabeth smiled coyly and said, "When we are married, we shall make every day an adventure, you and I!"

Charles appeared slightly stunned by this rather broad hint that his proposals seemed to have become an accepted matter of course. He stammered, "I—that is—of course I should endeavor—it is only that we are hardly well-acquainted, not but what I don't find you a devilishly charming young lady—"

Lizzie reached a hand toward him and pressed his arm slightly. "Why, how sweet of you to make your intentions so very clear. Only yesterday my maid was saying that it had become generally known that we would be wed before summer drew to a close."

When Charles turned bright red, Lizzie giggled and again cantered away from him, calling over her shoulder, "You must accustom yourself to the notion, for I mean to marry you, Mr. Charles Burnell!"

Charles looked back at Meg, a somewhat befuddled smile on his face as he gave a slight shrug then raced after Lizzie.

Worthen, who had remained beside Meg, said, "Like a lamb to the slaughter. I don't like to mention it, but that boy's in the basket, or very shortly will be. She's no wife for him. He had by far better marry Hope Norbury and save himself a lifetime of misery."

Meg, who had been thinking something of a similar sort, could not bring herself to admit she actually agreed with Lord Worthen and, with a slight tilt of her head, responded, "I am certain Elizabeth would make Charles a very fine wife indeed. They are of a similar temperament, you see. They both have a love of adventure and daring. You see how lively she is, and as for Charles, he has long been known as a veritable fire-eater!"

Worthen gave a short bark of a laugh and said, "Don't try to bamboozle me, Miss Longville. I saw your look of shock and surprise when Lizzie said she meant to have him. And as for their similar enjoyment of adventure, I should hardly think such a preference a rational foundation for a marriage."

Meg could not keep from responding hotly, "And I suppose your notion of a sensible union would be for a gentleman to force an unwilling lady into a marriage she did not at all desire."

He held her gaze for a moment, his black eyes burning into her own. "You forget one thing, the gentleman has cause to believe the lady is not indifferent. Her *willing* lips have exposed the truth of her heart."

Meg felt a faint blush creep up her cheeks, and she could find no words to answer him.

He chuckled softly and leaned over to stroke her cheek lightly. "Come, let us at least cease our quarrelling until after this day's escapade, which, I might add, has begun to disturb me. What, for instance, is Devil's Path? You must admit it has something of an ominous ring."

Meg, who had had two days to review her entire association with Worthen, glanced up at him quickly, aware that his words held a familiar note of caution that did not entirely please her. She wished suddenly he had a little more spirit, like Lizzie, and she again felt the persistent nag of disappointment she often experienced when she confronted his character. She tried for a light tone as she said, "It is not so dangerous as it sounds. Why, I doubt you would even scuff your boots upon such a hike, if that is what you fear?" Even to her own ears, however, a biting quality had somehow invaded her words. She knew instantly Worthen had heard it as well, for he merely lifted a brow and inclined his head slightly to her. He then shifted his attention away from her, his eyes blazing, his chin mulish.

Meg now had every reason to dislike him, for besides proving yet again that he was more interested in his safety than in enjoying even the mildest of adventures, he was now positively sullen.

She tried to smile to herself, to feel pleased by the evidence before her, to convince herself again that she had every reason to despise Worthen, but she could not. As she glanced at him, she realized that some of her reasonings had grown quite hollow.

Well! She would not think on that and instead trained her eyes upon the spirited play between Charles and Lizzie. About a hundred yards ahead of her, she watched Elizabeth slap her riding crop playfully on Charles' arm, then again dash on ahead of him. She was leading him a merry chase.

Meg thought of Hope suddenly. She knew Hope had taken her advice to heart as she remembered how lovely she had appeared at the ball three days ago. But as she again heard Lizzie's laughter float back to her, she feared Hope had been too late in her efforts to recapture Charles' wandering affections. Who could possibly compete with Lizzie's flirtatious manners and brilliant smiles?

Meg flicked her reins lightly, and Bluebell responded by breaking into a canter. Worthen joined her, and very soon the party was again moving forward together.

The final approach to the quarry was over a grassy carttrack that topped a hill. It almost seemed as though once they reached the summit, the hill disappeared, falling sharply away to a darkened chasm below. The quarry, having been worked for centuries, was wide and deep, clumps of beech trees and shrubs knotted in various places about the rim of the quarry, all appearing ready at any moment to tumble over the edge. The rock was an exquisite, red sandstone that traversed many of the hills about Staplehope. The cliffs sloped but slightly and were tufted here and there with grass. From the top of the hill, Devil's Path began—a slow, narrow descent to the bottom of the quarry that could only be accomplished by foot.

The party dismounted, tethered their horses to nearby shrubs and trees and approached the path.

Meg cried, "Good heavens! It is much narrower than I remember!"

Lizzie, who had gathered up her red habit into one hand, instantly began the descent. "What nonsense, Meg! If it were one inch wider, why, it would not be the least fun at all."

Charles, who followed behind Lizzie immediately, cast Meg a challenging glance. "Henhearted, Meggie?"

"Of course not!" she cried, and began gathering up the long skirts of her own habit.

She was stayed by a hand upon her arm as Worthen held her back from the path and, with a frown, asked, "Do you think it at all wise, Margaret? You must use one hand the entire time merely to hold up your skirts. What if you tripped? You'd pitch headlong down the path or into the quarry itself!"

Meg sniggered. "You are being oversolicitous, besides not trusting in my or Charles' judgement. We were used to traverse this path a dozen times a summer when we were children."

"Several severe storms betwixt times could certainly have altered the condition of the path, you must agree with that."

Meg strained against his constricting, sensible advice and responded tartly, "I have always thought you were rather lacking in boldness, Lord Worthen. Now I am convinced of it. And how it is you have enough bottom to even sit a horse, I shall never know."

Worthen, again confronting her wretched opinions, gripped her arm severely and said, "Do be careful in your

217

judgements, my dear. You are grown quite headstrong and reckless. As for the courage I somehow glean from the pitiful makings of my own soul, let me tell you that I have a peculiar method for allaying most of my fears. Horses, for instance! The horses I choose to ride, you see, I am fully acquainted with. I have usually trained them myself, for one thing. For another, I know their limits as well as their hearts, and I never supercede either, for to do so would endanger either my life or the safety of the horse. Furthermore, I would no more think of mounting an unfamiliar, irritable beast than I would consider descending a path that looks both treacherous and steep and for which I am neither properly clothed nor equipped to achieve safely." He gestured to the path down which Charles and Lizzie had long since disappeared. "I shouldn't think of attempting such a descent without a rope at the very least! Of the moment, my only desire is to keep you from going, but I can see that you are set on it and would despise me forever were I to constrain you. Instead, you are most welcome to this adventure of yours. But if you come to grief, you cannot accuse me of having failed in my duty to at least try to protect the woman I love from harm."

Meg's cheeks were already flaming with fury as she turned abruptly on her heel. Too much of what he had said was strong sensible advice, and she could not be comfortable with what she realized was her own somewhat childish attitude. At the same time, her heart ached to have him prove, as gallantly as Charles was willing to do, his love for her.

She had just taken three steps when Lizzie's frantic cry pierced the air and a horrendous silence ensued.

"Oh, God, no!" Meg cried, aghast. Somewhere in her mind she expected Worthen to berate her for the stupidity of their proposed adventure. Instead, the viscount ran swiftly by her, his coat a quick, russet blur as he hugged the wall of the path and began descending to the chasm below.

Meg began picking her way carefully, following some distance behind. Her heart was beating wildly in her breast. She heard Charles' cry for help, but she heard nothing from Lizzie. What if Elizabeth had fallen from the path? Oh, dear God, she could be dead! No, she mustn't let her imagination run away with her. Slowly, steadily, she inched along the path, until she heard Worthen's voice. He was shouting at her.

"Stay where you are, Meg! The path is not reliable! You must listen carefully!"

The path turned sharply some two feet ahead of her, and Meg dropped to her knees, easing herself slowly toward the edge. It was then that she saw Worthen some fifteen feet below, where the path had snaked back and was directly beneath the spot upon which Meg knelt. He and Charles were bent over a heap of red velvet, and Meg pressed her hand to her mouth as she saw Lizzie's still form, her white face, her neck bent at an awkward angle.

"Is she alive?" Meg whispered and then repeated her question, for she realized Worthen couldn't possibly have heard her.

"Yes!" Worthen responded. "But you must be very careful. Return to the horses and ride to the nearest farm. Fetch a cart or some other conveyance. Lizzie is near to death. Hurry, Meg!"

Meg felt dizzy suddenly. She could not tear her gaze from Lizzie's lifeless face. She thought she might be sick. Had she really wanted to experience an adventure such as this? And why had it never occurred to her that someone could get hurt? What was it Worthen seemed to understand so clearly that she did not?

"Meg! Why do you hesitate?" Worthen shouted at her. "Go at once! *At once!*"

Meg finally shifted her gaze to Worthen's face, and as he came into focus, shouting at her again to fetch a cart, that Lizzie was still alive, Meg finally found the wherewithal to move away from the edge of the path and begin her ascent. She tripped once on the long flowing skirts of her train and remembered Worthen's warning. Had Lizzie tripped on her skirts, lost her footing and plunged over the side? She felt dizzy again and pressed her hand to her forehead, pausing for only a moment as she again clambered back up the path.

Once she was astride Bluebell, she struck her riding crop hard on the horse's flank and headed for a farm just north of the quarry. The journey seemed to take forever as she traversed the slopes of the hills, jumping small brooks and low rock walls. At last she arrived at the farm. Mr. Shaw, a stooped sheep farmer, immediately harnessed his horse to a cart and was soon rattling down the carttrack. Meg gave him directions to which the aged farmer clicked his tongue and began expostulating on the stupidity of anyone who would tempt fate by visiting an abandoned quarry.

"The rains—t'were five years back—" he said, as he rubbed a dark snuff on his yellowed gums, "done washed out half the path. Dinna ye hear about the boy what nearly died?"

"Too late, I'm afraid," Meg whispered, her heart sitting in her throat. "I must return to my friends. Come as quickly as you are able."

"Aye, missy, I will at that." He nodded as he slapped his reins hard upon the back of his plodding horse.

Meg raced ahead of the farmer, and by the time she returned to the abandoned quarry, the men had brought Elizabeth safely up the path. Charles was holding her cradled upon his lap. Worthen was just returning from a brook, his kerchief wet and dripping. His gaze was fixed upon Lizzie as he asked Meg whether or not she had secured a cart. She told him about Mr. Shaw, assuring him the man knew of their location and that he would be along shortly.

Worthen knelt beside Elizabeth and held the damp, cold cloth to the side of her head. "There is a knot forming here, but otherwise, she seems uninjured. I can find no broken bones. We must be grateful for that."

Meg approached him and asked, "Has she awakened—even for a moment—since I was gone?"

Charles looked up at her, his blue eyes brimming with tears, his brow drawn together in an expression of anguish. "No! I thought she was dead. I thought she was dead. I thought I'd killed her by letting her come on this foolish expedition."

"You didn't know. How could you have known the paths were badly damaged."

He said, "I should have known when I saw how narrow they'd become. But it wasn't just that. Lizzie was moving too quickly. She was practically running, and then her boot caught in her habit just as she was turning." He closed his eyes as though reliving the accident again in his mind. "I reached out for her, but she was just beyond my grasp and seemed to slip over the side. Oh, God, if the path had not turned back as it did, she would surely have fallen all the way to the bottom of the quarry. She would be dead." His voice was low and frightened. "What have I done?"

Lizzie stirred slightly in his arms, and they all waited in a tense silence for her eyes to flutter open. Nothing. Meg bit back her tears, her hand on her cheek.

Worthen, who turned the cloth over and kept it pressed tightly upon her head, addressed Charles: "You could not have prevented a spirited, heedless young lady like Miss Priestley from doing precisely what she wished to do." He glanced at Meg, his expression hard, his eyes trying to convey an unspoken message.

At that moment, the farmer arrived, a scowl on his face. But as he saw Lizzie, he shook his head and cried, "So it be her, eh? No wonder! She's more bottom than sense, that un!"

Meg was surprised that the man knew who Elizabeth was, and when he caught her gaze, he added, "I've watched her a dozen times ride across them hills, crammin' her horses and takin' every hedge and fence with inches to spare. I've thought a dozen times she'd be brought home on a hurdle, her neck broke."

Worthen interjected with no small degree of asperity, "You will do well, however, to keep your opinions to yourself, my good man. As for now, we have only one wish, to see Miss Priestley returned safely to her aunt!"

Both gentlemen relinquished their coats in order for Lizzie to lie comfortably upon the hard wood of the cart. Charles rode with her, still cradling her in his arms. She moaned several times, and once, her eyes fluttered open. She looked up into his face and said, "My beloved one!" then returned to lie quietly against his shoulder.

The journey to Norbury House seemed to take hours, though Meg rather thought they had been on the road for little more than one hour when they passed through the gates. Worthen had ridden on before the unhappy party, and the moment the cart entered the drive, half a dozen manservants ran to meet them. Lizzie's eyes again fluttered open, and Meg heard her cry, "Oh, dear, such a bother!" Her hand clung to Charles' lapel and could not be removed so that Charles was forced, not unwillingly, to carry her into the lodge himself.

The barest suspicion entered Meg's mind, but she dismissed it as ridiculous. Lizzie had suffered a severe bump on the head. She simply could not have recovered enough to have decided already to make use of her weakened state in order to bind Charles more securely to her. Or could she?

Meg followed Charles and the servants into the hall. Hope and Mrs. Norbury met them there. The latter wrung her hands a dozen times while Hope drew close to Meg, begging to know what had happened to poor Lizzie! Meg, Hope and Mrs. Norbury followed Charles up the stairs. Meg spoke in a quiet, subdued voice, informing them as best she could of how the accident had occurred.

When they reached Lizzie's bedchamber, Mrs. Norbury—who also could not pry Lizzie's fingers from about Charles' coat—instructed Charles to put her in bed just as she was. He then sat in a chair by the bed, leaning over

Lizzie, his expression boyishly distraught.

The ladies clustered about the bed, waiting, hoping that Lizzie would awaken at any moment. But she remained still, her face serene and beautiful, though quite pale. A maid appeared and drew the curtains together so that the chamber dimmed appreciably.

Silence reigned for a long time, until Mrs. Norbury leaned over to Meg and whispered, "I presume you tried to arouse her with your vinaigrette?"

Meg met Mrs. Norbury's eyes, feeling quite astonished. "No, I did not! I never carry my vinaigrette when I go out riding."

Within seconds, Mrs. Norbury was beside Lizzie, opposite Charles, and wafting her pungent vinaigrette beneath her niece's nose. Much to everyone's surprise, Lizzie began coughing and sneezing and batting the small silver box away from her. Only then did she release Charles' coat and said, "Oh, my goodness. What happened?" She pressed a hand to her brow. "Now I remember. I moved too quickly and was suddenly tumbling down the side of the path! I was never more frightened." She lay still for a moment and swallowed hard. "I feel as though I have been travelling in an ill-sprung coach for hours. I feel battered and bruised, and my head aches dreadfully."

Meg sat straighter in her chair and tilted her head slightly. She then let out a great breath, a huge sigh of relief. "Thank heaven you are all right, Elizabeth. We thought you had perished."

Hope stood up and moved to stand beside her mother. In a quiet voice, she added, "Yes, Lizzie. We were frightened out of our wits!"

Lizzie looked at each of them in turn, her gaze finally coming to rest upon Charles. Her expression softened, and she reached up to touch his face. She spoke dreamily: "And the last thing I remember was that you, my dearest, sweetest Charles, had just asked me to become your wife."

Chapter Sixteen

Once the doctor had given his pronouncement that aside from several interesting bruises as well as a nasty bump on the head, Miss Priestley would no doubt live to see her own grandchildren happily wed, Meg quit the bedchamber. She made a slow progress down the grand staircase, only vaguely aware that her costume was considerably bedraggled: Her ostrich feather hung limply beside her face, her velvet skirts were soiled where she had knelt on the treacherous path, and she had ripped the sleeve of her riding habit in all the mad rush of finding a cart for Lizzie. She felt intensely relieved that Elizabeth was safe.

When she had reached the bottom step, she stopped suddenly, a vivid memory assailing her, the vision of a russet coat rushing by her. She tilted her head and realized with a start that Lord Worthen, regardless of consideration for his own life and limb, had plunged down the track to rescue Elizabeth.

Pressing a hand to her cheek, she realized he had actually behaved in a heroic manner!

The thought bowled her over completely. A tingling raced from the top of her head to course over her in wave after wave of excitement. He wasn't cowardly then, as she had kept supposing. He was merely circumspect. He could behave as a gentleman ought to behave, when he wished to. Then, perhaps with a little guidance, he might become as chivalrous as Montford and then—

Her thoughts collapsed one upon the other. Whatever was she thinking? Could she then truly love him, were he to become the imaginary knight that had suddenly taken possession of her mind? In a daze she realized she could love him; she could give herself wholeheartedly to such a glowing vision. She must seek him out. She must find him and tell him that she was proud of how bravely he had acted on Lizzie's behalf. He must know that she esteemed his bold rescue of Elizabeth. But where was he?

After searching several of the principal receiving rooms of Norbury House, Meg found her betrothed seated on the terrace, staring blindly into a grove of walnut trees, his arms folded across his chest. A deep, intense frown creased his brow, and for the life of her, she could not imagine what had caused him to fall into a brown study. Well, she would soon put that to rights.

She approached him quietly, so much so that when she spoke his name, he jumped to his feet.

"You startled me, my dear!" he cried. "But do tell me at once—will she live?"

Meg remembered Lizzie's manner of clinging to Charles' lapel, and she said, "Oh, yes, she is perfectly well according to the good doctor, and from everything that I could see." She laughed shyly. "I have the worst suspicion that somewhere along the journey home, Elizabeth awoke fully but did not wish her improved condition generally known. I do not think she wished to disengage herself from Charles."

Worthen appeared visibly relieved. He turned away from her and walked slowly to the terrace, where he sank his head in his hands. "Thank God!"

Meg watched him, aware that he was suffering a terrible pang of conscience for having refused to make a push to aid the ladies in their descent down the path. She walked up to him and patted him gently on the shoulder. "You mustn't blame yourself, my lord." She spoke softly, her heart full of hope that he was at last becoming the sort of gentleman she could esteem. She wanted him to know how much she respected his impetuous act in rescuing Lizzie. She said as much, her fingers caressing his sleeve. "You were remarkably brave today, Lord Worthen. Any Lady of Quality would have been proud to have called you her betrothed on this day."

She then lowered her lashes and, in a whisper, said, "You may kiss me if you like. Consider it a lady's favor for a knight's extraordinary courage." Only as she lifted her face, in order to present him with his reward, did she realize that somehow, in some inexplicable manner, she had erred—gravely so.

He placed his hands upon her arms, but not to embrace her. His eyes were dark with anger as he gave her a single, hard shake. He spoke sarcastically: "And so I have won *Lady* Margaret's admiration at last! Well, how very gratifying, indeed! One of your acquaintance must nearly perish because of her own stupidity and foolhardiness, and because I do what any other man would have done in such a situation, you call me brave." He gestured wildly to the air with an upflung hand. "I am honored beyond words! Oh, Meg, did it ever occur to you that Charles could have perished because of Elizabeth? Not to mention the fact that I am particularly fond of my own existence and have the most peculiar dislike of having my life threatened because some pea-goose decides she will race headlong over a cliff! I would tell you precisely what I think you ought to do with this most gracious salute you have offered me, but even the most slatternly female residing in the East End of London would blush to hear the words spoken that rise now to the tip of my tongue. And so, if you don't mind, I shall leave your revered presence, *Lady* Margaret, and perhaps when my temper has cooled, we might converse again on this delightful subject—or perhaps never!" He did not wait for a response, but turned sharply on his heel and stalked away.

Not that Meg was even able to respond to his cutting diatribe. In fact, she was so stunned that she merely stood staring after his back as he disappeared into the morning room. The ostrich feather tickled her nose, and puffing air from her compressed lips, she blew the feather away from her face.

Hope Norbury waited in the shadows at the end of the hall, her heart beating strongly in her breast. She wanted to speak with Charles alone if she possibly could. As she watched the door to Lizzie's bedchamber, her knees trembled and her hands felt as cold as the morning frost. Her mother had already told her that she would be sitting with Elizabeth for the remainder of the afternoon. The doctor had long since quit the lodge which meant that as soon as Elizabeth fell asleep, Charles would emerge from the bedchamber.

Hope swallowed hard, clutching the soft green sarsanet fabric of her morning gown. She wore a dark green velvet ribbon about her throat, pinned with a pearl broach. Her hair swirled about her face, and she was grateful for her papa's insistence that she alter her mode of dressing her hair as well as the cut, color and style of her gowns. The truth was, she actually felt pretty. She knew she could never possibly hope to equal Lizzie's dash and sparkle, but within her soul, she knew that she would make Charles a far better wife than Lizzie could ever hope to.

The door to Elizabeth's bedchamber opened slowly. Hope waited, her fingers still wrapped tightly about the fabric of her skirts, until a figure emerged from the room.

It was Charles, and she let out a sigh of relief. Had her mama found her standing in the hallway, she would certainly have divined her purpose and sent her instantly to her own bedchamber. Mrs. Norbury did not approve in the least of machinations, and she had far rather perish than see her daughter stoop to using anything broaching

Lizzie's tricks and flirtations.

But Hope was desperate. She knew her cousin would go to any length to secure the object of her pursuit— including capturing Charles. She watched Charles stand thoughtfully for a moment in the hallway. She had seen how tightly Lizzie had clutched Charles' coat. Lizzie had somehow turned even a near-fatal accident into an opportunity to wheedle her way into his affections.

She waited for Charles to look up and see her standing at the far end of the hall, but he kept his head bowed. He was obviously quite distressed. When he neared the landing, Hope moved swiftly to intercept him before he began his descent down the stairs.

"Hope!" he cried, startled by her sudden appearance.

She caught his arm with one hand, and with the other she placed a finger upon her lips, silencing him.

Charles followed her lead easily as she led him back down the darkened hallway. Hope opened a door and nearly shoved him into a large, well-appointed library. All about the square, spacious chamber, handsome mahogany shelves and row upon row of leather-bound books stood solidly in the glow from the afternoon sun. At intervals, portraits of many of the Norbury ancestors had been placed to brood over the occupants of the room.

Once inside the room, Hope shut the door behind her and leaned against it for a moment. Her heart felt compressed within her. She had never done anything so bold before, and the very newness of her actions had nearly frightened her to death. She could hardly breathe.

Charles, who had been looking up at a portrait of a brown-eyed man who wore a long, curly, black wig, must have realized she was behaving oddly, for he turned back to her and said, "Why, Hope, what is it? You look quite distressed, my dear. Are you feeling well?" He rubbed a hand over his forehead and continued, "Of course, you mean to berate me for Lizzie's accident, and I can't blame you. I deserve such a dressing down. You need not spare me in the least!"

228

Hope cried, "Oh, Charles!" And though she thought her heart would burst because of her unmaidenly intentions, she followed her instincts anyway and threw herself upon him. She slipped an arm about his neck, quite awkwardly punching his cheek in the process.

He stumbled backward slightly, laughing at the abruptness of her embrace, and cried, "Hope! Whatever are you doing, silly chit! You ought not to be—"

She placed a kiss upon his lips, then kissed his cheek. "—doing this. *Oh, my love!*"

Whatever momentary inaction her surprise attack had caused Charles, he very soon recovered his wits and instantly clasped her in a crushing embrace. His lips were upon hers, warm and painfully hard. Hope sighed softly, the yearnings of her heart fulfilled in this moment. Her fears disappeared entirely as she gave full expression to her love, returning kiss for kiss.

After a time, she pulled away from him, though refusing to release her arm from about his neck, and said, "I love you, Mr. Burnell."

"Hope, my darling. I have loved you for so many years now; only why did I not discover how much until this very moment? I mean, I always knew I wished to make you my wife, but I don't think I realized how precious my love for you was, until—" He pulled away from her slightly, his face contorted with pain.

Hope refused to let him retreat further from her and held firmly to the nape of his neck, kissing him again tenderly upon the mouth. She said, "And I did not comprehend the depths to my regard for you, until I thought I had lost you!"

At these words, Charles gripped the soft hand that encircled his neck, and pressed it hard. "I love you to the point of madness, but I fear we are both too late! I have offered for Lizzie, shortly after the doctor left. Lizzie expected me to. Indeed, I have made a great cake of myself in pursuing her so avidly over the past sennight." He paused for a moment, leaning his forehead against her

229

own. When he began speaking again, his voice was low and anguished. "You see, it is my fault that Lizzie nearly died this afternoon."

Only then did he try to pull away from her, and Hope let him go. His face was drawn and pale, his blue coat and breeches soiled from riding in the back of the cart, his white neckcloth stained and his hair dishevelled. She wanted to run her hand through his hair, to tell him he ought not to pay heed to Lizzie, but she knew he must speak the words that had already shaped his decision to offer for her cousin.

He continued, "Why was I so careless of her safety? Hope, you were right to think me unsteady and unworthy of your hand in marriage."

"Charles, no! I was very wrong—"

He lifted a hand, cutting her off. "Don't you understand that I caused Lizzie's accident through my reckless unconcern for her safety? I should never have suggested we go to the quarry, but how could I know the paths had fallen into such decay! At any rate, Lizzie was moving far too fast. I begged her to slow down, but you know what she is—"

Hope interjected, "Yes, I do. The moment you tell her to sit, she will stand, and if you tell her the sun is shining, she will tell you 'tis the moon.' And I am certain that the moment you told her to take care of her steps, she undoubtedly picked up her skirts and began skipping down the path."

He looked at her over his shoulder, his expression slightly sheepish. "Well, you have the right of it. And though she wasn't skipping precisely, she did quicken her pace and caught her boot in the train of her habit."

Charles stopped in his recital, cocking his head and stretching out his hand as though he could see Lizzie again, just as she appeared shortly before the accident. He said, "It was like a horrifying dream. I reached out to grab her, but she just disappeared over the rim of the path—and—good God, she almost died." His shoulders slumped as he buried his face in his hands.

Hope felt brazen and unconscionable at what she meant to do next, but she could not simply permit Charles to succumb to her cousin's wiles. She spoke firmly: "But she did not die. She is lying in her bed, and if I do not miss my mark, she will be up and about by tomorrow morning, despite all of the doctor's warnings. Charles, don't you see that trying to curb an impetuous, thoughtless creature like Lizzie is like trying to stop the storms from advancing past the Welsh mountains. You must believe that!"

Charles lifted his face to look at her, his clear blue eyes despairing. The soft afternoon light streamed through the west windows, coloring his eyes with a bronze glow. He shook his head. "Whatever Lizzie's faults may be, they cannot exonerate me from my duty in this situation." He crossed to the windows that overlooked the walnut grove and stared out at the Shropshire countryside. "I have been foolish beyond permission. I have pursued Elizabeth openly and recklessly, and is there one of our neighbors who would not be scandalized were I to jilt her now? Lizzie so much as told me that the servants here expect us to marry before the summer is out."

Hope wanted to point out that the same general opinion had been held not a sennight earlier with regard to herself and Charles, but she held her peace. She realized he was responding more to his sense of guilt in the situation than to society's expectations of him. She knew arguing would prove fruitless; his sensibilities were too disordered from recent events.

Instead, she walked slowly to the window, where she stood slightly behind him and said, "Charles, I honor you for your noble intentions, and I can see that there is nothing more to be said. Will you not, then, grant me a kiss in farewell?"

He groaned slightly and turned to face her. He gathered her up gently in his arms and kissed her sweetly once upon the lips.

Hope smiled and clicked her tongue. "I am afraid, Mr. Burnell, that won't do at all." She held him tightly as she pressed her mouth upon his, gently beckoning him to return her kisses. Her efforts were well rewarded as he slipped his fingers into the short curls at the nape of her neck, kissing her hard, his arms imprisoning her about her waist. Finally, he pulled away, breathless and miserable.

"I am a fool!" he proclaimed as he set her roughly aside. Within seconds he had disappeared from the library.

Hope stood rooted to the floor, afraid that the various portraits of the Norbury ancestors which crowded the walls of the library would cry out against her for playing so fiercely upon Charles' passionate nature. But her predecessors were silent, and after a few minutes, she actually began to smile as she strolled from the room.

She realized she had not been so long in Lizzie's company without having learned something of use afterall.

When Charles reached the entrance hall, having run down the stairs, he nearly collided with Meg, who emerged at the same moment from the drawing room.

Meg stopped abruptly and cried, "Good gracious! Charles, what is the matter! What is amiss?" A sudden fear struck her. "Lizzie—?"

Charles lifted an impatient hand. "No, no, Elizabeth is doing quite well."

Meg breathed a sigh of relief. "Thank heavens. For a moment, the expression on your face—I thought—"

"Rest assured Lizzie shall survive us all!"

"I am greatly relieved!"

Charles walked to the bellpull and tugged sharply. "I should be happy to escort you home, Meg, if you so desire." He glanced up the stairs and in a low voice said, "I have much to tell you."

Meg, who was still bristling from Worthen's sharp words, responded, "And I, you!"

When their mounts had been brought round and they were trotting together through the lodge gates, Charles told Meg all that had transpired: first that he was now engaged to Lizzie and secondly that he had, at this most unfortuitous moment, come to realize the extent of his love for Hope, who had actually pushed him into the library and kissed him rather fiercely.

"Hope?" Meg cried, unable to conceive of her proper friend doing anything so daring.

Charles nodded as he led his horse around a large hole in the road. "Good God, this curst track is worse than ever! I only wonder that Norbury doesn't have it macadamized. It's devilishly hard to navigate even when it hasn't rained for a fortnight!"

Meg ignored his comments on the condition of the road and said, "I am sorry that matters progressed so quickly between you and Elizabeth before you had a chance to know your own heart. I think it mightily ironic, too, that both you and I are engaged to persons we do not, or cannot, love."

Charles looked over at her as he pressed his hat down upon his head. "What are we to do, Meggie? We are both bound by the codes of our society to marry, but what choices do we have, really? I cannot jilt Elizabeth, certainly not after the accident, and as for you, why, I daresay if you did run away from Shropshire, you might never see your father again, or Staplehope, not to mention all your London acquaintance."

"I should not hesitate to spurn society were I to truly love the man who would be the cause of such a separation."

Charles shook his head. "Pitching it a bit rum, Meg. You could no more part with your family and friends, than you could elope to Bristol without a half dozen bandboxes!"

Meg frowned at him. "You needn't be so cruel as to put me in mind of my only near-successful attempt at extricating myself from this marriage. Besides, it was all your fault for having brought that absurd racing curricule!"

Charles, who ordinarily would have delighted in continuing what no doubt would grow into a grand quarrel, merely shrugged. "I suppose it was my fault. Afterall, I know your penchant for every comfort imaginable. The fact is I should have brought a fourgon to cart all your indispensables."

"How's this?" Meg queried. "You don't mean to brangle with me?"

"No. What I wish to know is what Worthen said to you while I was, er, attending to Hope."

"Oh, Charles," she sighed. "I am sick to death of his perpetual derision of my love of honor and everything chivalrous. I told him he was brave, and in response he flew into the boughs, flung up his hand and shouted at me!" Bluebell sensed Meg's distress and began sidling toward the edge of the road, her ears twitching. "There, there, old girl," Meg said, addressing her horse with a click of her tongue. "I am sorry. Afterall, it is not your fault Lord Worthen is a beast!"

Meg was silent for a moment, then continued, "But the worst of it was, Charles, that for a brief moment, following Lizzie's rescue and Worthen's part in it, I had actually been drawn to the notion of becoming his wife. I was even prepared to make one or two allowances for his general reluctance to defend his honor. But you will not credit what he had the audacity to say to me! It was very bad; I cannot repeat it!" A fire burnt on each of her cheeks, partly from anger and partly from humiliation. He had rebuffed her advances in the worst ungentlemanly manner possible.

Charles appeared shocked. "Did he curse at you?"

"No, not precisely, though he gave every indication he wished to."

"But why? I don't understand."

Meg said, "I can hardly explain it to you myself, especially since I do not fully comprehend the workings

234

of his mind. Somehow he seemed to feel that he had not behaved at all in an extraordinary manner and that for me to extoll his bravery was absurd! But beyond this, he was particularly angry that Lizzie had endangered his own life because of her recklessness and without saying so accused me of the same fault. I know he blamed me in part because I had had every intention of following you both to the bottom of the quarry. You see, we had been arguing on just that subject when I heard Lizzie cry out. Worthen had positively refused to set foot on the path."

"Oh, I see. I had no idea he had been that determined against the descent."

Meg's heart grew very still for a moment as she asked, "Charles, are we as careless as Worthen seems to believe? Do we take unconscionable risks?"

Charles sighed. "I have been wondering the very same thing. This I will say, today's expedition may have been a mistake, but I know that you would never have been as reckless as Elizabeth. You've a bit more sense than she has."

"I don't know what to think anymore, but this I know, Worthen and I could never be of one mind. I detest him thoroughly! He is the most disagreeable man I have ever known! At least Montford stands with me; he has promised to help me if he can."

"What will you do, Meg?"

"I don't know, but I shall contrive something. I think I ought to confer with Lord Montford. He has always comprehended my diffidence where Worthen is concerned. I only wish I loved Montford. He said I had but to say the word and he would steal me away from Shropshire. He wishes to marry me, you see."

"I thought as much," Charles answered softly. "And I think it poor-spirited in you not to have tumbled violently in love with him. Why, you could have had a dozen children, and besides, you know that piece of property your mother left you would have rounded out his estates to perfection."

For some reason, Meg was startled by these words. "I

235

hadn't thought of that." By now they had reached the High Street and could give the horses their heads a little. The horses lengthened their strides, both willing to run. It felt good to be flying into the wind. The ostrich feather on Meg's hat snapped off suddenly, and she let it go. Before long, the gates of Staplehope Hall came into view, and Meg drew Bluebell to a trot.

As they progressed together up the drive, Meg frowned, a disquietude possessing her heart. It was something about Montford and her dowered lands. She remembered suddenly a time when she was a little girl. Her father had been involved in a roaring argument with the first Lord Montford. His son, the present Lord Montford, had attended his father on this occasion, and at the time he was but a young man about to enter Oxford. Meg shook her head realizing that sixteen years had passed since that day and her papa had never forgiven the first baron for his sharp, coarse words. Only now, however, did Meg remember the subject of that quarrel: Montford had wanted to purchase the very piece of property Charles had just mentioned to her. A wretched suspicion entered her brain, and she spoke aloud: "No, it could not possibly be!"

"What, m'dear?"

"Charles—that is, oh, I am certain it is nothing, merely the unfortunate workings of my over-vivid imagination." She refused to give utterance to the disloyal thought which had streaked through her mind. Instead, she flashed a mischievous smile to her long-time friend and said, "I shall race you to the stables, and the loser must purchase the winner a new riding crop!"

Of course she gave Bluebell a firm kick as she spoke, and before Charles was even aware that a wager was in progress, Meg was flying up the long drive.

When Charles left Meg, he had no desire whatsoever to return immediately to his home. Meg's conversation, so full of her own concerns, had had at least one temporary though soothing effect: For some twenty minutes he had not thought once about his own impending marriage.

Now, however, he was alone, astride his favorite horse, and a thousand unwelcome thoughts dashed madly about in his brain. Uppermost was the realization that had he been more circumspect with regard to Lizzie he would not now be engaged to her.

He huffed out a frustrated breath into the cool evening air, angry at his own stupidity for having been beguiled by Lizzie's mischievous, sparkling eyes and her practiced dalliance. Good God! How did a chit of nineteen summers gain so much experience in flirtation? The most wretched thought crossed his mind that when he did become leg-shackled to her, he might find keeping her in tow a difficult task indeed.

There was only one thing to do, of course. He must go to The Vine Inn and drain a tankard or two of Mr. Crupps' home-brewed ale. Suddenly, he realized he was both thirsty and hungry, and he rapped his riding crop across the chestnut's flank.

Once inside the inn, he ordered a tankard and drained it immediately. Just as he was about to order a second one, he heard a shout of laughter come from within the parlor and recognized Montford's voice.

A brilliant inspiration struck Charles. He turned to Mr. Crupps with a smile and said, "I'll have another, if you please, and something for Lord Montford, too—whatever he is of the moment imbibing. I have some rather happy news for him."

When he stood in the doorway, he saw Montford grouped about a small table with three other local bucks, enjoying a game of whist. Montford looked up and called out a contented greeting: "Well, my good man, you look like a cat who just got into the cream pot!"

Charles said, "Get rid of these rascals, Montford, for I am about to tell you how you may win your lady fair!"

Chapter Seventeen

On the following day, Meg sat upon the hard stone bench in the center of the yew-hedge maze, a strong wind whipping at her red curls even with the protective hedges surrounding her. Her head was bent over a small wooden lap desk. Her mind worked feverishly, for a final inspiration for the last chapter of her novel had struck her, and she could not scratch the words upon the paper before her quickly enough.

Thick ropes burned into Rosamund's delicate wrists. Her hands were bound painfully behind her. She was trapped within the confines of Fortunato's heinous town chariot, and the count leaned over her, his foul breath upon her innocent neck.

She was gowned exquisitely in a white satin wedding dress, orange blossoms laced through her blond hair which had been coiffed in a myriad of angel curls atop her head, cascading in wave upon wave of golden brilliance down the pearl-beaded back of her gown. Her tiny feet were encased in silver shoes with little wings across the toes and decorated in mother of pearl.

"At last, no one can prevent us from this marriage! Whitehaven is dead, and Vulcan awaits us at his palace atop Lemnos. Why do you tremble, my precious one?"

From the corner of her eyes, Rosamund could see the mole upon Fortunato's cheek, and her heart turned cold within her.

"I am not trembling," she responded bravely. "The earth trembles for this dreadful deed you are wreaking upon me. This poor coach trembles, Olympus trembles, but not I!"

He laughed low and mocking. "You will not think the deed so very dreadful in the morning, my dear."

Rosamund tried to maintain her composure, but the coach seemed so stuffy of a sudden. She couldn't breathe, her vision grew hazy, and as Fortunato's face moved nearer, she fell back against the squabs and fainted.

When she awoke, the swaying of the coach had ceased, and a voice which was dearer to her than any other she had ever known—save her dear mother's and father's of course—could be heard outside the coach. Only then did she realize that Fortunato was no longer beside her. She leaned forward eagerly, her heart beating rapidly. As she looked out the window, she saw a sight that thrilled her.

Whitehaven was not dead, but this very moment held a sword to Fortunato's throat.

Meg could go no further. Her wrist was cramping dreadfully, and her heart was exhausted from experiencing the sheer exhilaration her heroine had felt at being rescued by her beloved. She closed her eyes, savoring the moment, as the characters drifted slowly from her mind. The novel was almost complete, and she knew a sorrow that these characters would very soon be living out their lives encased in calfskin instead of residing prominently within her brain. She would miss them tremendously.

A voice broke the silence. "Dare I hope that your

expression reflects at least one meager thought of me?"

Meg opened her eyes abruptly, startled by the sudden presence of Lord Montford. A strong gust of wind swirled into the center of the maze, catching the ruffles about the hem of her light green muslin walking dress, and scurried away to topple the baron's beaver hat from his head.

Montford chased it, sporting an awkward figure as he clumsily reached for the hat several times, the wind delighting in rolling it over the gravel.

Meg giggled slightly and felt grateful that the stiffening breeze had saved her from what could only prove to be an awkward moment. She did not wish to explain to the baron either what she was thinking or why he was not in her thoughts. She hastily stuffed the several sheets of paper into her writing desk, covered the inkwell tightly and dropped the pen onto the papers.

Setting aside her desk as Montford dusted off his hat, Meg rose quickly and extended her hand to him. "How very agreeable it is to see you today, my lord. And how do you go on?"

He took her hand, but instead of merely shaking it and letting it go, he held it firmly within his own strong clasp. "I will not waste a moment of this precious time in exchanging pleasantries with you. I have come upon a mission of great import. I spoke with Charles, you see, and he told me—" The baron paused briefly, almost uncertain of what he ought to say. "He told me of the most unfortunate accident that befell Miss Priestley."

Meg leaned toward him slightly. "Oh, Montford, I was never more frightened when I saw the tumble of poor Lizzie's skirts on the path below mine. Her face was as white as death!"

"Had I been there," he said, his voice low and passionate, "I would have calmed your tremblings and fears. Would that I had been present to save you from the horror of that moment. My heart collapses within me at the very thought that you, too, might have perished upon such a dangerous expedition." He lifted her hand which he still held imprisoned within the circle of his own. He pulled her toward him, clutching their joined hands to his chest.

Meg did not hesitate to follow his lead and stepped toward him. These were words of comfort she longed to hear. His eyes were the clearest, most brilliant blue she had ever seen. He was a handsome gentleman, and his speech worked strongly upon her heart. Had only Worthen addressed her in such a manner, she was certain she would have swooned at his feet and begged him to elope with her on the instant.

Montford said, "Only tell me that you did indeed escape all harm. When Charles told me what had happened, my mind refused to believe you were safe."

"I was not hurt in the least, and now you may be easy."

He smiled as though she had poured a soothing balm over his soul. Breathing a deep sigh of relief, he shaded his head with his hat in hand and said, "You do not know the misery I have suffered for the past day. I was in the most dreadful state of apprehension, you've no idea! I would have come to you last night, but I knew that above all things you needed rest after such a difficult trial. Alas, had I only been there to support you at such an hour!"

He led her to the bench and begged her to sit down. He still held her hand pressed against him. Regarding her steadily, his eyes piercing her own, he said, "Only tell me what I can do for you, my dearest, sweetest Meg!"

Perhaps it was the breeze that afflicted her common sense, or it could very well have been the fading euphoria from having written a scene from her novel, or perhaps it was merely that Montford was so sympathetic, but whatever the case, Meg felt tears tremble upon her lashes as she responded, "Please, oh, please take me away from Lemnos—that is—Shropshire!"

"Meg," the baron breathed. "How long have I waited for you to speak such words to me. We shall go at once."

He leaned toward her in that moment, and Meg's heart began beating hard in her breast. She felt frightened by

241

what he meant to do, yet she remained where she was, her face turned up to him. He again breathed her name, then kissed her upon the lips.

The pressure of his mouth against her own lasted but a few seconds, and afterward, he quickly pulled her to her feet and said, "Come! We should go at once! I know precisely what we must do."

He took her arm and held it firmly about his own. Meg guided them both quickly from the maze, her thoughts in considerable disarray. She did not know what to think! His lips upon hers should have lit her entire world; instead, a chill had passed through her in that moment, a sensation that Fate had descended brutally upon her in a manner she did not comprehend in the least! And yet, it was just a kiss. Surely, she was imagining her response to him. Surely!

She stumbled and instantly felt his strong arm slip about her waist, supporting her. She knew a desire to run from him.

But what nonsense!

He said, "My dear, you are trembling."

Oh, why did he have to speak those words precisely? "I am not trembling. The earth trembles, Olympus perhaps, but not I!"

He said, "Well, I shall take you away from all your difficulties, and you will feel a great deal better in the morning, I assure you."

Meg looked up at him, startled, feeling as though Fate had just taken a club and struck her a hard blow upon her back. She felt breathless and scared.

By now, they had reached the exit to the maze, and instinctively, Meg turned toward the house: but Montford guided her toward the hill behind Staplehope and said, "No, no! My curricle is situated in a concealed place upon the carttrack up there. We shall be gone from this wretched place, and I daresay not a single person will see us leave!"

Meg, whose heart was now failing her, murmured,

242

"How very delightful."

Montford did not seem to hear her as he hurried her up the path, toward his waiting curricle. Meg now felt completely panicked. She wanted to bolt, to run as fast as she could away from Montford, yet at the same time she kept telling herself how silly her thoughts were. The baron was her friend of many years; they shared the same values and beliefs; he would never harm her. Like freezing snow upon tender fingertips, Meg remembered something Worthen had said to her not long ago: *Be careful that you do not mistake your man!* Why did she have to recall his words now!

When they reached the curricle, Meg knew she could not go through with the elopement. She forced him to stop and said, "I can't go with you, my lord." Meg looked up at him, her chest painfully tight, hoping he would understand.

An odd light passed through Montford's clear blue eyes, and he smiled suddenly. "Why, Meg, whatever do you mean—" he broke off. Laughing slightly, he continued, "You do not think—that is, you cannot possibly believe that I would—oh, my dear, I know that we talked about eloping, but I hope you don't mind very much if I spirit you away to my—my aunt's house in Lincolnshire. She will know far better what to do in this awkward situation than I. And as for an elopement, I think I've grown quite henhearted, for suddenly I cannot abide the notion."

Meg nearly fainted from relief as she leaned into his shoulder and said, "I knew I could rely upon you. Yes, let us repair at once to your aunt's house."

When the shadows began to lengthen, Lord Worthen mounted his horse and slowly made his way to Staplehope Hall. For a full day, since Lizzie's accident, he had been torn apart by the realization that he and Meg were from two different worlds—hers of her own creation, part fantasy, part genuine love of adventure. And he—his peculiar and horrendous dislike of most matters pertaining to chivalry—had set his views continually at odds with hers.

When she had approached him on the terrace, her face aglow with pride in his manly conduct, he knew that with but a few carefully chosen words he could have won her to him entirely. But his conscience could not permit him to let her believe, even for a second, that he approved or gloried in any aspect of the accident. And worse, for his temper had certainly conquered him in that moment, he had spoken cruelly to her, not from an honorable desire to instruct her, but simply because he was furious that she still thought so little of him and found his efforts in helping to rescue Lizzie almost a miraculous change in his otherwise cowardly behavior.

But beyond this, he had begun the process of concluding that perhaps Meg was right afterall—that a marriage between them could only be forever fraught with just such disagreements as this. He meant to visit her now, to suggest they end their engagement.

His heart weighed heavily within him, because for all their differences he loved her and always would.

When he finally arrived at Staplehope, he met a flustered Caroline in the entrance hall. Her purple silk skirts swished toward him, her brow puckered, her emerald eyes filled with concern. "I am glad you have come, Worthen. Sir William is not yet returned from an angling expedition, and I fear something is amiss. You see, no one has seen Meg for several hours. Charles arrived about a half hour ago and searched the grounds for her, but all he found was her writing desk in the center of the maze. I have such an uneasy feeling, you have no idea!"

Worthen spoke lightly, though a certain unhappy notion began bludgeoning the edges of his mind. Montford had been amazingly polite to him yesterday when he chanced upon him in the taproom. Afterward,

Mr. Crupps expressed a grave concern that some foul scheme was afoot. Montford and Charles, it seemed, had been deep in conference bandying Meg's name about at least a dozen times—and that within his hearing.

Crupps had said, "An' I don't like my lord Montford, an' I never will. There's a light in his eyes what bespeaks somethin' without a conscience, if ye see what I mean. He's not paid fer one whit of ale or food he's partaken of these two years and more!"

Worthen did not wish to alarm Caroline, and he spoke evenly: "Perhaps she merely went for a very long walk. You know she enjoys traversing the hills and countryside."

Caroline shook her head. "No, I don't think she's merely traipsing about her favorite paths. According to her abigail, she was dressed only in a morning gown and sandals. You know what the terrain about Staplehope is; she would have worn a sturdy pair of half-boots at the very least, not to mention a coarse gown to keep clinging bramble vines from pricking her skin. But where could she be?"

Worthen said, "Do not distress yourself. I'll find her. Only where is Charles now? I would like to speak with him."

"He's in the library." Worthen turned to head that direction when Caroline said, "And Richard, there's something peculiar about Charles this afternoon. I don't know what it is because, though he expressed a concern that Meg had been gone for such a long time, he's smiling too much." She laughed suddenly and added, "Do but listen to me! I sound quite addled. But I am worried. Meg always let me or the staff know where she was and when she meant to return."

Worthen walked quickly to the library and paused in the doorway. Charles stood by the window, the afternoon sun on his face as he stared at the hills behind the yew maze. He wore a blue riding coat, his neckcloth in neat folds, his shirtpoints pressed firmly against his cheeks.

He was reputed a fine, though hot-tempered, young gentleman, reliable, honest, and loyal. And he was smiling.

Worthen studied him carefully. He knew that Charles was great friends with Montford, and it suddenly occurred to him that Charles might have been the one who informed the baron of Meg's engagement. But whatever the case, he was not certain precisely how he was to persuade Charles to tell him where Meg had gone.

He entered the room, speaking in a light tone, "You seem rather content, Mr. Burnell."

Charles, who had not heard the viscount enter the chamber, started forward, an expression of shock on his face. He stammered his response: "I—that is, you have cause to wish me joy, of course. Elizabeth and I are to be married. I was just contemplating the happiness our union will afford me." He bowed slightly, a red flush covering his cheeks.

Worthen gave a crack of laughter and cried, "What flummery!" He was now convinced Charles and Montford had hatched some odious plot together. He knew he must progress warily if he was to gain Charles' confidence. Taking his snuffbox from his pocket, he slowly helped himself to a pinch and smiled in a friendly manner. "If you do actually wed Miss Priestley, I sincerely doubt that joy will be the uppermost emotion pervading your home. You might be surrounded with hysterics, or tantrums, but joy? You will have nothing of the sort with her as you very well know!"

Charles, whose temper was never far from him, fired up immediately, clenched his fists and took a step toward the viscount. "I say! You've no cause to speak in that manner about my betrothed! She is a fine young woman, though perhaps a trifle coltish at times. And once we are married, she will no doubt make a very agreeable wife!"

"More humbug," Worthen said, lifting a slightly bored brow. "But I wish you to know that my intention was not to insult either you or Miss Priestley. I was referring rather to her inability to make you happy. It is of course only my opinion, and I will retract it if you wish."

Charles, who for some time had been of a similar mind, threw up his hands in despair. "I'm sure it would be quite useless for me to try and persuade you otherwise."

Worthen seated himself in a wing chair facing Charles and said, "Yes, I think it would be, particularly when I can see by your expression that you quite agree with me. Good God, man, how did you let such a hoyden entrap you? Country work, m'boy!"

Charles, incurably honest, replied, "It all happened quite suddenly after the accident. Meg thinks Lizzie feigned part of her illness, long enough at least to declare to everyone in the sickroom that we were to be wed. What recourse does a man of honor have in such a circumstance? I was not guiltless! I had been dangling after her for days, sitting at her feet and reading poetry to her. I had already kissed her half a dozen times, and once her uncle came upon us in the walnut grove just as I was releasing Lizzie from a passionate embrace. Lord, I thought he'd run to get his blunderbuss and blow a hole through my head."

Worthen felt a growing impatience. If Montford had somehow convinced Meg that she was safe to elope with him, every second he delayed harnessing four prime bits of blood to his curricle drew Meg farther away from him. He wanted to interrupt Charles and ask him directly where Meg had gone, but he knew he must wait a little longer. Instead of leaping to his feet as he wished to, he laughed lightly at Charles' history of his encounter with Mr. Norbury. "You cannot mean to end your recital there," he said. "Pray, tell me what happened? What did Norbury say to you? Did he demand you marry her?"

"Lord no! In fact, he called me a green schoolboy to be so taken in by such tricks, and walked on his way. Lizzie pulled a face at his retreating back and told me to pay no heed to her contentious uncle. But by then—well, you know the sort of girl Elizabeth is! You get one kiss and damme if all you can think about is stealing another!"

Worthen threw back his head and laughed. "What a cawker, Mr. Burnell." When he saw that Charles was again bristling, he waved a hand and said, "I only laugh because I did something very similar in my salad days. Only, her name was Daphne." He slipped an elbow on the arm of his chair and set his chin in hand. "Can you imagine anyone by the name of Daphne not being irresistible? I had my poor parent in the worst stew over her. She was an eligible female—just as Lizzie is—but as heartless and ungovernable as a bad-tempered mule." He fell silent, his gaze landing suddenly upon Meg's lap desk which sat on the hearth next to his chair. He picked up the desk, frowning. Caroline had said that the desk had been left in the maze. Montford must have found her there, then took her away immediately. He opened the lid and glanced quickly over the brief passage. He was struck by the reference to a mole on one of the male character's cheeks, and he reached up absently to touch the mole on his right cheek. How many times during the season had he found Meg looking at his face—at his mole! A sensation of shock travelled over him. As though Charles were standing a great distance from him, Worthen heard Charles ask a question, but he could not quite make out the words.

Worthen's attention was riveted to the passage before him, and he now read it carefully. The mole, it seemed, belonged to a villainous creature by the name of Count Fortunato—an evil man who was apparently coercing a delicately nurtured female by the name of Rosamund into marrying him. The similarity, both in person and in circumstance, struck Worthen hard.

He let the wood lid drop suddenly, and he returned the lap desk to the hearth. Awareness, cold and painful, dawned on him. Meg had been scrutinizing him throughout the London Season in order to imbue the villain of her latest novel with his characteristics. And all

248

this time, he had believed that her intense expressions as she would observe him were the result of her love for him! Good God! He had been exceedingly vain, then, to have supposed she regarded him with great passion. Instead, he had been her literary inspiration for her latest villain! What a complete sapskull he had been. No wonder, then, that Meg had been trying so desperately to end their engagement.

Charles' voice intruded again. Worthen looked up, staring unseeingly at him for a long moment. Finally, he said, "I am sorry! I'm afraid I was caught by something Meg had written. What were you saying?"

"Whatever happened to her!" Charles cried.

"Who?"

"The irresistible Daphne?"

Worthen laughed suddenly. "Oh, yes. Well, she eloped with a dashing young lieutenant of the Horse Guards. She followed the drum, gave birth to eight children and is now as stout as the Regent himself. I saw her Christmas last. She seemed content enough, though her voice had grown quite shrill, no doubt from reprimanding her brood of halflings!" And with all the adroitness of a skilled boxer, he popped one over Charles' guard and asked, "And while we are discussing elopement, will you please tell me where Meg and Montford have gone? You see, I can't possibly let him have her."

Charles opened both his mouth and his eyes wide with surprise. He appeared ready to argue, color again suffusing his face. But Worthen cut him off, his tone firm: "None of your whiskers, now. The fact is Mr. Crupps told me you had been deep in conference with Montford yesterday. He had not meant to listen to your conversation except that Margaret's name had come up repeatedly. He doesn't trust Montford, you see. The good baron has not paid his shot at The Vine for over two years. At first, I thought little of such a meeting between the pair of you, until now, when I stood in the doorway and saw you smiling as though you were greatly pleased with yourself. Have you hatched a plot with Montford?"

Charles frowned deeply and turned away from Worthen. He clasped his hands behind his back, his neck stiff as he again regarded the beech-laden hills beyond the maze. "I felt I had no recourse but to aid Margaret. She was desperately unhappy. I am sorry if your own schemes have been overset, but I would do it all again. She does not wish to marry you—she never has!"

Silence fell heavily between them. Worthen stared at Charles' back, considering his next words carefully. He sensed that Charles would fight to the death to protect Margaret if necessary, and he felt a need to choose his attack with great skill. Finally, he said, "I know that Montford wishes to marry Meg, but I was never convinced, in all these months, she desired to wed him. If they have eloped—"

Charles turned back slightly and looked at Worthen over his shoulder, his shirtpoints biting into his cheek. "Lord Montford is a gentleman. He would not coerce Meg: he loves her far too well to use her so ill. But I will tell you this, he has not eloped with her. Granted, he has taken her away from Staplehope, but not to marry her. His intention is far nobler. He merely means to put her beyond your reach. And now you may call me to account for my part in aiding Margaret, but I should do it again if it were necessary."

Worthen regarded Charles intensely. "Why should I call you out for standing fast as Meg's good friend? Could you tell me at least where they have gone? I promise I will not pursue them unless I can persuade you to come with me."

Charles said, "What do you mean? Why do you think I would ever wish to betray Meg in such a fashion?"

Worthen rose to his feet and slipped his snuffbox back in his pocket. He said, "I am convinced Montford has helped Meg escape from me for no other reason than to wed her himself. I am convinced he means to have her at any cost."

Charles cried, "There you are out! I know precisely

where they've gone. Montford is taking her even now to his aunt's house in Lincolnshire. His only desire has been to prevent Meg, strictly as her friend, from being forced into a marriage she does not want."

Worthen moved to stand by the fireplace and said, "To my knowledge, Lord Montford has no relatives living in Lincolnshire. And as for his *aunt*, he hasn't one. Oh, he used to have one, but she perished of a cancerous growth some ten years past."

Charles turned fully now to face him, the sunshine streaming in the window and lighting his red hair with a gold blaze. He wavered on his feet slightly as though stunned. Narrowing his eyes, his face pale, he cried, "Do you know what you are saying? You are calling Montford a liar! What do you mean he has no relations in Lincolnshire? And how can you possibly know that?"

Worthen replied, "Some months past, Sir William realized that Montford's pursuit of his daughter had grown extremely particular. He believed Montford was trying to fix his interest with Meg. He told me that his former association with the first Lord Montford had prejudiced him against the family as a whole. As a man of honor, he felt it not entirely fair to the son that his own dislike for the father should be transferred so quickly. As a measure to prove the baron's character to himself, he had a former Bow Street Runner—who now operates privately—investigate the baron's family's history as well as his current financial obligations. The results were less than agreeable. Montford it seems had run through his inheritance more than two years prior and appeared to be living upon the expectation of marrying an heiress—Meg, as it happens."

Charles stood very still, his arms tense, his fists still clenched. He stared at Worthen, unseeing. "Are you telling me Montford's creditors actually told the Runner that his marriage to Margaret Longville would be forthcoming? You must be mistaken. The Runner must have erred somehow."

Worthen held Charles' gaze steadily. "Montford is a

251

true gamester and must marry soon before his creditors disassemble his estates!"

Charles squeezed his eyes shut. "Hope told me only the other day that he was a gamester, but I didn't believe it. Though now that I consider the matter, he was always winning or losing unthinkable amounts of the ready." He stopped for a moment, swallowing hard. "What have I done?" He began breathing quickly and spoke in a rasping voice: "So, what you are saying is that I aided a gamester and a liar to escort Meg to Lincolnshire, to an aunt who does not exist. Montford told me she would be safe; he said he would merely escort her there until such a time as you could be forced, 'as a gentleman,' to relinquish Meg's hand in marriage." He shook his head vigorously. "Worthen, do you think then that he's abducted her?"

"I'm afraid so," Worthen responded, his voice low. "You know him better than I. Tell me what you think. Where would he have taken her? To Gretna Green or to Bristol and on to Paris? To Dover then Paris? What is your opinion?"

Charles, who was overwhelmed by the news Worthen had just related to him, began pacing the floor by the window. His movements were hasty and broken. He was obviously deeply distressed. "I love Meg. She's like a beloved sister to me. We played at ducks and drakes together on the River Tun. Oh, dear God, first Lizzie and now this! I shall never, never forgive myself if he should—"

"Stubble it, man!" Worthen called to him sharply. "If we are to discover her in time, you must tell me what Montford means to do! Think!"

Charles waved a hand in front of his face as though trying to dispel the panic that pressed on his mind. He said, "Of course, of course. Montford." He swallowed hard. "I don't know. I haven't the faintest notion, except—I remember once, a long time ago, we were all at White's playing at whist. Montford made mention of disliking sea travel immensely. Perhaps he would then avoid any such elopement to Paris."

Worthen added quickly, "And if he needed her funds, he would not wish to leave England."

"A true gamester, I am thinking, would not want so much time, as a journey to Paris would afford, separating him from a newly acquired source of the ready. Gretna it must be! But Worthen, are you certain of your information?"

"Without question. But there is one more thing, a certain property the Montford's have always wanted—"

"Meg's dowered lands."

"Yes. Precisely. I think this was the reason he chose Meg as opposed to any other eligible female."

Charles disarranged his red locks by running a wild hand through his hair. He was still pacing the floor as he cried, "Why, I mentioned that to Meg only yesterday, and even she found the idea of her lands rounding out Montford's to be a rather prickly bit of news. I just didn't see it at the time."

Charles straightened his shoulders and began moving toward the door. "I have been acquainted for a long time with Montford. I still find a great deal of what you have told me difficult to credit. However, I know that Sir William holds Montford in dislike, and if these are the reasons, then I can comprehend his wish to prevent the baron from marrying Meg."

Worthen said, "Come with me, then. Help me find them."

Charles nodded and moved swiftly to the door. They fairly marched into the hall where they rang for the butler. Caroline appeared suddenly and, looking from one face to the other, cried, "What is it? What is the matter?"

Worthen glanced at Charles and then at Caroline. He wondered just how much he ought to tell her. The fact that she was breeding was now obvious, and he did not wish to upset her. On the other hand, he knew Caroline, that she was made of stern stuff and that she would want to be informed of precisely what was going forward.

Before the butler arrived, he explained briefly what he and Charles believed had happened.

Caroline listened, her face growing constricted as he spoke. When he had done, the butler appeared, and Worthen ordered their horses brought round.

Caroline did not hesitate to dismiss the butler, and the moment the long tails of the servant's coat disappeared from view, she drew close to Worthen and whispered, "But it cannot be true. Montford cannot be so very bad. We were once such good friends, and though I can claim only an acquaintance with him now, I cannot credit what you have told me! If he is indeed a gamester, if he has eloped with Meg when she is engaged to you, then he is without a conscience. Richard, do you know what this means? He might even have betrayed—" Caroline broke off, turning away from Worthen slightly, an expression of horror taking possession of her face. She pressed her hand to her mouth.

Worthen, startled by the sudden paling of her complexion, caught her arm and asked, "What is it, Caro? What is wrong? There is something more."

"Yes, that is, no!" She gave her head a toss. "It may be nothing, but the truth is, it has little bearing upon our current distress. Go quickly, find Meg and bring her home. Oh, Richard, do you really think he eloped with her?"

Worthen released her arm and began pulling on his gloves of york tan. "Yes," he answered simply. "I believe him capable of such a dishonorable act." He turned away abruptly and walked briskly to the front door. He continued, "We'll take care of everything. You needn't worry. We have cause to believe they're on the road to Gretna, in which case we shall find them!"

"Richard," she called to him softly, "you must bring her home tonight. All will be lost, otherwise!"

"Make no mistake, I shall have her back in Staplehope before dawn's light!"

Chapter Eighteen

Meg dozed fitfully, her arm cradling her head against the squabs of Montford's travelling chariot. She wished they would soon arrive in Lincolnshire. She had been too nervous in the early part of her journey to realize that her stomach was upset because of her habitual carriage sickness. But later, after she had become accustomed to the fateful step she had taken in leaving her home with the baron, she had grown increasingly nauseous. For the past hour and more, she had been on the verge of casting up her accounts, with nearly every jolt of the vehicle. Somehow, she had prevented anything so disastrous as that from occurring, but she wasn't certain how much longer she could endure it. In addition, the springs of the baron's coach were poorly sprung, and every muscle in her body ached unceasingly. She awoke with a start as the coach hit a deep hole in the road, the body of the vehicle lurched forward and the entire equipage came to a sudden halt. Meg drew in a sharp breath and nearly toppled to the floor of the coach as she slid forward from the erratic movement of the vehicle.

"Good heavens!" she cried, her mouth dry, her head aching. "Whatever is the matter? Oh, my it is so very dark. I am quite ill, my lord, and cold. How much longer do we have to travel until we reach your aunt's home? I trust we are nearly there. But what is wrong with your coach? Why are we not moving?"

Lord Montford spoke quietly, though a slight measure of irritation laced his words as he said, "I am sorry I have not been able to see to your many comforts as you have so reminded me for the past several hours. I wish I could tell you we were close to our destination, but alas, it would seem that my coach has been rendered useless by that last jarring plunge into a hole. Hell and damnation, this must be one of the worst roads in all of England."

"Sir!" Meg reproached him. "It is not my fault the roads are ill-maintained."

Montford glanced at her, his expression one of mild irritation as he opened the door to the coach. He ignored Meg and leaned out the doorway, calling to the postillion, "It is not the pole, is it?"

"Aye, sir. I'm afraid it is! There's a hamlet not two miles ahead. I'll just unharness one of these horses and be back before the cat could lick her ear."

"Yes, yes, quickly man!" Montford cried. "We must reach the bord—that is, we must be at my aunt's house very soon or she will wonder at our late arrival."

Meg leaned her head wearily against the window glass beside her. A strong fragrance filled the coach suddenly as a breeze swept through the open door. Montford's temper had grown increasingly thin, and several times, when they stopped to change horses, he would pace nervously about the yard as though a specter were about to appear.

"Heather!" Meg cried softly, the scent a pleasant caress to her senses. "Why, I don't recall so rich a bouquet since I was in Cumberland's Lake District some two years past."

Montford spoke quickly: "You will like my Aunt Henry! I always called her Henry, even though she despised it, or at least pretended to."

Meg turned to face Montford. The coach was very dark, though a faint light from the carriage lamps glowed dully upon the many prominent bridges of the baron's

256

features: his broad, handsome forehead, his nose, his strong chin. She sighed, wishing that her heart were not so indifferent to him. "You are very good, my lord, to be helping me in this selfless, chivalrous manner. I will be indebted to you forever!"

When they had first left the safe valley within which Staplehope was situated, Meg experienced an uneasiness bordering on panic. Twice she had told Montford she wished to return, but he sweetly patted her hand and told her not to be such a henhearted pea-goose and that with just a bit of pluck, she would be free forever from Worthen's clutches. His warm, friendly manner of speaking to her had calmed her fidgets immediately, and very soon she had been able to enjoy the passing scenery, that is until her carriage sickness claimed more and more of her attention.

Her nervousness again returned, however, when they stopped at the small village of Lilleshall, some twenty miles from Staplehope. Here, Meg was greatly surprised to find that his lordship had sent his own private travelling coach ahead for the somewhat lengthy journey to Lincolnshire. This blatant evidence of the fact that he had planned their journey brought forward all her former fears. How could he have been so certain that she would accompany him? She remembered asking him, "You were so much assured that I would agree to accompany you that you even sent your coach ahead to this village? I must admit that I am rather taken aback by your foresightedness."

He laughed lightly. "You will soon learn that I take infinite care when I choose to elope with a lady!"

Meg's heart froze within her. "But we are not—"

He laughed outright. "I am only teasing you but a little. Of course we are not eloping. But I shall put it to you this way. Charles told me you were desperate for help, and I merely took the liberty of seeing to our travelling arrangements just in case you needed my assistance. And you can see I was right to do so."

257

Meg felt very foolish. She was grateful, too, that he continued to reassure her as he did. Afterall, they were travelling alone, without even her maid in attendance, and if he were of a mind, he could abduct her. But that was utterly ridiculous, Meg realized as she looked upon his warm smile and congenial expression. He was her friend, and she was now at ease enough to admire his foresight.

Two hours later they had stopped to dine at another small village in what Montford told her was the county of Staffordshire. Once inside, however, with the door closed upon them, he dropped to his knees before her and begged her to marry him, to elope with him, if she would, to Gretna Green, now, this very instant!

Meg's eyes filled with tears at the sweet supplication in his face and in his words. He held her hands in his quite tenderly, pouring his heart out to her, expressing the full extent of his love. Meg wished, nay longed, to tell him she would be his wife, but her heart remained stubbornly aloof. She touched his cheek lightly with a gloved hand and, as gently as she could, refused his passionate plea to become his wife. He lowered his eyes quickly as he reached for the hand that touched his cheek. He pressed her hand against his face and then turned to place a warm kiss into the palm of her hand.

His voice was very low as he responded, "I promise you, Margaret, I shall never importune you again."

An awkward silence ensued as he rose to his feet and settled her into a chair by the fire. But very soon he had recovered his obviously wounded spirits and engaged her in conversation. Evening began to fall over the pretty countryside, rolling hills bearing an expanse of beech trees having given way to softer hills dotted with sheep. Outside the inn, a gaggle of geese trailed by the window, heading toward a large, shallow pond where their nests were concealed in a thatch of tall reeds. A honeysuckle vine covering the front of the hostelry sent a rich fragrance into the open windows. Meg felt peacefully dreamy, her stomach settling down nicely to enjoy a repast of turtle soup, slices of cold venison, pies of pigeon and kidney, fresh bread, jellies, creams and afterward a dish of raspberries. She felt relieved that all the struggles of the past fortnight were now behind her. A sole difficulty remained, that of reconciling her papa.

However, not half an hour after they resumed their journey eastward, the charming dinner began tossing uncomfortably about in Meg's stomach. A chill invaded her entire body, for though Montford covered her with his cloak, she still shivered—the raspberries refusing to settle kindly within her. Only by remaining very calm, taking deep breaths and trying to sleep as much as she could was Meg able to retain her composure. Mile after mile, she regulated her breathing and kept her nerves as steady as possible.

And now the pole was broken. Well, at least she could be at ease for a time until the coach was mended.

Meg sighed deeply and again leaned her head against the window glass. She stared out at the darkened countryside and noticed the faint outlines of a steeply rising tor. She frowned. Lincolnshire, to her knowledge, was a country of somewhat flat fenlands. She had no idea the landscape would contain such a dramatic sight as this. The moon appeared suddenly between sheets of clouds, and the countryside was bathed for a moment in a white glow. The tor towered above the road, and the smell of heather from the surrounding rocky countryside again assailed her nostrils. The fragrance jarred her memories.

Suddenly, she sat up very straight. The tor, the hills that marched to the foot of the tor, the rocks, and the heather all bespoke the Lake District. If she did not know better, she would swear she was in Cumberland, far north of Shropshire, and not so very far from the border with Scotland.

A wave of shock poured over her, of stunning awareness, of fright. She knew she was no more in the north midlands than she was in Dover! She looked sharply at Montford, who stared straight ahead, all the warmth from his expression gone, his jaw a solid, determined line.

He said, "I had hoped you would sleep for the remainder of the journey. I want no hysterics, which I deem unworthy of you anyway. By tomorrow you will be my wife, and I think to be Lady Montford would not be an unfortunate circumstance for any young woman. You will be a Peeress of the Realm."

Meg could scarcely believe what Montford was saying to her. She was in Cumberland, then, and he meant to elope to Gretna Green with her. She cried, "You are not serious. But what of all your protestations of friendship? What of your aunt?"

"She died some ten years ago." He smiled slightly and patted her arm. "She will not miss us at all."

Meg knew a strong desire to faint, but resisted the impulse. Rosamund of Albion might be able to enjoy such a luxury, but Meg knew, as she watched Montford, that she had best keep all of her wits about her. If Montford was capable of such treachery, then he was very likely capable of worse things yet!

Her heart beat loudly within her breast as she continued to watch him, trying to determine what she ought to do next. "You are a scoundrel!" she cried at last.

He said, "My dear, you simply must understand that I had no choice. I had determined a year ago that you would become my wife, and when this occasion presented itself—your need to escape from Worthen—what could I do but oblige you and accomplish my own desires at the same time?"

"Worthen even warned me, but I was so headstrong. Besides, in my own vanity, I was convinced I knew both of you to a fault, when I have known nothing of the sort. Fault, indeed! It would be more to the point to say that I have known you both to a misconception!"

"Come, come, m'dear," Montford said wearily. "Do not berate yourself. You are a good woman, with an uncommonly trusting soul."

"Yes," Meg agreed numbly. "Only why did I trust you and not Worthen? Of what value is such a virtue as trust if it is perpetually misplaced?"

Montford laughed. "I have always enjoyed your peculiar view of life, Miss Longville. As for Worthen, I have no great opinion of him. He is unfit to sport the name of gentleman. How many times have I called him everything short of a skulking coward, and he simply ignored me?" He clicked his tongue. "However, I must say there is a measure of satisfaction in having stolen the prize from him!"

Meg looked away from the baron, shocked by his manner of speech, by the evidence of his blackened heart. What irony, Meg thought, that he should speak of Worthen being unfit to be called a gentleman and all because the viscount refused to be goaded into a duel. Meg had judged both men's character on this point alone.

A chill passed through her, not of fear or of cold, but of self-knowledge that disturbed her more than being trapped in a broken carriage with her abductor. She had erred so greatly that not only was she facing the possibility of being married to a truly wicked man for the rest of her life, but she had left behind in Staplehope a gentleman who grew hourly more dear to her than she would ever have believed possible. Then she knew the truth about herself, a revelation that shook her soul to its depths: She was a fool. A silly, vain, fanciful, easily manipulated simpleton. And she had prided herself on her principles and beliefs when she was nothing, afterall, but a ridiculous compilation of her favorite poems, novels, and characters.

She spoke quietly: "How could you ever respect a woman who let herself to be stupidly beguiled into joining you for a supposed jaunt to Lincolnshire?"

He turned toward her, leaning his shoulder into the squabs. Chuckling softly, he reached a hand out to touch her arm and said, "I don't need to respect you, Margaret.

I have other various and sundry needs."

Meg jerked her arm away from him and glared at him. "My dowered lands, for instance?"

He pursed his lips as though he wished to give the matter some thought. After a time, he said, "Yes, of course. Your dowry, too, for I am considerably under the hatches as it were."

"Cur!" she spit beneath her breath.

"You ought to be grateful, my dear, that I am at least being candid with you."

Meg stared at him, shaking her head slightly, unable to credit her ears. "But you spoke so convincingly to me. I believed you loved me. Montford—" she broke off, laughing with utter bewilderment—"you were on your knees at the inn where we dined. I believed every word you spoke to me."

He leaned toward her slightly, a charming smile on his face, a captivating, boyish expression. "Ah, but there you are wrong about yourself. You see, I know my own abilities, and I can win the heart of a true simpleton. But I never touched yours, not for one moment, did I?"

Meg was startled by this question, but she realized it was true. "No. And I could never understand why. You see, I find your company charming, your intellect witty, your beliefs all that I could desire. You are handsome and dashing, and you possess a daring spirit. But not once did I feel as I did—with—" Meg broke off, tears suddenly filling her eyes. The worst, most painful revelation of all hit her with all the force of a sweeping, northerly wind. "With—"

"Worthen?" the good baron interjected helpfully.

Meg's voice caught on a sob. "How absurd, how utterly, miserably absurd! To learn at this late hour the nature of my sentiments! He even told me to be careful that I did not mistake my man! Oh, what a wretched fool I have been!"

"And you do not even know the half of it." He leaned closer to her, as though they were intimates of long-standing, exchanging daring secrets. "You cannot imagine what delight I take in seeing your heart wrung in this manner. To think I finally captured the prize your betrothed wanted—it is so poetic after a fashion, though it is a great curiosity to me that Worthen and I have a similar predilection for certain females. Caroline, for instance."

The conversation had taken so many abrupt turns that Meg was not surprised at this one. She remembered, too, how Worthen and Caroline had shared one or two secretive laughs from days gone by. Meg brushed away a tear that had rolled down her cheek as she said, "So you had an interest in Caroline as well. Somehow I am not surprised."

"Oh, yes," he said, the tone to his voice almost wistful. "I had hoped to make her my wife, you see, some ten years past, which makes the events of the past fortnight almost too amusingly ironic to endure. I have enjoyed myself immensely."

"But you did not win her."

"Alas. She seemed to feel toward me the way you do. I could not comprehend it then; I do not really understand it all now. Why don't you love me? I make love prettily, you've said as much. This is a mystery."

She wiped away another tear and cried, "I do not even have my reticule with me!"

He took pity on her and handed her his own kerchief. She took it, blowing her nose soundly. "Thank you," she said, sniffing several times. After a moment she frowned slightly and said, "I don't precisely know why I never tumbled in love with you, though I can hazard a guess, my lord. Perhaps you are lacking some essential goodness that however much your veneer commands both respect and, to some degree, friendship—"

"Oh, do let me finish!" he cried, his voice full of mockery. "You mean to say that though I am covered in a gleaming Town Bronze, the heart of a virtuous woman can discern the hardened soul beneath that outer armor." He then drew very close to her, his eyes blazing with anger. "Well, let me tell you what I really think. You are as pitiful as the rest of them, especially your father. All you really care about is lineage and breeding, and instinctively you despise the fact that my forebears made their fortune in trade. I am too newly arrived at my consequence to be worthy of either a Caroline Bradley or a Margaret Longville, families with a lineage that no doubt goes back to the Conqueror."

Meg was taken aback by his anger and would have immediately tried to convince him how wrong he was, but at that moment, the postillion returned driving a small cart and pony.

The moon had again disappeared, and the countryside was blanketed in dark shadows. The light had shone brightly upon her mind for a long, harsh moment, then it was gone. She wondered briefly if Whitehaven, that is, if Worthen was following after her, whether he would rescue her, whether he would even *want* to rescue her.

Meg pressed a sudden hand to her cheek. Why would he wish to help her when she had told him she valued his manliness so little? Her spirits fell even further. No one knew where she was or whither she had gone. She had no chance at all of being discovered, and if she was to keep from becoming Montford's hapless bride, then she must escape from him.

But how? She had no money in her possession, and any hostelry used to serving The Quality would scorn such a tale as she might tell them. A lady travelling alone, without a maid or a proper chaperone, would be suspect. How could she explain that a Peer of the Realm had actually abducted her from her own home?

As Meg clambered aboard the ancient cart, she was grateful to find that the cold night air did a great deal to keep her carriage sickness at bay. Unfortunately, however, she was squeezed between the postillion and the baron. Already, she could tell that his demeanor toward her had changed. He held her very tightly about the waist, ostensibly to keep her from tumbling over, and took every opportunity that presented itself to hug her. Meg held the kerchief to her mouth, feeling very ill, not so much from the jolting of the cart as Montford's heinous advances. She never thought she could dislike anyone so much, but when he leaned over and kissed her neck, she did not hesitate to slap him roundly across his face. He laughed softly, apparently not in the least disturbed by this harsh rebuff.

The wind blew hard over the moorish hills, and Montford's laughter died eerily away. He said, "What fun we shall have together, you and I. You may pretend to be a lady, but I know a great deal better. I know the fire that burns in you!"

Meg was about to call him a beast when she realized that for weeks now she had used such an epithet to refer to Worthen. Somehow, out of a newborn respect for Worthen, she was unable to call Montford by any such term. Instead, she sat very stiffly beside him, even though the cart jolted her about more ferociously than ever, and said, "I will never marry you, Montford. I would rather die first. You are not a gentleman."

Montford leaned close to her, his hot breath on her cheek. "And I suppose now you will tell me that Worthen is a man of honor for having arranged with your father to force you to marry him? What is the difference, Meg, if I steal you away to Gretna Green, or Worthen signs marriage settlements unbeknownst to you? What a hypocrite you have become!"

Meg could not answer him for a moment. "It is not uncommon for fathers to arrange marriages for their daughters. I have been singularly unladylike in not bowing to my papa's wishes. I am at fault."

"And Worthen is not?"

She remained silent until they reached the inn, refusing to let him goad her into any further discussion of Worthen. Once he had seated her in the very dirty parlor of an inn curiously named The Bell and Mermaid,

Meg breathed a sigh of relief. Even to be apart from him for a few minutes while he saw to their travelling arrangements was a profound relief. Montford meant to oversee the repair of his vehicle himself and to ascertain whether or not he could hire another carriage suitable for the remainder of the journey to Scotland.

While he was gone, an overworked serving girl brought Meg coffee and a loaf of stale bread. The cup was dirty, and Meg swallowed hard, her former sickness again assailing her. When the servant left, she pushed the tray away from her and rose to stand by the fire. Black smoke belched every now and then from the chimney and stung Meg's eyes. Of course they were watering anyway because she was cold and miserable, aware that she had committed the worst folly of her life in leaving Staplehope with Montford.

A fear began rising in her heart that she would be unable to extricate herself from this wretched predicament. In front of her, a brass stand containing a brush, bellows and a poker to make up the fire rested against the stone fireplace. If she had to, she would willingly defend her virtue with the poker. She shivered with fright, realizing that she had written dozens of scenes where her heroines had to suffer just such a plight as this. But never had she imagined the harsh emotions that must intrude upon an innocent lady's heart when she was trapped. Somehow, her novels seemed silly to her, now that she was facing a true villain of her own.

The door to the parlor creaked upon rusty hinges, and Meg turned to face Montford. He smiled somewhat contentedly as he stood for a moment in the doorway, his hands pressed against either doorjamb reminding her that she was his prisoner. She squared her shoulders and said, "I will never marry you, Montford, you may be assured of that. No matter what happens this evening or—or tomorrow, I shall never agree to wed you. I had rather live out my days in disgrace than be married to the likes of you."

"Such noble words!" Montford cried as he sauntered into the parlor. "But after tonight, I fancy you'll take quite readily to the notion of accepting my hand in marriage." His speech was slow, and Meg realized with a start that while he was gone, he had been partaking of the landlord's stock of liquid refreshment. He smiled broadly and began walking slowly toward her. He was obviously enjoying this moment.

"Our coach will not be ready until tomorrow morning, my dearest Meg. You and I will simply have to make the best of it. I was at first distressed, as you may very well imagine, but then I realized we could be quite content in this tidy little inn—"

In a cold voice, Meg interjected, "The fireplace smokes, as I am certain do all the rest of the chimneys in this wretched place, the bread is stale, and no doubt we will be bit thoroughly the entire night through by bugs in our bedchambers! Oh, yes, a tidy little inn, indeed!"

Montford shook his head. "I will not permit you to cast aspersions upon this charming love-nest." He gestured about him, smiling more broadly still. "The truth is, you cannot imagine how long I have waited to take you in my arms. You are quite a bewitching creature, you know—so innocent! And yet do you know how often I have seen your eyes sparkle with passion. I am very much in love with you, Meg, despite the sordid nature of this elopement."

"If you love me, then let me go."

He chuckled softly. "Never," he said in response to her plea, advancing slowly toward her, a devilish light in his piercing blue eyes.

Meg reached behind her and grasped a thick handle. Her heart was sounding loudly in her ears. Montford was nearly upon her, and it was all she could do to keep from bolting in panic. She knew she would be lost if she tried to run from him. She had but one real chance to save herself—by striking the baron hard on the very first attempt and rendering him unconscious. She felt dizzy,

267

her heart pounding against her ribs.

"How very brave of you," he said, "to stand so firm and straight against my advances."

He was upon her now, and just as he slipped his arms about her, she pulled the object from behind her and struck the baron forcefully—a hard blow to the side of the head.

Unfortunately, she had removed not the poker, but the hearth brush, the bristles glancing off the baron's ear. Montford gave a shout of surprise, and when he realized he had been hit with a small broom, he laughed aloud, rubbing his ear, the short bristles having stung him.

Meg held the brush out before her and blinked several times.

"Why!" she cried, addressing the traitorous brush. "Why could you not have been the poker, you ridiculous thing! Must it only be in novels that the heroine can remove the proper implement from a stand by the hearth?"

Montford ceased laughing abruptly and moved to sweep his arm about her waist. Meg continued to strike him with the broom, but he laughed at her, finally catching her arm in his and twisting her wrist until she dropped her weapon.

"You should not have tried to fight me, Margaret. It only increases my desires to possess you."

"I never knew you! How could I have called you friend! I—"

He cut her off, pressing his mouth hard against her lips.

Meg felt her former sickness return to her again as tears began trailing down her cheeks. She struggled against him, pushing hard against his chest. But Montford was a strong man, a hardened Corinthian, and her efforts failed miserably. His kisses grew increasingly demanding, bruising her lips painfully.

When he drew back for the barest second, she found herself short of breath and cried, "Montford, desist at

268

once or I vow I shall be violently ill!"

He merely laughed in response and continued his assault upon her person, pushing her against the stones of the fireplace. This was a happy circumstance for Meg because she realized she was still standing in the same place and the poker was yet behind her. She felt the brass stand pressed against her legs. How careless Montford had been in keeping her so close to the hearth. She reached behind her, but this time she felt carefully for the poker. It would not do at all to try to hurt Montford by striking him with the cumbersome, rounded bellows.

When she felt the thin rod of the poker, she carefully brought it high over head and, with great difficulty, crashed it over Montford's skull.

The baron did not drop unconscious to the floor. Instead, his knees buckled slightly as he held a hand to his head. Immediately, the smooth planks beneath his feet were dotted with drops of blood. A swift-flowing rivulet poured through his fingers, down his ear and face and spread in a growing stain onto his white neckcloth. He groaned, stumbling backward, and fell into a chair by the table. "Damn!" he muttered. "You murderous witch! You shall pay dearly for this!"

Meg, who had taken a step toward him, regretting that she had struck him so forcefully, now gasped at his horrendous words and ran from the parlor. She moved blindly out the back of the inn, rushing toward the stables. Her one thought was to secure a horse and ride away from Montford and the seedy Bell and Mermaid.

She heard him call to her from inside the inn. She found the stables lit by a lantern where a single stableboy was carefully grooming the post horses. When he caught sight of her, his eyes nearly popped from his head.

"Quickly!" she cried, in a low commanding voice. "You must saddle a horse for me. Please. I must escape from here at once. At once!"

"Margaret!" Montford's voice reached her from the stable yard.

"Please!" Meg pleaded as she stepped toward the boy. He was staring hard at her, clearly confused as to what he ought to do. She cried, "I must have a horse!" But the stableboy remained standing where he was as though frozen by the mere sight of her.

She pleaded yet again, and just as the boy started forward, moved by the urgency in her demeanor, Montford stumbled into the stables. He caught Meg easily, laughing, one side of his face streaked with blood.

"Vixen! Yet, what great delight you are proving to be." At that moment he saw the stableboy, and with a lift of his brow, he cried, "Get out at once, you mealy-mouthed whelp!" He hefted a leather harness from a peg on the wall and slapped it against his leg, his expression sneering.

The boy glanced wildly from Montford to the harness the baron held in his hand. He inched away from both of them, finally turning to spring from the stables.

Montford threw the harness into the hay and slowly turned Meg within the circle of his arms to face him.

"Leave me alone, Montford. I'll ruin you, I promise you that. Let me be!"

He merely laughed very low, his hands pinning her waist. His head was still bleeding sluggishly, and Meg realized he must be very foxed indeed to be accosting her when his wound required attendance.

Suddenly, Meg felt all the fight drain from her as she surrendered to the inevitable. Her legs no longer supported her. Montford held her in his arms, his face a blur over her own, and yet without warning, he pulled away from her, causing her to stumble slightly and fall to her knees. She sank to the stable floor, sitting on the hay, and buried her face in one hand. She was about to negotiate with him, to offer him money for her release, when she realized they were not alone.

A familiar and most welcome voice asked, "Meg, are you injured?"

Meg turned sharply and saw Worthen standing over

Montford, who was lying on the hay and groaning slightly. The viscount stood rigidly still, looking at her and waiting for her answer, but remained purposely beside Montford.

She was stunned, for it had seemed so unlikely that he could have either learned of the abduction in time to be of assistance to her or followed in her wake! But he had managed it somehow, and never had she been happier to see him. Her eyes filled with tears as she cried, "I cannot believe you found me. Oh, thank God you've come, my lord! I was lost. He meant to—to—"

Worthen hesitated only for a moment, then went to her immediately, pulling her to her feet and gathering her up in his arms. "Meg, oh, my darling, my darling—"

Meg held him very tight, burrowing her head into his shoulder, his coat cold and damp against her cheek. "I was lost!"

Behind Worthen, another voice cried, "Get up, you miserable cur! Get up, I say!"

Meg drew away from Worthen and saw Charles standing over Montford, his hands on his hips, his expression outraged. He barely controlled his temper, his hands clenched into tight fists as he cried, "Stand up, you drunken lout!"

Montford rolled on his side and groaned but did not rise to his feet. He stared up at Charles, squeezing his eyes shut for a long moment. He said, "I didn't mean anything by it. I meant only to keep her here until Worthen could be forced to relinquish her. You must believe me, Burnell! I would never harm Meg. You know that I love her. You must know that!"

Margaret could not credit what she was hearing, and she cried aloud, "You despicable cretin! After you accosted me so brutally, to lie there and actually speak such falsehoods. I have never despised anyone so much as you!" At this point, she knew she was hysterical as she broke into a sob.

Worthen placed a firm arm about her shoulders and

said, "Gently, my dear. Let us get over this rough ground as lightly as possible."

Montford rose slowly to his feet, slapping hay from his coat and breeches. He swayed on his feet as he said, "I don't know why she is telling you such a whisker." He stumbled slightly and touched the wound on his head.

Charles started forward as though he meant to plant Montford a facer, but Worthen cried, "Come, Charles, that will settle nothing. Let us repair at once to the parlor and tend to Meg. Now!"

Margaret was startled by the urgency in Worthen's voice. She glanced up at him, astonished. His face was marked by a familiar determination, and though he spoke of wanting Charles to attend to her, she knew his purposes were quite different. Yet she could not comprehend what he meant to accomplish by diverting Charles from his path.

Charles' voice intruded on her thoughts as he continued to address Montford: "And tell me, my lord, do you have an aunt residing in Lincolnshire? Answer me that?"

"I—that is—"

"No, he does not," Meg interjected harshly. "He lied to you and to me. His aunt has been deceased for years now." She felt Worthen tighten his grip about her waist as though he meant to warn her, but she was far too angry with the baron to remain still and silent. She wanted him punished, severely so, for his unkindnesses to her, for his treachery. "This man," she added, her voice full of scorn, "is both a liar and a gamester. He meant to take me to Gretna Green, to force me to marry him!"

Montford looked at Meg and smiled. He spoke cryptically: "I suppose one way or another you will afford me pleasure, Margaret!"

"What do you mean? I will not marry you now if that is what you are hinting at!"

Montford laughed lightly as he gestured in his habitual stately manner to both men present. "These gentlemen," he said, a congenial smile on his face, "know precisely what I mean."

Meg glanced up at Worthen, whose expression had become stoney in appearance, his dark eyes, in the yellow light of the lantern, cloaked and hard.

Meg still was not certain what Montford meant until she turned toward Charles and saw that he was very pale. His aggressive stance had not altered since his arrival in the stable. He had all the appearance of a fierce animal ready to engage in battle.

All at once, Meg understood Worthen's warning and Montford's hints. Charles meant to call him out. Margaret opened her eyes wide with horror, a stunning awareness striking her that if Charles were to engage in a duel, in all likelihood he would perish. He was no match for Montford.

She opened her mouth to speak, to prevent matters from progressing so far, but Charles' voice preceded her. "You'll not go unpunished for this night's work."

"Burnell!" Worthen called to him sharply. "Do not commit this folly!"

Charles turned toward Worthen and bowed to him slightly. "I honor you for the vow you have taken; but I took no such vow, and I will have satisfaction in this situation." He turned back to Montford. "You are an insult to your rank and to the privileges your forbears in their industry and ambition conferred upon you. You have but to name your seconds." And because he was angry beyond words at having been both a dupe as well as having endangered Meg's life, he tore the glove from his hand and flung it at Montford's feet.

Meg saw the glove of York tan lying crumpled in front of the baron's dusty black boots. One of the horses blew and stamped his hooves. Worthen released her to stand beside Charles, and the gentlemen began immediately establishing the form for the encounter. Worthen would act as Charles' second, and Montford said his dear friend, Mr. White, was due to arrive tomorrow at Staplehope and would no doubt be pleased to act as his second.

These words registered but slightly in Meg's brain. Her hearing had grown quite dull as she continued to stare at Charles' glove. It looked so vulnerable lying there in front of Montford's hard leather boot, hay and other stable debris a poor background for her dear friend's gauntlet.

She looked up at Charles, who stood very erect, a man of honor. He was clearly several inches shorter than either man present, but in this moment he appeared manly and true, a brave gentleman, the very thing Meg had been demanding all this time of Worthen. She looked at Worthen, who wore an expression of intense concentration on his face. He, too, stared at the glove on the ground. She realized he had tried to warn her, that with a little effort a duel could be avoided.

Meg felt a chill surround her. Charles had just committed himself to a duel with one of the best shots in England. She tilted her head, a new realization dawning upon her, a knowledge she shared with hundreds of women who abhorred the practice of duelling: She could lose her dearest, most beloved Charles to a stupid pistol ball. Not that Charles wasn't an excellent marksman, but for all his dash and fire, somehow he'd managed only one duel in his long career and that a farce with a friend that ended in the pair of them adjourning to a nearby tavern and getting completely foxed.

She tilted her head again, glancing from one face to the next, at the gentlemen who were now deeply involved in settling this matter honorably. She knew precisely how it would end, too. Charles would be buried because of this night's work. Charles would die because she had foolishly subscribed to a set of beliefs that every sensible woman in Mayfair denounced. She, and she alone, had created this horrible affair. If Charles died, she would be responsible for his death, no one else.

Chapter Nineteen

When Worthen escorted Meg back to the parlor, Montford retired to a private chamber on the first floor of the inn. Charles, upon the viscount's request, remained in the taproom while Worthen settled Meg beside the dirty, smoking fireplace and chafed her cold hands.

Meg looked at him, wanting him to speak to her, to take her to task for her stupidity so that at last she might agree with him and prove how greatly her opinions had changed, indeed how they had been in the process of changing over the past fortnight. But he would not look up at her. He seemed completely buried in his thoughts, and Meg had the worst sensation that he was searching for a way of telling her something dreadful. Lines of fatigue were creased about his dark eyes, and she resisted the impulse to reach out to him, to touch his face and kiss him. She loved him so much, she realized, but a cold fear had entered her heart. He was too silent for her to be comfortable, especially since his habitual mode when he was displeased with her was to rant and rave at her follies.

If only, Meg thought with great irony, he would fly into a passion. She could tolerate his anger: instead his gravity tore at her heart, leaving her bereft of words.

At last she could bear his silence no longer, and she said, "I fear I may have lost your regard forever, my lord. Only just a few minutes ago, when I finally saw Charles' glove lying upon the soiled hay, did I truly comprehend all that you have been trying to tell me these past several days."

He looked up at her hopeful, yet distant. "But you expected me to call him out, to face Montford in a duel in order to avenge your honor, did you not?"

"Worthen, I—"

He silenced her by placing a finger upon her lips. "You don't need to say anything. I am well-versed in your sentiments. Since yesterday, as it happens, I have been giving your request to release you from this engagement a great deal of thought, and I have concluded that you are right—we should not wed, we are indeed ill-suited." He released her hands then and rose to his feet to move to the small, filmy windows of the parlor. For some reason he could not resist swiping a hand across the window and looking at his soiled glove. In disgust, he cried, "Good God! Could not Montford have done better than this? I have never seen a worse rat-trap in my entire existence!"

Meg remained sitting where she was, her gaze fixed to a dark red spot on the floor. She realized suddenly that she was staring at a droplet of Montford's blood, and her head began to reel. She could not believe that she was ready to part with her beliefs at the very moment when Worthen had just ended their engagement.

She spoke quietly, unwilling to look at him: "Would it make a difference to you, my lord, were I to tell you that my affections have undergone such a change as to make me desirous of—of becoming your wife?"

He did not answer her at once. She could not know what he was thinking, and when he did not speak, she turned toward him and found his head was lowered, his aspect somber. "You speak," he said at last, "because you feel you owe me some reward for rescuing you. But what you do not seem to realize is that I am equally to blame in this despicable situation. I provoked you—in a hundred different ways—to flight." He turned toward her and said, "You owe me nothing, Margaret, on that score, so you needn't pretend that your heart has undergone such an abrupt change." He smiled faintly. "I do, however, appreciate the gesture."

"But it is not a mere gesture on my part, I assure you."

"Meg," he said, the smile disappearing from his face entirely. "I had an opportunity before I left Staplehope of stealing a glance at your latest novel. I understand now, how much I have erred almost from the beginning."

"You know then that I write ridiculous novels of love and adventure?" Her throat felt constricted as she spoke. "I suppose Papa informed you of my identity?"

"Yes, he did. But you are grievously mistaken if you think your stories are ridiculous. They are delightful, at times enchanting, amusing and frequently flawed but never ridiculous. I read all three of them, and the last I had just finished on the night you and Charles arrived at The Vine, brangling and clawing at one another. But when I referred to your latest novel, Meg, I meant your fourth novel."

Meg rose quickly to her feet, her hand flying to her cheek. "Oh, no!" she cried. "Then you have discovered the extent to my foolishness!"

He moved toward her, the quietness in his demeanor disturbing her infinitely more than all of his former angry outbursts. Each step he took as he advanced on her bespoke a finality and a separation she did not want to see. He asked, "Do you remember several weeks ago, at Mrs. Norbury's musicale, when I first proposed to you? I was so astonished when you refused me, because I had believed you were in love with me. Instead, I now understand that you had been merely memorizing my features and flaws for your latest novel. Do I have the right of it?"

"Yes, but you don't understand."

He was with her now, his hands holding her arms gently. She did not want his gentleness in this moment; she wanted him to hold her roughly as he was wont to. She wanted him to kiss her again as was his habit.

Instead, he looked sorrowful, yet as stubborn as ever. Only now, his wretched determination was set against their marriage.

He said, "But I do understand, only too well. I release you, Meg." He stepped away from her, and in a different tone of voice, one of business, he said, "In little more than an hour, a post-chaise will arrive to escort you back to Staplehope. I have hired a serving girl to accompany you on the return journey, and for your sake, Charles and I mean to return tomorrow at a separate time. I wish it were possible for you to remain here, to rest tonight, but I am certain you understand how important it is for you to be ensconced in Staplehope by morning's light. Caroline will be waiting for you."

Meg did not try to argue with him or to stop him from quitting the room when he had completed this speech. Instead, she asked him to send Charles to her, that she wished to speak to her dear friend.

Charles entered the room, wearing a tired smile as he crossed to her and kissed her lightly on the cheek. Meg asked him to please sit down with her on the settle by the fire. When he had done so, sighing heavily, she possessed herself of his hands and asked, "Were I to beseech you with all my heart, my dearest friend, to forget this wretched, hateful duel, would you do so?"

Charles, whose complexion had remained exceedingly pale since he offered Montford his challenge and was accepted, ground his teeth together slightly and averted his face toward the blackened hearth. In a quiet voice, he responded, "You know I cannot. I am a man of honor, and no one has impuned that honor more than Montford." He took a shallow breath, as though to prevent unwanted words from rushing forth. He paused for a moment, then said, "I counted him friend, and this is how he repays me. I have no other course open before me."

"You have one," Meg said. "To love, in order that you might marry Hope and have children and grow old and—

278

and withered together."

Charles looked at her upon these words, his eyes misting slightly. "I am not such a poor shot, if you must know. I can generally give an excellent accounting of myself when the occasion requires it!" He laughed and said, "And how is it that suddenly you stand in opposition to this ancient, noble form of settling gentlemanly conflicts?"

Meg held his gaze steadily and said, "Ever since I gave up my childish beliefs for a woman's heart."

The journey back to Staplehope was very cold and desolate. The serving girl, as it happened, suffered a degree of carriage sickness far worse than Meg had ever endured, and she found herself caring for the poor child the entire way. She had not tried to argue with either Charles or Worthen, for she had finally come to understand something of the mettle that comprised both men. Neither gave, nor withheld their word without great integrity. And what tears or arguments of hers could ever hope to alter that integrity? No, she must find a different way of ending the duel between Montford and Charles.

When she arrived home, it was but an hour before dawn. She had travelled the night through, and Staplehope had never appeared more welcoming. Her first duty was to see the serving girl tucked into bed with a warm posset, and afterward she found her father snoring in the library. Caroline was seated by a window and rose at once to embrace her.

"Was it Montford?" Caroline whispered in her ear, so as not to disturb Sir William.

Meg nodded, tears smarting her eyes and rolling down her cheeks. "Oh, Caroline," she responded, her voice low. "I have made such a wretched mull of my life. I have lost Worthen. I held to my beliefs until I lost him, and I will lose Charles, too. Montford will kill him!"

Caroline held her very tight. "Do not tell me Charles is

to face Montford in a duel?"

"Yes," Meg cried. "Pistols."

Caroline shuddered but said nothing. Finally, she released Meg, then slipped her arm about Meg's shoulders, guiding her gently toward the door. "I will have one of the servants waiting to tell your father of your safe arrival should he awaken soon." She chuckled beneath her own tears and glanced back at the baronet, who was stretched out upon the settee, lying comfortably upon his back, his mouth wide open and snoring contentedly. "Though I doubt anything less than a brigade of cannons could awaken him now!"

Meg gave a watery laugh and let Caroline draw her out of the room and into the hall. Here Caroline began speaking in a more normal voice as she led Meg toward the entrance hall. "I have spent the entire night thinking about you, Margaret. There is something I have wanted to tell you for so long now, but I never quite knew how to tell you properly. You see, I was in love with Worthen at one time, ten years ago. He and his brother were my favorite suitors. Montford was a suitor as well. I was very giddy in those days, not unlike Elizabeth, and I thought nothing could be more romantic than having a duel fought over me. I encouraged the brothers to spar, nay fight, for my attentions!"

Meg walked slowly beside Caroline and upon these words looked at her sharply. "You? But I cannot imagine how you could ever have been like that. You are so steady, and you wear your hair in braids and you are reserved—" She broke off suddenly as she remembered how Caroline fainted when she saw Geoffrey Blake. Meg stopped her stepmama in her tracks. They had reached the bottom of the staircase. Caroline still held an arm about Meg's waist, but Meg clutched Caroline's other arm in a hard grasp and cried, "Then you did have two gentlemen do battle for you. It was Mr. Blake, was it not? Worthen told me he had been lamed in a duel. Caroline, did Montford shoot him? Did he engage in a duel with Montford?"

Caroline looked stricken, the expression on her face stiff as she stared into the past. "It is worse than that. And worse, I think, than even I knew. You see, Worthen shot Geoff. He shot his own brother."

Margaret felt all the lessons of the past several weeks roll over and over her: Montford, a liar and a libertine; Phillip, a gamester; and her dearest Charles to perish in a duel that she caused! And now this, a final blow—Worthen hated duelling for the simple reason that he had nearly killed his own brother in a thoughtless, hateful duel! And afterward, he had vowed never to duel again. That must have been what Charles meant when he referred to Worthen having taken a vow.

Meg nodded her head slowly, comprehension filtering through all the jumble of her thoughts. On and on, the events of the past few days brought her entire life sharply in line. Somehow, Meg realized, the untimely death of her mother had left her own thinking twisted, disjointed, trapped in a little girl's mind and afterward never properly guided to maturity. Now she looked back at all of her encounters with both Worthen and Montford, and she wondered how she could have honored the unworthy man and scorned the one whose heart held all that was indeed honorable? How could she have not known these men for who they really were?

Meg could no longer stand, and she sank slowly to the bottom step of the stairway. She took a deep breath, cradling her head in her arms as she said, "I've been such a foolish little girl all these years. I only wonder that I have not come to a worse pass than this much sooner. Oh, Caroline, what have I done? I have cost Charles his life."

Caroline said, "There is something more in all of this that I want you to know. The night before Richard and Geoff were to engage in their duel, I asked Lord Montford to take a certain letter to Worthen. The letter asked Worthen to stop the duel. In it, I told him that I loved him, that I had been foolish beyond permission in

281

encouraging the brothers to spar for my affections as they did, and that if he wished for it I would become his wife."

Meg lifted her head and in a soft voice said, "I thought you were in love with him, or had been at one time."

Caroline laid a hand upon Meg's shoulder as she, too, dropped to the stair and joined Meg. "That is not to say that I do not love your father. You must remember, what passed between Richard and me occurred some ten years ago. At any rate, Montford returned to me with the awful news that the duel would take place anyway. He told me that Worthen had read the letter and had responded curtly, 'You may tell her she is too late in her supplications!' I believed Montford, that is, until now. Meg, I don't think he ever delivered that letter to Worthen. The truth is that after the duel took place I did not exchange one word with either of the brothers for an entire year. We were all to blame, but I suspect that Montford has been guilty of treachery. I mean to ask Worthen whether or not he ever received my missive."

Meg sat quietly for a moment, considering all that Caroline had told her. Suddenly, with a laugh edged with the slightest note of hysteria, she said, "Do you know what I would do, were ladies permitted to behave as men?"

Caroline smiled. "What?"

"I would call Montford out, this very instant!"

Caroline slept the better part of the morning and into the afternoon. When she awoke, she lay quietly in her bed for some time, giving careful thought to all that had happened. Finally, she decided that above all things she wanted to ask Worthen outright whether or not he had received her letter the night before his duel with Geoffrey.

Later that evening, after having explained her intention to Sir William, Caroline received Worthen privately in the baronet's study. He stood now beside a large cherrywood desk, fatigue etched into the lines of his face. Caroline sensed in his bearing the fierce tautness of an internal struggle of no small magnitude. She had meant to address the issue of Montford's letter immediately; instead she said, "I have not known you all these years without comprehending you a little. Pray tell me what is the matter."

Worthen glanced toward Caroline and spoke in a mocking voice: "Nothing of consequence, really! Only that Burnell will be killed in a duel that I ought to have started! I should face Montford, not Charles. He will be killed." In sudden exasperation, Worthen slammed his hand down upon the desk.

Caroline frowned slightly, fingering the soft white lace fichu draped over the bodice of her gown. She was standing by the window that overlooked the clipped gardens, and she said, "You must stop the duel, of course."

"Yes, somehow I must do at least that." His dark eyes grew grave and hard in the candlelight of the small, panelled chamber. "I should not have permitted Charles to issue his challenge in the first place, but I knew he was in a towering rage and would not have let his honor go unavenged—he had been duped by his *friend!*" Worthen shook his head. "And Burnell is no match for Montford, either pistols or swords! It will be nothing short of murder." He moved to stand by the fireplace, where his attention was caught by Meg's lap desk. He continued, "If only I were free to face Montford myself."

Caroline turned away from the window and seated herself in a small chair covered in a faded needlepoint of rose and green. She wanted neither of the men to engage in a duel, and as for Montford, she well knew that his dissolute ways would eventually take him down his own path of destruction—punishment enough for any man.

Changing the subject slightly, she asked, "And what of Margaret? She seemed to feel you no longer wished to marry her."

Worthen lowered his gaze, his chin stubborn. "I was

wrong to have forced Meg into an engagement she did not desire. Very wrong. But beyond this, I pinched at her and provoked her so much over the past several days that is it any wonder she eloped with Montford? I caused her to flee Staplehope in his company. I am to blame for what has happened, just as I was to blame for the events of ten years ago—for Geoff's lameness. I nearly killed him in that absurd duel, and only last night I barely saved my betrothed from suffering a defilement too horrid to even think about. And now, Charles might perish because of my stubbornness."

Caroline knew an odd impatience with Worthen's almost martyred attitude. In a quiet voice, she rebuked him: "Why, how very noble you are, Richard, to bear everyone's faults and take them as your own." He looked at her, a little startled, and she continued, "I share culpability for your brother's lameness, and I know that Geoff shares an equal guilt. Why must you then sport this false piety and tell me you are entirely to blame? And does it not occur to you that my lord Montford has been, in both cases, far guiltier than any of us? If you must accuse someone of wrongdoing, accuse Montford."

Worthen frowned at these last words and asked, "What do you mean—in both cases. He had nothing to do with my duel with Geoff!"

Caroline's voice dropped very low as she said, "I never believed so until recently. But given this new evidence of his unhappy character, I fear that he was very much involved, indeed."

Worthen asked, "How so?"

Caroline said, "Let me ask you something first. Had I begged either you or Geoffrey to abort your duel, would you have obliged me?"

Worthen nodded. "He and I were speaking of that only the other day. We both wondered, in retrospect, why you did not make a push to get either of us to stop the duel."

Caroline took a deep breath. Then, it was true—Montford had never delivered her letter. "But I did," Caroline responded, her voice lower still. "I sent you a letter."

Worthen shook his head, unable to credit what he had heard. He said, "I never received it. Who failed to deliver this message to me? One of your servants?"

Caroline looked up at him, her eyes slowly filling with tears. "Not a servant. Cannot you guess? You see, I have the same blindness of perception as Meg does."

Caroline had never seen Worthen's eyes grow so black or fierce in appearance as in this moment when he said, "Montford!"

Caroline rose to her feet and stepped toward him. "So you see, you are not to blame. You do not possess the power to prevent a dishonest man from acting dishonorably."

Worthen nodded slowly and said, "But I can at least make certain he does not do further injury to anyone again."

Caroline opened her eyes wide and pressed a hand to her bosom. She said, "Whatever are you saying, Richard? You cannot possibly mean to call him out yourself? What of your vow to Geoff?"

"Were it anyone but Montford, I would not consider such a course. As it is, I feel no compunction whatsoever, given the baron's treachery in this situation, of issuing a challenge to him. Had he presented that letter to me as you asked him to, my brother even now would be whole!"

Caroline sat very still, her mouth slightly agape. Why had she not foreseen this? She folded her hands in front of her and said, "I am sure there is nothing I can say to you that would cause you to change your mind, so I will therefore wish you well." She moved toward the door and paused in her steps. "Oh, yes, there is just one thing. Meg has asked to speak with you before you take your leave tonight. She is in the morning room."

Meg had already paced the morning room a dozen times and now sat before her small writing desk, anxiously going through her manuscript and scratching out every reference to Count Fortunato's mole that she could possibly find. She was waiting for Caroline to send Worthen to her, and every minute that passed seemed an eternity. She was anxious beyond measure and frequently patted her red curls to see that they were all in place.

She had dressed carefully for this meeting between herself and the viscount, knowing that time would quickly separate her forever from him. He would no doubt stay in Shropshire, acting as Charles' second, until the duel took place. Afterward, she was certain he would leave immediately. She had, then, this small opportunity to attempt to change his heart. She knew his mind was unalterably fixed against marrying her; but she knew he loved her, and she meant to appeal to his love. For this reason, she wore a soft, white muslin gown that clung to her womanly form; she had even dampened the fabric of the skirts to enhance her feminine aspect. The serving girl, Bonnie, who had recovered sufficiently from her ague to help her dress, had created a cloud of Meg's hair, so that though it was caught high upon her head, it cascaded in a thousand tendrils all about her shoulders. Even Bonnie had exclaimed that Meg appeared goddess-like. If only Worthen would find her appealing enough to kiss her good-bye—upon this prospect she based all of her hopes.

She heard footsteps on the tile down the hall, and she immediately leapt to her feet, her pen falling to the desk and rolling onto the floor. She faced the door wide-eyed as the steps drew nearer still. Suddenly, she wanted her haunt to be less well-lit, and she turned to extinguish the entire branch of candles that sat upon her desk. She did not have sufficient time to tend to either of the other branches, but this effort most certainly softened the appearance of the room.

A knock sounded quietly on the door. Meg crossed to the fireplace, where she sat quickly down upon the wing chair to the left of the hearth and said, "Enter."

The door opened, and Worthen was in the room,

standing at the threshold, his expression somber and as distant as it had been on the night before.

Meg rose to her feet, aware that both the glow of coals behind her and the branch of candles on the mantel lit her entire person with a warm glow. She watched with satisfaction as Worthen's gaze, now opening wide, travelled down her figure even to her feet.

She took a step forward, then stopped. "I hope you don't mind my receiving you privately in this manner since we are no longer engaged. It must seem, to some degree, very improper of me."

On these words, Worthen advanced into the large chamber. He spoke quietly: "I am certain that since your stepmama has permitted me to attend you here, society can find little to object to."

Meg smiled and took another step toward him. She did not want him to sit down, so she began speaking quickly. "I have a small favor to ask of you before you leave. You see, I am in the most awkward of predicaments."

He seemed concerned suddenly and drew close to her, taking her by the elbow, apparently with the intention of settling her in one of the chairs by the fire. She felt panicky and pulled her arm away from him saying, "No! If you please, I had much rather stand, thank you!"

He seemed surprised but inclined his head to her, saying, "Of course. Whatever you wish. Now, how may I oblige you?"

They were standing within a few feet of the fireplace, and the light from the candles softened his features. She looked into his dark eyes and felt her heart cry out to him. She loved him so very much. He appeared for just a moment, as she held his gaze, to lean toward her, then abruptly shifted his gaze from her face and turned slightly toward the fireplace.

He asked, "What favor, Meg? I will do anything that you require in this moment."

Meg took a step toward him and laid a hand upon his chest. He looked back at her sharply, a look of surprise on his face. He caught the hand that touched his coat, and pressed it very hard. Meg said nothing, but merely looked at him, trying with all her might to convey her sentiments to him without speaking.

His voice was low and hoarse as he said, "Why do you look at me in that manner? What are you about, Meg?"

Finally, Meg drew very close to him, the skirts of her gown touching his breeches, and said, "If I must live forever without you beside me, never knowing again the sweetness of your lips on my own, never hearing you take me to task for my nonsensical thinking, then I want this last parting moment with you. Worthen, this is the favor I ask of you—will you not kiss me good-bye?"

Worthen still held her hand clutched in a painful grip. "I should not," he said, searching her eyes, her face. "I should not do this when we will never be man and wife." He lifted his free hand to touch her hair. He let his fingers ripple over just the edges of her curls, and he said, "Your hair is so soft—"

"Spun copper," Meg breathed, leaning toward him, lifting her lips to his. "Remember?"

"Are you seducing me?" he asked, his eyes clouded, his hand moving restlessly over her hair.

"Yes," Meg answered, her lips parted slightly as she reached toward him and gently began brushing her mouth against his. His breath was sweet upon her lips, and she said, "I love you, my lord. Will you not love me but a little?"

He waited no longer but sank his hand deep into her hair, forcing her head toward him as he kissed her painfully upon the lips. Meg had never given herself, even in kissing Worthen, so completely as this. Her heart felt overflowing with her love for him as she held him fiercely close. "I love you! I love you!" she cried, when he kissed her cheek again and again.

"And I you, my darling Meg."

Suddenly he drew away from her, aware that he was speaking words that could only make their parting more difficult. He said nothing more, but turned abruptly on his heel and hurried to the door. When he again stood in the doorway, he held the doorhandle in one hand, preparing to close the door, but looked back at her first and said, "I will call upon Caroline just before I quit Staplehope."

"Worthen!" Meg called to him. He shut the door firmly, and as his footsteps echoed down the hall, she picked up an old book, which she despised very much, and threw it at the door, saying, "You are the most foolishly stubborn man I have ever known."

And because she feared desperately that she would be unable to win him from his current position, tears overtook her, and she sank into her red chair, covering her face with her hands.

After a moment, she was surprised to hear another knock upon the door. She leapt to her feet, hastily wiping the tears from her cheeks and cried, "Worthen! Oh, my dear—"

But the door opened, and Caroline stood framed in the doorway.

"I'm sorry, Meg. He's gone. But never fear, we have a great deal of scheming to do, you and I, before we can undo all the harm that has been done."

Meg sniffed once and hurried to her desk in search of a kerchief. When she found one crammed into the corner of one of the drawers, she quickly blew her nose.

Caroline moved to stand beside her and asked, "Did he tell you, then?"

"What? That he means to leave Staplehope very soon? Yes."

"No. I mean about the duel?"

"He said nothing of the sort." Meg met Caroline's intense gaze and drew in a deep breath. "Tell me at once!"

"He means to face Montford himself!"

Meg blinked rapidly several times, and with all the weak spirits of a Rosamund, she crumpled to the floor.

Chapter Twenty

On the following day, Caroline and Meg paid a morning call upon the ladies of Norbury House. Mrs. Norbury, they discovered, had the headache and was laid down upon her bed. Elizabeth and Hope, however, were found in the walnut grove in the midst of a grand quarrel.

When Caroline and Meg approached the grove through a break in a yew hedge, they heard Lizzie exclaim, "Well, I for one am delighted that my betrothed has given so brave an accounting of himself. I honor him for having called Montford out! And it just proves, Miss Prim, that he is a man of dash and fire and will suit me admirably!"

As soon as Meg stepped to the edge of the grove, she saw Hope wave a hand dramatically in the air as she responded hotly, "And it is just like you, Elizabeth, to be thinking only of how Charles' involvement in a duel would affect you! But have you considered the possibility that Charles may not survive this duel?"

"Oh, pooh and nonsense, Hope! Charles will not die! He told me himself that he is a reasonably good shot. He might suffer a slight flesh wound and perhaps even lose a dram of blood, but only the thoroughly unskilled ever go to their grave because of duelling!"

"You are the most unfeeling creature I have ever known!"

Lizzie smirked. "And you are quite the most *hope*lessly priggish female with whom I have ever had the misfortune to be connected!"

At this moment, Lizzie, who was seated in an unladylike manner as she straddled a fallen log, caught sight of Meg and Caroline. She waved her hand in much the manner of an excited child and cried, "How glad I am to see you, Meggie, for you at least will appreciate how thrilling it is to have Charles actually engaged in a duel with Montford! Only do tell Hope she is being uncommonly missish!" She glanced at Caroline, and with a cooling of her spirits, she spoke politely: "Oh, hallo Lady Longville, how do you go on?"

Caroline merely inclined her head to Lizzie, waiting for Meg to answer the sprightly female.

Meg said, "I am sorry to say, Lizzie, that I shall disappoint you grievously today. I have only one desire, as it happens, to see that none of these gentlemen spill even the smallest speck of blood in anything so foolish as a duel!"

Lizzie's mouth fell open most unbecomingly. She looked as though she wished to speak, but Hope interjected quickly, "I only learned of this heinous situation this morning. Gossip has already circulated throughout the principle houses of the valley to the effect that little else is discussed. At first, I didn't believe a word of it, but Elizabeth said she had discovered the truth from Charles himself last night."

Meg turned to Elizabeth and asked, "Charles actually told you about the duel?"

Lizzie responded with a slight furrow between her black, arched brows. "As it happens he did, and he was being awfully morbid about the entire affair. He kept saying something like, 'should anything happen to me,' until I was ready to scream with vexation!" She cast a sly glance toward Hope and said, "Although I did permit him to kiss me—just once, of course!—since he would very soon be facing Montford with pistols at thirty paces."

When Hope merely lifted a disgusted brow, Lizzie sighed. "I only wish I knew why they were fighting a duel! Charles would tell me none of it."

Meg did not hesitate to inform both Hope and Elizabeth about all that had transpired since the night Montford tried to abduct her. Hope listened to Meg's recital, as she stood beside a walnut tree, with a look of pained fear upon her face. Lizzie, still astride the log, leaned forward, her entire body a picture of excitement as she took in every word Meg spoke, even interjecting a few pointed questions in order to enlighten the various aspects of the elopement or precise nature of Montford's treachery. At the end of Meg's recounting, Lizzie clapped her hands together and cried, "Oh, but it sounds like it must have been such famous fun! What a glorious lark!" She trilled her laughter. "You are the most fortunate of creatures, Meg! I only wish someone would abduct me!" She sighed gustily. When she realized that all three ladies were staring at her with expressions of reproach, she opened her hands wide, palms up and exclaimed, "Well, I cannot help it if I have more spirit than all the rest of you combined!"

Hope rolled her eyes and turned her back on her cousin while Meg stood staring at Lizzie for a very long moment. Until recently, her own views had not differed very much from Lizzie's, and she felt conscience-stricken suddenly, awareness growing within her hourly of how much her schoolgirl fancies had brought about this desperate situation. She glanced at Caroline, an unspoken plea in her eyes.

Caroline reached a hand toward her and pressed her arm. She said, "We shall set everything to rights. You'll see."

Meg smiled faintly and turned to address Lizzie. "My opinions have changed so much that I hardly know how to answer you. However, I don't think it at all necessary that any of us agree upon whether or not duels and elopements are either harmless or dangerous. We each, save Caroline, have a concern in this forthcoming duel: Hope may lose the man she loves, I may do so as well, and as for you, Elizabeth, you may forfeit a very excellent chance of becoming a peeress."

Hope, who had remained turned away from Meg, now whirled around and asked, "Are you saying that you have actually fallen in love with Worthen?"

Hope's voice was warm and sweet and somehow brought all of Meg's sentiments to the surface of her heart. Meg felt tears rush to her eyes, and she nodded, searching hastily about in her reticule for a kerchief.

When she had dabbed her tears away, she continued, "I love him very much, more than I ever dreamed possible." She paused, thinking also that she had lost him because of her refusal to comprehend how childish her thinking was, but this she did not say aloud. Instead, she took a deep breath and continued, "Lord Worthen, as it happens, gave Caroline a strong indication that he intended to prevent the duel between Charles and Montford by crossing swords with Montford himself."

Lizzie cried, "But what of Charles, then? Will he not have an opportunity to avenge his honor?"

"Not if Worthen has his way!"

"Well!" Lizzie cried, indignant. "I call that shabbily done!"

Caroline, who had been silent, stiffened upon these words and addressed Lizzie sharply: "You would not think so, Miss Priestley, were you to stand over Charles' grave. Think on that for a moment. What would you say to him? 'Well done! You got yourself killed, but you acquitted yourself admirably'?"

Lizzie merely smiled in an obnoxious manner and said, "You make too much of the matter."

"And you make too little!" Caroline snapped in response. She let a sigh of exasperation escape her lips and then said, "Well, I certainly did not come here to argue with you. As a matter of fact, I am here in hopes of persuading you to relinquish your claim upon Charles."

Lizzie was shocked as she sat up very straight and said, "Why, whatever do you mean? I would never give up Charles. I love him. I intend to marry him."

"Why would you want to do that, Lizzie?" Caroline cried. "When Montford so desperately needs a dowry— one such as yours, for instance? I have reason to believe, because of all that my husband learned of his current financial distress, that he would be most interested in a female of your exceptional charm!"

Meg glanced at Caroline, wondering if her stepmama had been right about Elizabeth—that she could be persuaded to pursue Montford if she thought she had a reasonable chance of winning him.

Elizabeth cocked her head, regarding Caroline with a surprised expression on her face. "How very curious, Lady Longville! So you suppose that I have an interest in Montford?" She rose to her feet and slipped a leg from over the log, brushing shards of bark off the skirt of her peach muslin walking dress. "You presume a great deal."

"Miss Priestley," Caroline responded, a hint of amusement in her voice. "I know very well that you would not hesitate to elope with Montford were he to give the barest hint that he desired to do so. And this is the very thing Meg and I wish to propose to you—an elopement, in fact."

"I am affronted!" Lizzie cried as she pressed a hand to her pretty bosom. "And deliciously intrigued. You simply must tell me more."

Hope, who had been listening to this exchange with an anxious expression on her face, moved to stand beside Meg and whispered, "What is Caroline about? Oh, Meggie, do you know what this would mean for me? But would Lizzie actually give up Charles so easily?"

Meg inclined her head toward Lizzie, but addressed Hope with a very simple question: "What do you think?"

Hope smiled suddenly, a twinkle appearing in her large doe eyes. "How silly of me! Of course she would!"

Meg then leaned very close to her and whispered,

"There is only one thing: If we are to prevent a duel between Charles and Montford, you will need to be very brave as well, for you must act a part in our forthcoming intrigue!"

Hope looked at Meg, her expression sincere. "I will do whatever is required of me, you may be assured of that!"

Later that afternoon, Meg saddled Bluebell and rode with a groom in tow over to Horsley Mill where Charles' duel with Montford had been arranged to take place. The grounds seemed desolate compared to her recent visit there with Worthen. Leaving the groom to rest the horses by the stream, Meg traversed the yard in front of the mill, trying to gain a sense of just how the duel might be conducted.

Her heart was both heavy and continually pressed with fear. Her thoughts, day and night, were consumed with Worthen, her love for him, his recent stubborn refusal to respond to a request she sent him to call upon her, the blackness of his intense eyes, the strength of his arms, and the ever-present sensation of impending loss that dogged her heels.

Caroline's scheme was simple, and she was certain it would succeed. Each of the ladies had but to hire a carriage, steal her beau away from the duel, and all would be well. But Meg could not be easy. She did agree that Montford, given both his character and his need for Lizzie's dowry, would no doubt respond to such antics from Lizzie. But what of Worthen and Charles? After several hours of deliberation, Meg concluded that neither man would be satisfied with being torn from what he believed was his duty. Charles in particular, aside from his need to avenge his honor, would never permit Hope to be so disgraced by an elopement of any kind.

As Meg walked off distances, counting off thirty paces from various points, she knew again a need to re-orchestrate coming events. She went inside the mill, light filtering through the broken window in a thick ray, illuminating the perpetual dust of the mill. The dank smell remained, of disuse and rats. Meg could not keep from glancing at the floor where the rat had died from a pistol ball. It was not so many days ago that the unfortunate picnic had taken place, but so much had happened that within the framework of Meg's heart, she felt as though years had passed. If only she could find some way of reaching Worthen before the duel. The very thought of losing him made her dizzy with fright, and she left the mill to again look about the grounds.

What was she searching for? she wondered. Some inspiration, perhaps as to how she could bring the entire situation about? A few hundred yards away, she could see the groom sitting on the side of the creek, the horses nibbling contentedly at the grass about their hooves.

Meg thought back on all her association with Worthen, and one memory came to mind that jarred her—the moment on the terrace when she had told him precisely how she felt, that she did not esteem his character because he so frequently permitted Montford, and his like, to browbeat him, that he would not avenge his honor by duelling.

How perfectly ironic, Meg thought, and how poetically just to have Worthen now both ready to engage in a duel and prepared to give her up forever.

She felt a slight tingling across her neck as a breeze swept down the hill and whipped the skirts of her riding habit. A wonderful, familiar sensation travelled quickly down her spine and caused her to shudder. She remembered at the same time a comment of Worthen's upon the same occasion. "You must face a pistol at thirty paces." He had meant, of course, that until she had lived through the same circumstances as any man—or woman, for that matter—she had no right to sit in judgement on that man's actions or beliefs.

Worthen had been correct of course; but in this

situation, Meg tilted her head as she glanced about the level, open ground, and she saw herself dressed in man's garb, holding a pistol in an outstretched arm, and slowly pulling the trigger.

As though the fact indeed happened, Meg felt the gun recoil in her hand and heard the loud crack of the pistol rip through the air. She covered her ears, squeezing her eyes shut. She could not do it! She could certainly not fool any of the men into believing she was Charles, or could she? It would be very dark; she could wear a woollen scarf wrapped several times about her neck and feign a cold—and she looked like Charles to some degree! If the only lighting present were limited to one or two lanterns sitting on the ground and casting shadows upon everyone's face. . . . Meg picked up the train of her habit and began walking quickly toward the horses. And if Worthen's arrival were delayed, and if she was very careful, it might just work, it could work, it had to work!

If Meg felt frightened before, now she felt petrified. She knew, in her heart of hearts, that if she was to reach that stubborn man of hers, it would have to be in this shocking, dangerous manner. Only, what if Montford shot her dead? Meg stumbled as she reached the stream, something of the reality of her decision affecting her ability to maintain her balance. Well, she would not think on that! Finally, she reached her horse, mounted quickly and headed swiftly back to the hall.

When she arrived at Staplehope, she went immediately to her morning room and tore through a drawer full of various correspondence until she found an ancient, inexpert letter from Charles. Then she set about writing three letters, two of which she forged Charles' handwriting. An hour later, she sat back and admired her efforts. The script was remarkably similar to Charles', and she was pleased with the results. The first letter was addressed to Montford, and in it she scorned his character with several pithy comments on libertines in general—her intention to make certain Montford arrived at the duelling site hot-to-spur. The second letter she sent to Worthen, telling him, in Charles' offhand manner, that the meeting would take place one half hour later than originally scheduled. The third letter she wrote in her own hand to Lizzie, telling her to be certain to arrive in a timely fashion, otherwise the duel between Worthen and Montford could not be averted. Lizzie, as everyone knew, had a propensity for arriving late since she loved making a grand, exciting appearance whenever she could.

In the early hours of the morning, before dawn, a fine mist crept among the thickly grown bluebells in the wood that separated Burnell Lodge from Staplehope Hall. Meg stood in the doorway of the morning room, listening to the growing chatter of the early rising birds. She was waiting for her groom, James, to return through the woods with the news that Master Burnell had harnessed a horse to his curricle and was in the process of quitting the lodge.

In the distance, Meg spotted her groom and her heart immediately began beating loudly in her ears. What if her scheme failed? She had chosen not to confide in any of the other ladies because essentially she was the only one affected by the alteration in their plans. But now, on the verge of going herself to Horsley Mill, Meg had no one to support her in what she meant to do. She stood trembling in the doorway, wishing she could tell Caroline, who was seated by the fire, all of her woes. But if Caroline learned of her real intentions, she knew very well her stepmama would never let her leave the hall quietly.

Caroline's voice called to her from the wing chair: "Do you see James yet?"

"Yes," Meg called over her shoulder, whispering. "He is coming now!" She turned around to look at Caroline and asked, "Do you really think I look sufficiently like Charles to fool Worthen or Montford?"

Caroline, who was crocheting a baby's cap with a small hook, stopped the dippings and risings of her hand to say,

"As long as you remain in the shadows as much as possible and do not speak except to cough into your kerchief and complain of having the ague, I'm certain you will fool them because it is so dark. At least long enough to give Hope sufficient time to spirit Charles away and for Lizzie to force Montford to decide between her dowry or this stupid duel with Worthen." She smiled suddenly. "It is a brilliant plan, do not you think so?"

Meg answered quietly, "Yes, of course."

Caroline rose to her feet and approached Meg. "You are uncommonly nervous, as you have every right to be. Now, let me have a look at you." She smiled suddenly. "I had not realized until I saw you dressed in this manner that you do, indeed, bear a resemblance to Charles." She then stood in front of Meg and adjusted the folds of the thick white neckcloth which encircled Meg's neck. Meg wore a black coat and waistcoat, black pantaloons and top boots. In addition, Bonnie had carefully groomed her hair so that when Meg settled a black beaver hat over her red curls, she appeared to be sporting a cut *a la Brutus*.

Caroline grasped Meg's arms and gave her a firm, encouraging shake. "Tell Richard you love him, Meg. Tell him a hundred times until he kisses you and agrees to marry you."

Meg hugged Caroline to her, saying, "You are the very best of women!"

Caroline released her and gave her a little push. "I shall tell your papa everything later this morning. I've little doubt he'll be happy to know you are to wed Worthen at last." She chuckled. "Of course, he will do nothing more than lift a brow at your escapades, and shortly afterward he will disappear with his wicker basket, his favorite angling rod and perhaps a beetle or two!"

These final words caused Meg to laugh, and a little of the tension in her heart eased away. But James was at the doorway suddenly, his face flushed as he cried, "Master Burnell is heading toward the High Street!"

Caroline helped Meg to adjust the hat securely atop her

curls, and within little more than a minute, Meg was seated in her own post-chaise and bowling down the avenue as James rode postillion.

When they had been on the highway for what seemed like but a few seconds, James brought the post-chaise to a stop. Meg peered out the window, and in the distance she could see both Charles' curricle as well as what she presumed was Hope's own hired carriage blocking the road. She watched Charles leap down from the curricle and cross to the other vehicle, and Meg smiled at how surprised he would be when he discovered Hope within.

Charles stared at the hooded figure secreted in the depths of the carriage, and in a voice of exasperation, he cried, "Lizzie, what are you about? You know you should not be here!"

"And what, Mr. Burnell, makes you think I am Elizabeth?"

"Hope?" Charles queried softly, disbelieving. "No, but it is impossible—you would never!"

Hope pushed back the hood of her cape and said, "I had to see you before—" she broke off, tears filling her eyes. "Charles, I am so afraid for you, and I couldn't bear the thought of not seeing you one last time!" She bowed her head and began sobbing in her cambric handkerchief. This action had the happy effect of drawing Charles neatly into the vehicle.

Charles pressed the hood of her cloak back even farther and began softly stroking her hair. "My darling, I wish you had not come. You make this even more difficult for me, and I do not like to see you cry!"

Hope turned toward him, laying her hand on his arm and pressing it hard. "You are so very brave, Charles, while I—I am frightened beyond words that I will never see you again. And I don't care a rush if you marry Elizabeth; I just do not want you to die." She again gave herself to a hearty sob, and he slipped an arm about her shoulders.

"There, there, my pet, please. Nothing will happen to me, you'll see! And as I already told Meg, I am a tolerably good shot!"

Hope looked up at him and said, "I know you are! Why, you're the best shot in the county, in England!"

Charles looked into Hope's brown eyes, so filled with love and admiration, and he was overcome with his affection for her. He was hardly the best shot in Shropshire, nonetheless England, and he knew it quite well. He was as frightened as Hope was that he would not live to see the day out. And as such thoughts poured through his mind, he suddenly grabbed Hope, holding her in a crushing embrace and saying, "My darling Hope. I love you. I'm so sorry for all that has happened."

Hope pressed him back slightly, looking up at him with her eyes misted with tears. "Kiss me, then, my love."

Charles leaned down and placed a kiss upon her willing lips. Hope slipped her arm about his neck and held him fiercely to her, returning kiss for kiss until she was breathless.

After a moment, she pulled back from him and asked, "Do you intend to drive to the village? I could take you there, myself. Is Worthen to ride with you? Oh, Charles, I am so frightened!" She clutched his arm, holding the fabric of his cloak tightly in her hand.

Charles said, "I—I am meeting Worthen at the appointed place."

"Horsley Mill," Hope said, nodding sadly.

Charles suddenly felt a little exasperated. "I say, how is it you seem to know so much about this deuced duel!"

Hope replied, "I learned of it from Lizzie, and you know what she is. Once she knew a duel was in progress, she badgered all of the servants until one of them was able to discover where you were to face Montford." She then said, "Oh, please Charles, will you not permit me to take you there myself? As you can see, I brought an outrider with me this morning, and he could easily drive your curricle behind us. Please, Charles?" Tears trickled down her cheeks as she pressed his arm.

301

"No!" Charles cried. "You cannot! Ladies are not permitted to attend such affairs."

Hope smiled sweetly, leaning her head on his shoulder and said, "I thought you might say that. Well, then, let me take you as far as the lane, and then you may proceed the rest of the way to the mill by yourself."

At first he refused to do any such thing, but when Hope pointed out that they may never see one another again, he acquiesced. Charles then instructed the outrider as to how he ought to handle the prime bits of blood harnessed to the curricle. When he was satisfied that the servant would do no harm to his horses, he rejoined Hope, and the cavalcade set off at a brisk pace. Once they were moving, Charles held Hope close to him, and Hope did not hesitate to burrow her head in his shoulder. Charles said, "I've been such a fool, Hope, you've no idea. Had I to do it all over again—"

"Hush!" Hope cried. "I was to blame, too, if you remember. I nearly forced you into Lizzie's arms with my missish manners! I was a veritable pea-goose, and you know it!"

These words set Charles at ease, and he began relating to her the harrowing journey into Cumberland in search of Meg. ". . . and after we had got past Lancashire, my horse threw a shoe and went lame. Fortunately we were but a mile from the next village—I say—" he broke off, having glanced out the window. "Staplehope is but a few hundred yards before us. Damn and blast, we've missed the turn-off! Postillion!" Charles cried to the driver. But the man did not appear to hear him.

When he called to him a second time and still received no response, he turned to Hope and asked, "Is he deaf?"

"No," Hope replied softly. "Except to your entreaties."

Charles cried, "What do you mean?"

"Only that I am abducting you, Charles Burnell. By tomorrow night, we shall be wed over the anvil."

Chapter Twenty-One

The moment Hope's coach disappeared around a bend in the highway, Meg called to James to "spring 'em," and her post-chaise moved swiftly toward Horsley Mill. When she arrived at the mill, Montford and White were already there, standing beside the baron's town chariot. Meg was pleased to find that only one lantern lit the yard, and she let out a small sigh of relief. There was an excellent chance, then, that she could bring her own scheme to fruition.

She hoped to protect her identity by insisting upon the confrontation immediately, before the dawn could arrive fully and expose her deception. She also meant to speak only with Mr. White if she could possibly manage it since he was less known to either her or to Charles than Montford was. Her identity then would be safeguarded even further.

James drew the post-chaise to the far side of the level yard in front of the mill, the door to the carriage opening away from the lanterns. Meg signalled to him to bring Mr. White to her, and she swathed her neck with a black woollen scarf.

Mr. White, a short man of one and thirty, with a balding pate and curly light brown hair, crossed the yard on a quick step and seemed taken aback when Meg spoke to him from the window. She coughed several times first, keeping her head down, then lowered her voice as far as she could. "White, I've had word from Worthen. He has been taken ill and will not be coming! I insist upon facing Montford now! See to it." She coughed once then waited for White's reply.

He stood facing the carriage as though struck dumb, and finally said, "But it isn't the proper form! We should wait until you've a second who will check the weapons."

Meg rasped, "I will have satisfaction now, I tell you! If Montford has the stomach for it!"

White sniggered and responded, "As you wish, Burnell!" He snapped a formal bow, turned on his heel and returned to the baron.

Meg followed White with her gaze and watched the two men discuss the matter for a few seconds. Meg motioned to James to come to her so that she might give him her father's pistols to take to Mr. White for inspection. They were fully loaded, an operation that had taken her an hour to complete.

James took the case from Meg's hands and said, "Miss, I don't like to mention it, but these men seem mighty serious fer someat that ye said t'would be a lark. Where's my lord Worthen?"

"My lord Worthen," Meg answered with a smile, hoping that she did not appear in the least nervous or anxious, "will be along at any moment, rest assured! And as for Mr. White, do you not think he is playing his part with great vigor?"

James frowned at her and then glanced at Mr. White. He'd seen a great deal of odd and mysterious games what the gentry were like to play on one t'other. And as fer Miss Margaret, why, he'd no more disobey her than he'd chew off his foot! He bowed to her and took the case over to Mr. White, then returned to see to the horses.

Meg suggested he take them back to the stream as he had done yesterday, and he nodded, saying that if she didn't mind overly much he would be quite happy to absent himself.

Meg watched Mr. White and Montford until all the pistols were properly loaded and inspected. Only as they both stood staring in her direction did she descend her coach. She pulled her hat low about her ears, muffled her chin and set her posture to resemble Charles' gait as well as she could remember it. She marched over to them, thinking as Charles might think.

When she stood before them, she made certain she was turned away from the lanterns so that her face was constantly in shadow. Neither man saw anything odd with her appearance, and she relaxed slightly, enough at least to remember to bow to both men and call Montford by name.

Montford, his head upright, his countenance stiff, said, "I found your letter, Burnell, to be quite beyond bearing. And I do not hesitate to tell you that I shall enjoy this duel immensely."

If Meg felt nervous until this moment, his words brought her anger rushing to replace her unsteadiness. Her stature grew slightly, her expression hard as she inclined her head in a sarcastic fashion. She did not even mind staring at him in silence, forcing him to make the next move. She wondered if he suspected anything. For a brief second, his eyes narrowed slightly, but beyond that he showed no emotion whatsoever.

Mr. White finally addressed her: "Burnell, since Worthen is not present, do you wish to check your weapon in Montford's presence?"

Meg coughed, but was in command of herself sufficiently to say, "I trust your judgement, White. If you have found everything satisfactory, I think we ought to proceed."

Montford and White exchanged a quick glance, and Montford said, "By all means. At thirty paces?"

Meg nodded.

Mr. White showed them where to stand to begin marking off the proper distance, and for the first time since she had hatched this scheme, as Meg stood back-to-

305

back with Montford, did she realize the enormity of what she was about to do.

Lord Worthen raced headlong down the High Street, sinking his spurred boots into the flanks of his chestnut stallion. He felt like such a fool to have received the letter from Burnell without the least suspicion. A servant had brought it to him earlier that evening, and though he had thought it somewhat odd that Charles had changed the hour of the meeting, he had no reason to disbelieve him. Only a few minutes earlier, when he was stamping into his boots, did he happen to glance at Charles' letter again and notice that a *t* in the last line of the note was crossed with a flourish, a style that seemed both unlike Charles and yet very much familiar to him.

All at once, Meg's manuscript flashed in his mind, full of flourishes, especially around her *t*'s. And just as quickly as he knew that the letter had come not from Charles, but from Meg, he comprehended that some horrendous scheme was afoot. Without hesitation, he left his vest and coat lying on the bed of his chamber, dashed from his room, and shouted for one of the stableboys to saddle his chestnut immediately.

He now flew down the highway, his head down, his heart pounding in his chest. Would he be in time to avert a disaster? He was not certain what Meg intended to do by involving herself in Charles' duel, or even whether Charles would be more at risk by her interference, but whatever the case, he was half-mad with fright—for both her safety and Charles'.

Meg marked off each step as Mr. White called them aloud, "Twenty-six, twenty-seven . . ."

A rushing sound had closed in on Meg's ears, one of sheer panic. What was she doing, walking and walking, holding this absurd duelling pistol, preparing to turn, cock her pistol and fire upon Montford! Of course she meant to delope, to fire high in the air, but what if he shot her through the heart? "Twenty-nine!" Meg felt dizzy with fear. "Thirty!" She whirled about, lifted her arm high into the air, heard the crash of a pistol and fell backward as a second shot rent the air.

Worthen heard the first pistol shot and then the second and spurred his horse on. "Dear God, don't let anyone be harmed!" Within seconds, he galloped into the clearing and saw Burnell's crumpled form at one end of the yard, while Montford and White stood at the opposite end, staring at Burnell. Smoke issued from Montford's pistol. Was Charles now dead? Where was Meg?

The baron saw Worthen and immediately cried, "I don't know what happened!"

As Worthen's horse burst past Montford, the viscount called out, "If you've killed Burnell, I'll see you buried!" The expressions of confusion on the men's faces registered but slightly as he drew rein next to Burnell's body and leapt from his horse.

He lifted the hat from Burnell's head and watched as a mass of red curls fell backward into the dust and leaves. "Meg!" he cried, disbelief and shock pouring over him. "Oh, my God, what happened. Meg! Meg!" He checked her head and her body for the blood he expected to be pouring from a pistol wound, but he found nothing. He felt confused and disoriented and pulled her limp form to his chest, holding her close. "Dear God, say you are all right! Tell me you are not dead!"

He felt her move against his chest and heard a muffled sound. He released her, supporting her shoulders with one arm and loosening her neckcloth. She was very pale.

Montford and White hurried to stand beside him, and Mr. White exclaimed, "Why, it's Miss Longville!" He then turned to address Montford. "Did you know, then?"

Montford said, "Only just before she turned her back

307

to me. There was something about her cheekbone that did not look at all like Charles—and then I knew."

"But did you shoot her?" White asked, incredulous.

Montford made a disgusted sound. "Of course not. But I could not resist firing into the air."

Meg fluttered her eyelids slightly. When she saw Worthen's face, she squeezed her eyes shut and, in a dramatic manner, said, "I must leave this earthly world now. How very dark everything is!"

Worthen laughed and held her. "Oh, my darling, ridiculous love! Of course, it's dark; dawn is just now breaking over the countryside."

Meg whispered, "You do not understand. I have been mortally wounded in combat with Montford. You told me once that I ought to face a man at thirty paces. I have done so, and now I must say—good-bye." She closed her eyes, wondering why Worthen was laughing. She expected momentarily for her spirit to begin drifting from the earth, but nothing even remotely related to such an occurrence happened to her. If anything, the chattering birds grew more distinct, the early morning air cooler upon her cheeks, and the feel of Worthen's arm as he supported her wonderfully blissful. In short, she did not feel as though she was dying.

She blinked her eyes open and swallowed hard. If she could describe the way she felt, she thought it more nearly resembled her former experience at the mill— when she had fainted. She groaned. "Do not tell me that I have not even been hit by a pistol ball!"

"I'm afraid not," Worthen said. "Montford fired into the air just to frighten you."

Meg pressed a hand to her forehead and cried with much anguish, "Oh, lord, I have become another Rosamund! Fainting every time I but turn around! I am mortified beyond words."

"Rosamund?" Mr. White asked. "Who is Rosamund? I know of no female by that name except a detestable aunt I had once, but she died just after I had gone off to Eton. Apoplexy!"

Worthen ignored White and asked Meg gently, "Do you mean you fainted?"

"Yes," Meg said. "Was there ever a poorer specimen than myself?"

"You have a great deal of courage," Worthen responded with a laugh. "What I question, however, is whether or not you are endowed with even a particle of sense."

Meg said, "I don't think so." She then begged to be brought to her feet, which Worthen did quite readily, though he kept an arm about her waist to support her.

He asked, "Where is Charles, by the way?"

Meg looked very self-conscious for a moment and then said, "I daresay he is on his way to Scotland with Hope Norbury if our scheme has worked at all."

"*Our* scheme?" Montford queried.

"Yes, we ladies who had an interest in the outcome of this wretched affair concocted a plan of our own to disrupt a duel that would have harmed one or more of us beyond repair. I refer, of course, to Caroline, Lizzie, Hope and myself. And you may all be angry if you like, but we were desperate, knowing that one of you was likely to be killed this morning!"

Mr. White made an attempt to rebuke Meg, but both Worthen and Montford silenced him. Meg seemed a little surprised that Montford did not take her to task, since he seemed so willing to do harm to anyone who crossed his path. He caught her expression and said, "I wouldn't have killed Charles, if you must know. I happen to enjoy my rank and its privileges, and I don't think an exile on the Continent would have been at all to my tastes."

Meg responded heatedly, "I suppose I must be gratified, then, that your care-for-nobody attitude would have actually saved Charles' life this morning."

He smiled in a mocking fashion and said, "You should at least be appreciative."

Meg was ready to do battle with this man whom she had once admired and had now grown to despise, but Worthen set her gently aside as he addressed Montford himself. "For some time now, I have taken your insults because I made a vow to my brother never to engage in a duel again. But I no longer feel that I must endure your slurs upon my honor or character, nor any similarly mindless defamations which your friends might decide to offer me. And you know I have cause to break my word to Geoff for reasons far greater than your obloquies."

Mr. White backed nervously away from both Worthen and Montford as the baron retorted, "I don't know what you mean."

Worthen advanced on him. "I am alluding first to Meg, of course, and your abduction of her. But I refer also to a matter ten years old—a certain letter, in fact."

Montford grew quite stiff upon hearing these words, and he said, "Ah, yes. A letter I never delivered."

"A letter, as it happens, that cost my brother the full use of his leg the rest of his life. I want you to know, I don't blame you entirely, because I was foolish enough to have pulled the trigger. But Geoff and I both agree that that duel would not have occurred at all had you fulfilled your promise to Caroline and seen that I received her missive."

Montford made no attempt to argue, but simply asked, "Your choice of weapons?"

Meg, who had been listening to this entire exchange with a mounting fear, heard these last words of Montford's and felt all of her former fears rush over her. Would she now, after so much time and effort, lose Worthen anyway? She stepped quickly between the men and cried, "No! I won't permit it! Caroline would not want this to happen either!"

Worthen looked at her, his face hard. "You were right in one thing, Meg. There does come a point when a man must defend both his honor as well as the lives of those he loves."

Meg tilted her head, tears starting to her eyes. "The woman who told you that was a foolish little girl! What is honor? Will it take a man's place in his wife's bed? Will it

310

father her children?"

Worthen opened his mouth to speak, startled by her words. An awareness coursed through him that what Meg had told him in the morning room on the day before was indeed true. Her opinions had indeed altered dramatically. He shook his head. "I never thought I would hear you give voice to such a sentiment."

Meg stepped close to him and placed her hands upon his chest. "I beseech you, Worthen. Don't make a second mistake. Not now, not when we truly have a future together.

For a long moment, as dawn began to edge over the hills to the east, he stared at her, his hands upon her arms. Meg could see that he was deliberating over her words as well as all that had happened in the past few weeks, in the past ten years. She waited, holding her breath, hoping that he would end this duel before it had begun. Finally, he said, "I did take a vow, did I not? I wonder what Geoffrey would want me to do."

Meg bit her lip, tears swimming in her eyes. She said, "To honor your vow. Oh, please, Worthen—let Montford go."

Worthen suddenly released Meg, the expression on his face lightening considerably as he turned to Montford and said, "I know that Margaret will not approve, for you see she has this tremendous dislike of taproom brawls, but I cannot let you go unpunished. I choose fisticuffs, here and now."

Montford, who had a tremendous dislike of boxing, sneered slightly. "I would never lower myself to such a common form of doing battle!"

He turned as if to walk away, but Worthen caught him by the arm, whirled him back around to face him and said, "This *common* form of sport is all the consideration you do deserve!" He then planted a flush hit alongside Montford's jaw and dropped him to the ground.

Montford sat there, rubbing his jaw and frowning. "If this is what you require, then so be it!" He began rising to his feet, when a feminine voice cried out, "I absolutely forbid it!"

"Lizzie!" Meg exclaimed. "Thank God you've come!"

Montford, to whom Lizzie had directed her remark, took great exception to a female telling him what he may and may not do, and he responded impatiently, "Oh, go to the devil, Elizabeth!"

Meg feared that Lizzie would be so upset by the baron's form of address that she would fail to fulfill her part in the scheme. But until this moment, she had never really understood Lizzie's character completely.

Dismounting her fiesty black mare, Elizabeth dropped to the ground. She approached the baron, clucking her tongue in a playfully disapproving manner, and cried, "I simply cannot permit you to speak to me in that horrid manner, especially since you are very shortly to become my husband!" She held the train of her cherry-red riding habit slung over her arm and a riding crop held lightly in hand. She continued, "But my goodness, what excitement! Oh, do look at you, Meg, all rigged out in pantaloons and top boots!" The dawn was emerging steadily as the dark shapes of trees grew more distinct and the air grew filled with the chatter of thousands of birds. "I am sorry I am late, but now that I am here, I shall be happy to take Montford off your hands." She turned back to the baron, who was now standing upright and dusting off the back of his coat and black pantaloons.

Montford snorted. "I have no desire to marry you, Lizzie!"

"You are being very hasty, Montford, don't you think? Afterall, I do possess something of which you are in dire need, do I not?"

Montford appeared as though he wished to speak, to send her packing, but his expression soon developed a decided grimace. "You do indeed," he said at last. "So, what do you propose."

Lizzie regarded him wide-eyed and innocent. "I think, my lord, that in the normal course of events, that task is

312

yours to perform." She laughed at the little joke she had made, then continued easily, "As for myself, I should think a delightful wedding at St. Michael's Church would suffice, let us say in a sennight's time. I do long to be married!"

Montford turned back to Meg and Worthen and bowed politely to each of them in turn. To Meg he said, "My humble apologies for a very foolish attempt at an elopement." To Worthen he said, "You are quite handy with your fives. My compliments." And he rubbed his jaw where a lovely purple shading had begun forming on his chin. Turning back to Elizabeth, he took her hand and began kissing each finger in turn. "Do you know that I have always admired the sparkle to your hair and the dazzling brilliance of your exquisite eyes!"

"My, how you do turn a girl's head," Lizzie cooed as she looked up at him adoringly. She then said, "I do indeed find your manner of making love enchanting, but what I wish to know is if you've ever considered developing a much larger political influence. I have several ideas upon that subject which I have been longing to discuss with you these past five weeks and more."

Montford stopped her in mid-stride and looked down at her. "Miss Priestley, have I all this time not seen the real treasure that you are?"

Lizzie laughed, and because they now were entering the baron's travelling chariot, their conversation grew distant and muffled.

Meg shook her head as they drove away. She could not resist saying with much irony, "Such a heavenly match and so well-suited!"

Worthen turned to her and was about to speak, but Mr. White approached him suddenly and said, "My lord Worthen, a word with you, if you please!" He was clearly perspiring heavily as he ran a hasty finger along the inside of his neckcloth, and cried, "About that incident at Almack's—good heavens, was it truly a year ago?" He laughed uneasily and continued, "I assure you that I

313

meant nothing by it. I offer you my apologies; I am certain I was in my altitudes. And as you know, one is not always aware of the untidy things one says in such a state. I, therefore, wish you to be assured—"

"Mr. White," Worthen responded, cutting him off. "If I ever have occasion to see you so much as speak to Miss Longville again, I shall be happy to make you account for each word you permit to escape your mouth!"

"Very good, sir!" Mr. White cried, forcing a smile. "Well, and I suppose one may say, all's well that ends well. Ah, yes, well, I daresay I shall take my leave at this time. Good day to you." He was about to bid Meg farewell, but stopped before the words were uttered, laughed lightly, and turned as though he expected to find a coach waiting for him. He realized suddenly that he had been so preoccupied with his need to apologize to Worthen that he had not joined Lizzie and Montford in their coach. His expression was so pathetically frightened that Worthen took pity on him and suggested he ought to ride Miss Priestley's mount back to Norbury House.

Poor Mr. White bowed several times to Worthen, then struggled first to catch the reins of Lizzie's skittish mare, and afterward, to mount the beast that apparently took great exception to his person.

Within a minute, he was gone, and Meg was left standing alone with Worthen, her hair tossed untidily about her shoulders, her pantaloons covered with leaves and dust.

They were both silent for some time. Meg began, "Worthen, I am sorry—"

"Sorry?" he queried, his expression strange. "Sorry?" And as though he suddenly realized just how close a brush with death Meg had really run, he grabbed her arms roughly and cried, "You ought to be drawn and quartered for this little prank of yours today! You might have been killed had Montford not recognized you. Faith,

314

I don't even want to think of what could have happened!"

Meg leaned toward him slightly and said, "You cannot know how much happiness it gives me to hear you shouting at me again!"

"What?" he cried, the timbre of his voice rising a notch. "Don't tell me you are at your schoolgirl daydreams again! I suppose now you mean to tell me that I am proving my love to you by giving you a dressing down."

Meg breathed, "Oh, yes!"

He gasped, the grip on her arms tightening. In a low, menacing voice, he growled, "Margaret Longville, if you do not stop this at once, I'll take a willow switch to your legs. Have you learned nothing in all these weeks?"

Meg responded, "I have, indeed. I have learned that all the heroes of my novels are meek and malleable in their treatment of the women they love and that they are dull dogs, every one of them!" She placed her hands on his chest and began smoothing out the wrinkles in his thin linen shirt. "Now tell me everything! In what other ways have I made a mull of things! Should I have worn breeches, for instance, instead of pantaloons?"

Worthen looked down at her clothing, at the slim line of her legs, and he opened his mouth in astonishment as though he had just realized how she was dressed. "Meg," he said, his voice sounding a little strange. "This costume—" He looked her over carefully as he gentled the grip on her arms. He had grown very quiet, except for his eyes which now scanned her face and hair. "You've dirt on your cheek." He touched her face lightly with his fingers.

Meg caught his hand and kissed it, then said, "I love you. If you leave me now, I'll perish, or worse yet, I promise you I'll restore every reference to the mole on Count Fortunato's cheek—and enjoy doing it!"

He laughed suddenly, slipping a hand behind her neck. "We may quarrel frequently, you and I. Are you certain that is what you want?"

Meg nodded, and he continued, "And I intend to read everything you write before ever you ship it off to a publisher. I'm persuaded you'll be miserable with me. And everytime you slip into a romantic fancy, I'll—" He leaned close to her, his lips nearly touching her own. "Meg, I thought you had been killed!" His lips touched hers lightly, drifting over her mouth in a teasing, beckoning manner. It was not a kiss, precisely, and Meg knew a growing urgency to have his lips pressed very hard against her own. Finally he said, "I'll never leave you, my darling Meg!"

And with that he kissed her painfully hard. Her arms fell to her sides as she leaned into him fully and let him bruise her lips. He slipped an arm about her waist and pressed her more firmly against him. Meg's thoughts drifted one into another as she gave herself completely to the enjoyment of his kisses and of his love. She was right, the heroes in her books would have saluted their hard-won heroines chastely upon the cheek or forehead, but Worthen—oh, my goodness!—his brutal manner of kissing her was far beyond anything she could have contrived in even her most daring daydream. Her heart overflowed suddenly with her love for him, and tears began trailing down her cheeks and into her neckcloth. She loved him, madly, completely, more than a Rosamund could ever possibly have loved a saintly Whitehaven.

The sun peeked above the rim of the beech-laden hills to the east, and the gentle wood about the mill glittered as the first rays of light hit the leaves of beech, ivy, and dogwood. Worthen held her fast, kissing her brow, her cheeks, the loose tendrils of her hair.

"I love you," he said, again and again, his words a soothing balm after the harrowing events of the past three weeks.

Meg laid her head upon his chest and rested quietly there for a long time. She could hear his heart beat, a comforting, easy rhythm.

She could have remained there forever, but the sounds of a carriage approaching the mill broke the spell of the moment. Together, they turned to watch Hope's post-chaise rattle up the pitted lane, and Meg smiled. She had suspected they would not get far toward the border, and in this she had been exactly right.

Once the dust settled, Charles leapt down from the coach and turned to help Hope descend. His cheeks were flushed, his blue eyes dark with anger. He led Hope toward Meg and Worthen and cried, "Meg, I'll never forgive you for this day's work! Good God! You are dressed in a man's clothes! What has happened here?"

Meg smiled. "I was pretending to be you and took your place in the duel with Montford!"

He stood staring at her, his eyes wide with astonishment. "But you don't know the least thing about firearms, you stupid chit! Don't tell me you actually fooled Montford or Worthen with this disguise!"

"It was very dark at the time, and I pretended to be quite ill and coughed frequently." She looked up at Worthen and added, "Besides, Worthen was not yet arrived."

Charles, whose temper had cooled a little, cried, "But you might have been killed!"

Meg nodded. "Yes, I know. But I felt, after all the trouble I had caused both you and Worthen, that I was guilty of the worst sort of heedless behavior. Why should you or Worthen have to suffer for my headstrong, reckless conduct?"

Meg's words, as full of sense as they were, momentarily silenced Charles until he bethought himself of Montford's betrayal of his own friendship. "I have my own score to settle with Montford apart from you, as you very well know. I will not be satisfied until I have crossed swords with him."

Meg did not know what to say to him and cast a beseeching glance toward Worthen. He took the hint readily and said, "I am afraid you are simply too late. I

317

had cause as well to do battle with the good baron, but Elizabeth arrived, ending prematurely what I had hoped would become a hearty bout of fisticuffs!"

"Elizabeth?" Charles cried, astonished. "What the devil was she doing here, and besides, I thought she, of all people, would have desired to cheer both of you on rather than end what must have been an extremely exciting contest!"

Meg said, "Well, she was rather upset that I forced the issue with her, but as it happens, she told Montford she positively forbade him to continue fighting if he wished to marry her. I don't like to be the one to tell you this, but it would seem your betrothed has jilted you for a Peer of the Realm!"

Charles stared at both Worthen and Meg with his mouth slightly agape.

Worthen added, "And as Mr. White said, 'All's well that ends well.'"

Charles lifted his chin and said, "As to that, we'll see. My honor requires that I seek Montford out, and I will!"

Meg cried, "And if you do, Charles Burnell, after I risked my life to make certain you would not die—and don't tell me you were a match against the finest shot in England!—I'll never speak to you again!"

Charles seemed quite stunned, his gaze shifting from Meg to Worthen. He seemed undecided, as though he ought not to yield to feminine persuasion, when Hope, who had remained quietly beside him now took a step away from him, her own countenance lit with a blaze of anger as she cried, "And how will I answer our children when they ask me why their father was killed in a stupid duel?" Everyone stared at her in considerable surprise because of her passionate speech and because of her faulty logic. She blinked several times and with a giggle placed her hand over her mouth. "Good gracious," she said. "How very silly of me to have said that. The fact is, if you perish in a duel—" her gaze grew sad, her brow puckering as she looked up at Charles—"oh, my love, we would never have children. Tell me you don't mean to leave me bereft of my own babies, do you?"

Charles appeared startled as he regarded Hope. He was with her instantly, possessing himself of both her hands as he cried, "My sweetest Hope! No, of course not, but I had never thought! Children! Our own children. Yours and mine." He smiled down at her suddenly. "Well, since you've put it to me in that most peculiar manner, I suppose I will have to oblige you. Besides, it would seem I owe his lordship a debt of gratitude. Were it not for him, I would still be engaged to Lizzie."

Hope laughed and, in response, said, "Yes, and I will most certainly send him a letter expressing my unutterable joy that he has done so."

Meg looked up at Worthen and realized that she, too, owed Montford a similar debt of gratitude. His perfidy had been the instrument by which she had finally come to understand the value of Worthen's character.

Later that afternoon, Meg sat at her writing desk in the morning room, her head bent over her manuscript. She was working steadily at removing the remaining moles from her fourth novel when she heard Worthen approach her from behind. He leaned over her, his hands gently stroking her arms. "Are you nearly finished with this disgraceful task."

Meg looked up at him over her shoulder and smiled. "Nearly so! Although I must say I regret having to do this at all. You see, I had wanted nothing more than to see your expression when everyone read the latest Hartshorn novel then began examining your face almost as earnestly as I had!"

Worthen shook his head. "You are a vixen, you know." Since he kissed the top of her head, Meg knew he was not displeased with her. He then reached his hand toward the desk and pulled forward a sheet of paper which was entitled, *The Fanciful Heiress.*

Meg tried to take the paper from his grasp, but he was too fast for her. He cried, "What is this?"

Meg felt her cheeks growing very warm as she responded, "The very beginning of my next novel."

He read aloud:

Eleanor gasped as the evil Duke de Monteforde bent over her red curls and cried, "You are mine, my precious flame-haired beauty. I shall take you to the ends of the world where I have a grand castle, and you shall preside there as mistress forever!"

"But I love another," Eleanor cried, wringing her hands and staring into the piercing blue eyes of her abductor. "You cannot mean to do this monstrous thing! Why, the Marquise de Verité will not hear of it!" Eleanor thought suddenly of the marquise, to whom she was betrothed. He was handsome, good and kind. His eyes were as dark as the night, his countenance was noble and determined, and upon his right cheekbone, he possessed a curious mole which gypsies had once told his mother meant he was endowed with all the wisdom of the gods—

"No," Worthen spoke firmly.

Meg cried, "But do you not think that if I were to—"

"No," Worthen reiterated as he tore the sheet into little pieces and let them all drift to the floor. "You are free to write anything you wish, save a story about a heroine with flame hair and a hero with a mole upon his right cheek."

Since he softened his words by drawing her gently to her feet and kissing her full upon the lips, Meg felt she could do little else but oblige him. Perhaps the hero could have a mole upon his left cheek. . . .